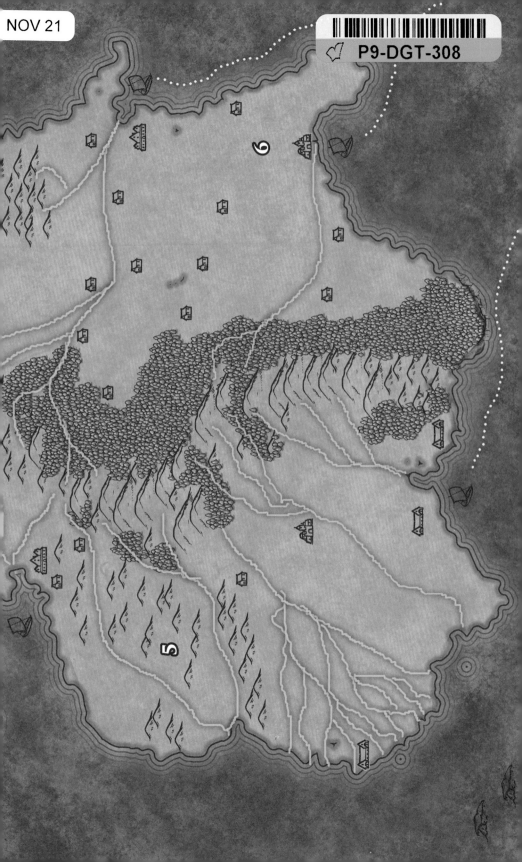

PRAISE FOR G. R. MATTHEWS

'Corin Hayes' adventure in *Silent City* in an altogether more visceral first-person adventure set in a far future where humanity has fled beneath the waves to live in undersea cities. The story is packed with action from the first page which has our hero preparing for a beating to the last where our hero is... (spoilers, as Riversong would say).'

Fantasy Hive

'Damn good fun, intriguing as hell, different and exciting, I devoured this book.'

Dyrk Ashton, author of *Paternus*

'Entertaining and exciting: *Silent City* is the start of a series I'll certainly be following with interest.'

Laura M Hughes, author of *Danse Macabre*

'It had plenty of twists and turns, and I was on the edge of my submarigine pilot seat once or twice. The ending left lots of room for more adventure but wrapped up this particular part of the tale. It was very well done. I like Corin's sense of humour too, so that was a plus.'

Super Star Drifter

'Corin, as a character, has been put through the wringer quite a bit and you feel for him or I certainly did. He's awesome!'

Rapture in Books

"Truly stellar world-building, which combines all the griminess of cyberpunk with the majesty and terror of the sea."

Paper Plane Reviews

First published 2021 by Solaris
an imprint of Rebellion Publishing Ltd,
Riverside House, Osney Mead,
Oxford, OX2 0ES, UK

www.solarisbooks.com

ISBN: 978-1-78108-913-2

Copyright © 2021 G. R. Matthews

The right of the author to be identified as the author of this work has been asserted in accordance with the Copyright, Designs and Patents Act 1988.

10 9 8 7 6 5 4 3 2 1

A CIP catalogue record for this book is available from the British Library.

Designed & typeset by Rebellion Publishing

Printed in the United Kingdom

SEVEN DEATHS
OF AN
EMPIRE

G.R. MATTHEWS

SOLARIS

To every Emlyn: you really are the heroes of our world, whom we should acknowledge more often, more fairly, and with more respect. You've all taught me more than I realised at the time, but it is never too late to say "Thank you."

I

THE GENERAL

TEN YEARS AGO:
The fist thumping on his door was the only warning, the only chance he had to prepare.
"I am so sorry, they were both killed in the raid."
"And what about the child?"

"CLEAR THE ROOM."

"But, General, we haven't yet—"

"Leave me," General Bordan repeated. He did not look up from the parchment in his hand. It took every ounce of willpower not to crush the paper and the poisoned words which were written in a neat, tidy hand upon it.

Around the polished wooden table, the men and women of the General's staff exchanged guarded looks.

"We'll reconvene this evening," Bordan repeated, choking down the sadness which tightened his throat and threatened to strangle his words. "Messenger, you stay."

The staff stood, gathered their papers, and shuffled from the room. No one spoke. Bordan calmed his heart and schooled his features into the mask of a professional soldier, someone who had sent hundreds to their deaths and would do so again.

"You've done the Empire a sacred service," Bordan said, scraping the wooden chair across the stone and standing as the door closed.

"Legion Arcterus commanded me to make best speed from the front lines and deliver the message to you alone, General," the messenger said. "He would not trust it to the magicians."

"And you've carried those orders out?"

"Yes, General." The messenger nodded. "I have spoken to no one of my mission."

"Not at any of the inns or way stations?" Bordan cast the messenger a glance and hooked his free hand into his belt.

"No, sir," the messenger said, a proud smile breaking across his face.

"You know the contents of the message?" Bordan asked.

"I was in the camp, General," the messenger said, his eyes focusing on the past. Bordan watched as a glassy sadness crept into them.

"And how fares the army?"

"It was a shock, General," the messenger said, his gaze returning to the present.

"I'm sure it was," Bordan replied, his own voice thick and the words catching in his throat. "How was the journey?"

"The weather held, and no one questions an Imperial Messenger on the roads."

"Excellent," Bordan answered with a smile, and stepping forward, drove his pugio deep into the messenger's heart.

The man's eyes widened in shock and with a cough of blood he slipped to the floor. His hand trailed along Bordan's arm from shoulder to wrist before his fingers lost their strength and the light faded from his brown eyes.

General Bordan, most excellent leader of the Empire's army, sighed and stepped over the body. Pausing, he retrieved a square of cloth from inside his tunic and wiped the blood from his hand and the blade of his dagger. Taking a deep breath and holding it to calm the racing of his heart, he opened the thick wooden door.

The guards to either side snapped to attention, spear tips pointing to the ceiling and their gazes fixed upon the painted wall opposite.

"The messenger has taken ill," Bordan said. "See to his comfort."

"Yes, General," the guard on the right said without inflection.

Both guards were Immunis, specialised troops whom he had selected personally from amongst the ranks of soldiers and paid double. They were loyal and trustworthy.

"Ensure it is done with the minimum of fuss," Bordan added, stepping past them.

"Of course, General," the guard replied.

The long corridor was decorated with plaster painted with squares of vivid orange and red, a reminder of the setting and rising sun which encompassed the reach of the Empire, and the flame which warmed them all with life. Between each square, a small alcove in which the stern but benevolent bust of a past Emperor looked out upon all who walked the military corridor of the palace: a line stretching from the founder of the Empire to the latest Emperor. They had overseen centuries of prosperity, of wealth, and a culture the likes of which the world had never seen.

As Bordan passed the first bust his posture straightened, his spine unbent, and his shoulders broadened. This is what it meant to be the General of the Empire's Army. To defend all that it was from any threat, external or internal; to maintain and expand its borders, and bring all under one banner—no matter what the means, methods, or costs. The years fell away, but the stone of sadness remained heavy in his chest.

He stopped at the most recent bust, that of the current Emperor, and spent a moment inspecting the carved face, letting the memories of the man's life swell in him. Below this bust, as with all, a small flame flickered at the end of an oiled wick. A representation of their Flame, of their ever-lasting life: it held a promise and reassurance. Yet today, he felt neither reassured nor the promise of a brighter future.

Doors of iron-studded wood sourced from lands which had once been outside the Empire, and constructed over two hundred years ago, opened out onto the courtyard of the palace. A great square of hard-packed grit and sand where soldiers paraded and Shields, the lowest of the officer ranks, shouted and screamed at their small units.

"Atten-tion!" A loud voice echoed around the square and every soldier snapped to attention.

Bordan, the warmth of the sun taking the chill from his blood, nodded to the officer who had spotted him as he stepped from the shadows of the doorway. She saluted and Bordan returned the gesture.

"Carry on, Cohort," Bordan said, his words carrying clear across the square without strain. A practised voice from the pit of his stomach, not used often in the past twenty years, but he was glad he had not lost the knack. Another day, another victory over age.

"Resume march," the Cohort shouted.

Keeping to the covered walkway which surrounded the square, Bordan ignored the sight of the soldiers drilling and forced his mind to consider his next words. They must be chosen with care, sympathetic but professional. Now was not the time to panic. Plans must be made. Cool heads must prevail.

In his mind the words spiralled and twisted in a sombre dance, but its rhythm and steps escaped him. He tore sentences apart and forged them anew. Formal gave way to informal and a moment later reasserted itself. These few words would be spoken to people he had known and cared about for more than three decades—a fact which made the task harder, not easier.

Passing through the palace towards his destination he did not see the stares directed at him, the puzzled looks, the salutes, or the servants scuttling out of his path. At the final door he paused, offering a simple prayer that the past could look after itself if he, with enough thought and planning, could control the future. The words settled into his mind, a thousand seeds drifting to the soil where the sentence would grow and flower.

"General," the guard said, "the family is at lunch."

"I'm sad to say I must disturb them, though I wish it were not so," Bordan said.

"Of course, General," the guard answered without emotion. His part had been played: he had challenged the need for the meeting and his superior had spoken. No blame could fall upon him.

"Ensure we are not disturbed," Bordan said.

"Yes, General." The guard knocked three times on the door and swung it open. He called into the shadowed interior of the rooms beyond, "General Bordan requests entrance."

"The General is always welcome," came the quiet reply.

"Thank you," General Bordan said, favouring the guard with a nod.

Stepping through the door, Bordan caught sight of the second guard inside as they slipped back into their dark hole. If he had not been announced and granted permission, the guard would have killed him—run him through with a sword without hesitation or care.

Conversation and a sudden eruption of high-pitched laughter sounded ahead. The scent of spice caught his nose and tickled the back of his throat before the aroma of cooked meat brought a hot wash of saliva to his mouth. Breakfast seemed a long time ago, though he had thought his appetite had been driven away by the messenger's note.

Turning the final corner, Bordan found the source of laughter surrounding a long dining table laden down with food from every part of the Empire. Roast fowl, steam rising from its crispy brown skin, competed with haunches of beef swimming in rich gravy. Sizzling dishes of thinly sliced meat bubbled away next to bowls of pasta drowned in a deep red sauce. Bread—long and thin, thick and dotted with seeds, or twisted into convoluted shapes—rested on large silver plates. Shrimps, prawns, lobsters, and fish decorated a large serving bowl embossed with the dream of the coast.

The imperial family and their guests sat either side of the table, though the chair at its head was empty. Next to the empty chair sat the woman he had come to see and, close by, her son and daughter. All heads turned as his heels clacked on the tessellated floor.

"General," called the Emperor's son. "If we'd known you were hungry, we would have invited you to our small lunch."

"My Prince, I would have been honoured to attend, but my duties did not permit such an honour to befall me," Bordan replied, focusing on keeping his tone neutral and his face calm, while behind it his mind raced and his heart beat loud enough that he was sure everyone could hear. It would do no good to betray the news to this gathering. Every noble, every power-hungry parasite and schemer who sat at this table with the imperial family had cause to hate the General, and many more would soon join that number, he mused.

"Yet here you are," the Empress said, her voice smooth with long practice.

"Indeed, Your Highness," he nodded. "I was unaware you were entertaining."

"You have something for us," the princess, a young woman with golden hair caught in curls upon her head, said a smile of welcome upon her face.

"Yes, Princess," Bordan agreed. "Though it can wait until you have finished."

"Perhaps the General would like to pull up a stool," Duke Abra offered, looking not at Bordan but at the Empress whom he sat next to.

"General?" the Empress enquired.

"That is kind of the Duke to offer me a seat at your table, Empress." Bordan stressed the words, ensuring the Duke knew he was aware of the implied insult. Only peasants and the lower ranks sat on stools. "However, I would not interrupt. I will await your pleasure, Empress, in the Emperor's study."

"It must be important to bring you from your duties," Abra said.

Bordan noted the tightening around the Empress's eyes and the stares of her two children.

"This is my duty, Duke Abra," Bordan answered stiffly. Transferring his gaze from the hard eyes of Abra, Bordan looked to his Empress. "With your permission, Your Highness."

"You have it, General. Please make sure the servants provide you with a drink. I do not think this meal will last much longer," the Empress answered, her face resuming its mask. "My appetite has quite suddenly fled."

Bordan covered his half-smile with a bow in her direction as a hush fell over the table. A smart turn and he retreated to a room close by, one he knew well, settling into a familiar chair and accepting the glass of wine offered by the servant.

He was satisfied when his hand did not shake.

II

THE MAGICIAN

TEN YEARS AGO:
The city was vast and even at night, from the back of the cart
which carried him through the gate, he could only wonder at its size.
It looked a lonely place despite the people bustling about. He was
already alone and this place held no comfort.

KYRON WALKED THE camp in a daze.

Soldiers sat around their campfires talking in muted tones, and not one face wore a smile. There were no voices raised in song. No laughter and no grunts of a soldier taking his ease with one of the camp whores.

Pots bubbled away unattended, burning the soldiers' morning porridge to the black iron of their base. An occasional arm would reach out to absently stir the food, but no one ate. Bowls full of lumpy white paste rested upon the earth, steam rising and carrying the scent of food to the noses of men with no appetite.

Few took notice of Kyron's passing and no one called to him. Each tent and bedroll, which on any other day would be packed before breakfast was started, was still in place. Today the army would not march. The first day since spring had descended upon them that they lacked the will and drive to advance further into the forests of the northland.

Even as the sun rose above the trees, turning morning's gemstone dew into a thin grey mist which drifted to the canopy above, the sense of despondency settled anew into his heart. The aroma of loss overpowered the smoke from the fires and the scent of porridge charring in the pots. He drew it down with every breath, feeling it sweep through his limbs on each pulse of his heavy heart, draining the energy from his legs, and every step became a struggle against lethargy.

Breaking free of the soldiers' densely packed tents brought no relief. Three tents clustered in this clearing and all were embroidered with pictures and symbols which paid little regard for regulations or a colour scheme. Whatever colour was required had been used and if they clashed, the designer seemed not to care. The sight always brought a queasy roll to his stomach and his eyes forever told him he was balanced atop the tallest tree, looking down upon the forest floor far below, about to fall.

This morning, though, the vertigo and sickness was lost beneath the mood of the camp. The tickle of energy which washed across his skin as he crossed the circle he had scratched in the earth last night usually brought a smile of accomplishment to his face, but today brought only a wave of sadness.

"There you are, Kyron," Padarn said from his seat on a large rock by the fire.

"Master," Kyron said, his voice falling flat on the air, "the Quartermaster wishes to remind us to renew the preservative markers on the stores."

"I'm sure he does." The older man ran his fingers through the short and carefully trimmed beard which framed his face. "Could you not have done it while you were there?"

"I offered, Master, but he wouldn't let me," Kyron admitted, moving to the fire and its bubbling pot of water, pouring in a hefty measure of oats.

"He wouldn't let you?"

"Said he didn't want no apprentice messing up his stores," Kyron said with an apologetic nod at his master.

"Can't have us all starving because you made some stupid mistake," a new voice croaked out.

He looked away from the already bubbling porridge to see Elouera emerge from her tent. Her grey hair was tied in a ponytail which fell down her back and the long grey robe she wore with its line of symbols running down one sleeve was, he knew, more to stave off the cold than for any magical energy they contained.

"Good morning, Master Elouera," he said, bowing in her direction.

"Don't go good morning me, Apprentice, and I'm not your master, he is." She pointed a wrinkled finger at Padarn, who favoured her with a smile. "And thankful you should be for that, young Kyron. I'd have set you aside for a candidate of quicker wits years ago."

"He's quick enough," Padarn said, coming to Kyron's defence as the younger man winced. "You train your apprentices your way, Elouera, and I'll train mine my way."

"Pah," Elouera spat. "He's got power, I don't doubt that, but he hasn't grown enough, neither in height nor intellect."

"It will come," Padarn answered. "I note your own apprentice has yet to rouse herself from bed. Mine has, at least, provided us with breakfast."

The last tent, smaller than the others, had its flaps still tied and sealed.

"I work better at night," Elouera said. "Don't sleep as much as I used to. You'll get there one day, when you're as old as me, Padarn. When you do, remember it was me that told you. Youngsters need sleep so much more than the old. So much time you waste in your early years."

"You don't let me sleep in, Master," Kyron said, a note of accusation entering his voice.

"If I let you sleep in, you wouldn't wake until next year, Kyron," Padarn chuckled. "Once breakfast is done, we'll go back to the Quartermaster and you can renew the preservative markers. It'll be good for you to practice."

"Yes, Master." Kyron felt the confidence his master had shown him should lift his mood, but it did not. "Master?"

"Yes, Kyron."

"What will happen now?"

"I don't know," Padarn answered in a voice as heavy as Kyron's heart. "I'm sure it will be fine."

From the other side of the small fire, Elouera snorted.

"You foresee problems, Elouera?" Kyron's master asked.

"Last succession happened in the city," she answered, kicking the pole which supported her apprentice's tent. "One before that was when I was but a child. As I recall, there was a lot of trouble in the city and countryside."

"Trouble?" Kyron asked, confused. "Doesn't the eldest child become Emperor?"

"It's not always that easy," she replied, stretching her back and groaning in pain. "Don't give me that look, young man. When you get to my age, you'll groan too. What was I saying?"

"Trouble in the city," he reminded her.

"Yes, well, not everyone is happy that an accident of birth makes a man an Emperor. Some feel that just having a few more coins than the soul next to them is enough of a reason to make them Emperor instead. A few drops of poison, a knife in the dark, or a riot or two... it all whittles the field down."

"Is that what happened when you were a child?"

"I remember hiding with my mother, Flame keep her, in the cellar while the riots went on," Elouera said. "In the end, it was the army who made sure the Emperor's son came to the throne. Don't you go forgetting it, young Kyron. Control the army and you can impose your will on a country or an Empire."

The rough-cut spoon in his hand stopped in its stirring of the porridge, and he felt a guilty stab in his stomach. "I'll remember, Master Elouera."

"See that you do," she said and turned to the tent from which her apprentice was just now climbing. "What time do you call this, Ayita? Sun's been in the sky for hours and you're just now waking. You'll amount to nothing if you don't study."

"We studied last night," the young girl said, her long dark hair a contrast to her master's grey.

"And we'll study tonight too," the old magician said. "Slacking off and laziness will just turn you into Kyron here, and we don't want that."

"No, Master Elouera," Ayita said with a smile, "we definitely do not want that."

"Thanks," Kyron muttered under his breath and returned to stirring the porridge.

When the food had come to the boil and the bubbling porridge began to rise towards the rim of the pot, Kyron lifted it from the fire. Four bowls of carved wood were placed upon an upturned log, and he spooned the porridge into them in equal measure. Taking his own, he retreated to the tent he shared with his master and sat upon the earth near its entrance.

Padarn, Elouera and Ayita collected theirs. The two masters sat upon logs, shuffling to get comfortable while the young girl sat on the ground near Kyron.

"Camp's quiet," she said, her dark eyes meeting his.

The familiar catch in his throat and the tightness in his chest caught him, as it always did, by surprise. He covered his reaction by taking a hot spoonful of porridge. It burned all the way down his throat and into his belly. "No one can believe it."

"People die all the time," Ayita said.

"Not Emperors," replied Kyron. "He wasn't old. Not as old as Master Elouera anyway."

"Older than Padarn?"

"I think so, but that's still young. Master Padarn is barely past his fortieth summer." The fire in his belly cooled, as did the heat on his cheeks.

"Has anyone said how he died?" she asked, her eyes fixed upon the lumpy porridge in her bowl.

"Not that I've heard." He lowered his voice to a whisper. "We've not fought a battle in weeks, and he wasn't wounded."

"Old people just die from age or being ill," she offered.

"Elouera doesn't look in danger of dying."

"The Flame couldn't burn her if it tried," Ayita answered with a giggle he found at once irritating and enticing.

"The Emperor was a strong man. A great man," Kyron said. "He shouldn't be dead."

"Even Emperors die, Kyron," Ayita said, speaking around her mouthful of porridge.

"Too soon." The sadness which had lifted while he had cooked breakfast returned. "He had so much more to do. Bringing peace to the north was a worthy deed. His name would have been spoken about for all time. Now that glory will go to his son."

"How do you bring peace by starting a war?" Ayita asked as she drew symbols in the porridge which slowly flowed back to level, obliterating each a few seconds after she finished. It was as if they had never been.

"They war with each other," Kyron protested. "Constantly. Petty tribal conflicts and clan wars. Once they join the Empire they'll be at peace, just as the rest are."

"My people aren't always happy to be part of the Empire." He noticed how her brow furrowed and nose wrinkled as she spoke.

"That's treasonous," he whispered furiously.

"Why?" Ayita turned serious eyes upon him. "To say you are not always happy, how can that be treason?"

"You speak poorly of the Empire and of the Emperor."

"The two are the same then?"

"The Empire is the Emperor and the Emperor the Empire." Kyron repeated the phrase he had heard so often at his grandfather's knee.

"But the Emperor is dead," she pointed out, a ruthless stab to his heart, "and the Empire continues."

"His Flame will never die," he protested. "It will be passed on to his son. They will merge and he, like those before him, will become immortal."

Ayita opened her mouth to reply, but the words did not come. She looked at something over his shoulder and her eyes widened. He turned sharply, dropping the spoon and reaching for the pugio at his waist.

From the trees five men in the uniform of the Empire appeared. None had weapons drawn and Kyron sighed in relief, letting go the hilt of his dagger and staring forlornly at his breakfast spoon now spotted with forest dirt.

"Magician Padarn?" asked the lead officer, a Cohort by the colours on his helm and belt.

"That's me," Padarn replied, standing up and moving around the fire. "What service can I perform for the Empire, Cohort?"

"Legion Arcterus has commanded you appear before him," the cohort said without ceremony.

"Does he need something particular?" Padarn asked. "I will need to gather the right supplies."

"He did not say so." A look of puzzlement passed across the officer's face. "I was ordered to bring you to him."

"In that case," Padarn said, "lead the way. One question though, if I may. Can my apprentice accompany me? If there is some task to perform, I can send him back for the right supplies. He will know what to look for where a soldier may not. It will save time."

The cohort glanced down at Kyron and Ayita who were sat on the earth. Kyron watched the man chew his bottom lip and his eyes narrowed. It felt as though he was being measured, assessed, and found wanting. It was unpleasant and a slow ember of anger kindled in his belly.

"Bring him if you wish." The cohort turned back to Padarn; a dismissive gesture which blew fresh air on the flickering coal.

"Thank you, Cohort," Padarn said. "Come on then, boy. Up you get. Dust yourself down as we walk. We cannot keep the Legion waiting. Bring your bag too. Just in case."

III

THE GENERAL

TEN YEARS AGO:
Scrawny, was the first word that entered his head as the boy was ushered in. A lump rose in his throat as the sunlight through the narrow window caught the young boy's face. He looks like his father.
"You've grown, boy," he said.

LIGHT FROM THE mid-afternoon sun fell heavy upon the large desk. Made of dark wood with graceful carvings of a stag in the forest upon its legs, it was the central feature of the room, drawing visitors' gaze back to it wherever they looked. Books and scrolls littered the shelves, and the cold fireplace in the opposite wall—alongside the faint layer of dust which covered the stone floor—said this room had not been used recently.

Despite the luxury of the Emperor's study, there was little chance of the General enjoying the peace and quiet. The letter, with its broken wax seal, lay folded inside his tunic: a weight upon his heart, colder than the glass of wine in his hand or the deep snows of the winters in the far north. The creases in the parchment were sharp edged, as were the words written upon it; and on each breath, he felt them slice into the barricades he had erected around his emotions.

The owner of this room had sat at that desk in months past and discussed the war with him. Servants brought wine and ale, sweetmeats and thin parcels of pastry to fuel them through the long

21

nights. Plans had been drawn up and discarded, maps inspected and the latest reports from the Legions read. Troop numbers, supply lines, and costs had been scrawled on parchment only to be burned in the fire.

A smile found its way to his face as the memories played out. A last great war, the largest conquest of his career, had been planned in this very room. Every action, strategy, and tactic had some mark of his about it.

As winter broke its hold on the south, the plans had been written up by the clear hand of a scribe and placed in the leather satchel which was guarded day and night. The excitement rising within him when the day had come. The glass in his hand trembled at the vision of the Emperor, leather satchel in one hand, the other resting upon his golden-hilted gladius, as he stopped at the top of the ship's ramp and turned.

"You should be coming with me," the Emperor had said.

"I'm too old, Your Highness," Bordan replied.

"Then I will bring back the glory in your name as well as my own," the Emperor laughed. His final words before disappearing into the distance, the oars of the long ship digging into the calm waters of the bay under the early morning sunlight. An auspicious beginning to the grand conquest.

A dream shared since the Emperor ascended the throne, now turned nightmare by the words inked on the folded parchment concealed close to his heart.

The glass of wine was almost empty when the door opened and the Empress swept in, her modest dress accented by threads of gold and bright gemstones. Bordan struggled out of his seat, grunting at the ache in his legs and the twinge in his lower back. Nevertheless, he executed a respectful bow and placed the wine glass down upon a nearby table.

"Sit, General," the Empress said and with a wave of her hand indicated the chair he had just clambered out from.

"You are gracious, Your Highness," he answered, settling back into the cushions.

"Now," she began, glancing around the empty room, "what news is so urgent that you disturb such a carefully orchestrated dinner? I almost had Duke Primal agreeing to reduce the cost of wheat bushels come harvest."

"Your Highness," Bordan said, the words cascading around his head as he sought to soften the blow he was to deliver, "a messenger arrived from Legion Arcterus of the First Army."

"Is something amiss, General?" She turned towards him with a raised eyebrow.

"Your Highness," he started, the words like boulders in his chest and heart, "Legion Arcterus is saddened to report the sudden death..."

"No," the Empress said, face draining of colour and her hand rising to cover her open mouth.

"... of your beloved husband, the Emperor of Sudrim," Bordan finished.

"No," the Empress, widow of the Empire, repeated.

He struggled once more from his seat, caring not for the aches and pains, and moved towards her. Her eyes were already filling with tears and her hand trembled as he took it in his own and guided her to the chair he had vacated.

"Sit," he said, pitching his voice low.

She followed his gentle command without thought or resistance, her dress gathering around her legs as she sank into the cushions. "No."

"I am sorry, Your Highness," he said. "The messenger had few details, though I expect further news to follow soon."

"Where is the messenger?" She looked up at him, the glimmer of a wish in her eyes.

"Hidden away, Your Highness," he answered. "The news must be contained until preparations are made."

"My sons." The wish died and a hard glaze fell across her eyes.

"Alhard is the heir," Bordan nodded.

"He must be guarded," she said, pushing herself up from the chair. "I loved my husband, General."

"I know, Your Highness," Bordan replied, though that was a practised lie. Both Emperor and Empress had done their duty and provided an heir and a spare, as Aelia was known in the taverns of the capital, but that had marked an end to their sharing of a bed. It was common knowledge that the Emperor had enjoyed the company of many during the long nights, some highborn who found his power erotic, and others chosen for their youth and looks who had little choice in the matter. Amongst those had been the occasional officer who caught his eye. But the Empress too had dallied with minor lords, young men and women who had been selected for a private audience in her chambers. Such things were the way of the Empire.

"But I must set that aside for now," she said, her tone turning as cold as the ache in his chest and as practical as the dagger on his hip. She smoothed her dress. "Where is the Amulet of the Empire?"

Bordan chose each word with more care than he sharpened his sword. A cut here would not be healed with a simple bandage, but could put him in a grave of his own, next to the messenger, no doubt. "As custom dictates," he said carefully, "the Emperor's amulet is with him, guiding his soul to the Flame and everlasting life."

"I would never question the Holy Flame, but, war is risk, General. I am not so foolish or naïve as to ignore that fact, and now we face an even greater peril with the succession."

"The Emperor's body is being escorted to Sudrim by an honour guard of five hundred hand-picked soldiers," Bordan said.

"This is not the time for custom, General," she snapped. "Is five hundred all that can be spared? His body and the amulet must be returned to us as soon as possible. Can we not, this once, use a ship?"

"Flame cannot travel over water," Bordan said, fighting to keep his voice level. "His flame of life, protected by the amulet, would be extinguished by such a trip, and could never be used to pass his soul and wisdom on to your son."

"Religion," she said, as if the word were a curse.

"And custom, Your Highness. Of these things is the Empire made and maintained. The succession must be carried out accordingly if your son is to ascend the throne, as is his birthright, without conflict." He stepped away and watched her pace for a moment. Her hands fluttered at her side, and he noticed she was chewing her lip in thought.

"The Dukes would not dare." Every word was bitten off by sharp teeth and spat into the air.

"Some might take the chance, Your Highness. Though support

for this war and your husband is strong amongst the people and the army, the Dukes are not always so fervent in their desires." His fingers clenched into fists at his side and he forced them to relax. "We must not give them an excuse to think such rash actions might win them power."

"Alhard is of an age to take the throne," she said. "The Dukes would do well to remember their place."

"I am sure they are all too aware of their place, Your Highness."

"Arrest them," she said with a sudden whirl towards him.

"The Dukes?"

"Yes." Her eyes flashed with fire and a cruel smile twisted her face, turning beauty into horror. It was gone in a moment, but in that second Bordan recognised the Empress of old: the young woman who had come to court and beguiled the young Emperor. The lady who had risen above all others to capture his heart, and barely a month into the marriage had poisoned it against her by deliberately choosing to fall pregnant, securing her position, despite the Emperor's decision not to father an heir until at least a year had passed.

During the years which had followed she had worked to soften the ambition and greed which all others had seen, but the Emperor had missed at first. It was a political marriage, Bordan knew, but the Emperor had been too young and trusting to see her for what she was—what her father, a King on the southern borders, had made her. The birth of their children had given Bordan hope that they could make their marriage work, but it had been forlorn. When the Emperor had declared the succession to pass to his eldest child and that the Ruling Council would act as regents should the need arise, stifling the Empress's powers, Bordan had considered it ill-judged for the marriage, but politically astute.

"Your Highness," he said, clasping his hands, now trembling of their own volition, behind his back, "such an action would surely lead to civil war and at this early stage we should tread carefully."

"You command the army, General." She turned away and stamped over to the cabinet containing the Emperor's liquors. The sound of liquid pouring into a goblet filled the pause. "With the army comes the power to do anything."

"Forgive me, Your Highness, but the Dukes pay for the army. They could withhold their taxes and we would lose the army's support. It is also worth noting that many of the senior ranks are filled by men who owe their allegiance to the Dukes. Rank is gained, though it pains me, not always with service, but as a reward, a bribe, or bought by a Duke."

She turned back to him, a cut crystal glass full of amber liquid in her hand. "Are you saying we cannot rely on our own troops?"

"No, Your Highness." He took a step towards her. "I am saying we must step carefully over the next few weeks until the body of our beloved Emperor is returned to us. The integrity of the amulet and the succession must be maintained, whether we believe or not. The customs which ensure succession passes from parent to child depend upon it.

"However," he added, his gaze sweeping the scrolls and books upon their shelves, "history tells us that succession is not always that simple. Sometimes, sadly, dynasties fall, and others rise. I would not wish that to happen here. There are others who would wish the throne and who could press the claim through force of arms or wealth."

"My son will sit on the throne, General," the Empress said and took a gulp of her drink, her lips curling at the taste. "We will see it happens, and if a Duke or two must die along the way, so be it."

IV

THE MAGICIAN

TEN YEARS AGO:

   "They said you are my Grandfather," he said, ashamed of the way his lips trembled, and his hands shook so badly that he clasped them together.

   "I am," the old man said. "I've not seen you since you were born and your family moved north."

   "They're dead," he said, and the tears came anew.

THE TWO MAGICIANS followed the soldiers through the camp. It was set in the regulation large square with sentries posted around the perimeter and a rudimentary palisade of sharp sticks to deter any of the local tribes from launching a raid. The outer ring of tents was for the soldiers, weapons and shields always within easy reach and with their own watch rotations in place. Making their way further in, they passed more soldiers' tents and those of the Immunis who specialised in looking after the mounts; the stores, familiar to Kyron from his daily tasks; the blacksmiths who repaired the weapons, and forged new arrowheads and points for pila; and the fletchers and bowyers who supplied the archers of the auxiliary. The tents grew larger and it was not strange to see servants carrying out chores instead of the soldiers themselves. At the centre of the camp, clerks and administration tents formed an inner ring around the largest tents of the Prefects, Commanders, and—in the very centre—the Legion's.

To one side of the Legion's tent were a collection of smaller tents embroidered with the sign of the Flame. Priests and acolytes—those not praying or tending the Holy Flame itself—milled around. As Kyron and his master approached, the priests began tapping each other on the shoulder or pointing in their direction. Some went so far as to make the sign of the Flame, fingers steepled and palms apart, in a gesture of warding.

"Wait here," the Cohort said, and stepped past the guards who stood either side of the entrance.

Kyron looked around again, more to take his mind from the flutter in his stomach and the sweat which matted his dark hair to his forehead than in any interest. Near the entrance and standing tall, held by the Aquilifer, was the standard of the Legion, its column of gold discs topped by the statue of the Emperor's Eagle, which gave him some measure of comfort. The priests still glared at him, though a few had returned to their duties. His master stared straight ahead with a calm, serene look on his face. The man was rarely flustered and there was no sign of sweat upon his brow.

A minute later the Cohort reappeared and beckoned them both in.

Torches in ornate stands illuminated the long tables which ran down either side of the interior, and clerks busied themselves shuffling paper and scribbling on scrolls. At the far end another table, more ornate and of a deeper, richer wood than those the clerks used, was surrounded by staff. Words and voices became more distinct from the mass of broad shoulders as they approached.

"Legion," one man with a bushy red beard was saying, "to send him back with only an honour guard is inviting trouble."

"We cannot spare any more," replied a different officer, a woman in a suit of lorica segmata, the Crest of the Flame emblazoned upon the tunic she wore over it. "We're deep in the northern forests with hostile tribes all around."

"And the honour guard will have to travel back along our route, through those tribes," Red Beard replied.

"Which are already pacified," a third voice joined the discussion. Kyron had to crane his neck to see the officer who had spoken. "The route will be clear."

"Pacified, Jevan?" Red Beard's voice rose in scorn. "Commander

Parthivi has just said we are surrounded by enemies. More than that, we left no garrisons to cement control."

"This army is moving forward, Commander Trebonius," a cultured, polite voice said, and silence fell across the table. "The Emperor's strategy is a sound one. We've discussed it many times and I intend to carry it out to the fullest ability of this army."

"Legion," Trebonius said after a moment, "I am not arguing that we turn the army around. My concern is that a Spear is not enough to secure the Emperor's safe passage back to Sudrim. Five hundred men is simply not enough to protect the Emperor, not with the tribes still active."

"And I appreciate your concern," Legion Arcterus answered and Kyron saw the man raise a placating hand. "Hearing opposing views is what makes this army stronger than the sum of its individuals. However, we've yet to run into a tribe whose numbers threaten the army—"

"We've had it easy," Trebonius interrupted.

"I agree, but that will soon change," Arcterus replied, and pointed to the table in front of them all. "The forests will thin and we will be in the foothills of the mountains which lead to the High King's Castle, which means we need all the strength we can muster. We can spare one Spear and I am convinced that, following the route we have taken, they will convey the Emperor back to the capital without delay or risk."

Trebonius opened his mouth to reply but closed it before any words were spoken. Kyron saw him settle for a simple nod.

"Good," Arcterus said, his bright eyes catching the flickers of the torches as he looked through a gap in the ring of officers. "I see my guests have arrived."

The Cohort saluted as the ring of officers turned. "The Magician Padarn and his apprentice..." The Cohort's introduction came to a halt as he glanced at him.

"Kyron," he supplied.

"...Apprentice Kyron, Legion," the Cohort finished smoothly.

"Thank you, Cohort. Your name?"

"Borus, of the 8th Spear," the officer who had escorted them to the Legion's tent said.

"Please stay," the Legion said, walking around the table to stand before them. He was not a tall man, but the breadth of his chest spoke of strength and the gladius at his hip was no ornamental statement of rank. The grip was worn and the leather belt from which it hung was wrinkled by age and use.

"Magician Padarn," the Legion began, "you are aware of the passing of the Emperor and know how important it is to escort him back to the capital for cremation and the crowning of his son, Prince Alhard." The Legion's voice quavered a touch when he mentioned the death, as if stating it was to acknowledge it for the first time.

"I am, Legion," Padarn answered.

"Good." The Legion took a breath before continuing. "The Gymnasium of Magic is, by tradition and decree, outside of the army's structure of command. Therefore, I must make this a request. Would you be willing to accompany the Emperor back to the capital and do your utmost to ensure his safe arrival?"

"It would be an honour, Legion," Padarn answered, his voice as calm and warm as it always was. "My compatriot Elouera can take over my duties without undue stress or difficulty. You have no objection to my apprentice accompanying us?"

The Legion turned to Kyron and the young man saw a flash of recognition pass across the officer's face, although he wasn't sure where the Legion would have seen him at close quarters. "Are you prepared to accompany your master?"

"I follow where he leads, my lord Legion," Kyron said, and offered a small bow of respect.

"Well said," Trebonius interjected from the table.

"Quite." The Legion allowed a small smile to crease his face. "A young man must learn at the knee of the wise. Master Padarn, bear with me for a moment. Cohort?"

The soldier standing next to them saluted.

"Spear Astentius will be leading the 8th in the honour guard to escort the Emperor back to the capital. Master Padarn and his apprentice will be joining your Cohort. You have any experience of working with magicians?"

"No, Legion," Borus replied, casting a sidelong glance at Kyron.

"Treat them as Immunis, outside of the duties of regular soldiers.

Astentius will want to consult with them regularly."

"Yes, Lord Legion," Borus replied, though the uncertainty in his voice was clear for all to hear.

"You'd be surprised how useful they can be, Cohort. There is much more they can do than just keep the supplies fresh and drive the biting insects away," the Legion said. Kyron saw the nods of the other commanders and his chest filled with pride.

"However, there is one more duty I must place upon you. As you will have heard my commanders discuss," the Legion said, glancing over his shoulder, "the route back is safe. However, there exists in any endeavour a calculated risk. Astentius recommended you as a level-headed officer who has the respect of his men, and can be relied upon to follow orders."

"Thank you, Legion," Borus said, standing a little straighter.

"Don't thank me yet, Cohort. Learn a lesson from one who rose through the ranks. When a superior offers you praise, it is wise to wait for the real message to be delivered before you allow his flattering words to cloud your vision," the Legion said dryly. "Spear Astentius is aware of the gravity of his task and to ensure it succeeds, a local guide has been assigned to the Spear."

"A guide, Legion?" It was Padarn who spoke, stroking his beard in thought.

"They know the tribes and their ways, and they will help to smooth the Spear's progress towards the capital. At least as far as the edge of the forests."

"Can we trust them, sir?" Borus asked, stealing the words from Kyron's throat.

"Yes," the Legion said firmly. "We have assurances in place. The guide will be part of your Cohort, Borus. There will also be priests accompanying the Emperor on his final journey."

"Are they to be part of my Cohort too, Legion?"

Kyron felt the sweat which had dried on his forehead begin to bead anew.

"That would not be..." the Legion cast a meaningful look at Padarn, "prudent."

"Thank you, Legion," the Cohort said with a sigh of relief, which Kyron echoed.

The Legion turned. "Trebonius, the guide?"

"Come here, girl," the red-bearded commander called.

A young woman with red hair so dark it was almost black appeared from beyond the torches. She sketched a stiff bow to the Legion, and Kyron noted the coldness in her eyes. Whatever assurances the Legion had obtained had not been welcomed by the woman.

"This is Emlyn," Trebonius said. "She will guide you safely to the edge of the forest. After that she is, as she knows, free to return to us here or accompany you to the capital. That decision is hers alone. Either way, a message will be delivered to us of your safe arrival."

Emlyn turned her hard eyes on Trebonius, who glared back. When she broke the stare and turned to Borus, her voice was cold. "I am ready to leave when you are."

"You leave tomorrow morning," the Legion said, ignoring the woman. "Master Padarn, please gather everything you will need from the stores. The clerks have a blank order scroll for you to collect before you depart the tent. Cohort Borus, Spear Astentius may have more orders for you. Please report to him. I wish you all a safe journey."

"Good fortune favour the Empire, Legion," Padarn replied. "Come along then, Kyron, we'd best get ready for a long journey."

Kyron looked from the guide to the officers and not knowing what to say, settled for a bow before trotting after the departing back of his master.

V

THE GENERAL

TEN YEARS AGO:
  He could see the boy's hands start to shake and when tears began to flow, he was unsure what to do. Years ago, he'd argued with his son, the boy's father, about the move to the northern plains, but stubbornness was a family trait.
  "Come here, boy," he said, reaching out to gather him into his arms.

"GENERAL." THE CALL echoed from the plaster walls of the corridor.
  Bordan stopped, the thoughts which had occupied his mind scattered to the winds, and turned. The man, face freshly shaved and eyes that saw too much, sauntered towards him.
  "Duke Abra," Bordan said, sketching a bow to cover the grimace which found its way onto his face. "How may I assist you today?"
  "The Empress has called a meeting of the Ruling Council," Abra said.
  "I am aware of that, your lordship," Bordan replied, struggling to keep the irritation from his voice. "I am on my way there now."
  "If you've no objection, I shall accompany you," Abra said, the smile which stretched his thin lips to almost invisibility never wavering.
  "Of course," the General answered a moment late, all reasonable excuses having fled his mind.

The two men, both with sheathed blades upon their belts, walked along the corridor. Ahead, a servant carrying a silver platter laden with cups and wine took a step backward into a doorway to give them room. Passing by, Bordan noted her wide eyes and partially open mouth before she ducked her head in a bow.

"Do you know what this council meeting is about, General?" Abra asked in a tone which any other could have viewed as conversational, but which long years of animosity had made Bordan wary of.

"I am sure the Empress will tell us in her own time," Bordan replied, keeping his gaze fixed upon the door to the council chamber.

"Perhaps it is news of the war in the north," Abra suggested.

"Perhaps," Bordan agreed, choosing his singular word with care.

"An announcement of some great victory over the tribes in the forests, or the clans of the hills," Abra continued, his words in rhythm with his steps.

Focused upon his breathing, keeping every inhale and exhale to a regular beat, Bordan did not respond.

"You think not?" Abra said and from the side of his eye Bordan saw the other man's smile twitch. "There was some strange news I received recently, General."

"Really?" Bordan responded automatically and inwardly cursed himself for giving the man another opening to speak.

"Most curious it was," Abra said. "Apparently, so I was informed, an Imperial Messenger reached the palace just yesterday morning. His horse was lathered and bore the mark of a coaching inn to the north."

"Imperial Messengers come and go all the time," Bordan pointed out.

"Absolutely true, General. True indeed. However—and this is the curious part of the news—no one has seen this messenger since he arrived."

"Perhaps he has already been sent to deliver another message," Bordan offered, pushing his thoughts away from the sensation of warm blood washing over his hand.

"I thought that, but no one seems to have seen him or knows who sent him back out into the countryside," Abra said with a shake of his head. "As you say, messengers are always coming and going, but there are enough to let one man rest his weary horse."

Bordan let his hand rest upon the buckle of his belt, not far from the hilt of the pugio dagger. "Is this what occupies your idle hours, Duke Abra?"

"Many things do, my dear General," Abra responded and a soft chuckle followed the words. Forced and strained, Bordan thought. "I would have thought a missing messenger would be one of your concerns. After all, often they carry important information and messages. Should one of those be intercepted by the wrong people?"

Bordan let his eyes rest once more upon the door to the council chamber, willing it to come closer so this conversation would end. "Do you wish me to task someone to look into this matter for you?"

"No. No," Abra protested, both hands raising, palms out in a placating gesture. "I wouldn't want to trouble you."

"It is no trouble, Duke," Bordan pressed. "Such matters can be easily solved and if the findings bring some relief to your curiosity, I would consider it a favour."

"It is kind of you to think of my well-being, General."

"I often find myself so concerned, Duke," Bordan said. "It will be a simple matter to discover who this messenger saw and where they were sent."

An investigation, even one as rudimentary as this, would enable him to create whatever story he wished to tell, to give credence to a fiction. Maybe the Duke's desire to invent problems and to stick his long nose into every aspect of palace business might be an advantage, this time.

"Let me get the door for your, General," Abra said, skipping ahead a few steps to reach the door to council chambers ahead of him.

"Thank you."

"A pleasure. You've served the Empire well and faithfully for your whole life, such a little service as this is nothing compared to your legacy."

Bordan allowed a little bow of his head to demonstrate the proper respect and thanks even though he ground his teeth together at the implication.

"And as for the investigation," Abra continued as Bordan stepped past him. "There is no need to bother. I know who the messenger saw. I am sure he was well rewarded for his diligence."

It was said with a politeness that only a truly political mind could muster that it caught Bordan unawares. He stumbled half a step before recovering his balance. Checking over his shoulder he saw the smirk; a knowing, vicious slash which bisected Abra's face and vanished in an instant.

"A loose tile, General?" Abra stepped forward, kicking the toe of his expensive leather boot at the offending stone. "I will mention it to the Palace steward. It wouldn't do for the Empire's foremost military mind to fall flat on his face in front of the council, would it?"

"You are too..." Bordan said, letting the pause stretch between the two men, "kind."

"Think nothing of it." Abra smiled, waving away Bordan's words.

"On the contrary, such kindness is to be treasured, Duke Abra."

A brittle silence which chilled the air between them was broken by the appearance of the High Priest at the door.

"Are you intending to take your seats, gentlemen?" The priest had a deep, sonorous voice which caught every falling shard of the broken silence and turned them to soft motes of dust which drifted to the floor.

"Of course, Your Eminence," Bordan said, smiling at the only other man on the council who came close to his age. Six decades was a good age in the Empire, especially for a career soldier. The High Priest was approaching his fifty-fifth summer and had let his moustache grow long and bushy in the manner of his people from the southern continent.

"You all right, Bordan?" the High Priest asked, squinting at him.

"The General tripped on a raised flagstone, Your Eminence," Abra said. "I was speaking and must have distracted him, for which I've offered my apologies."

"I'm fine, Godewyn," Bordan grunted at the High Priest. "I tripped."

The priest stroked his moustache idly for a moment before speaking. "Lift your feet, Bordan. Shuffling and tripping are the marks of age and you've never been one to give into that enemy."

"I can still give the recruits a good match," Bordan answered, feeling his spirits lift a little at the priest's words.

"I've still got the scar you gave me," Godewyn replied, a genuine smile creasing his face.

"You'd have made a good Legion, Godewyn," the General admitted.

"The Flame found me and took my path elsewhere, General. We each serve where and when we can. Sometimes we trip and fall on our path, but we must always seek to rise above such failures in the service to the Flame and the Empire. Isn't that true, Duke Abra?"

"Of course, High Priest," Abra responded quickly, looking away from the two men and back down the corridor.

Bordan noted the nervous swallow of the younger man and faintest twitch of his fingers towards the knife at his belt. The reaction was gone in a moment and when Abra turned back, the smile was on his face as if it had never left.

"I suggest we take our seats," Godewyn said, unruffled and calm. Secrets were stock-in-trade to both the Army and the Priesthood, and Bordan knew well enough that Godewyn would take his to the grave. Still, Abra's reaction was interesting.

Looking down the table, the Emperor's high-backed chair was at its head and to either side were lower, but ornately carved, chairs for the Empress and two children. Today plates and cutlery had been set in front of those chairs, a sure sign the imperial family would be in full attendance.

Bordan's position, to the left of the imperial seats, was as traditional as it was practical. The Empire prized military might. All citizens were made to serve for two years and many stayed longer, finding the discipline and order suited them, or contained and focused their youthful energies towards something other than trouble. A position near the top of the table reflected that ideal of servitude, of duty, and honour.

It also served to put a soldier's sword arm—the right for all soldiers, even those who were born favouring the left—towards the council. Though no physical swords were permitted in the council chamber, it made sense to have your best and most favoured warrior able to draw their knife and defend the imperial personages without the disadvantage of having to turn or have the table get in their way.

Opposite the General's chair sat Godewyn: the spiritual and physical on opposing sides of the long council table. In reality there was no such opposition, only mutual respect: but in past centuries, Bordan knew, that had not always been the case.

Duke Abra had taken his seat further down the table, not far from Duke Primal. The other councillors, nobles, and senators of standing took their own chairs and conversation became a muted buzz which fluttered around the room on the edge of hearing.

The door opened once more and a portly man in a robe too small for his frame bumbled in. His thick beard hid much of his face and from beneath bushy eyebrows, which appeared to be mounting a successful invasion of his forehead, piercing blue eyes stared at the gathered council.

"Apologies," the man said, with not a trace of shame or embarrassment. "I thought I'd given myself enough time, but it is like the finest sand of a master glassblower. You hold it in your hand, sure you have enough for the task at hand, but do not notice the subtle trickle between each finger until too much is lost."

Bordan snorted and even Duke Primal, a man not noted for his sense of humour, allowed a small smile to pass across his lips. Godewyn said nothing but glared at the newcomer.

"Come, sit," Duke Abra said, indicating the empty chair at the far end of the table. "The Master of the Gymnasium of Magicians is always welcome at the council table."

"And often late," Bordan heard Godewyn mutter. It was a truth hard to deny, but between priesthood and magicians little love was lost.

Another door opened and a hush fell across the table. A moment later, they all stood and bowed as Prince Alhard and the Empress, followed by the golden-haired Aelia, entered the council chamber.

VI

THE MAGICIAN

TEN YEARS AGO:

He felt the warmth of the embrace, of the old man's arms around him, but it was distant. He did not recognise the man's smell although there was something about his face, a memory or similarity which held an edge of comfort.

Hot tears fell down his cheeks and his fingers dug into the man's clothes, drawing forth what comfort was offered.

TRAVELLING THROUGH THE forest was boring, Kyron decided. There were no long views across grassland, no peaks rising from the horizon to take giant bites from the sky, no rivers winding through valleys or across plains to draw the eyes into the distance. Instead you were faced, constantly and unendingly, with trees—one after another, each swarming with spring's young leaves which drank the sunshine and dripped pools of chill shadow upon the track.

Five hundred soldiers, some carts, and the few horses the army could spare tramped through the woods, following the trail they had broken on their way north. It had been one used by the tribes of the forest; however, the army had widened it by cutting down the saplings and branches which encroached upon their freedom of movement. It was now a cart and a half wide at its narrowest, and in places would allow three carts to travel side by side. Kyron looked forward to those parts.

Hemmed in by the trunks of tall trees and being unable to look up and see anything but the narrow ribbon of light afforded by the burgeoning canopy was unpleasant. The tribes moved through these forest mazes with a stealth and silence no one could match. Kyron found it hard not to imagine a tribesman behind every tree, in every dip and shadow, bow drawn and selecting his back as their target. He started at each shaft of sunlight which pierced the clouds and leaves, eyes darting to the slightest hint of movement.

In amongst the full strength of the First Army, the march through these trees had been… if not relaxing, at least comforting. The tribes had hardly struck. An arrow here, a quick raid there, nothing the army could not repulse with ease. Further on, as they moved north through the great forest towards the hills and mountains, the attacks had grown in strength and ferocity as if there had been, finally, some organisation to them. After a time and after heavy losses on the part of the tribes, the attacks had ceased.

Now, in the middle of the marching order, one cart back from the covered waggon carrying the Emperor's body, he felt exposed. To make matters worse, the carts which led the funeral procession were full of priests whose low, chanted prayers drifted back to his ears with every step. The creak and groan of the axles punctuated each verse, creating a discordant rhythm which grated on his teeth.

"Master?" Kyron said, looking up from his lonely walk to the cart where his master sat next to the driver.

Padarn looked away from the leather-bound sheaf of papers he was studying and sighed. "Yes, Kyron?"

"It's not fair," Kyron said, the words he had meant to say slipping from his grasp, and he heard the whine in his voice.

"Which particular part is not fair, my apprentice?"

"Her." Kyron gestured with the point of his chin towards the front of the column.

"It is her forest."

"It is part of the Empire," Kyron said. "The Emperor has brought civilisation to it. It is ours now."

"Ours?" Padarn said with a chuckle. "Which bit do you own, Kyron?

Which tree is yours? Choose wisely."

"The Empire's, I mean. You know what I mean."

"I do, Kyron. My apologies. I do not make fun of you, but you should think before you let words fall from your mouth."

"Is it not part of the Empire? Is that what you mean?"

"One day it will be," Padarn acknowledged, "but today is not that day."

"But we've conquered it," Kyron said. "This bit anyway."

"We've marched through it," his master corrected, a chuckle softening the words. "We've fought some battles and taken forts and villages. Conquered, though? It is a word filled with many meanings and vague because of it. All of which leads us away from your feelings of unfairness related to Emlyn."

"Why must she stay with us?" Kyron stepped around a pile of horse dung left by one of the cart horses or an officer's mount ahead.

"Where would you like her to sleep, Kyron? With the priests?" Padarn tucked the sheaf of parchment away in his pack. "They like her even less than us. Heathen gods and strange ways which don't conform to their view of the world. They have little in common, and I'm sure they'd be bound to try and convert her to the Flame."

"Would that be so bad, Master? The Empire follows one religion, the true way." Kyron answered without thought, the words drummed into his skull at the feet of priests in the capital city.

"You know better than that," Padarn chided him, casting a glance at the cart driver next to him. "All those years of study and you fall back upon rote learning. I taught you better, as did your grandfather before you joined us."

"He believes," Kyron protested.

"I don't doubt his faith. I merely praise his questioning mind and practicality." The Master Magician shook his head and looked back down at Kyron. "So, not with the priests. What about with the army and officers?"

"Why not?"

"The very same people that burned her village, took her fort, and stole her friends' lives away?"

"Did her village burn?" Kyron turned his gaze in the direction of their guide.

"I don't know, Kyron. I haven't asked her, but one of those things, or more, is likely to have happened. You would force her, or the soldiers, into the position of sleeping so close to an enemy? How many nights until one or the other fails to wake in the morning? A knife in the night cuts quick and deep."

"She wouldn't." He choked the words out, half shocked and half appalled.

"They might," Padarn replied. "I don't know for sure, but neither does Spear Astentius. It is better to make sure everyone is safe, and our journey continues without incident."

"But we don't need a guide," Kyron protested, trying another tack. "We just have to follow this track back out of the forest."

"And how far is that? The army marched for weeks to reach its present position. Fifteen thousand soldiers, camping, guarding, watching out for each other. A force that few, even in the far south, would choose to stand against. Now we are five hundred strong, a better target, an easier target."

"Then Legion Arcterus should have sent more with us," Kyron answered. "Not just us and a guide."

"And weakened his forces to the point where the campaign would fail? Where the army might be defeated?"

"You just said fifteen thousand was a force no one wanted to face, and now you say they could all be killed," Kyron pointed out, a smile creasing his face. "You cannot have it both ways, Master."

Padarn clapped and smiled. "At last, you are thinking again and with your brain rather than your prejudices. The Empire army is used to fighting on plains, where the shield wall is unbreakable, and the swords run red with the blood of those who stand against them."

"We don't lose," Kyron nodded.

"On land of our choosing," Padarn said, raising a finger as he always did when he wanted to have Kyron take careful note. "The mountains of the north won't allow the legion to deploy its full strength all in one go. You've been to the low hills to the west of Sudrim. Take those wide valleys and gentle slopes, make them as narrow as a cart and the slopes as steep as castle walls. The legion marches through those to reach its goal. All of which, again, leads us away from your initial complaint."

"I'm not complaining, Master."

"Of course not." Padarn smiled. "You are questioning?"

"Yes, Master."

"And have you come to an answer?" Which was how almost every teaching session ended, Kyron having to come up with the answer he'd wished to receive from his master.

"She is with us because we can keep her safe and no one likes us much anyway," he answered with a sour tone. On the cart, the driver snorted and Padarn chuckled.

"Wisdom is gained one step at a time," Padarn said.

"Just don't step in horse shit," the driver added with a loud laugh.

THE SMALL FIRE between the two tents sent shadows capering through the trees where they joined those conjured by other fires to dance with each other beneath the new boughs of spring.

"Don't burn your fingers," his master advised.

"I can cook the ham without burning anything, Master," Kyron answered.

"Ham," Emlyn, the guide and tribeswoman said, "again."

"You don't have to eat it."

"You're going to cook something else?"

"Not for you." Kyron looked through the flames to the young tribeswoman sat across from him. She returned the look without expression.

"Then I'll eat it," she answered. It was difficult to read her tone and her eyes had given little away on the journey so far. She left every morning, packing her basic shelter away, a simple sheet of waxed cloth that she tied to a tree and then pinned two corners to the earth.

"You could help with the cooking." He looked over towards Padarn for support and found none forthcoming.

"Why? You do what your master tells you, boy," Emlyn said.

Through the flames Kyron could see she was occupied with something in her hands. "Master, why doesn't she help with the cooking?"

"I don't know, Kyron. Have you asked her?"

"Well..." he began, replaying the words he'd spoken.

"Then ask," Padarn said, looking up from his book. A spark of light hung above the pages, illuminating the words.

"Yes, Master." Kyron sighed. "Emlyn, would you help with the cooking?"

"No."

"Why?"

"It is not my custom," she answered, her hands moving in her lap.

"Your custom?"

"Tradition. Way of life. Is that not the right word?" Emlyn glanced up at him.

"Well, yes, it is," Kyron conceded.

"Good," was all she said returning her gaze to her task. "The ham will be burning."

"What?" There was a sizzle and single tendril of grey smoke rose to his nose. "Damn."

Dragging the pan from the flames, Kyron wafted the hem of his robe, tied short for walking, over the smoking ham. Using a knife, he first lifted one slab of meat and then the others, sighing once more when he noted the edge of each was charred.

Extra flavour, he decided.

"Master," Kyron said, carrying the pan to the seated magician and spearing a hunk of ham, sliding it onto the plate.

"Thank you, Kyron," Padarn said, "and not as burnt as usual."

"Yes, Master," Kyron said and stepped around the fire to Emlyn. Her wooden plate rested on the forest floor and next to it a curved knife with one sharp edge. "Your food."

"Thank you," she said, holding the plate up for him to place the ham upon.

"You do have manners," he said, biting down on the words too late.

"I'm not the savage," she replied, looking him in the eye with the hard, sharp gaze she wore much of the time.

"What are you doing there?" He nodded towards the short lump of wood that sat on her lap.

"Carving," she said, moving the wood, its bark gone and the creamy white of its flesh exposed to the night air.

"Carving what?"

"This piece of wood."

"I meant, into what?"

"You should say what you mean," she answered, plucking the knife from the floor and slicing it quickly through the ham. Stabbing the thin section she had cut off, she held it up to the light and inspected it.

"What's wrong?"

"Where did you get the meat?"

"Some of the soldiers will have caught it in the forest," Kyron replied. "We've got some salt cured, but fresh is better."

"Stolen it, then."

"Stolen it? There is no one around to steal from," Kyron said.

"You stole from the forest and people who live here." She dropped the meat on her plate and ran the knife across the rest until there were ten slices.

"No one owns the boar. The soldiers hunted it. Caught a few, I heard," Kyron said.

"Who says no one owns it?"

"Well," he started, suddenly unsure, "the soldiers."

"Did they ask the boar who owned it?"

Kyron snorted. "You can't ask a boar anything."

"Really? You're sure."

"You're making fun of me," he accused. "Boars can't speak."

"All boars belonging to someone are branded with their mark," she explained, lifting a slice to her mouth and chewing slowly. "Did you see its skin?"

"What? No! Of course not," Kyron said.

"And you say it wasn't stolen," she answered, selecting another slice and placing it in her mouth.

"It wasn't," he protested, but felt the argument slipping away.

"Yet you cannot say for sure," she said. "You take too much for granted and ask too few questions. Those you ask seem to be the wrong ones, and of the wrong people."

With that she looked back to the wood in her lap, turning it over with careful hands as she chewed.

Kyron stood still for a long moment, his brain trying to find the right words, the correct argument to use, but he might as well have been killing gnats with a bow and arrow. Every word he loosed had missed its mark: the target too small, too quick for his mind's eye.

He turned and stamped around the fire to his own plate and dumped the last of the ham onto it. He wolfed it down, barely tasting the meal he'd spent time cooking, only the simmering anger which he tried hard to swallow. Pouring some water from their supply into a tall pot, he set it over the fire to warm.

"Master," he whispered, and Padarn looked over to him. "Did we steal the boar?"

"Probably." Padarn nodded. "There is a lot we don't know about life in the forest. Although she might just enjoy making you angry and frustrated."

"Why?"

"I don't know, Kyron." Padarn sighed. "Perhaps she is bored, or maybe it is because we've invaded her land and changed her life forever."

"That's not my fault." Kyron shrugged, drawing a breath to say something else but finding the words fled once more.

"Then whose is it?" His master looked at him with sad eyes and half a smile on his face. "We're here in her forest, marching with an army, stealing their food. Who should she blame?"

"The soldiers," Kyron answered quickly.

"Who do their duty to the Emperor," Padarn replied a moment later. "We're all here at the Emperor's order and he is dead. She can't argue with him. You're a substitute."

"A poor one." Her voice wafted over the fire.

VII

THE GENERAL

TEN YEARS AGO:

"This is your room," he told the sniffling boy. "There is a chest for your clothes, and the mattress has been stuffed with fresh wool."

He watched the boy look around the room, take in the bed, the painted plaster walls, the empty shelves. A memory of decades ago surfaced and the well of sadness opened in his belly.

"It was your father's when he was a young lad."

"YOU MAY SIT," Prince Alhard instructed the council, glancing to his mother as he spoke. "We have much to discuss today, and I am looking for your support in the matters before us."

At the head of the table, the tallest chair—the most ornate and carved with scenes of the Empire's long history—sat empty. Bordan stared at it for a long moment and tried not to sigh at the symbolism which would become all too clear to the rest of the council within moments.

The Empress and Princess Aelia took their appointed chairs while Alhard, the oldest son and heir, remained standing. The rich tunic of imperial purple the Prince wore caught the flickering light from the lanterns hanging on the walls as Bordan slipped into his own chair beside the Princess. The others of the Ruling Council sat and the General could almost see their minds turning over the few words, searching for their hidden meaning and how they could best benefit from whatever it was.

Both children's faces were hard, carved from stone, and their eyes made a slow sweep of the council. In Alhard's eyes flames leapt and flickered, dancing and cavorting in anger and rage; Aelia wore a fragile mask to hide her grief, but it was clear in her eyes for all to see.

However, it was the Empress's eyes which drew Bordan's. Her stare was cold and the flames which simmered within were ice blue.

Bordan's heart beat a quick march while snakes coiled around in his stomach. He took a deep breath, forcing his heart to slow and the snakes to hibernate. It was like this before a battle. The waiting and the knowing that very soon your life blood could be spilled upon the earth. That amongst the press of bodies, the stench of sweat mingled with urine, blood and fear, the screams of dying and roars of the frightened, you would be scrabbling just to stay alive.

He shuddered, waiting for the clarion call to battle even if today, here, the note would be delivered by a woman who had never seen battle, who had, to his knowledge, never killed, let alone felt the keen edge of a blade bite into soft flesh. Worse still, he thought, this battle would be fought not with swords and spears, but with words, subtle actions, secrets and hoarded knowledge, favours and bribes. His hand ached for the feel of his sword's worn hilt.

"We have received some troubling news from the north," Prince Alhard began, once more glancing to his mother who gave the slightest of nods. He held up a hand before anyone could fill the silence which followed that statement, and then rested it on the empty chair at the head of the table. "My father, your Emperor, has died."

Bordan watched the council members for a reaction, gauging their faces and words. With no information on the cause of the Emperor's death it was possible that one of these had something to do with it. Assassins were expensive, but each member of the Ruling Council was rich.

Abra's face was a picture of surprise and Bordan squinted. Was that face too good, too practised? The Duke knew of the messenger; did he know of the message too? Had he been expecting it? A possibility.

Duke Primal let go a gasp which turned into a cough, drawing Bordan's attention. The older man, his thinning grey hair and island of a bald spot reflecting the lantern's flames, was bent over the table struggling to catch his breath. Next to him, Lady Trenis had reached out to pat his back with one hand even as the other took hold of the goblet and offered him a drink.

Across the table, Godewyn raised a single eyebrow but no other emotion crossed his face or showed in his eyes. Even so, Bordan felt the weight of his friend's question upon him and nodded in confirmation.

At the far end, the Master of the Magicians, stood from his chair in shock. The chair teetered on its back legs for a moment before clattering to the floor, the sound of wood striking stone echoing around the room. "No. It cannot be true."

"Calm yourself, Master Vedrix," the Empress said, her voice a warm breeze which dispelled the harsh echo, speaking before her son could. "In war, people die."

"Empress," the fat man said as he drew a handkerchief from his belt and wiped his eyes, "my deepest sympathy for your loss."

"And the Empire's," the widow added. "I am sure we will all miss his presence and his leadership."

Of them all, even Godewyn, Vedrix had the most to lose and was, Bordan concluded, the least likely to have anything to do with the death. If indeed there had been something untoward about it. Curse the messenger for not bringing better information. Perhaps killing him before questioning him more had been a mistake: but the death had bought a day to prepare, to act and gain securities before the news spread throughout the city and beyond.

"Be assured, the next Emperor," the Empress laid a hand upon Alhard's arm, a gesture no one in the room missed, "will continue to support your work and that of the Gymnasium of Magic, Master Vedrix. We recognise your worth to our Empire and the benefits you bring our society."

"Your Majesty," Vedrix responded, the hand holding the handkerchief fluttering about, "that was not my first concern. The Emperor is... was a great man and I am shocked by his passing. It is..." He paused and Bordan saw the man search for the right word, "untimely."

"Empress," Duke Abra said, his voice greased by fake sympathy and oiled with ambition, "no man would say different. Alongside my obvious sympathies for your grievous loss and that of the Prince and Princess, I must enquire as to the cause of the Emperor's demise?"

Bordan caught the subtle nod of the Empress and cleared his throat, going over the story once more in his head before speaking. "We believe he fell in battle against the tribes of the forest. An arrow from one of their bows passed through the slit in his helmet and took his life. A misfortune of battle, but sadly they happen more often than we wish to acknowledge."

The image of the Emperor standing alongside his soldiers and losing his life while fighting the heathen unbelievers of the forest would play well with the populace. There was no chance of keeping the death a secret. Every mouth in here, bar a few, would be blabbing about it to their wives and husbands, with aides and servants overhearing every word. The news would spread like wildfire on parched grassland through the inns, taverns, brothels, and beyond as sailors left for other shores, other ports. Better to control the story before rumours were birthed and grew beyond your grasp.

And though there may be wounds upon the body already, when the Emperor's shell arrived in the capital, there could be one more if needed, as evidence of this story. Bordan himself, his fingers curled into his tunic, would inflict it.

"The Emperor is being transported back to the capital for cremation and for the coronation of Prince Alhard," Bordan finished.

The Empress nodded. "Prince Alhard will be crowned Emperor as is right and proper, as our traditions dictate and it was the Emperor's wish."

"My father," Alhard said as he sat down in the Emperor's empty chair, his voice deep and even, "was a great man. His deeds will be spoken of in every tavern and trade house, in every town and village. His presence will be missed, and the populace saddened, but I, his son, learned at his knee what it was to govern and lead this great Empire. His work shall continue, and we will honour his name in all we do."

Bordan watched the Prince meet the eyes of every council member as he spoke and saw each nod in return. When it came to his turn, Bordan too nodded, but the image of flickering fires behind the dark pupils of the Prince would not leave him.

"The council has much to do," Prince Alhard said, his words measured as if learned by rote, which Bordan knew they had been, "and I will leave you to the discussions, though I expect the reports to be with me as soon as you are finished. General Bordan has been briefed as to my requirements. You have guided me in my father's absence and will, I am sure, continue to do so without fail."

Alhard stood from his chair, his hands resting again on the carved wood while his sister and mother stood from their own. The council stood also and bowed to the imperial family as they departed the room. As Alhard stepped through the door followed by Aelia, a faint sound drifted to Bordan's ear and though it was incongruous with the mood in the room, he swore it was a chuckle. Glancing around the room he saw every member of the council still bowing and, perhaps, hiding their faces from view. The sound had come from inside the room, he was sure of it.

As they retook their seats, servants carried in platters of food and jugs of wine. No one spoke as the platters were lowered to the centre of the table and a single plate with an accompanying eating knife was placed before them. Goblets were refilled and the servants filed from the room.

"You knew," Abra said, speaking first in accusation.

"Of course," Bordan answered. "Such news necessitated secrecy and it was only proper that you, the loyal council, were told first. As the Empress stated, we have a lot to discuss and plan for."

"Where is the body?" Godewyn asked.

"An honour guard is bringing it back to the capital," Bordan answered.

"Across the land?"

"Yes," Bordan said, using his knife to lift a thick slice of steaming ham onto his plate.

"Is that not slow and dangerous?" Abra asked. "I could have one of my ships to a nearby port much quicker, and the coronation could be accomplished before much strife spreads."

"When an Emperor dies there is to be sadness, not strife," Bordan responded though, in truth, it was his greatest fear. An army was disciplined and possessed a clear hierarchy. There was always someone in control, someone able to make decisions and give meaning, purpose to a life, to an action. Death was a natural result of war. The civilian population were unlikely to be so calm about it. So much rested on Alhard's shoulders. The young man had been at his father's side for much of his life and had sat at the Ruling Council meetings, though he had offered little and the burden of rule had fallen on Bordan, Godewyn and the Empress. He had been tutored in religion, politics and war, however learning from scrolls was no substitute for experience. "I'm ready to hear of your worries and suggestions."

"An honour guard?" Duke Primal broke in. "Is that sufficient considering what they guard?"

"The Legion of the First Army has considered the importance and also has first-hand knowledge of the route to be taken. Arcterus knows what he must do to ensure the safe return of the Emperor and maintain the safety of his own army as they continue northwards."

"The war continues?" Lady Trenis said, her voice high in surprise.

"The Emperor and I had considered the possibility of his incapacity or his recall to the capital in the plans, my Lady. Though his tragic death was unexpected, there are contingency plans in place," Bordan said. "In those eventualities the army was to continue its push north. To retreat would embolden the tribes which would only lead to more battles and bloodshed. Should they be so bold as to follow the army they may reach as far as our own borders to the north. Your own holdings are in that direction, are they not?"

She fired him a sudden look of venom. "As you well know, General, my lands are in the north and supply much of the food and fodder for your excursion into the forests."

"For which we are grateful, and it is our duty and honour to ensure the continued safety of your land, Lady Trenis," Bordan said.

"The amulet," Vedrix said, his voice travelling the length of the table and every ear it met turning in his direction. "It is with the Emperor?"

Bordan took a breath, holding it for the count of three before sighing it out. This was the question he feared. Not because the answer was complicated—it wasn't—but whoever possessed the amulet held the Empire, so entwined with the history of the Empire was it. The Flame of each previous Emperor was contained within its facets, and they would pass the knowledge to whomever owned the amulet when the coronation ceremony was complete. More than one dynasty had held the Empire's throne over its existence, and the amulet cared nothing for bloodlines or heritage.

At least, so the stories said. The jewel held some power beyond its symbolism: of that Bordan was sure. Too often he had seen the Emperor appear to drift off into daydreams only to come back to the present with a piece of wisdom, or a moment from history when the Empire faced similar struggles and from which lessons could be learned.

"It is," Bordan said, painting a target upon the honour guard should any here wish to take power. "We will be sending a force of our own to escort the Emperor."

"From the Third Army or Second?" Abra asked, leaning forward.

"The Second cannot be recalled in time," Bordan replied. "Their campaign on the southern continent continues and our borders are strengthened by their presence there. We will do our utmost to keep the news from them until their own battles are won. Morale is as important as sharp swords to an army."

Which Abra knew, Bordan thought. The man who controlled the seas and the ships had a good deal more knowledge of the Army's movements than was comfortable. He shook his head, clearing away the worries for another day.

"The Third then?" Abra pushed.

"Yes," Bordan acknowledged.

"It is my understanding that the Third Army is our reserve," Abra said, looking along the table to Bordan, his nostrils flaring a little on each breath. "Made up of our youngest and oldest soldiers."

"Our recruits with veterans to lead them," Bordan corrected, snapping the words off like thin icicles in the depth of winter.

"But they are spread about the Empire?"

"At present," Bordan said, "better to protect against outlaws and give confidence to the people."

"And you've enough to spare," Abra continued, "to send north to meet the honour guard?"

"I cannot foresee a problem," Bordan answered, though in truth he had dreamed of nothing but problems last night.

The Third Army was an army in name only. Under the command of Legion Maxentius, it was broken into small forces which patrolled the borders, and were stationed in towns and forts far from the capital. The city itself had force enough to defend itself, but to march it north would strip that safety away and the worry gnawing away at Bordan's innards told him he would need that force before long.

"Perhaps we should speak first of the coronation, High Priest. Could you reacquaint us with the ceremonies and rituals so that we might plan and ensure a smooth transition from one beloved Emperor to the next?"

VIII

THE MAGICIAN

TEN YEARS AGO:
He watched the old man close the door, and then he was alone.
Wiping his eyes free of the stinging tears, he saw the room was bigger
than his old one. Sitting on the bed, silence crowding his thoughts,
he ran his hands across the decorated headboard of embossed bronze
depicting galloping deer.

"HERE," EMLYN SAID. "Put this in the water and bring it to the boil."

"What is it?" Kyron plucked the twisted root from her fingers and peered at it through blurry morning eyes.

"A wicked poison," she answered.

"What?" His fingers jerked open and the root fell towards the forest floor, but her quick hands snatched it from the air.

"You don't think and have no sense of humour," she said, shaking her head and pushing past him. "We call it Asaraum. I don't know what you call it, even if you have it. It flavours our tea and gives energy for the day ahead."

She dropped it in the boiling pan of water before he could reply or move to stop her.

"No." He reached out a hand anyway, knowing it was too late, but making the effort to convince himself he had acted properly.

"Your army trust me to lead them safely through the forests and you will not even let me make tea," Emlyn said, straightening up, then arching her back. "You seem to have no end of faults, young man."

"I'm hardly younger than you," he snapped back.

"It takes more than years to make someone older," Emlyn replied. "Give the tea a few minutes to infuse."

"Are you two arguing already?" Padarn said, stepping out of his tent into the predawn light and mist which filtered between the trees. All around, the night's camp was coming to life and the sounds of men grumbling drifted alongside the mist.

"She is making tea, Master," Kyron complained.

"I'm glad someone is." Padarn stepped up to the fire and held his hands out to catch the warmth which spilled from the flames. "The weather isn't looking good and I need something to warm me for the long march today."

"But I don't know what she has put in the tea," Kyron said and lowered his voice. "It might be poison."

Padarn snorted and glanced back at him, a wry smile on his face. "If she wanted to kill you or me, as I told you before, a knife in the night would be simplest. She could be gone from the camp before light and no one would find her. Isn't that so?"

Emlyn smiled up at him from her seat on the ground. "They would never find me."

"The army has excellent trackers," Kyron said, puffing out his chest.

"Not good enough to find me," Emlyn answered, and there was a simple honesty to the statement which deflated the young magician.

"What is in the tea, young lady?" Padarn asked, leaning over the boiling pot and sniffing.

"Asaraum."

"Wild ginger," Padarn nodded. "I've not tasted that in a long, long time. Years, at least, if not a decade."

"You know what it is?" Emlyn's look changed from one of victory, to one more wary and guarded.

"Travelled a bit when I was younger," Padarn said, stepping to a log and sitting down. "Broadens the mind, and experience is the best teacher. You'd be surprised what you can learn from the simple act of sharing a meal."

"You came to the forest?" she asked.

"Not this bit," Padarn said, looking around. "Though, if I am honest, I can't be too sure. One tree looks very much the same as another to me."

"You came here before, Master?" Kyron prodded.

"I've been to a lot of places, Kyron. Part of the reason I agreed to accompany the army was to travel, to expose you to the world. Too much time in the capital blinds you to the world around. You have to understand it all if you want to realise your potential," the magician said, then paused and added, "The preservation charms on the Emperor's wrappings will need to be checked today."

"I checked yesterday, Master," Kyron whined. "The priests weren't happy that I was there. The charms will be in effect for a few more days."

"They'll be even more unhappy if the Emperor's body is not kept in the best condition possible," Padarn replied. "The Empress even less so."

"Then the priests should get the blame," Kyron complained.

"And you know that they will not, Kyron. You can put up with the priests for a little longer," Padarn said. "The Imperial Family are the patrons of the Gymnasium of Magic. Without the Empire's support of our studies for the past centuries we would not even possess half the knowledge we do now. The least we can do is preserve his body, and deliver it whole and unblemished to his family."

"How did he die?" Emlyn asked. "I've spoken with the officers, when they bother to talk to me, but they won't say."

Kyron lifted the boiling water and, holding the root back with his knife, poured the tea into three clay cups, passing them out and taking his own. The story he had heard of the Emperor's death was full of rumour and no substance, little more than soldiers' gossip. Assassins from the tribe had used magic to disguise themselves and sneak into the Emperor's tent, stabbing him to death, seemed to be the story most shared. No one could agree on how many assassins there had been, nor how many the Emperor had killed with his bare hands before succumbing to their blows. Worse still, Kyron had been unable to find anyone who had seen the assassins' bodies and no guards had been disciplined for the lapse in security.

But he knew the two master magicians had been consulted when the body was discovered, and now he leaned forward, hardly breathing, waiting to hear the truth from someone who knew.

"His heart stopped," his master answered.

"Why?" Kyron breathed. There must be more. The Emperor was a great man who had changed the world, whose actions had expanded the Empire and brought peace and prosperity to thousands. Behind his death there would be a valiant story of a struggle. There had to be. All the old stories which his grandfather had filled his head with during his youth had been full of shining heroes and dark villains. The Emperor was a hero, so there must be a villain.

"It happens," Padarn shrugged, taking a sip of his tea and sighing in contentment. "He was an old man with a lot to think about and do. Sometimes that's all it takes."

Kyron stared at his master, waiting for more which did not come, and a sense of emptiness flowed from his toes to the top of his head. An Emperor deserved a glorious death, a story to tell the next generation. "Is that all, Master?"

"Sometimes simple answers are the truth," Padarn said. "Take a razor to complicated knot and it comes apart easily enough."

IX

THE GENERAL

TEN YEARS AGO:

He sat in his room, alone, and heard the heart-wrenching sobs being drawn from the boy's small frame. In his hands he held a toy chariot. One of the wooden wheels refused to spin, the soldier had one arm missing, and the horse's ears were broken off.

Is this who I am? he muttered to himself. Shaking his head, and placing the small toy back on the shelf, he strode to the door.

"HOW FARES THE city, General Bordan?" the Empress asked.

"Restless, your Majesty," Bordan replied, sighing. Three late nights of reading reports from the watch and the troops deployed to keep order in the city felt like an eternity. "No rioting or particular disorder. Those in the wealthier areas of the city have begun to increase their own security."

"Where is disorder greatest?" Alhard looked up from his plate of food, a tower of meats and slow cooked vegetables. A family of six could happily dine on that amount and consider themselves full at the end of the meal.

"In the poorer quarters, Your Highness."

"Ride the troops through the slums and string a few up, Bordan," Alhard said, waving his eating knife to punctuate his command. The chunk of sausage which the Prince had stabbed only moments before described a precise arc through the air and bounced on the stone floor. One of the dogs—a dark, muscled beast which Alhard favoured—scurried across the floor and gobbled it up, licking its lips in appreciation of the unintentional gift.

"A fine idea, my Prince," Bordan said, taking care with every word and watching the Empress for clues. "I will certainly deploy the troops with those orders should the need arise."

"Law and order are important for the city," Alhard said, already tucking into another sausage.

Aelia stared at her brother for a moment before shaking her head. "What of the Dukes, Bordan?"

"Princess?"

"The poor are a nuisance, but surely little more. If, as my brother suggests, we feel the need to send in the soldiers to set a few examples, they will quickly give way. It is the Dukes who worry us more, is it not?"

"It is, Princess," Bordan said, taking another look at Aelia, noting the younger woman cast a glance at her mother and the way her fingers fluttered against the table. "I've set some rotations to ensure that the troops within the city are from the rural areas of the Empire. Legion Maxentius, of the Third Army, is keeping a tight grip on his troops. He knows them well, and has the new recruits commanded by veterans. Both of us know that soldiers do as they are ordered, but it would be folly to order them to kill their childhood friends."

"Well done, General," the Empress interrupted. "However, as Princess Aelia asked, the Dukes? This news of increasing their own guards, should it worry us?"

"They have insufficient numbers, even banded together, to pose a serious risk to the troops within the walls, Your Highness."

"And individually? We know that they will not threaten the army, General. However, should they kill you, they may be able to place someone more amenable to their aims in charge," the Empress said.

"Then what?" Alhard said, though the words were muffled by the quantity of food which he had just stuffed in his mouth and was attempting to swallow.

"I'm guarded, Your Highness, and risk is part of a soldier's life. There is an established chain of command should an accident befall me. Maxentius will take over my duties, as he will upon my eventual retirement," Bordan said, shifting his shoulders under the armour he wore today. There was a small ache at the base of his spine, a sure sign that he was not used to the additional weight.

"And our safety?" Aelia said, glancing once more at her mother.

"The Immunis of your imperial guard are charged with your protection, and I've doubled the guard around the perimeter of your quarters," Bordan said. "I've also got each of the Dukes who may think themselves a future Emperor under a close watch."

"Do they know that?" Aelia said, pushing her plate away. Most of the food on it was untouched.

"I hope so," he replied, allowing a smile to cross his face. "I've put some of my most obvious men on that duty."

"A warning?" the Empress asked.

"That, and if the Dukes are concentrating on the obvious, they might not spot some of the informants I have placed in their households."

"You did all this in the past three days?" Alhard looked up from his food, his knife pausing in its butchery of a lamb's leg.

"No, my Prince," Bordan acknowledged. "I've had people within their households for many years. However, they expect me to do something to keep a closer eye on their activities, so I have given them someone to watch. It confirms their suspicions and guards my true spies."

"Clever," Aelia said.

"Thank you, Your Highness." Bordan bowed. "If there is nothing else, I have an appointment with Duke Abra to discuss the rotation of troops to the western reaches."

"You're meeting with him?" Alhard said, coughing on a mouth stuffed with food.

"We need his ships to supply the army in the north and our troops elsewhere. The southern continent remains important to trade and the tax earned pays for the army," Bordan explained, holding back a sigh. "Much as I might wish the crown had control of the seas, the merchants are more numerous and better suited than the few warships we maintain."

"General, we should have a strong navy to protect our borders and ports," Alhard said.

Bordan nodded and looked to the Empress. She waved a hand in permission.

"Protection from who, my Prince?" Bordan clasped his hands behind his back, constraining his usual tendency to gesture and point when teaching. His son had cautioned against it and his grandson, a wilful boy who soaked up knowledge but rarely listened, had argued with him incessantly every time. He took an extra moment to tell himself this was the next Emperor and not to be treated like an unlearned child.

"Raiders and pirates," Alhard answered much as a child at a tutor's knee would, with the learned and oft repeated answer.

"And the last time we were subject to such attack?" Bordan said, stepping forward.

"Well..." Alhard cast a look around the room, seeking an answer from his sister or mother. Neither were forthcoming and the man's face screwed up in obvious thought. "I don't know."

"And you might argue, might you not, my Prince, that it was our navy that has brought us this peace and safety to our ports?"

"Of course," Alhard exclaimed, latching onto the idea and almost leaping from his chair in excitement, a large smile spreading across his face.

Bordan smiled at him. The tutor's trap had been simple and Alhard should have known better than to fall into it. Aelia would have neatly side-stepped it, Bordan knew, and he sighed. "Our fleet is more for show than anything practical. Five large warships to sail into ports, show the flag of the Empire, and thirty or so smaller vessels to secure the shipping lanes at the behest of the merchants."

"Then why haven't the raiders attacked?" The smile gave way to a look of confusion on Alhard's face, one he'd seen too often before.

"Because we conquered them," the Empress interjected.

"About two centuries ago," Bordan added, tipping his head to acknowledge the Empress's answer. "It was from them we learned to build the smaller, faster vessels we use now. Sooner or later, every nation becomes part of the Empire."

"And Duke Abra?" Aelia asked, when her brother fell silent, her eyes narrowing and sharpening.

"Knows this," Bordan agreed, "as do many of the lords, Dukes and other nobles of the Empire. It is no secret."

"Which would mean that the Duke knows how important his ships are to us?"

"Undoubtedly." Bordan nodded. "However, by tradition and law his vessels cannot carry much in the way of defence or weaponry except in times of war, at which point they fall under the control of the military."

"Abra knows his worth," the Empress said in her quiet voice. "However, he understands it would take just a simple declaration to strip those ships from him."

"And he would lose everything," Aelia said.

"Indeed. Also, tax revenues would fall and there would be hardship for many," Bordan agreed.

"And so we are caught," the Empress said.

"Trapped," Aelia said.

"To a degree," Bordan said, "but so are they."

"And on such devices does our Empire stand and fall," the Empress said, her tone solemn.

"I don't like it," Alhard grunted. "The Dukes always want more power."

"Would some dream of being Emperor?" Aelia took a sip from her goblet and Bordan saw the Princess's eyes go distant for a moment.

"It is not unheard of," Bordan said.

"I'm the next Emperor by birth, tradition, and my father's decree." Alhard slammed his open palm down upon the table causing the plates and goblets to jump and rattle. "They cannot take that from me."

"They will not, Prince Alhard." Bordan looked to the Empress for support but received only a small shake of her head. "But it is no secret that they wish to have more of a say in how the Empire is run."

"Filthy ingrates," Alhard spat, tossing the eating knife he held onto the table where it slid for a distance before coming to rest against a haunch of steaming meat. "They want to take our power. Who, General? Which ones? Abra, Primal or more of them?"

"Abra certainly," Bordan said, swallowing his irritation and keeping his voice level, "though he has done nothing overt nor spoken of his desires. With his control of the merchant fleet, it is feasible that he could engineer some way to make a play for the throne, but it is not likely. He is not a man prone to rash actions. To hire his own army—enough mercenaries to pose a threat to our two armies on this continent—would be hard to disguise. There will be others."

"Trenis?" The Prince stood in a rush, his chair legs scraping across the stone.

"Possibly, my Prince. We will keep watch on them all. Once the ceremony is complete, you will be Emperor," Bordan explained. "If we need to take action before, we will."

"Arrest them now," Alhard said. "Take Abra's ships. I'll issue the declaration. The risk is too great. Let's put them back in their place before they get too bold."

"We cannot, my son," the Empress said. "The Empire is based on the rule of law. If we break it then everyone else is free to do so."

"We have the army," Alhard argued. "We command and they obey. Bordan, summon troops back to the capital. The peasants will fall into line quick enough if we march troops through the city's streets."

"And in the countryside where many Dukes hold land and have mercenary groups alongside their own guards?" Bordan paused for a moment, taking a drink from his goblet, watching the thoughts stray across Alhard's face. "Would you give up the farms and forests where our food and fuel comes from? It would give a Duke such as Abra greater leverage, and we cannot fight a war on the plains and the oceans at the same time." He paused, examining the shimmering reflection on the surface of the wine. It hid the lines around his eyes, but not the sadness. "In the city, they are contained, Prince Alhard, and under careful watch. The traditional period of mourning will make any action stand out to our watchers. I know it is difficult, but better to be calm and consider all options and strategies before launching an attack. When you are crowned Emperor, the Dukes will fall into line, my Prince, and your throne will be secure."

"But..." Alhard began.

"Should action be needed, it will be taken at the right time, and when we are sure of the support of others. For that we need proof. General?" the Empress asked, cutting off her son's response.

"My spies report daily, Your Highness," Bordan said, offering the Empress a grateful nod.

"A summary of their findings would be useful."

"I will bring it every morning, Your Highness," Bordan agreed.

"I don't like it," Alhard said, sinking back into his chair and staring at the ruins of his meal.

"What, my Prince?"

"That they want to take my place, to steal my birthright and throne."

"They will not, my Prince," Bordan assured the young man. "Your father was a man of patience who knew the right time to strike was not always at the outset of an endeavour. You are his son, his heir, and have that same blood running through your veins. Be guided by us, your mother, sister, and myself, until the amulet is yours and the souls of every Emperor joins with your own. You will be Emperor, my Prince."

"I must be," Alhard said, reaching across the table for his discarded knife and stabbing it into another slab of meat. "And once I am, we will deal with the traitors properly."

"A show of force, a parade, might settle the people, General," Aelia said, though her eyes were fixed upon the last of the evening light streaming in through the window opposite. "And my dear brother should be seen by the people. At our father's side he was, forgive me, just the heir. Now he can ride at the head of the column."

"Yes," Alhard said, his sullen mood evaporating, and the food forgotten once again.

"It cannot be... too big a parade," Bordan cautioned. "The period of mourning must be observed, and the people expect certain things of us all at this time. We cannot step too far from the rituals and rhythms of the Church. There have been reports of some unrest amongst the people as well. It might be best to—"

"A procession," Aelia mused, talking over the General, her gaze still distant. "An observance."

"To the Church?" Alhard's tone was less than enthusiastic and Bordan could only agree.

"To an ancestor," Aelia's voice rose and she turned to face them. "To the statue of this city's founder. Pay respects."

"And forge some links to our past," the Empress added. "The people would understand the symbolic journey."

"It is a good suggestion," Bordan replied, though deep in his belly a worm of worry began to burrow. "We would need to plan it most carefully."

"Tomorrow," Alhard said. "We will go tomorrow. I cannot stay locked away forever behind these walls, only attending Ruling

Council meetings. The people should see me and the troops." The Prince held up a hand as Bordan opened his mouth to argue for another day to prepare. "I have made my decision, General. You now obey me as you did my father."

Bordan glanced at the Empress but her face was impassive, giving nothing away. "Of course, my Prince. I will have the troops assembled for you in the morning."

X

THE MAGICIAN

TEN YEARS AGO:

No one woke him. No one called his name. No warm arms enfolded him, and no soft kiss was planted upon his forehead. They were gone.

He pulled on a tunic, his only one, and stumbled down the stairs of the unfamiliar house. The scent of baking bread wafted to his nose and he breathed deeply, a memory of a home no longer standing. Bittersweet.

"KYRON."

His master's voice broke him from a daydream and the image of dark eyes fled back into the recesses of his mind. "Master?"

"It is time to renew the markers on the Emperor's funeral bier," Padarn said. "Daydreaming is all well and good, but if you're not going to study you may as well be of some use."

"But, Master, you know the priests don't like me," he protested.

"They are not overly fond of me either, Kyron, but the Emperor requires our service and he was long a supporter of the Gymnasium when others counselled him against it," his master replied. "Do not give them the shot to sling back at us, my apprentice. Renew the preservation wards, be polite, and serve the Empire."

"I know about service," he snapped back and regretted it immediately. "I'm sorry, Master. A word I heard too often used as a reason growing up."

Waiting for admonishment, he was surprised to see a small smile crawl across his master's face. "Master?"

"I met your grandfather, briefly, when he presented you at the gymnasium," Padarn mused. "A man of dedication, but a pragmatist too. He saw your path was not his. To some men service is the pinnacle of their expectations, to others it is the core of their being, and yet to a rare few it is just the beginning. The Emperor understood that; at least I choose to believe so. Where you stand is yet to be determined, Kyron. However, right now, at this moment, your master is giving you a task and you will carry it out to the best of your ability." The words were tempered by the smile which still creased Padarn's face. "Don't let any of us down."

Kyron took a breath. "Of course, Master."

He stood, brushing the leaves and dirt from his clothes. He threw the leather strap of his satchel over his shoulder, settling the weight against his hip and giving it a reassuring pat.

"Be polite and don't rise to anything they say or do," Padarn warned him. "Remember, they need you if they are to fulfil their own duties."

"Master, what if…" he began.

"And no magic but that which the markers require," Padarn said, raising a finger. "Not even an itch or bee sting should befall the priests."

Kyron sighed. "Yes, Master."

"Good boy. Off you go," his master said, "and don't take too long. We'll be moving again soon."

This time he contained the sigh and settled for a nod of acknowledgement. Trudging through the resting column towards the funeral bier and the priests who clustered around it, he was forced to step across the deep muddy ruts left by the waggons ahead. On both sides of the track, soldiers sat, chatting and eating their rations of hard bread and cured meat, swigging from water skins and checking the fit of their armour. Despite the relaxed atmosphere, Kyron knew there were scouts out amongst the trees and other troops keeping watch.

Too soon the Emperor's bier came into view: a waggon painted in the Emperor's colours with a ring of guards stationed around it.

These did not sit, chat or eat, but kept a watchful stare at the forest. Clustered together, a short distance from the waggon sat the small cadre of priests who had been chosen to accompany the body back to the capital. Kyron saw one look in his direction and nudge the priest next to her.

Gritting his teeth and forcing a neutral expression on his face, Kyron kept his steps even and his eyes focused upon the waggon. The priests did not call out, but their stares weighed as much as a merchant's cheating thumb on the spice market's scales.

Stopping before the soldier who stood between the tracks, he looked up into the man's hard eyes.

"Immunis," Kyron began, cursing the crack in his voice, "my master sent me to renew the markers."

"Pass, Kyron," the Immunis said without looking at him.

"Thanks," the young man said and stepped around the soldier.

"Don't let them get you annoyed," the Immunis added in a quiet whisper. "You're serving the Empire with honour. Don't forget that."

Kyron stopped, level with the Immunis but looking towards the waggon and the priests who had lined up before it. "Always service."

"What else is there to life?" the Immunis replied.

Kyron bit back his initial response. "Thank you for the advice."

"Anytime, Apprentice."

Kyron moved again, thinking over the guard's words and forgetting to look at his feet. The churned-up mud was slippery and his foot skidded, his balance abandoning him. Wheeling his arms, he lurched forward and down onto one knee. Both hands slammed into the mud to prevent him going any further and there was a burst of laughter from the line of priests.

Standing, he looked at his dirt-covered hands while the laughter rang in his ears. A fire of anger flashed down his throat and warmed his belly, but he damped it down, remembering his master's words.

"Here," the Immunis said, handing him a cloth which Kyron used to wipe most of the dirt from his hands. "I've slipped twice today myself."

"Thank you," Kyron said, returning the cloth.

"Keep it," the Immunis said, "at least until you've had a chance to clean it."

"I'll bring it back to you," Kyron promised. "Immunis?"

"Juncus," the man said.

"Thank you again, Immunis Juncus." He folded the cloth into a square and tucked it inside his clothes.

"Welcome, Apprentice," one of the priests said as Kyron turned back to them. His robe was like the others but trimmed with a grey the colour of ash.

"Deacon," Kyron replied adding a small bow. Scanning the other priests, he saw there was one other wearing the grey trim of rank, every other robe was plain black. The highest priest of rank amongst the honour guard was absent and the three Justices had stayed with the main bulk of the army, for which Kyron was grateful. "How fares the Archdeacon today?"

"His arm is healing," the Deacon replied, his eyes narrowing as he focused on Kyron.

Under his own clothes, the young apprentice began to sweat. "I am glad. If you would permit, I am sure I can..."

"No," the Deacon snapped. "The Archdeacon's arm will heal without the taint of your magic."

Kyron swallowed down the response and settled for a calm nod and the words, "Of course, Deacon. It shall be as you say."

The old man had tripped over something on the first day of the journey—exactly what no one would say or seemed sure—and in the fall had broken his arm. The cry of pain had echoed along the column and they had halted, letting daylight pass while they treated the man. Padarn had offered his assistance but was rebuffed just as Kyron had been now. It was important, his master had told him, to make the offer nonetheless.

"The markers?" Kyron prompted when no one else seemed to want to speak and risk the Deacon's temper.

"Yes," the Deacon said. "Curate Livillia, go with the apprentice and see he carries out his duties appropriately."

"Yes, Deacon," the voice of a woman floated out of the hooded cowl she wore.

"Don't touch anything else." A bony finger with its sharp nail tinged with unhealthy yellow punctuated the Deacon's words, jabbing at Kyron upon every word.

"Of course, Deacon," Kyron said, his hands curling into fists and spine stiffening as he forced himself to bow to the priest.

"I'm glad you've been taught proper respect for the priesthood," the Deacon said, oil dripping from every word as he swept away followed by the other priest.

The lonely figure of Curate Livillia did not move for a long moment, but once the Deacon and followers had rounded the corner of the waggons a deep sigh emanated from the cowl. "Come then, Apprentice. Let's get this unpleasant duty done."

"I know where the markers are, Curate," Kyron said. "You don't have to watch me."

"Much as I don't wish to, Apprentice, the Deacon has ordered it," she said, "and to be a priest is to always follow the higher order. Even one as unpleasant as this."

Without another word, the Curate turned and led Kyron to the corner of the Emperor's bier. Even from the length of four horses away, the scent of magic, the power contained and re-purposed washed across him. It was a dry smell, an old aroma—not of the grave or decay, but of the ancient and treasured. His grandfather had owned swords: some were gifts from other kingdoms, some were from the Empire, but all were too old to be used. They had a similar smell and feel, not of magic but of time.

The markers themselves were nothing more than symbols painted upon each corner of the bier. Permanent preservation—or at least as his master explained it preservation which would last so long as to be viewed as permanent—was possible, but expensive. The materials needed to contain the magic, to prevent its essence from eroding the material, was rare and only a few knew the correct combination of minerals, metals and gems along with the forging technique.

Most magic, that which was designed to last, was written on parchment or painted on objects. Constant upkeep and maintenance was required, but that kept the magicians in employment—so Padarn said.

Kyron breathed deeply as he knelt before the first marker. The shape was stylised, somewhere in-between a picture and a letter and each observer read it differently. Beyond that it had no meaning or special power. It was part of the artifice of magic, the outward show of the years of study.

Taking a pot of ink and brush from his satchel, he painted over the symbol, defining the lines a little more and adding a twist of his own. It was a moment of stillness, of calm and practice which helped to focus his mind.

Closing his eyes, he placed the implements upon the floor, and let his mind drift to the magic. The sounds of the world melted away, the whinny of horses, the scrape of whetstone on metal, the chatter of the soldiers, even his own heartbeat faded from his consciousness.

Yet around him the world buzzed. With eyes shut, he could not see the landscape and forest, but the magic outlined it all in his mind. The priest who stood close by, the shape of the bier, its fabric and wood, the trees and dirt. The further away, the less distinct it became until the world faded into a blur of impression and mists.

Only the minute specks of magic remained, passing through and bouncing off all that surrounded him. They were everywhere, in everything, a million tiny flies buzzing past his ears, a billion minuscule stars wheeling around the sky. They called to him and he to them, commanding, cajoling, explaining, demanding, and controlling.

This was magic. This was where he existed.

XI

THE GENERAL

TEN YEARS AGO:

The soft footsteps intruded on his thoughts and he looked up from the scroll. The boy had cried himself to sleep last night in his arms, his little body wracked with sobs. It had been an easy decision to let him sleep late. He put away the pot of ink and rolled up his journal, tucking it into a desk drawer.

"I AM STILL not convinced this is wise, my Prince," Bordan called over the sound of horseshoes on cobbles.

"We are surrounded by your best guards, are we not?" Alhard replied, sweeping his hand in a gesture which encompassed the ring of soldiers who surrounded them.

"We are."

"And you said it yourself, General, to keep the peace it is important the people see their future Emperor," Alhard said.

"From castle walls, my Prince, at feasts, attending the theatre, at the Colosseum. Not riding amongst them." Bordan looked across at the heir. They had argued for a short time, but the Prince had finally agreed to wear the lorica hamata, the vest of chain, beneath his tabard. "The Dukes need to see you out and about. The lords and ladies who control the trade, the tax collection, the flow of food into city. The guild masters and merchants, those are the people who need to see you, who you need to talk to and impress."

73

"Impress, General? I am their Emperor. I don't need to *impress* them. They just need to do what they are told," Alhard grunted.

"They will, my Prince, but sometimes you will find their support will come with more… alacrity if they find you agreeable to their interests," Bordan suggested.

"Agreeable?" Alhard turned in his saddle to wave at a resident who gazed out at them from a window. "Once I am Emperor, General, are not their interests mine?"

"Of course, my Prince," Bordan said. "I am sure they will always follow your directives. It is they who will be dealing with the people at large and what they say to each subordinate will work its way down to them. Rumours and stories, those which we've worked to control, can make your rule easier or more difficult."

"Then better to be about amongst the people, letting them see the truth," Alhard said.

"We are at a dangerous time, my Prince."

"And I am wearing the armour you insisted upon and we have guards," Alhard pointed out, his voice taking on an edge of irritation. "Where is this unrest you mentioned most pronounced, General?"

"We have much of it contained, my Prince," Bordan said.

"But where, General?"

"The southern quarter, adjacent to the docks."

"The Fishers? Where the statue is?"

"Yes, my Prince," Bordan said, surprised. "I was not aware you knew so much of the city."

The Prince's high-pitched laugh rang out through the street. Two soldiers turned as they marched, but a barked order had them facing the front once more.

"My father made me study, General. I know each area of the city and trade for which it is named," Prince Alhard said. "However, I have visited very little. This is my city, General Bordan, the heart of the Empire my father ruled and has passed to me."

"Cohort Timet," Bordan said, "what is the current situation in the Fishers?"

"Tense, General," Timet, a thin man upon which the armour he wore looked too large, replied. "Though we have increased patrols and it is the calmest it has been."

"Safe enough?"

"That would be hard to say, General. The city is nervous, and the people are talking about the Emperor's death. They're worried and the delay in the coronation is only increasing their fears." Timet leaned forward and nodded in the direction of the Prince whose gaze was elsewhere. "Everyone wants the Prince to take the throne without delay."

"I'm sure they do, Cohort," Bordan said, acknowledging the unspoken words. There were factions in the city, amongst the people and the nobility, who had not been happy under the old Emperor's rule. They would take the chance to make their feelings known. "Prince Alhard, we can visit the Fishers should you wish."

"I thought that was my order, General," Alhard said, surprise in his tone as he turned back to face Bordan. "I did say that was where I wished to go, and my wishes are to be taken as commands, are they not?"

"Of course, my Prince. However, your safety is our prime concern," Bordan replied, adding a short bow from his saddle. "Cohort, lead the way."

As Timet called out orders, Bordan checked the position of his sword hilt. It felt good to have the weight on his hip and his own lorica hamata encasing his chest. A shield would have been welcome but would have felt too much like heading off to war, and a battle in the city was the last thing he wanted. The soldiers were, as always, dressed for battle and the people expected that, welcomed it as normal. However, it would not be seemly for the General or the heir to the throne to go about kitted out for war. It would send the wrong message.

Around them, Sudrim went about its business. The tall, ornate buildings of the nobles gave way to the shorter, plainer homes and businesses of the merchants then to the single storey dwellings of the clerks, administrators, and money counters as they began to descend from the hill upon which the palace sat.

Citizens moved aside as the patrol approached, the soldiers with their spears and shields forging a path for the horses which followed. The scent of the sea rose to meet them, and the homes grew in size once more as the slope levelled off. Here were the factors and warehouses, the trading houses, markets, and navigating it all, like the great sharks of the open water, would be the Emperor's tax collectors, hated and feared in equal measure.

Through the buildings, Bordan caught a glimpse of the tall masts of ships at harbour. The source of Duke Abra's wealth and power. His horse flicked its head, and it took an effort of will to relax his grip on the reins. A deep breath, letting the salt air wash away the fetid scent of rotting fish, rubbish, and anger.

"We turn here, General," Cohort Timet said.

The soldiers led them along a road which headed off at right angles and ran parallel, though a few streets away, to the docks. The street narrowed and Bordan felt the weight of stares upon him. Expecting rotten fruit, a stone, or an arrow between his shoulder blades at any moment, he kept his hands on the reins and away from his sword.

"The Fishers is just ahead, General," Timet said. "Are we sure we wish to visit the market... the statue this morning?"

"We are, Cohort," Alhard said in a loud, clear voice. "I believe I was clear in my wishes."

"Of course, my Prince," Timet said, a tremor in his voice and Bordan noted the way the man's eyes twitched and throat reddened.

"It will be fine, Cohort," Bordan assured him. "Lead us through the district. Any information you can give on landmarks, buildings, or how trouble here has been dealt with, would be very much appreciated."

"Yes, General," Timet said, the words whistling out between clenched teeth, before he called to the soldiers around them. "Tighten up the ranks. Keep a watch out."

"Where is the statue, Cohort?" Alhard asked. "My father spoke of the statue to an old Emperor, the founder of this very city."

"It is in the district market, Prince Alhard," Timet replied. "I believe it is to one of the early Emperors, when the city was smaller. If I had known earlier that it was to be our final destination, I would have made better preparations."

"Didas," Alhard said, waving away the officer's excuses. "Emperor Didas. The fourth or fifth Emperor. It was he who moved the capital to Sudrim. Constructed a fleet of ships to carry the court across the seas from the southern continent and secured the trade routes."

"He founded the city?" Timet asked, leaning forward in his saddle.

"Yes, Cohort," Alhard answered with a chuckle. "There was, I seem to remember from the interminable scrolls one of my tutors made me read, a town or perhaps just a small village already here. Didas expanded it and began the building of the palace and castle. I would very much like to see the statue of my ancestor, Cohort. Lead us there."

"As you wish, Prince Alhard," Timet said.

Bordan glanced across at the Cohort. He sat straighter in his saddle, the rebuke forgotten or forgiven and a look of pride upon his face. A lowly soldier spoken to by the heir to the throne as almost an equal had given the man a sense of worth. It was a trick Alhard's father had deployed with the troops, a sharing of knowledge, a conversation, a meeting of minds, and they had loved him for it. Perhaps, Alhard had inherited some of the skills he would need to rule. For the first time since the Emperor's death, Bordan found a spark of hope in his heart.

The flow of people increased as they approached the market and the soldiers in the lead began calling out to clear the way. There were angry mutterings and a few shouted insults, but they meant nothing to the troops and the Prince, to his credit, ignored them all. No one would ever have knowingly spoken to him in such tones, and when the people realised who rode amongst them the shouts dwindled to a sullen silence.

The market here was not the permanent structures of the docks or the wealthier areas. Some had set up tents and awnings from which to sell their wares. Others, more transient and desperate, had spread blankets upon the ground which they covered with scattered belongings, hoping someone would offer them a penny so they could feed their families.

"We'll need to dismount," the Cohort said. "The horses won't be able to get through the stalls to the statue."

Bordan swung his legs, wincing at the ache in his hips and frowning at the way his muscles trembled as his feet met the earth. Getting old and out of shape, he thought and rested his hand on the sword hilt, angling it for a quick draw in an unconscious gesture.

"Lead the way, Cohort," he said, gesturing with his free hand. The groups of soldiers and the Prince began to pick their way through the crowd.

"Meat for sale, fresh yesterday."

"Trinkets and jewels."

"Cloth. Best you'll get."

"Spices and herbs."

"A penny for the bread."

Sellers crowded around the soldiers, the aroma of wealth which wafted from Prince Alhard drawing them all closer with the promise of profit. Their shouts and imprecations to buy grew louder.

"We will soon have a riot on our hands," Timet said, casting a nervous glance at the crowd.

Bordan nodded, wary of the press of people and the growing demands to buy, to spend, to give a little to the poor. In the centre of the pocket, surrounded by the soldiers, the Prince's face wore a smile almost beatific. General Bordan took a step closer, hand not leaving the scabbard of his sword and noted the way the Prince's eyes swept the crowd, soaking in the faces and noise. There was no fear, no tremor or nervous tick, no sweat upon his brow. He is enjoying it, Bordan realised, he thinks they are here for him, not for his money.

"It is just through here," Timet said as the soldiers rapped the butts of their spears upon the stone and clashed their shields with the hafts. Around them the crowd began to part a little, enough for the group to move forward.

They emerged from the stalls and tents into a small clearing set about a low wall which contained a pond of stagnant water. From the centre rose a statue, carved in dirt-smudged stone. It depicted a man dressed in the ancient fashion, a toga gathered around his waist and draped over the leather cuirass which covered his chest. The statue's legs were bare, the man's hand upraised and pointing. Bordan followed the direction of the outstretched finger and knew that way lay the palace. Didas's head was encircled by a crown of laurel leaves.

However, the statue had not been well treated. It was missing an arm and its feet were covered in the green brown sludge of dirty water. Straps and ropes had been wound around its body to secure the thick pole which rose above the Emperor's head. From this, awnings were tied which stretched across the pool and made up the first rows of market stalls.

"Who has done this?" A strident voice, full of outrage, rang out in the clearing.

All eyes, soldiers, and citizens alike, turned towards the source. Prince Alhard stood with his own finger pointing not in the direction of his palace but at the statue.

"Who has defiled my ancestor? Who is so craven, so unthinking, as to blind the rest of the city to its founder? Who drags his memory through the sludge and mess of this stagnant water? Who has tied their profit to his memory and uses his stature for their own ends?"

Bordan watched as the Prince's eyes were consumed with anger and rage. He saw Alhard's finger tremble and his lips peel back from gritted teeth.

"You have." The Prince turned on the spot, to point at the stall owners and people of the market. "Such affront cannot be allowed to stand. Tear it down, General. Tear it all down. Arrest those men. Arrest them."

Spittle flew from the Prince's mouth. Where a moment ago he had seemed to be enjoying the crush of the crowd, the presence of the people calling to him, now that man was gone and in his place was a tower of rage. Red-faced and the tendons in his neck showing clear and proud against stretched skin, mouth open shouting orders.

"General?" Timet said, stepping to his side.

"My Prince, we can take down the awnings and return the statue to its former glory," Bordan began, eyeing the fearful crowd and soldiers who looked to him for direction. "Given another day of preparation and we would have cleared the marketplace for your visit."

"Bordan, you can see what they have done. It should not have been allowed in the first place. Tear them down, scatter the market. I forbid them ever to use this space again."

"These people earn their living here," Bordan tried to point out as the murmurs in the marketplace grew louder.

"They can earn it elsewhere," Alhard countered. "Or they can starve for what they have done. A punishment for their neglect and abuse of my ancestor."

"My Prince," Bordan tried again, struggling to keep his voice low and calm but still be heard above the crowd, "the people have used this square as a market for centuries. It is their livelihood and how they feed their families. I agree," he added hastily as the Prince's furious eyes turned on him, "that the statue has been poorly treated, but we can remedy that now and into the future."

"General, I want those awnings down and this square cleared forever." Alhard pointed at the obscured statue. "It will become a place of honour in the city. All Emperors should come here to remember how we began. It will not now or in the future be used as a marketplace by these..." Alhard waved his hand towards the stall holders who were being held back behind a line of soldiers, "...people."

The first stone sailed out from the crowd, bouncing on the stones by the Prince's feet. Both men looked down upon it as it came to a halt by a market stall. The next landed on an awning then more followed, as did scraps of fruit, sticks, and anything the crowd could find.

"Get the Prince out of here!" Bordan called, drawing his sword and once again wishing for his shield. He looked to the Prince who stood staring at the angry mob who were pushing forward, trying to break through the line of soldiers. "When you are safe, my Prince, we will return to do your bidding."

"General," Alhard said, "what is happening?"

"Timet, get them moving!" Bordan shouted.

The crowd were screaming. Many tried to barge through the small alleys between stalls and others simply trampled their way out. At the front and to the sides, the soldiers laid about themselves with their pila, though Bordan was pleased to note they used the hafts and not the sharp heads of their weapons.

"To the horses," Timet ordered. "Look smart and keep tight ranks."

As they emerged from the awnings, the first stones began to fall.

"Raise shields," Timet shouted. "Quick time."

The missiles bounced from the wooded shields and Bordan drew his cloak above the head of the unresisting Prince. With luck, they would make it out in one piece and few citizens would be harmed. But luck was never a weapon a good soldier relied upon.

He did not see the stone, but it struck him a sharp hammer blow to his temple and blood began to flow down his face. His vision swam and he stumbled, his hands refusing to come up and block his fall.

"I've got you, General." Hands grabbed him and he heard the voices fade as the world dimmed.

XII

THE MAGICIAN

TEN YEARS AGO:
He screamed. The moment the door opened and before he was even aware of taking a breath, he screamed.

The man possessed a livid scar running down one side of his face and moved with a limp. A grimace pulled at the scar, closing one eye and drawing a snarl from his lip.

"Don't go scaring the lad, Gressius," said a gentler voice.

"WHAT ARE YOU doing?"

Emlyn's voice cut through his concentration, slicing apart the threads of thought which bound the construct he had spent the last three turns of the timer building. His grasp on the magic, the tiny motes which danced and cavorted, fled, and it collapsed. A sigh escaped his lips and his shoulders slumped.

"What were you doing?" she repeated when he looked up at her.

"Practising," Kyron said, taking a square of cloth from his tunic and wiping the sweat from his brow.

"Magic?"

"What else?" He unfurled his legs and stretched them out across the carpet of pine needles which shrouded the earth beneath.

"What can you do with magic?"

He stopped shuffling, trying to find a comfortable position, and favoured her with another look. "Why do you want to know?"

She stepped towards the fire and sat down, moving some branches out of the way. "I'm interested."

"You don't have magicians?" He squinted at her outlined in the flames. Was she trying to get information to take back to the tribes? At the outset, in the Gymnasium, he had heard talk of magicians amongst the tribes, though no one seemed to know much. There were legends and myths from the pacification of the tribes to the west, but that was so long ago they could not be relied upon.

"Not like you or Padarn," she offered, drawing a stick towards her and placing the edge of her knife against it.

"What is it you want to know then? I will tell you what I can, if you'll tell me of your magicians," Kyron said. No learning was ever wasted and sharing knowledge was the path to true understanding: two of Padarn's many teachings.

"What can you do with your magic? Is it useful?"

"Everyone is a bit different," Kyron began, "but the only real limit is imagination and force of will."

"Will?"

"I can't think of a better word," he admitted. "To get the magic to do what you want, create fire, lift an object, or whatever, you have to make it do it."

"Make it? Is your magic alive?" The shavings from her whittling were piling up before her.

"No," Kyron said, confused for a moment. He shrugged, "I don't think so. It is a natural force, something that's always been here."

"And you can control it?"

"Yes."

"But other people cannot. Why?"

He frowned. "We don't know. Some people are born with the gift, the ability, and others aren't. It is just the way it is."

"How do you know?"

"Know what?"

"Who can use your magic? How do you find out who has this gift and who does not?" She stopped whittling for a moment and fixed him with a questioning stare.

"The Gymnasium has a test," Kyron said. "If you pass, you have the gift."

"And you passed," Emlyn nodded. "How many people do they test?"

"Not very many," he admitted.

"That doesn't make any sense," Emlyn said and began whittling again. "If magic is powerful, and you say there are no real limits to it, then it would make sense to have lots of magicians. The more people you test, the more you would find, the more powerful your Empire would become."

Kyron glanced around the clearing and lowered his voice. "The Church does not like magicians very much, so not many people come forward for the tests."

"Why not?"

"They think it goes against their teaching, their holy books."

"But you say it is natural and has always been there," Emlyn replied, flicking another shaving into the fire. "If that's the case then their god, who they say built the world, put it here."

"Well," Kyron said, trying to put the ideas he had learned at a young age into words that made more sense now that he was grown up, "the priests say that the magic left here is a part of the god's power and that by using it, we are defiling it."

"But if their god built the world, and left the magic, they surely did it for a purpose?" She held the stick up to the flame and inspected it closely.

"Just not for our magicians," Kyron said with a shrug. "Either way, they don't like us using it. They claim we are trying to become a god, that we have too much power."

"Too much power?" She applied the tip of her knife to the stick once more. "If I stabbed you with my knife now, could you stop me?"

"I... I..." he stuttered, unsure. "I don't know. Possibly."

"But possibly not," she said, not looking at him. "I could kill you now, in your sleep, as you walk, with nothing more than this," she held up the blade for a moment, twisting it so the flames danced along its edge, "and there wouldn't be much you could do about it. Is that not 'too much power'? To hold your life in my hands, at my whim and control?"

"It is not the same," he said, knowing the argument was weak.

"And if you decided to kill me with magic, there is little I could do about it?" She met his eyes for a moment before looking back at the stick she was carving. "We share that power over life and death, do we not?"

"Yes, but it is still not the same," he argued.

"To me, it is," she replied and glanced over her shoulder. "Your master is coming. I had better let you get on with your practice."

Kyron watched her stand, an economy of movement and grace, and slip the knife back into its sheath. He returned her nod and followed her with his eyes as she stepped around the fire and headed off into the dark. When she had disappeared from view, he looked across at the place she had sat, her words fresh in his mind and saw the stick she had been carving throughout their conversation. One end had been thrust into the ground so the other, shaped to look like a hand, reached up to the stars.

Before he could shift and reach for it, Padarn came into the clearing.

"How goes your practice?" his master asked.

"The construct is difficult," Kyron said.

"It is supposed to be, Kyron," Padarn said. "Binding the magic to markers is simple. The structure is there already; you're merely filling in the gaps, making it smoother with magic. To create a complete structure from magic is supposed to be difficult."

"I create a section," he complained, "and move to the next, but the magic keeps trying to escape."

"And you must hold it in place with your mind, your will, your confidence and belief," Padarn said.

"But I can't hold it all at the same time," he whined.

"You have to," his master replied. "Watch."

Kyron focused his gaze on the fire where his master pointed. The flames flickered and shades of yellow and orange pranced before his eyes, beautiful, ephemeral, an illusion of light and heat that existed for a moment before it vanished.

Under his master's command, the flames rose, and a wave of heat washed over Kyron. He squinted against the sudden brilliance and when his vision cleared, he saw five separate strands of the flame hanging in the air above the fire. They wavered and danced but did not fade from view.

"A construct, created and held, can change the world. This flame," Padarn waved his hand in the direction of the fire, "should have gone out, but it has not. Why not?"

"Magic, Master."

Padarn sighed. "All these years and still you do not listen. We know it is magic, Kyron. I want you to look at the magic that holds the flame."

"Sorry," Kyron said, his cheeks reddening. He closed his eyes for a moment, letting his senses widen and the heat from the fire warm his face. As it always was, he felt it first on the edge of his mind.

Looking once again at the filaments of fire, he saw the weave of magic which his master had placed about them. The shape, elegant and twisting, forever moving and yet staying the same, was the one he had been tasked to create. His master had done it in the blink of an eye, a heartbeat of effort—not the difficult, tense age which Kyron had spent.

"Years of practice," Padarn said, seeming to read his apprentice's mind. "You will be able to hold this simple construct soon, but it will take practice. Like the others you have learned, you will come to hate it and love it."

"One day, Master," Kyron said.

"By the end of tomorrow, Kyron," Padarn said and the construct vanished as did the flames. "I want you to focus all your time on this construct. It is the basis of all which follow along this line of learning, and from it you can develop your own constructs."

"By tomorrow? Master, I'll never be able to do what you did," he protested.

"I want you to be able to build it and hold it," Padarn corrected with a smile. "I do not expect you to do it as quick as I did. Not for a year, at least."

"I will try, Master," Kyron said.

"You will succeed, Kyron," Padarn answered. "You have struggled in the past as any student does, but I have confidence in you."

"Thank you, Master," Kyron nodded.

They sat in silence for a moment enjoying the warmth of the fire. Kyron watched as his master reached down and plucked Emlyn's carving from the dirt. Padarn stared at it, turning it over in his hand and holding it up to the light.

"Who made this, Kyron?"

"The guide, Emlyn," Kyron answered. "She carved it while she sat there talking to me just before you came."

"What did you talk about?" Padarn asked, raising the carved stick to his nose as if breathing in the scent.

"Magic. She asked what I could do and promised to tell me about the magic of her tribe."

"And?"

"And what, Master?"

"What did you learn from her?" Padarn asked and Kyron heard the sigh implicit in the tone.

"Nothing. She left just before you arrived," Kyron said. "I didn't get a chance to ask anything."

"Yet she gave you an answer, Kyron," Padarn replied, passing the stick across to him. "That young lady needs careful watching."

Kyron looked down at the intricate carving, not understanding. A state of being he was used to.

XIII

THE GENERAL

TEN YEARS AGO:

"You met Gressius," he said as the boy cowered against the wide table in the kitchen. "He won't hurt you."

"It's true, lad," the woman said. "He might look uglier than a rat, but that scar's an improvement. Been married for more years than I want to remember. Never could work out what I saw in him."

"Honour, Decima," he said. "That's what you saw in him. Honour."

"How is your head, General?"

"The pain has mostly gone, Your Majesty," Bordan replied.

The council table was full of steaming platters, and, though the smell was heavenly, the mere thought of eating made his stomach roil. Around the table, the members of the Ruling Council were selecting their own slices of meat, roasted vegetables, and delicately sliced pieces of fruit. Abra picked at the fruit on his plate, nodding as Duke Primal spoke into his ear. Vedrix had piled his plate high and was eating with a contented smile and the occasional grunt of pleasure. Opposite, Godewyn's plate was as empty as his own.

"Your appetite has not returned?" Alhard asked.

"Not yet, my Prince. Head wounds can be strange. I eat and drink enough. I do thank you for the concern."

"How fares the city today?"

"The fires are under control, Your Highness." Bordan nodded.

Immediately the room swam, and blood pounded in his temple. He raised a hand to the lump on the side of his head, wincing at the contact. "Most citizens are staying in their homes and soldiers are patrolling in greater numbers. No one attacked them yesterday which is a good sign. Not so much as a single stone."

"That is good news," the Empress said when Alhard did not respond. "It would not do to lose control of the capital at this time."

"I think it was more an expression of fear," Bordan said, and thought carefully about his next words before continuing, "at the delay to the coronation. The people like certainty and the city is an uncertain place at the moment though the period of mourning continues, and the Churches are, I understand, speaking of calm and continuing the rituals." He looked to Godewyn who nodded in agreement. "I am more concerned with the reports from the countryside. It seems the riots have spread outward, and there are armed groups in villages, even some towns."

"And these groups do not support us?" Aelia asked.

"No, Princess," said another voice. "My shipmasters, who have travelled the ports, report that sentiments are turning away from the throne."

"Are they, Duke Abra?" the Empress cut in. "And what do your shipmasters give as the reasoning for this change in sentiment?"

"They are unsure, but I suspect it will be the usual matters surrounding tax and poverty," Abra answered, unruffled.

"Much comes second- or third-hand, however. My crews do not stray far from the docks and it is the carters, traders, and waggon masters who pass on the news to us."

"Should we see this discontent as insurrection yet?" Princess Aelia asked.

"My own reports suggest not," Bordan answered, "and it is difficult to see it ever becoming so. Neighbouring countries may see a chance to destabilise the Empire, but they rely on us for trade and security also. Maxentius has sent word to the commanders of the Third Army to increase their patrols but do nothing to inflame the situation further."

"Quite a balancing act," Aelia said.

"Indeed, Princess," Abra interrupted. "However, my own sources, as I mentioned, have reported stirrings in the countryside. Especially in the forest communities which line the western mountains."

"They are far from the ports, Duke Abra," Bordan said.

"True enough, but the waggon masters who bring the wood and crops to the ports have a good knowledge of those towns and villages," Abra pointed out. "It is integral to their work."

"Forests?" Alhard spoke around the food which filled his mouth. "You mean the tribes my father went to conquer?"

"Not quite, my Prince. Duke Abra refers to our people who dwell in the forests to the west. Once, many centuries ago they were of the tribes, but no longer," Bordan explained. "It would be hard to see them having sympathy with those in the north, not after all this time."

"Traditions run long and deep, General," Abra said. "I would not put it past them to see a chance to reclaim their old ways and worship."

"Pagans." High Priest Godewyn leaned forward in his seat. "The Flame is the true religion and they have only prospered since they came to know the warmth which binds the Empire together."

"Some may not see it that way," Master Vedrix said, his hands fluttering in apology as he spoke. "Hard to believe, I realise, as the Flame has kept us safe all these years, but some beliefs may be hard to let go of."

"And the wealth they share is nothing compared to that of the farmers on the plains or in the cities and towns," Duke Primal joined the conversation, his pinched face animating for a moment as the thought struck him. "News travels fast, faster than any horse, and it has been some days since the troubles in the capital. Perhaps they see a chance to carve out their own kingdom?"

"Unlikely," Bordan said. "They know the power of our army and enjoy the security it brings."

"But the bulk of your army is far away," Abra pointed out.

"As I said, we've troops enough in the outlying towns and villages to deal with any trouble," Bordan insisted.

"But what if they group together, General?" Alhard asked, picking up the nerves and worry which were emanating from the two Dukes. "What if they put down their saws and pick up swords and axes? My father said there were a lot of people living there. In small villages, but they lived close enough together. If they banded together, General, they could march on the plains."

"And if they did," Primal continued, "they would disrupt planting and the next harvest would be reduced. Prices would rise and the people of the city would go hungry. The tax collectors would have a harder job and our revenue will fall. We need the farmers much more than the foresters. The trees will grow regardless."

"If they go to war, Your Highness," Abra began, "not only will the farms suffer, trade from the ports will decline. We will be forced to import more food and prices will rise further. The poor will suffer more than any other. It might encourage them to further acts of rebellion."

"And," Lady Trenis added, as Bordan opened his mouth to intervene, "if there is war on the plains might they not venture further north to attack your husband's funeral guard."

"This," Bordan managed to interrupt, feeling the fear of rebellion sweep the room like wildfire, "is a very unlikely scenario."

Aelia spoke, her words slow and thoughtful, as if trying them out on those listening, "There is clearly a problem in the countryside, General?"

"Yes. However, Maxentius knows what to do," Bordan pointed out.

"But the city is calm once more," Aelia continued, "and I know I would be reassured, as would my brother, no doubt, to know that matters were in your capable hands."

"I have some good—" Bordan was cut off by Alhard's raised hand.

"My sister is right, General," the Prince said. "We must secure the countryside and the forests."

There were a thousand reasons why this was not necessary, but the heir had commanded and a General must obey, especially when such an instruction was given in front of the Ruling Council. Division would only sow further seeds in their minds, and it was hard enough keeping track of the little ploys and schemes they were all engaged upon. "As you say, Your Highness."

"Thank you, General." The Empress favoured him with a small smile and for the first time he noted the dark circles beneath her eyes. "My son is well served by you."

"I'll have Maxentius task a small force from the city, Your Highness, and they can gather more troops along the way. I'll send riders with orders," Bordan said.

"Brother?" Aelia said, and Bordan had feeling he had fallen into a trap of another's design.

"I should lead it," Alhard said, puffing out his chest. "I would like to see the plains and forests of my Empire."

"A splendid idea," Princess Aelia said, smiling. "An Emperor should know his lands and his people."

Alhard's spine straightened as he gazed down the table. The Empress looked much less sure, but Bordan noted the glance between her and Aelia.

"This would reassure the merchants, my Prince," Abra said, and both Primal and Trenis nodded along with his words. "For goods to be moved, money to be made, and taxes paid, the lands need to feel safe for all. More than that, I am sure the people in the countryside will be gladdened to see you take charge."

"Did you wish to go along, Duke?" Vedrix asked from the end of the table, brushing the crumbs from his beard. "I am sure room could be made."

"Me?" Abra barked a laugh and covered his mouth with his free hand. "My apologies, Your Highnesses. I am merchant, Master Vedrix, my only skill at arms is with a stylus and balance sheets. Swords and war, I leave to the General and his fine soldiers. I am sure with General Bordan along, no harm shall befall the Prince if that is your worry."

There was also the manner in which Abra, Primal, and to a lesser extent, Lady Trenis had spoken, that set a knot of worry in Bordan's stomach. None of his people had reported anything unusual going on between them. No messages passed, no secret meetings, no feasts or coincidental visits to the same theatre during which to conspire. Nothing to suggest they were working together, but all the same, it had the aroma of a setup. A dirty, unhealthy smell that wormed its way down to his stomach and made him ill. Worse still, they had all played into it; Aelia, the Empress, even his own words had done little to distract and deflect the issue away.

Removing the heir from the capital might be a good way to reduce the tension. Many amongst the people, and the city army, blamed him for the past few days. The events in the marketplace had been the spark falling on already dry tinder, and it had taken a lot of effort to damp it back down.

Removing the heir and the General from the capital, which Abra had now neatly boxed him into, was also a good chance for one of them to meet with an accident. If Alhard died, the blame would fall on Bordan, no matter what the cause or reason.

With little else to discuss, the meeting broke up and the nobles filed from the room, leaving only the imperial family, the High Priest, Master Vedrix and himself still seated.

"You're worried," Godewyn said when the last had departed.

"Always," Bordan grunted.

"The city is calm," Vedrix pointed out. "The troops and the priests have been quelling the fear and worry."

"Which Abra and Primal have been stirring up," Bordan stated.

"I don't think," Vedrix began, casting a quick glance in Alhard's direction, "that you have cause to worry in that direction."

"You have some proof?" Aelia asked as Alhard tucked into another slice of meat.

"No," he admitted. "Nothing at all."

"But you are worried?" the Empress asked.

"The talk of discontent in the countryside has me worried," Bordan said.

"And it will be good for the army, and me, to be seen in the countryside, General," Alhard spoke, his mouth - as ever - full of food. "It will settle the people to know a strong leader is looking out for them."

"For all their scare stories, there may be a kernel of truth amongst the chaff. Each has something to lose from a rebellion in the countryside, even a small one may set a fire we cannot contain or give others a cause to rally around. A show of might, a reminder of imperial power in places where only tax collectors and few troops visit is in order," Bordan conceded with a sigh.

"We'll show them," Alhard grunted. "Ride into a few villages and towns, they'll soon back down."

"If they are doing anything in the first place," Bordan said.

"You don't believe the Dukes and Lady Trenis?" Godewyn asked. "Should I?"

"They are protecting their own interests," Aelia admitted, a thoughtful furrow to her brow, "but those align with our own at present, do they not? If your spies had any proof or suspicions, you would know and we could take action?"

"If only it were all that simple," Bordan said, rubbing his temple as the headache, forgotten for a moment, returned.

"It will all be fine, General," Alhard said, nodding and smiling. "I'll ride with you. The next Emperor and the famed General riding out to deal with rebellion. As it should be."

"As you say, Prince Alhard, though I really should caution us all not to believe everything a carter or waggon driver says. Everyone likes a good story and all inflate the numbers and danger with each telling," Bordan said.

"My son," the Empress said with a sigh, turning to Alhard, "be careful and learn from the General. This will not be the last time you will sit the saddle and ride to war. Even your father said he learned the most valuable lessons in warfare from General Bordan. With your permission, I will look after the Ruling Council in your stead until you return."

"Excellent," Alhard said. "When do we leave, General?"

"In the morning, my Prince," Bordan said. "I will need some time to get the riders sent out. It would be better to have the troops ready when we arrive in the towns. The forest is three days distant at its closest. We can collect intelligence from the villages as we travel and adjust our course as needed."

"I will bless your troops upon departure," High Priest Godewyn said.

"Will you need a magician to accompany you?" Vedrix asked earning a scowl from the High Priest.

"I think not," Bordan said. "Not this time. Though I thank you for the offer."

"The Gymnasium of Magic serves the Empire, General," Vedrix pointed out, fixing his gaze upon the High Priest's.

"Of course," Godewyn's words were forced out between clenched teeth.

"Until tomorrow," the Empress said. "Though, General, if I could have a private word with you about the journey. Just to set my mind at ease?"

"Of course, Your Highness," Bordan replied.

XIV

THE MAGICIAN

NINE YEARS AGO:

He dressed in the white tunic laid out for him and, struggling to contain the yawn which stretched his mouth wide, descended the stairs. The room to the small house shrine was open and the other three were waiting for him. A flame burned in the bowl upon the altar and the aroma of spices filled the room.

"A joyous birthday," the old man said.

A ROUGH HAND shook his shoulder and Kyron struggled to open his eyes.

"Get up." His master's voice sounded so very far away and the fog of sleep obscured his vision.

"What time is it?" he mumbled, trying to have his tongue obey the sluggish commands of his brain.

"Wake up, Kyron. We are being attacked," his master said and the hand on Kyron's shoulder retreated.

The clash of metal on wood, the shouts and cries of violence made themselves known as his mind gave into the reality of the waking world.

"Get your satchel," Padarn said, gesturing towards the embers of the fire, and they roared back to life, "and keep your wits about you."

Kyron struggled out of his blankets, kicking them away as they sought to tangle his feet. His legs ached and there was a kink of pain in his lower back as he bent down to grab his boots, forcing his feet into them.

"Here," Padarn called and a leather jerkin sailed across the space between them. "Put it on."

There was a tingle of magic across his fingertips as he caught the armour, thrust his arms through the holes and settled it onto his back. His fingers fumbled at the toggles, but the energy imbued within the garment sparked his mind much as Padarn had done to the fire.

He glanced around their small camp, noting the absence. "Where's Emlyn?"

"She woke me and has headed to the front where the fighting seems to be," Padarn answered, fastening the last of the toggles on his own jerkin. "Come. We must get to the Emperor's waggon."

"Yes, Master," Kyron answered, drawing the strap of his satchel over his shoulder and following the older man from the campsite.

Amongst the dark of the trees beside the track they followed, everything was a shadow. Figures of mottled grey and black flitted and darted between the pines and hardy birch trees which could survive the winter climate this far north. Padarn's form as he ducked around the trees, heading for the track and the Emperor's waggon, was just visible ahead and Kyron worked hard to keep up. Breath misted before his face and the scent of old pine tickled his nose, coating his throat with its astringent tang as he ran.

Emerging onto the open track, Kyron saw soldiers, some dressed in full uniform, while others frantically dragged theirs on and some barely dressed, yet carrying spears and shields.

"This way!" Padarn called, pointing in the dim waves of light emanating from the torches high up on their night stands.

Jumping out of the way of a troop of soldiers, Kyron stumbled and slipped across the cart tracks and muddy footprints as he trailed his master along the line of waggons. Carters, porters, and the others who were not soldiers, but not so foolish as to travel the wilds unarmed, were gathering around their vehicles ready to defend them if needed.

Ahead, and the brightest lit of all waggons was the Emperor's. Clustered around it were the priests, all of them dressed in their robes with the flame of their faith glowing on their chests in the reflected torchlight. It was not magic: Kyron had checked many years ago. It was simply a trick of the material the flame was made from.

The Deacon stepped forward as Padarn and he entered the ring of light. "Why have you come here, magician?"

"It is our assigned position," Padarn replied, not looking at the priest but outward into the forest. "Have they come close yet?"

"Not yet," the priest grunted, "but they are out there."

"Master," Kyron said, "the fighting sounds like it is coming from up the column. We should go and help."

"Our place is here," Padarn said, and Kyron caught the slight nod of the priest's head beneath the cowl. "If we're needed, they will come and get us. Deacon, your priests can fight if needed?"

"Each has had martial training," the Deacon affirmed. "They were chosen for their devotion and skills."

"If they come, it will be arrows first," Padarn said, taking half a step forward and squinting at the dark of the forest. "I can shield us from those. For a while, at least, but they will follow the first salvo with swords and axes."

Kyron put his hand on the leather jerkin, comforted by the magic he felt running through it. It wouldn't stop an axe, but it would turn a clumsy sword or deflect an arrow—though only once or twice, after that the magic would be drained. He brushed his hand down the leather adding a little more power, making sure that it was fully charged.

"Don't add too much," Padarn said, turning back to him. "You can overcharge it and it will fail. Now, help me set up some shield markers along this side of the waggon."

"Yes, Master," Kyron said, taking the offered spikes of wood from Padarn's outstretched hand.

"Dig them deep, Kyron," Padarn instructed. "I don't want them coming out of the ground when the arrows hit."

Kyron nodded and ran to the far end of the Emperor's bier. Kneeling, he took the first of the spikes and, raising it high, drove it deep into the earth. The damp soil parted without resistance. Pushing it in as far as he could, Kyron drew on the motes of magic which flowed through the air, binding them to the pattern carved into the wood which stood proud of the soil.

Shuffling a few steps to the right, he repeated the act. Drawing more motes to him, he cast a line of magic to the first marker, then looped it around and into the pattern, binding the markers together. Three more times he carried out the same task and with the last, sweat dripping into his eyes, the line was complete.

In the blur of the vision granted by the magic, he saw the shapes of figures amongst the trees. Narrowing his eyes and focusing his will, he could see the bows they carried and pick out the shape of their armour.

"Master," he cried, letting go of his concentration, "they're coming."

"I know, Kyron." Padarn's comforting voice sounded close by and a soft hand came to rest on his shoulder. "Ignore them for a moment and pass the leash on to me."

Kyron took a breath, returned his concentration to the line of magic which he had strung from marker to marker, then unpicked the thread from the last spike and held it out to his master.

"I've got it," Padarn confirmed and Kyron saw the line picked from his hand and tied to the longer, brighter line which Padarn carried with him. A pulse of magic flowed along the length of the line and a shimmering wall, invisible to all but those who carried the gift, rose above him, curving to meet its reflection from the other side of the waggon. "Help the priests and don't get hurt."

"Master!" Kyron cried as the first flight of arrows erupted from the dark forest. Beside him, Padarn grunted as the iron tipped missiles shattered against the shield they had erected.

"Send up a signal," his master wheezed. "We'll need help."

Noting the sweat already pouring down his master's face and the way in which the cords in the older man's neck stood out, Kyron knew it was taking all his effort to hold the shield against so many arrows. Once the tribes realised their arrows were failing to get through, they would change tactics and charge. A small arrow carried a lot of energy as it hit the barrier, and many of them striking at the same time was hard to shield against. Men, heavy in armour and wielding swords and axes, would be impossible to stop.

Kyron looked up to the clouds above the trees and punched the sky, throwing a small carved wooden sphere over his head. A shaft of green light left his hand with a cry of release and shot upward, passing the height of the canopy in less than a heartbeat. At the apogee of its arc the spear exploded into light. There were cries from all around and, a moment later, a silent breath as the darkness reasserted itself.

Opening his eyes, spots of orange and red playing against his vision, he saw the closest of priests pawing at his face and stumbling to the side. Those in the forests, if they had followed the trajectory of the flare, would be in the same plight: night vision ruined and likely to hit a tree or each other with an arrow.

Even so, the slap and snap of bow strings echoed once more and sparks erupted across the magical barrier. Now the sound of running feet and cries of war came from the tree line and the first tribesman, leather skin shield and axe held high, leaped across the dirt towards Kyron.

The barrier shook under the impact and he saw spider webs of energy crackle across its surface. Held back, the tribesman's face wore a mask of surprise for a moment before his axe came down once more to smash at the barrier.

"Kyron," Padarn grunted.

Focusing his mind, Kyron drew the motes of magic around his fist, forming them into a simple spear point which he threw at the tribesman. It passed through the barrier, invisible, unseen, and plunged into their attacker.

A spray of blood from the wound and the axe fell from the man's limp fingers. Kyron watched the warrior stagger back and clutch both hands to the wound in his chest, but he was dead before he hit the dirt.

"More are coming, Master," Kyron called, and from the forest stepped at least twenty tribesmen and women. Each bore a shield and a weapon, and they advanced slowly upon the barrier.

The priests stepped up beside Kyron, but their presence gave him little comfort. They were armed but dressed in the robes of the priesthood and carried no shields, wore no armour.

"Don't cross the barrier," Kyron warned them. "Stay still."

"Don't tell me what to do, boy," the Deacon said, his grey trim fading to black in the shadows of the torches.

"Step past it and die then," Kyron spat, feeling the wave of guilt wash through him a moment later. His grandfather's words and admonishments called to him from the memory of youth. "They can't get through, Deacon. We're safe."

"For the moment," Padarn grunted and fell to one knee. Warriors of the tribes were hammering at the barrier with sword, axe, and spear, and the sparks of magical motes were visible now even to the priests. "Be ready."

"Hold on, Master," Kyron called, kneeling next to Padarn. "The soldiers will be here in a moment."

"No time," Padarn whispered.

Kyron watched as his master dug one hand into the dirt at his feet and reached back with the other over his shoulder towards the Emperor's waggon. As a scream tore from Padarn's throat, the barrier ahead of them came apart. Axes and swords passed through the air which had a heartbeat ago defied them. The warriors of the tribes stumbled forward.

It was a short-lived advance. Only Kyron saw what his master did, tearing one side of the barrier down and dragging the other over the waggon. Its edge, no longer bound to its reflection, was sharper than any knife. Padarn's outstretched hand came forward, clawed and the muscles in his arm bunched as if pushing a heavy weight before him.

The edge of the barrier sliced down at an angle, cutting through shield, armour, flesh and bone as it sought the reflection which his master had buried under the earth. Cries of war turned to screams of pain and anguish as bodies were cut in two, as legs were sliced from bodies, as hands were severed from arms, and weapons tumbled to the floor.

Again, there was silence. And in that moment of still Padarn collapsed, sinking to the dirt, and Kyron called out his name.

When time began again, there were shouts and prayers, the sound of metal on flesh, and the taste of ash in Kyron's mouth as the magic poured out from him towards the surviving attackers.

XV

THE GENERAL

NINE YEARS AGO:
The boy had grown, and though he would never be a giant, there was a hint of nervous speed about him.

"They would be proud of you, lad," he said, resting a hand on the young man's shoulder.

"I hope so," the boy replied, staring at the flickering fire.

"Make an offering to the Flame," he said, picking a sprig of sea dew and placing it in the bowl. "We'll tend the tree as well. It is a good day to remember them both."

"THERE IS A town ahead, General," said the scout.

Bordan had seen him coming from a distance, the trail of dust kicked up by his horse's hooves from the dry tracks which traversed the plains. The lesser-used tracks had been covered with new spring grass, but this was a well-worn road between the towns.

"At last. I feel like I've in this saddle for weeks," Prince Alhard said, shifting in his saddle.

"What is the disposition of the town?" Bordan said, distracting the scout from the Prince's grumbling.

"There are troops on walls, General," the scout answered. "The gates are open."

"Did you tell them of our coming?"

"I did, sir. Said they knew you were coming and that they would meet you in the town square," the scout said.

"It isn't a market day?" Bordan asked, shading his eyes with one hand and peering in the direction of the town. It would still be a few hours' march away and appeared as nothing more than a faint smudge on the horizon of the plains.

"I didn't ask, General," the scout replied.

"A few farmers in the fields but no one else, General," the scout said pulling on his horse's reins, turning the beast away.

"Thank you," Bordan said. "Go and see to your horse and take a meal. The rest of the road is clear?"

"You think something is wrong, General." The man who spoke rode behind the Prince and had a round shield hooked over the horn of his saddle.

"Unless I have my days wrong," Bordan began, "not unheard of at my age, I would swear today should be a market day, Spear Sarimarcus."

"I think you have the days right, General," the Spear replied after a moment.

"Yet they wish to meet in the town square where the market should be?"

"They know I am coming, General," Prince Alhard said. "The market is inconsequential to that honour."

"That may be the case, my Prince," Bordan allowed, suppressing a sigh. "Though we did not proclaim your presence in this troop. If they know you are with us, it can only have come from someone in the city, or sat at the table of the Ruling Council."

"We will know when we get there," Sarimarcus said, ducking his head so as not to meet the Prince's gaze as the man turned to him.

"We won't be able to take the full army into the town," Bordan said, scratching at his nose. "Spear, select the best fifty men you have, those that can follow orders but can think for themselves a bit too. They'll come with the Prince and I into town."

"Yes, General," Sarimarcus replied.

"And find ten more to go to the town barracks. I want these to be your brightest and best gossips. They're to be friendly, make themselves known and find out what they can of the town and lands around. Give them some spending money, just not too much."

"What is the matter, General?" Alhard said, lifting himself from the saddle and rubbing his legs.

"It always pays to be careful, Your Highness. A little care and thought now might save us some trouble later on."

"But a town would not rebel against the throne and not against the next Emperor," Alhard stated as if the truth was his to decide.

"Perhaps not, my Prince," Bordan replied, choosing his words with care. "However, this will be the last town before the forests and the old tribes. A Prince, especially the next Emperor, as hostage would be a good prize if there truly is a rebellion brewing."

"Duke Primal's farmers and Abra's waggon masters said the land was safe," Alhard pointed out.

"Exactly, my Prince. I am sure they are as trustworthy as ever, but even their information is more than a few days old and things can change rapidly."

"Did you and my father have these discussions?"

"All the time, Prince Alhard. All the time—and he listened carefully to my words."

"If there is rebellion in the town, we will burn it to the ground," Alhard said, a snarl entering his voice, slapping the neck of his horse and dislodging a cloud of dust. "It cannot be allowed to grow and spread."

"If there is something going on, my Prince, rest assured we will take every action we must. However, let us not go making trouble where none may exist," Bordan said. "Spear, go and select your men. We've a few hours of marching ahead of us, but I'd like to be ready."

"Yes, General," Sarimarcus said, reining in his horse and dragging it around to face the army which followed.

"General, I do not intend to let my Empire fall about my ears through lack of action," Alhard said once the Spear was too far away to hear.

"I agree, my Prince," Bordan answered, turning in the saddle to meet the other man's gaze, refusing to back down. "However, it is better not to imagine difficulties where none may be. Also, the talk of killing civilians is not one which a military man or woman enjoys."

"You mean they won't follow orders?" There was a note of surprise in Alhard's voice.

"They will follow my... our orders," Bordan stated, "but let us not start rumours and stories amongst the troops."

"You have," Alhard said and now there was petulance and a sulk in the tone.

Bordan held his breath for a moment, careful of the Prince's fragile ego. Losing a parent was always a shock, compounded with the pressure of ruling an Empire, meant that allowances must be made. However, the heir's actions in the marketplace showed that he had yet to start thinking like a leader, letting his words fall from his lips without much thought, and his anger loose without the tempering of mercy and compassion. Inexperience was an excuse that few would countenance if it was not accompanied by some learning. "I have made preparations, my Prince. Given the troops some direction and tasks. It is normal when approaching the front lines. They will be expecting it to occur more and more as we come closer to the forests. It will reassure them that we take their safety seriously, that we are thinking, and have a plan."

"Should there be a rebellion in the town, General, we must put it down and make an example to all others across the Empire," Alhard said, a flush of red at the base of his neck, just above the collar of his hauberk.

"I serve the Empire, my Prince. I always have and always will," Bordan replied. "Your father and I had discussions, even arguments about strategy, but neither of us forgot our first duty was to the Empire. If there is a rebellion, we will deal with it accordingly."

"See that you do, General," Alhard replied and clucked his horse to a slow canter, taking up the lead of the army.

Bordan sighed but kept his thoughts close and mouth closed for the rest of the ride. Behind him, the few mounted troops they had brought kicked up dust upon which the marching army coughed and choked. It would do them good to find a river and clean the dust from their throats and armour.

A clean army was a wonderful sight to behold. Colours resplendent in the sunshine, heads held high and pila tips glinting as the troops marched. Sometimes the mere sight of a well-disciplined army was all that was needed. It struck fear in the hearts of those who worked against the Empire, and pride in those who served it. Also, it reminded people that their taxes were well spent on their safety and security.

His back ached and the pain in his hips had lessened over the days on the road but climbing down from his horse at the gates to the town still brought a grimace to his face. Spear Sarimarcus had stepped forward to assist, but he had waved him away. It felt good to be out of the capital and on the road at the head of an army again, but this would be, he knew, the last time. Age was an enemy no one could defeat with cunning strategy, clever tactics, or sharp sword. It cut through armour, flesh, bone and blood without pause or care.

"General," a tall, thin man dressed in fine clothes called to him from between two stocky guards.

"General Bordan," he introduced himself. "You are?"

"Kendryek," the man answered with a bow. "I am here on behalf of Scribato the Mayor. He awaits you in the town square."

"He did not see fit to meet us here?" Alhard said, striding forward, hand on his sheathed sword.

Kendryek looked to Bordan for instruction.

"Allow me to introduce His Highness, Prince Alhard," Bordan said.

The tall man gulped and fell to one knee, as did his guards either side.

"Forgive me, Your Highness," Kendryek said. "We were not notified you were with the army."

"Yet here I am," Alhard said. "Lead me to your Mayor with whom I need some words about protocol."

"Of course, Your Highness." Kendryek unfolded himself to his full height and waved the guards to lead the way.

"Approach with calm thoughts, my Prince," Bordan whispered. "They did not know you were coming, and for that we should give thanks to the Flame."

They followed them through the town, nosy inhabitants staring down from windows, others scurrying out of their path. Every face looked fearful and worried, and many were pinched and grey. A small child ran into the path of the soldiers, his tiny hands upraised in a pleading gesture. The town guard raised the butt of his spear to swing at the child, but the mother grabbed the child's thin arms and pulled the boy out of the way.

Bordan noted the troops on the wall, some dressed in the uniform of the Empire and others who looked like local militia. All followed their progress with interest. From behind, he could hear the sound of the assigned troops falling into line and the others heading off about their instructed tasks.

The town square was empty of market, but full of militia who appeared relaxed, sat on the fountain's wall in the centre or leaning against the buildings to either side. Near the fountain, an ornate affair which appeared to be a dark stone carved into the shape of sea beasts spraying water from their mouths, stood a small group of men and women talking animatedly to each other.

One woman, grey hair tied in a ponytail which reached to the small of her back, was waving her arms at the wealthiest dressed man among them. He was holding his hands up placatingly and trying to get a word in when his face changed as he caught sight of the approaching group.

"General!" the man called, a voice deep and booming, full of welcome and friendliness. It put Bordan's teeth on edge and he wanted to reach for the hilt of his sword. Too many men covered their true intentions with a veneer of confidence and friendship while concealing a sharp knife behind their backs. Abra and Primal were such men, but long association and custom replaced the knife with rumour and hard-won secrets. "It is good to meet you. We knew of your coming, of course, from the messages sent ahead and the watch on the walls saw your scout earlier."

"Messages?" Bordan spoke before anyone else could open their mouths.

"From your office, General." The mayor looked perplexed. "That your troops were coming and we were to prepare a welcome."

"Excellent," Bordan replied. He sighed and felt some of the weight lift from his shoulders.

"This is General Bordan and may I introduce," Kendryek gulped, "His Highness, Prince Alhard."

A wave of whispers and was quickly followed by a silence which washed out from the circle of people. The mayor's face drained white.

"Explain why you did not come to meet us at the gate?" Alhard said without preamble.

"Forgive me, Your Highness," the mayor said, "we were not made aware of your presence amongst the troops. Please, let us adjourn to somewhere out of the sun. I'll have refreshments brought. Some food too."

"Acceptable," Alhard said, gazing around the square, accepting the stares of his subjects as his just due.

"Excuse me, Mayor," Bordan began. "Why is there no market on market day?"

"You don't know?" The mayor seemed confused.

"Should we?" Bordan asked, even as he reached out to draw the Prince's attention back to the conversation.

"We sent reports to Duke Primal," the mayor said. "I thought that is why you came?"

"Duke Primal hinted at some news, but perhaps was not aware of the complete situation," Bordan said, unwilling to give too much information away. "What is happening?"

"There is trouble in the forests and on the edge of the plains," the mayor said, his eyes darting between Bordan and the Prince. "Not open rebellion, not yet, but our carts have been turned away or arrived here empty. The town is hungry, our own farms are not sufficient to feed everyone, and our supplies are not extensive. The tax collectors came through like—forgive me, Your Highness—a plague of locusts and we have not had the time to replenish the stocks. I fear there will be trouble in the town soon. Already there are whisperings of discontent."

XVI

THE MAGICIAN

NINE YEARS AGO:
The tree was a stubby thing, scrawny almost, and cast a shadow across the dry soil behind it. He knelt, accepting the clay pot of water from the old man, and poured it around the base.

He stopped when the jug was half-empty and held it up to the old man. "Did you want to pour some around Grandmother's tree?"

"HERE, MASTER," KYRON said, lifting the spoon of broth to Padarn's lips. "It's hot. Be careful."

"I'm not an invalid, Kyron," Padarn snapped.

Pulling the spoon away, Kyron looked down at the bowl and swallowed his own response.

"I'm sorry, boy," Padarn said, his tone calmer and quieter. "I just need to rest."

"Of course, Master," Kyron said, setting the soup bowl down. "I'll leave it here for when you're ready."

"How many people did we lose?"

"I don't know the full count, Master. A few soldiers near the front where the first attack came before they had a chance to get their shields up. One or two down the line, but that's all," Kyron answered.

"Injuries?"

"Quite a few. Cuts, bruises, and some broken bones amongst the soldiers. One of the priests had his nose broken by a tribeswoman before the soldiers arrived and drove them off," Kyron said, half a smile playing about his lips.

"They were after the Emperor?"

Kyron looked back up, noting the dark smudges under his master's eyes and the grey pallor of his skin. The furs he had wrapped the man in should have kept him warm against any element yet even now the older man shivered.

The shield against the arrows had been held a long time and against a larger force than just one magician should have faced. The construct was designed to shield a single person—the magician—or a small group if they crowded in close. That Padarn had broken the construct and held it together to reform it below the earth was a feat which Kyron was still in awe of.

Standing over Padarn's unconscious body, Kyron had watched the priests tear into the stunned warriors of the tribes. Showing no mercy to the fallen and injured, the priests killed with abandon. Once the initial shock had worn off, the tribes had fought back. For a moment it had looked as though the priests would be overrun, but the thunder of feet and clash of swords on shields announced the arrival of the imperial soldiers. The tribes had lost heart and faded back into the dark of the forest.

Having two soldiers help him with Padarn, Kyron had trodden carefully between the pools of blood already seeping into the soil, the severed limbs, the injured and dying. He had to cover his nose at the stink of battle and death. Beside the waggon, the priest whose nose had been broken tried to stem the flow of blood with a rag.

"The soldiers thought so," Kyron said, shaking off the memories. "The attack at the front was a distraction, but I don't think they expected to find a magician and priests willing to fight when they came upon the Emperor's waggon."

"A magician?" Padarn's tired eyes met his. "You did not help in the defence at all?"

"I did what I could," Kyron admitted. "A few spells to deflect blows and to slow down the attacks upon the priests."

"More than that," Padarn said, and the quiet calm in his voice was an invite to talk.

"Little more, Master," Kyron said, looking away, unwilling to see the flesh which had charred, or the whites of eyes turned bloody, the open, screaming mouths of agony. A shiver ran through him.

"Well," Padarn said, "when you want to talk, I'll be here. Now, I think I should sleep."

"Yes, Master. Rest," he agreed. "We won't be moving till tomorrow. The soldiers have set a strong guarded perimeter and scouts are out to track down those who attacked."

However, Padarn was already asleep, his breathing shallow and even. Kyron sighed in relief. His master would recover in a day or two of rest and already one of the carters had agreed to make room for him to sleep.

"Kyron." It was Emlyn's voice from outside the tent and he sighed once more.

Flicking open the flap he saw she was not alone, but four soldiers stood near her. None had swords drawn, but there was distrust in their eyes.

"You survived, I see." He heard the bitter note in his voice but was satisfied with it and would not recall it even if he could.

"They were not my tribe," she pointed out.

"Your tribe, their tribe, still a tribe."

"You possess a strange world view, Kyron. Is that common to everyone in the Empire?"

"Is what common?" he snapped back, standing up.

"To view the world in such absolutes. Them and us. Empire and not Empire. How far do you take that, I wonder?"

He ignored her question, not sure how to answer or what she truly meant and spoke to one of the soldiers. "Have you escorted her back to us?"

"Shield Lepida," the soldier replied, "and no, Apprentice, she is with us by order of Spear Astentius. He orders your master and her to his tent."

"My master cannot be moved," Kyron protested.

"He was wounded?" The soldier took a step towards the tent, worry on her face. "The Spear did not know."

"Not wounded, not in body at least. Just very tired. The spell he used to protect the Emperor's waggon was very tiring. He needs quiet and rest," Kyron answered.

"I was told the priests did most of the fighting," the Shield said, arching an eyebrow.

"And I would never go against the word of a Priest of the Holy Flame," Kyron answered, gritting his teeth.

The Shield smiled and nodded. "Wise. It seems you will have to do then, Apprentice. Come, the Spear is waiting on us."

Casting a last glance at his sleeping master's tent, Kyron followed the troops through the temporary camp, noting the addition of fortifications between the trees. They would not stop a determined warrior, but the sharp spikes, the trip pits, and the piles of broken wood which blocked routes would slow them down and put them at the mercy of a thrown pilum or sharp gladius.

Spear Astentius had set his tent near the front of the camp and surrounded it with a ring of soldiers. Each carried a sharp spear and shield, but it was their hard faces and cold gazes that instilled fear in Kyron's chest. His heart fluttered as they inspected him, judged him, as he came closer. He reached for the calm concentration needed to build the constructs of his magic to calm his pulse and was only partially successful.

"Spear," Lepida said as he stepped into the tent with Emlyn and Kyron a step behind, "I've brought the guide and the magician's apprentice."

"Where is the magician himself? I ordered him to appear, not his apprentice," Spear Astentius replied, turning from his discussion with another officer.

"My master was injured in the attack, sir," Kyron said, swallowing hard and stepping forward to be seen. "He needs to rest."

"How serious?"

"Not a physical injury," Kyron clarified, "but protecting the priests and the Emperor's bier took a lot out of him. A day of sleep, perhaps two, and he will be fine."

The Spear nodded, satisfied. "We had reports of the battle. Your master killed a lot of the forest warriors. Some of my officers were impressed by the fire and light which came from that direction. A few lost their food to the sight of the charred and severed bodies. He did well to defend against so many."

Kyron settled for a nod of agreement and looked around the tent.

Much larger than his own, though smaller than the Emperor's, there was room enough for a table and bed.

"When he wakes, tell him we are grateful," Astentius said.

"I will, sir," Kyron answered.

"Though you did not fight in the attack?"

It took a moment for Kyron to realise that the officer was speaking to Emlyn rather than him and a sigh of relief escaped his lips.

"I was instructed to guide you through the forest, not to kill my own people," she replied, her stare meeting and matching Astentius's.

"And they did not attack you at all?" Kyron spotted the trap in the question and, to his own surprise, hoped Emlyn did to.

"Why should they attack me when there are all these Empire soldiers around with their shields, spears, and dreams of invasion written plain across their faces?" Her voice did not crack or waver, a feat Kyron could never have managed when faced with Astentius's hard edged, measuring stare. "Attack the threat first, leave the non-combatants till last. Is that not good tactical doctrine, Astentius?"

The officer grunted and turned back to the table, but Emlyn had not finished her answer.

"Not that your soldiers follow it very well. Attack a village and kill everyone without a care. The elderly, women, and children are the deadliest of opponents to your troops."

"Enough," Astentius snapped, turning back to her, a red flush creeping up his face and his hand resting on the knife at his belt.

Kyron reached out, betrayed by his own hand, and gripped Emlyn by the elbow trying to pull her back. She wrenched his arm out of his grip and refused to budge.

"You are here..." Astentius started to say, but Emlyn cut him off.

"I know full well why I am here," she answered, her tone cold and brittle, "and I'll do as I was told to, but that's it. Don't expect me to take up my blades against my own people."

The two of them glared at each other for a long, uncomfortable moment and everyone in the room held their breath. Just as Kyron was opening his mouth to say something, anything, to pierce the expanding sense of violence, Emlyn stepped back to his side and broke the stare. There was a collective, unspoken sigh from the others present.

Keeping a close watch on the guide, Kyron said, "You called us here, Spear?"

"Yes," Astentius snapped and paused to take a deep, cleansing breath. Kyron saw the man's hands unclasp and much of the tension left his frame. "I asked for your help to question one of the prisoners."

"Us?" Kyron said, unsure.

"Me?" Emlyn asked at the same time.

"Yes," Astentius said and spoke to Emlyn in a tone much more level than their last exchange of words. "You are of the tribes and might be able to keep him calm. We wish him no harm, he is no longer a threat, and our mission is to return to the Empire not wage war."

"And me?" Kyron asked, cursing at the break in his voice.

"I understand magicians have a way to compel people to tell the truth?" The Spear's eyes held the question as much as the words.

"Some do," Kyron admitted, "though the art is forbidden in the Gymnasium and beyond. No good magician learns such magic. The penalties for its use are high."

"Does that mean you, or your master, cannot do it?" Astentius said, adding, "Speak freely, none here will judge you harshly. We are at war and what weapons we have must be sharpened for use."

Kyron paused. It was true there was a way to compel people to follow instructions, tell the truth, or do whatever the magician desired, and it was forbidden to study and use. The trick, for that is what Padarn called it, was not particularly difficult and with small adaptations it could be used effectively for other, more benign purposes such as taking away pain or inducing slumber.

However, the realisation that a magician could control another with a simple trick was one which scared a great many people, the Emperor and Church amongst them. Hence the magic was forbidden. The Spear's assurance meant little if the troops truly knew what the magic could do. Fear of losing oneself was a primal one and often resulted in uncontrollable anger.

"I'm sorry," Kyron said. "I do not know it, nor does my master. No one teaches it in the Gymnasium and those discovered in the wilds who have the knowledge are executed as an example."

"Then you cannot help me," Astentius said, disappointed.

"I can tell when someone is lying, Spear Astentius. The magic for that is not difficult, but much more reliable than guesswork," Kyron added, trying to be helpful.

"That is something, at least. Come," Astentius said, beckoning them from the tent. "We have a warrior to talk to."

XVII

THE GENERAL

Nine years ago:

*"I've arranged for you to join a class led by Grammaticus Flaccus,"
he said, dipping the bread into the dark vinegar and taking a bite.*

"You don't want me here anymore," the boy whined.

*"I want you to learn," he answered, keeping his voice calm and
placid. "Your father attended a Grammaticus also. I expect you to
learn all you can and make the family proud."*

"How far to the forest and those villages, General?" Alhard asked
him.

"We will reach them by this afternoon, my Prince," Bordan
answered. "Once we are in sight, we can set camp and a watch, I'd
much rather start our sweep of the villages in the morning when we
have the benefit of time and daylight."

"You're scared of the forests?" Alhard looked across to him, one
eyebrow raised in a question.

"It is their ground, my Prince," Bordan said. "They chose it, they
live there, and they know its secrets. Our legions are better on open
ground and at a site of our choosing."

"The legions are strong, General," Alhard said, his voice brimming
with confidence. "No matter the ground, we will be victorious."

"I have no doubt of that," Bordan replied, shifting in the saddle to
ease the pain in his hips, "but I would not spend their lives needlessly

or casually. The men are the most important part of the army. Without them we cannot fight."

"Surely the leader is the most important, General," Alhard countered. "How many times over history has an army been defeated because its leader was killed?"

"Many times, my Prince, but follow the path of history a little further and you will see a new leader always arises to continue the fight," Bordan said, shaking his head and looking along the line of troops ahead. "Without the soldiers there is no army. Without a leader it may lack direction for a time, but there are many who could take on the mantle."

"I am not sure I like what you're suggesting," Alhard said, lifting himself in the saddle to see better over the head of his horse.

"I am not suggesting anything, my Prince," Bordan answered. "In a war, both killing soldiers or the leader are valid tactics, depending upon the overarching strategy being employed."

"Now you sound like my tutors," Alhard complained.

Before Bordan could answer the faint brown line of the forests appeared on the horizon and a village—no more than a few houses surrounded by freshly tilled land and cattle wandering freely about the plains, chewing on the spring grass—came into view. Raising the seeing glass to his eye, Bordan twisted the tube, extending it a little further and bringing the homes into better focus. Still blurry, but recognisable as the homes of farmers and labourers, he saw thin wisps of smoke rise from two of the homes and there were the shapes of people working in the fields. One or two appeared to move and look in his direction, though they could just have easily been looking back at the village.

"We'll stop there," Bordan said. "Sarimarcus, send the scouts ahead. I'd rather have the village forewarned and ready to accept us."

"And if the rebellion has spilled this far from the forest, we can prepare an attack," Alhard said.

"They're farmers, my Prince. A few homes, less than twenty men, women and children," Bordan said as Sarimarcus began calling orders.

"I will not have treason in my realm," Alhard said, kicking his horse into a canter.

Bordan let his horse pick its own way along the dirt track, watching the Prince catch up to the front of the column, his back straight and head held high.

"Do you think he means to attack the farmers, General?" Sarimarcus asked from his side.

"I'm sure he doesn't, Spear," Bordan answered in the same low voice. There were a thousand other thoughts running around his head that he left unspoken.

The Prince seemed to enjoy being with the troops and many of the soldiers were in awe of the man. It was not often a member of the imperial family rode with the soldiers on patrol, and even on a mission such as this, it was unheard of. Bordan knew that getting the Prince away from the dangers of the capital, one or two of them of his own making, was a sensible decision. However, his actions in the market had shown Alhard to be a man of impulse and emotion, but a leader must be calm and thoughtful.

Anger had its place in battle. It blanketed your fears, overcame your nerves, and drove many a soldier to a feat of bravery or sacrifice which could turn the tide. In the front line, controlled, contained, and well-utilised anger was as much a weapon as a spear or sword.

In a leader, it was nothing but a hindrance. Anger clouded thoughts, narrowed vision, and blinded you to the truth by overwhelming you with lies and your greatest fears.

In the privacy of his own thoughts, Bordan could acknowledge Alhard's in inexperience, and it worried him. An Emperor needed to be calm when faced with anger, merciful when faced with dissent, and understanding when faced with ignorance. The road ahead was uneven, undulating, and shrouded in the dusts which only time would settle.

He sighed. Time was the enemy which he faced every day and knew would defeat him far too soon.

"General!" The shout came with urgency and Bordan's thoughts scattered upon the sound of hooves heading in his direction.

"What is it?" Spear Sarimarcus called back.

The scout pulled on the reins of his lathered horse, bringing it to a halt in front of Bordan, blocking the road ahead. Over the man's shoulder, the General caught sight of Alhard riding back to find out what had caused the alarm.

"General," the scout said, "the villagers are fleeing towards the forest."

"What?" Bordan snapped. "Why?"

"I don't know, sir. I was still a distance away when I noticed them all start to leave the fields, race to their homes and start running towards the forest," the scout said.

"They could have mistaken him, and us, for bandits?" Sarimarcus offered.

"Possible," Bordan allowed, though his heart knew it was untrue.

"They are in league with the tribes in the forest," Alhard spat and his horse skipped from hoof to hoof under him.

"There are no tribes, my Prince," Bordan replied, holding his temper. "Those in the forest are people of the Empire and we're not sure what their reason is."

"Only the guilty run." Alhard stated it as fact, his eyes fixed on the village ahead.

"Or the scared," Bordan countered. "However, it would be wise to be cautious. Spear, draw the men into a column, set some outriders to protect our flanks."

"I'll ride at the front," Alhard said, moving to swing his horse about.

"My Prince," Bordan, guiding his horse up alongside Alhard's, lowering his voice, "the soldiers at the front are walking. Your horse would be in their way."

There was a moment when, Bordan felt, the Prince might argue, but for once the younger man held his tongue for a moment, before nodding and having the grace to look slightly abashed.

"Of course, General," Alhard said.

"The cavalry would be glad to have your horse and sword," Bordan offered, gesturing to the group of ten mounted soldiers who followed the soldiers. Perhaps the boy could learn to lead if he began to heed advice. Learning that silence, that taking a moment to think before speaking, did not make one appear slow but rather deliberate and considerate, even if you had no idea what the right decision was. Aelia had been the more thoughtful, studious child, but she had been given time to follow her interests. Alhard had been groomed to be the Emperor, and all which that entailed.

Three of the soldiers left the column as the Spear called to them, acting as outriders, and the scout, his own horse still blowing hard from the ride, cantered to the fore of the column and headed back towards the village.

"The Empress ordered me to bring you back safe and it would not do to lose the heir to the Empire in a skirmish over a tired farming village," Bordan said, adding a smile to soften his tone.

Alhard nodded and pulled his horse to the side to await the small band of cavalry.

The small force, numbering barely half a cohort, drew into formation with parade ground efficiency and the supply carts which followed closed up to the back of the column. It was a sight which filled Bordan with pride and sent a tremor of excitement through his bones. The air felt fresh and clean in his lungs.

Through the dust the village came into sharper focus as they progressed. Homes became clear and what had looked idyllic through the seeing glass now looked dirty, unkempt and desperate. Wood smoke rose into the still air, but the overriding stink was of animals, dung, and rot. A few scrawny chickens clucked around in their small enclosure and Bordan heard the snorts and gruffs of a pig as it snuffled around in the dirt.

Years as a soldier, on campaign as he rose through the ranks, had made him immune to a hard life, but decades of luxury living in the capital had eroded his appreciation for true poverty. His nose wrinkled and he found himself looking down upon the wood, wicker and mud plastered homes until the faint memory of his own childhood floated to the surface of his mind.

The troops spread out amongst the dwellings, checking and searching, while a hundred or so men set a perimeter between village and forest.

"Empty," Sarimarcus reported. "There is food cooking on the fires, but no one is here, not even the children."

"They've gone to warn the tribes," Alhard said.

"If so," Bordan said, finding no explanation other than fear, "we form our camp around the village. We'll have food, water and can secure the ground between the forest and here."

"They'll have time to prepare and plan," Alhard said. "I say we clear the forest of rebels while there is still light."

"My Prince," Bordan said, biting his tongue in front of the soldiers, "we don't know that your subjects have rebelled, nor that those in the forest have turned against you."

"The camp will be a target to their archers," Sarimarcus added.

Bordan nodded, though the intervention of the Spear rankled. "Which is why we should secure the land between. I accept both of your points and I have no wish to leave us vulnerable and exposed. However, to fight on their terrain, if fight we must, in the gathering dark would be folly."

"General..." Sarimarcus began, but Bordan waved him to silence.

"Spear, have the men begin to fortify the village. Standard precautions but double the watches. It looks like a clear night so it will be difficult for any to creep up upon us."

"Yes, General," the Spear answered.

"The Prince and I will take fifty men to patrol the edge of the forest," Bordan continued, nodding towards the Prince whose face split in a wide, eager grin.

"I will have them ready in a few moments," Sarimarcus said as he clambered down from his horse and began to issue orders.

Moving to the edge of the village with the Prince beside him, away from the stink of rural life, of memories best forgotten, Bordan gazed towards the forest. A wall of green which separated the plains from the late afternoon sky, he knew it was closer than it appeared. The subtle rise and fall of the plains, the shimmering grass, and the lack of human built structures distorted a sense of perspective.

"Have you ever been in the forests?" Bordan asked.

"Not since I was young," Alhard confessed. "Father had less time to take us hunting when the war heated up."

Bordan nodded, more recent memories of war and battle crowding his mind. "We will have to leave the horses behind. There will be tracks, but nothing wide enough for a horse and being mounted amongst the branches will make it impossible to ride anyway."

"You expect me to walk all the way to the forest?" Alhard said, his mouth falling open in surprise.

"And back," Bordan nodded. "It is not as far away as you think, barely two leagues."

"So close?" Alhard leaned forward over his horse's neck and peered at the forest as if seeing it for the first time.

"The land around here plays tricks on your eyes," Bordan said, sliding from his horse with a groan of pain. "And hopefully the walk will do us some good. Take a shield, my Prince, and, if you'll forgive me, remove any signs of rank and lineage. Amongst the trees, if there are rebels, they will mark you out as a target. Your mother would be less than pleased if I returned you to her with a few new arrow holes."

Alhard laughed, and when Bordan heard an innocent, childlike quality in the deep voice of the Prince, once more hope flared in his heart.

"I will, General," Alhard agreed. "My mother is more frightening than a whole army of rebels. However, I am riding as a Prince, not walking as a common soldier."

XVIII

THE MAGICIAN

NINE YEARS AGO:

"Ah," the Grammaticus said, as they approached. "I see you've brought the boy."

He watched as the old man handed over a pouch which jingled as it came to rest in the Grammaticus's hand.

"I am Grammaticus Flaccus," the man said, "and have been told a little about you. Come. Sit. Join the class. You speak the language of the far southern continent?"

He shook his head, scared to open his mouth, and his hand tightened in the old man's grip.

"No matter," the Grammaticus said, "I will teach you."

TIED TO A tree, the rope wound around his torso and knotted at the back, the warrior of the tribes was unbowed and ready to fight. Straggles of blond hair dripped over his eyes, but the set of his shoulders, the strain on the muscles in his arms as he sought to free himself, spoke of a stubborn will.

Spear Astentius positioned himself in the man's eyeline and issued a sharp command to the guards stood either side of the tree. At his voice, the prisoner stopped struggling and looked up.

Kyron gasped. The warrior's face was a mass of purple bruises and dried blood. Even so there was no give, no surrender in his eyes: just hate.

"If you stopped struggling to get free, the guards would not beat you," Astentius pointed out, his stance relaxed but one hand resting on the worn hilt of his sword.

"Life is a struggle," the warrior said.

"We only stop when we are dead," Emlyn finished and the warrior's gaze snapped around to her.

"Who are you to know the sayings of the forest?"

"I am of the forest," she answered.

"Yet you stand with them," he accused.

"Not through choice."

"Then you struggle," he said.

"I am not yet dead," she answered.

"Quiet," Astentius said, taking a step between them. "You're alive to answer my questions, don't forget that."

"You speaking to me or her?" the warrior grunted.

Kyron saw Astentius stiffen before he answered.

"You," the Spear said. "You and your warriors attacked my force. Why?"

"Because you are here, invading our lands." The warrior hawked and spat at the Spear's feet.

"Apprentice?"

"Yes, Spear Astentius?"

"Is he telling the truth or not?" The officer turned his glare on Kyron, who shrank a little from the look.

"Not the whole of it," Kyron said, holding his nerve. It was a safe answer and he reached for the motes, constructing a web of them about the warrior. Next to him, Emlyn snorted.

The Spear turned to her. "You've something to add?"

"There is no such thing as the whole truth."

"Perhaps not," Astentius said, "but he will tell us all of it he knows."

"He would rather die than give up his secrets," Emlyn said.

"I'm sure he would," the Spear answered, a sneer plain on his face. "And he will wish death had come swifter by the end of my questions."

"You will execute him?" Kyron said, his voice catching and breaking.

126

"He knows there is no escape," Astentius said and the warrior nodded, "and we have no capacity to carry prisoners."

"Then he gains nothing by speaking," Kyron said, not understanding.

"Like our guide, he will have few choices left to him," Astentius replied. "Tell me if he lies, it is all you have to do."

"Yes, Spear," Kyron said.

"Why attack us?" Astentius asked once more.

"You are here to be attacked," the man answered.

"Truth," Kyron said.

"Just the lies, Apprentice," the Spear said without turning. "How many of your warriors were with you?"

"Not enough," the warrior answered.

"How many more are there?"

"More than enough," the warrior said, and Emlyn snorted once more.

"Guide," Astentius said, "you know these forests?"

"I know of them," Emlyn said, "though, as you know, my own village was much further north."

"How many villages are there around here?"

"I don't know," Emlyn replied. "I just told you these are not my lands."

Astentius grunted. "Are there plans to attack the caravan again?"

"We're always planning to attack," the warrior answered, glancing over the Spear's shoulder to stare into Kyron's eye.

"Are your forces planning to attack again tonight?"

"Yes," the warrior said.

Kyron felt a sweat break out across his body as the man answered and he could not look away. "A lie, Spear."

The warrior grunted and Kyron realised it had been a test.

"Tomorrow?" Astentius asked without a pause.

"No," the warrior answered.

"The day after?"

"I don't know," the warrior answered.

"That's a..." Kyron faltered. "I'm not sure. Some of that was a lie."

The warrior tied to the tree laughed, a rich sound at odds with his predicament which rang through the forest.

"You are playing with us," Astentius said, though there was no rancour in his voice, just resignation. "I had so much wished to avoid this. Bring it up."

The warrior's laughter tailed off as more troops entered the small clearing. Between two of them, and held off the ground by two stout poles, they carried a burning brazier of wood. Flames licked the brim as it was set down and a wave of heat washed over Kyron.

Another soldier approached with a wrapped leather bundle in his arms. Laying it down upon the earth he pulled at the straps which held it closed and flicked the covers aside. Rods of iron, blackened and jagged at one end, were revealed and the soldier took one up and plunged it into the flames.

"Are you sure you wish to do this?" Astentius said to the trapped warrior.

"I struggle," the man replied, gritting his teeth.

"I applaud your bravery," Astentius said, sweeping his hand to point at the brazier, "but your stupidity astounds me."

"Life is disappointment," the man said.

"And death the escape," Emlyn added.

"All that matters are our choices."

"And the memories we leave behind," Emlyn said, shaking her head.

"Which last forever in the heart of the forest," the warrior finished.

"Pagans," Astentius spat. "Immunis Surus, at your pleasure."

"Yes, sir," the soldier answered. "It will take a few moments to heat the iron."

They waited without talking as Surus judged the proper moment to withdraw the iron from the fire. Twice he took it from the flame and inspected it much as an artist would a portrait, seeking the imperfections and correcting them with a deft brush. Except here and now, Surus settled for spitting on the iron and listening to it sizzle as it turned to steam.

"Ready, Spear," the man finally said.

"Thank you, Immunis," Astentius said. "Guide, you can go."

"I will stay," Emlyn said. "To witness his struggle and collect his memories."

Astentius shook his head. "Whatever you want."

"Spear?" Kyron queried.

"Apprentice, what?"

"Can I go?" The thought of a man tortured, his flesh blackening under the kiss of hot iron, was turning his stomach and adding the sweat already pouring form his forehead.

"No, Apprentice, I need you to tell the truth from the lies," Astentius replied. "Believe it or not, I've no wish to inflict pain, and torture sickens me as much as it does you, but our mission is too important."

"But…" Kyron said, trying to find the words which would help him escape from his fears.

"If the warrior can face it with stoicism, so can you," Astentius snapped. "You will not show cowardice in the face of the enemy, Apprentice, and you will follow orders."

"Yes, Spear," he gulped.

Emlyn moved a pace or two away and settled to the forest floor. Crossing her legs underneath her, she picked up a fallen twig as round as two fingers, drew her knife and began to whittle. The dark shavings of bark soon gave way to the pristine white of the wood beneath. Her movements were smooth, untroubled and she was focused upon her task.

"Where is your village?" Astentius asked the warrior.

"So you can destroy it like the others?"

"Immunis," Astentius said.

The stench of burning flesh filled the clearing and the black smoke which rose from the prisoner's bare leg made Kyron's stomach heave.

"Where is your village?"

"I…" the warrior panted, "am not telling you."

"Immunis."

This time a choked cry rose from the warrior's mouth and Emlyn's smooth strokes of the knife faltered for a moment.

Kyron covered his mouth with his hand and focused upon the net of motes he had wound around the man. Even they recoiled from the man's pain and it was an effort of will to keep them contained in the construct.

"Perhaps a different question," Astentius said, his voice cold, calm, devoid of emotion. "What was the focus on your attack last night?"

"To kill you," the warrior said, his face white but his eyes aflame with pain.

Kyron swallowed, feeling the tremor in the construct. "A lie."

"Thank you, Apprentice," Astentius said. "Immunis."

Another sizzle and cry as more flesh was burned and the clank of metal as the iron was stabbed back into the fire.

"You enjoy the pain, perhaps?" the Spear said. "You lie, the iron burns. You refuse to answer, the iron burns. You do not tell me what I want to know, the iron burns. When your legs are charred and the blood flows too heavily, we will start on your fingers, hands, arms, and from there it will only get worse. Your mouth and tongue will be last so you can still gasp out your truths and lies."

Kyron stumbled to the edge of the small clearing where sharp pine branches wove a wall with few breaks and threw up. Bile and breakfast spattered at his feet mixing with the fallen needles into a foul soup of disgust.

"Your youth has no stomach for this," the warrior said. "My memories will become part of the forest, but his are poisoned by these actions and you have only yourselves to blame."

"Immunis," Astentius said and this time a scream of pain was torn from the throat of the woodsman. It bounced and echoed from the trees and Kyron, looking away from the sight, saw the leaves shiver and rustle as the pain wracked the warrior's body. "Get up, Apprentice. Each serves as we must, and you will be stronger for witnessing."

Kyron, sweat dripping down his face, turned back to the prisoner and saw the cauterized wounds on the meat of his thigh. Wisps of smoke rose from each and twisted through the pine boughs above. Each tendon in the man's neck and arms was caught in sharp relief, straining to escape his skin, to escape the pain being inflicted upon his body.

"Will your people attack again?" Astentius pressed.

"Yes." The man spat a globule of blood and saliva which landed upon the forest dirt. "And again, and again until you are driven from our lands."

"You have an army?"

"No," the man said between gasps.

"Spear," Kyron said, dragging the words from his throat, knowing the consequence of them, "he is lying."

"Hold," Astentius said to the soldier who had dragged the iron from the flames. "An army awaits us or follows us. Even with your lies, we can find out the truth. Save yourself the pain and tell us what you know."

"Life is a struggle," the warrior said, a line of blood dribbling from his mouth.

"Immunis," Astentius sighed and another scream was torn from the warrior's throat. Kyron's stomach roiled once more and the acrid, bitter taste of bile flooded his throat, but he could not look away.

On and on it went, the burning, the smoke and screams, and the questions. Kyron spoke only when the lie was plain against the construct while beside him Emlyn looked on unflinching but with her hands balled into tight fists.

After a time, as the iron caressed the man's face, the screams became hoarse and whispered. The man of the tribes was a mess of burns and weeping sores, and his throat had given up or torn itself to pieces with the pain. He had bitten through his lips which were puffy with blood, pink flesh poking through the rents his teeth had made. Every few moments, the man coughed and more blood, darker and thick, fell from his lips. His head bowed against the ropes and each breath was a tortured rattle followed by a sucking, wet rasp.

"I think we have learned all we will," Astentius said, wiping his hands on a rag, clearing away the stains of red where he had held the man's face up to his own. "Immunis, put him out of his pain."

"His memory will go to the forest," Emlyn said, "and it will not forget."

"Trees can be cut down, burnt, chopped into firewood or shaped into planks, guide," Astentius said. "A forest can be destroyed, as can your people if they continue to struggle against the Empire."

"Life is a struggle," Emlyn repeated as the Immunis stepped forward to drive his dagger into the broken warrior's heart. The bound man sagged against the ropes and a soft sigh escaped his throat, a last whisper of a life.

XIX

THE GENERAL

NINE YEARS AGO:

"How was your first day?" he asked as the boy slipped into the chair at the table. Decima slid a bowl of meat smothered in a thick gravy across to the boy who looked at it with narrowed eyes. "You must be tired. Learning can be very tiring."

"They all speak a funny language," the boy said, stating it as fact and challenging him to argue.

"I know," he answered, a small smile playing across his lips. "You'll learn it quick enough. Now, eat up. Decima's cooked your favourite."

AT THE EDGE of the forest they dismounted, handing the reins to a soldier who would stand guard over them. He was the lucky one, Bordan mused, not to have to traipse through the tracks of the western forest. It had been far too many years since he had been forced to wend his way along the trails of a forest, not since his grandson had left.

"We don't need to go too far in," Bordan said. "We find the villagers and discover why they fled. There's a good chance they saw us as bandits. The legion will not patrol out here too often and the nearby militia might be all they are used to. Do not underestimate a rural dweller's paranoia. It served them well in the past, kept them alive, whether that was against real bandits or just rotting food."

"There might be a tribal village in the forest," Alhard said, his eyes never leaving the narrow entrance to the forest and the dirt track which marked it out. There were fresh footprints in the mud which meant following the villagers should not be too much of a problem.

"I did not see a wide track or road as we rode up which would indicate one nearby," Bordan said, and the troops nodded their agreement. "However, it would not do us well to be complacent. We might have missed something obvious to those who live here."

Alhard looked away from the trees and Bordan caught the glow of excitement in his eyes. That would diminish as soon as they were amongst the forest where every shadow was a potential archer, where sight lines were poor, and the brambles of the forest floor caught and tugged at your armour. Worse still, the lack of a breeze would make you sweat, sticking woollen garments to your skin. Before long, the desire to scratch every itch would descend into a distracting madness.

"Let's get this over with," Bordan said. "You men stay and guard the horses. Keep watch along the forest edge. We might not come out here, though I intend to, and I would like you to be ready to assist us if needed."

"Come, General, let's show them what being part of the Empire means," Alhard said, clapping his hands together.

"My Prince," Bordan said, "your shield."

Alhard nodded and returned to his horse, unhooking a shield from the saddle horn and settling it on his arm. It was a plain wooden shield of the legions. His own, embossed and decorated, was left with the soldiers to guard.

Bordan nodded accepting his own plain shield from a soldier, slipping his arm through the strap and clasping his fingers about the handle. The weight was at once familiar and uncomfortable, tugging as it did on his shoulders and forcing his body to twist against itself. Better aching shoulders than an arrow in the belly, he told himself, shifting it again to try to reach some accommodation of comfort.

"Break the trail," Bordan said to the first group of soldiers, the second would follow Alhard and himself, protecting the rear.

Three of the front group carried no shields but had taken up the short bows of wood and horn which the legion favoured. Each carried their short stabbing sword on their hip, but now there was a quiver of arrows hanging from the other side. They scampered off into the forest first and after a few heartbeats the front line of troops followed.

Bordan entered the dark shadowed world of the forest and a sweat broke out on his brow. Resting a hand on his sword hilt, more for comfort than any desire to draw and swing it in anger, he followed the troops and the Prince.

The scent of spring was stronger here, but the odour of rot undercut it. New buds were erupting on the limbs of every tree and old leaves were decomposing underfoot. Wet dirt and the odour of oiled leather and mail. Sweat dripping down his face and the taste of the midday meal in his mouth. He swallowed, reaching for the waterskin and took a deep draught of the warm liquid.

A shadow to his left moved and he swung his head in that direction, the waterskin falling from his hand as he grabbed for the sword. It was nothing, light playing a trick with his imagination, creating danger where there was none. Better to react than not, he told himself. As every old soldier knew, the one you miss will be the one that kills you. He shook his head, imaginary threats and dangers would be playing on the mind of every soldier. Corking the waterskin, he let a rueful smile form on his face and turned to grin at the man behind him.

"I will be stabbing a tree in a minute," he said.

"Me too, sir," the soldier said.

"Get your own tree," Bordan said, his smile growing wider. "Plenty to choose from."

"I will, sir. I promise," the soldier replied with a low chuckle.

Bordan felt the pressure ease. His shoulders straightened and the breath in his lungs was full of life.

"Sir," a call came from ahead and Bordan saw a soldier waving him forward.

Keeping to the edge of the trail, he edged past the soldiers who, in good military discipline, turned to face the forest, their shields guarding the back of their neighbour. Say what you wanted about time spent on the parade ground, but the legions were made on those dusty squares through long hours of drill and discipline. He felt his heart swell with pride.

"The scout, sir," the soldier said. "He's got a report."

"Sir," the scout said, "we've found them."

Much quicker than he would have expected. "Where?"

The scout's right eye kept blinking and narrowing, giving his whole face an unfinished look, as if a painter was learning his craft and had sketched one side in before fully committing to the rest. "Just ahead. The other two are keeping a watch on the clearing."

"What are they doing?" Bordan said, looking past the scout and along the trail though he saw nothing but trees.

"Just sat there, sir," the scout replied. "They seem to be eating."

"Eating?"

"Yes, sir." The scout shrugged. "There aren't many of them, but they've sat down in the clearing and are eating whatever food they have."

"What is it?" Alhard said, coming forward.

"The scouts have found the villagers," Bordan said.

"Why are we waiting then? Let's go and demand they tell us why they are rebelling against my throne," Alhard stated.

"We will keep half the men back, in reserve," Bordan said, nodding towards the men at the rear. "We don't want to scare them, but the Prince is right to say we need some answers."

"They will talk if they know what is best for them," Alhard said.

"I am sure they will, my Prince," Bordan said.

Leading twenty men into the clearing, feeling the welcome touch of the morning sun on his face and the light touch of a breeze to carry the sweat from his forehead, Bordan saw that the scouts had spoken true. The families, for there were children amongst the adults, sat on the mossy ground and appeared to be finishing a sparse meal.

A ripple of shock washed through the villagers as they noted the presence of the soldiers. They stood hurriedly and retreated to the far side of the clearing. Parents shooed their children behind them, and the men folk raised their weapons, a club, a staff, a rice thresher, in protection.

Bordan stepped forward, feeling the Prince at his shoulder do the same, and kept his hands away from his sword. "We mean you no harm."

"Keep back," one of the farmers said, his face white and voice cracking as he spoke. Two others stepped forward, putting themselves at the man's side.

"My name is Bordan," Bordan said. "I am an officer in the Empire's legions."

"We don't want no trouble," the farmer said. "Leave us alone."

"Why did you run from us?" Alhard barked and the three men jumped, switching their attention to the Prince.

"We don't want any trouble," the farmer said. "Armies mean trouble."

"We are..." Bordan began, trying to regain their attention and to calm them down. The level of fear they felt was plain on every face and a child started to wail.

"Why did you run from us?" Alhard said, his voice cracked and echoed like a whip around the clearing.

"We... We came here to be safe," the farmer said, his hands twisting around the staff he clutched in both hands.

"You are rebels," the Prince said. "That's why you ran. Ran to the forest to meet the tribes, to form a rebellion against me."

"You? What? No." The farmer shared a look with the two men near him, their confusion clear to Bordan.

"My Prince," Bordan said, "they are villagers. Uneducated, scared..."

"They are armed rebels, General, and deserve only death," Alhard said, stepping towards the farmers and using his drawn sword to point at the farming tools held their hands.

"They are farmers with children," Bordan said, feeling the situation slipping away as Alhard's anger and fears swelled in the clearing.

"They are with the tribes," Alhard pointed, and Bordan noted the sword tip tremble in the Prince's hand.

"No, my Prince, I am sure they..." and his voice faltered as two newcomers entered the clearing. They were dressed in the leathers and furs of the forest folk. Axes, the tools of woodcutters and the weapon of the forests, were in their hands.

The lead farmer turned in horror to the newcomers, his mouth open to say something as Alhard's sword punched through his stomach. Whatever words the man had intended came out as an agonised scream. He slipped off the sword and to the floor, the staff falling to the dirt as he clasped his hands to the wound in his stomach.

"Alhard!" Bordan shouted and chaos erupted.

The Prince raised his bloody sword into the air, the farmers, the wives and children wailed, and the soldiers charged to protect the Prince before Bordan could draw breath to shout an order.

It was all the General could do to bring his shield around and take the blow from the farmer's threshing-flail. It bounced from his wood and the shock ran up his arms through his shoulders. Putting his other hand against the shield, he rammed it forward, catching the farmer in the chest and face. The man stumbled back, blood streaming from his nose and a soldier slipped past the General and sliced his sword across the falling farmer's chest.

He looked left and saw the two woodsmen step back into the trees. They looked shocked, confused, and terrified. Bordan called across to a soldier, pointing with his free hand towards the retreating men. His troops turned and began to chase the woodsmen back into the trees.

Ahead, Alhard was slicing his sword back and forth. The farmers that came against him were cut down. Even as Bordan watched the Prince began to slice his way through the women and children who had cowered behind the farmers. Their cries and wails were silenced with each slice of his sword and between each cut.

Bordan raced forward, putting his body and shield in front of the frenzied Prince. The other man's sword crashed into the General's raised shield, echoing around the clearing. Bordan twisted his body and shield, letting the force of Alhard's blow carry him forward. Dropping his own sword, he grabbed the Prince's sword arm and pulled it tight against the shield.

"Alhard. Stop!" he shouted.

All around the battle, such as the slaughter had been, ceased. A quiet descended upon the clearing, broken only by the quiet sobbing of the women and children who cowered behind Bordan.

Alhard, his eyes clearing, looked around at the fallen and broken bodies, young and small, women and children, in which he stood. The Prince let his sword hang dripping blood and ichor to the soil. His armour was painted red with spilled life.

Bordan saw Alhard's shoulders rise and fall as the man took great gulps of air, and the sobbing continued.

XX

THE MAGICIAN

NINE YEARS AGO:

"Who can tell me when the Empire was founded?" the Grammaticus asked.

He kept his hands by his side and glanced at the four other boys, all older than him. One, Linus, was almost fourteen and would be leaving soon.

"Over a thousand years ago," another boy said.

"And who founded the Empire?" the Grammaticus asked, his gaze flicking to each of the boy's faces.

"AN ARMY AWAITS us, Master," Kyron said as Padarn struggled out of his blankets. Yesterday had seen the magician regain a lot of his strength as the honour guard moved cautiously along the forest track. Another good night's sleep and most of the colour had returned to the older man's face.

"The forests are broad, but there are fewer people than you suspect, Kyron," Padarn said, dragging on his boots and stamping his feet into them. "Many have already fled north to join the clans of the mountains. Together they may be enough in the ravines and valleys to pose a threat to the legion. There will be few to face us."

"The warrior said there would be enough to beat us," Kyron said, "and he did not lie."

"No," Padarn answered, "but it may have been the simple truth of belief, not reality. The construct is a good one, but not infallible."

"There could be thousands?" Kyron said, his voice cracking and he cursed the betrayal of his throat.

"I doubt it," Padarn answered. "A few hundred possible, but likely less. They will make a stand, and they will fight, for that is their belief and way of life."

"Life is a struggle?" Kyron repeated Emlyn's words.

"True enough a statement," Padarn replied as he stood and stretched, a hand going to the small of his back. "However, we have soldiers of the Empire and they have us. It will not be an even battle."

"Master..." Kyron said, hesitating.

"Yes?"

"The Spear tortured the warrior, the tribesman," Kyron said, struggling to find the right words.

"So you said," Padarn replied. "Not a pleasant experience for anyone."

"I had to read him, Master." Kyron found a lump in his throat choking off his words.

"I'm sorry, Kyron." Padarn reached out and patted Kyron's shoulder.

"I felt it all." Kyron looked away, out into the forest. "Not as much as he did, but his reactions to the questions, to the pain. I could feel the fire in his limbs, the pain in his stomach, the beating of his heart. He screamed, Master. So loud. From the very pit of his stomach. I'm sure he almost tore out his own throat."

A tear welled in the corner of Kyron's eye and began to trickle down his face. It was cool on his hot skin and he let them come. His master stayed silent, but his eyes spoke for him.

"All through, the Spear kept asking him questions, and I had to read him," Kyron sobbed. "Emlyn watched it, Master. Her face didn't move. She didn't react, but she knew his sayings, his ways, knew him. I don't how she didn't cry or try to do something."

"Do what?" Padarn said in a warm, soft voice.

"Fight. Rescue him. I don't know."

"And if she had, what would have happened?"

"They would have killed her," Kyron admitted.

"You see her dilemma," his master said, his tone unchanging, not judging, praising or reprimanding. "But she stayed with him to the end. She offered her support, her guidance, to ensure his memories went to the forest."

"That's what they said, Master. His memories would go to the forest," Kyron said, looking up and wiping the tears away with the back of his sleeve.

"Their system of belief," Padarn explained.

"Paganism," Kyron said without thought.

"Just different," Padarn said, lowering his voice to a whisper, "and probably best not spoken of before a priest."

Kyron looked over his shoulder, a guilty shiver running through his body, as he checked for eavesdropping priests who would see him crucified for any words of heresy.

"She honoured him," Padarn continued, "as do you with your tears."

"She didn't cry," Kyron pointed out.

"Perhaps not in front of you, or him," Padarn pointed out, "but neither did you."

"No, Master," Kyron admitted and rallied his courage. "What will we do about the army?"

"If," his master raised a finger, "if there is an army of tribes waiting for us, we will fight."

"What if they beat us?"

"Then we will have done all we can," Padarn said, lowering his hand and Kyron saw the man's arm shake with weariness.

"You should rest, Master." Kyron stood and moved over to the older man. He paused as a thought occurred. "What will happen to the Emperor if we lose?"

"I'd imagine that the tribes will use the body to force the legion from the forest," Padarn said. "After that, I am sure they will push for further assurances and protections."

"The Empire will not allow it, Master. Surely the legions will do everything they can to get the Emperor's body back?"

"How?" Padarn asked, accepting Kyron's help in sitting down.

"Invade?"

"Isn't that what we are doing now?" Padarn shook his head. "If the legions invade, the tribes threaten to burn the body? Or slice it up and send it back to the capital piece by piece. Set it on a pyre and burn it in front of the legion? Take it and vanish into the forest, or the mountains? Their position is precarious: push too far and the legions will raze the forest to the ground, slaughter every man, woman, and child. The smoke would hang over the Empire for a thousand years and we would all lose something of ourselves."

"Then why would they try to take it? The Empire will kill them all to get it back," Kyron said. "There is nothing they could do."

"And what would they have to lose, Kyron? The Empire is already here, already killing their warriors, destroying the forest and their way of life is coming to an end. Would you not do all you could to protect what you had?"

"Well," Kyron said, then fell silent for a moment, pondering the words which would defend the Empire. Every word that his master said appeared to paint the Empire as villain, as the evil in this. Surely, bringing civilisation to the forests and mountains would benefit them all. The tribes would get richer, the clans of the mountains would be able to trade with the Empire. Their lives would get better. That is what the Empire did, it brought peace and change for the better. "We'll be making their life better."

"By killing?" his master countered. "By making them live as we do? Did they ask for this, desire it?"

"But, Master," Kyron complained, "if you didn't think the army coming here was a good idea, why did you come?"

"Because I serve the Empire, Kyron, just as you do," Padarn said. "I may not agree with everything we do, but I serve."

"And when their army comes to attack?"

"I will fight, as will you," Padarn said. "The Emperor's body must make it back to the capital. It is better for all if it does."

"You like the tribes?"

"I should hate them? What for?" Padarn's face creased and Kyron felt ashamed that he had asked the question.

"They are the enemy," Kyron said, the words sounding hollow to his own ears, but he was unwilling to give up the discussion.

"They are people, Kyron, with their own history, tradition and lives to lead," Padarn pointed out, but Kyron noticed the way his eyes scanned the immediate area. "Enemy is a strong word, an emotive word. I spent some time amongst the tribes when I was younger, and I have lived in our capital city for many years now. There is little difference between those who live there and here."

"But…" Kyron struggled to find the right words.

"If the tribes attack, we will be ready," his master said, "and that means you need practice. Let's work on your shield construct."

"Master," Kyron whined, "you know I can't hold it for long."

"My point exactly, Apprentice," Padarn said. "You need to be able to hold it with a part of your mind while you act with another."

"It is difficult," he complained.

"Of course, it is," his master said. "Everything is difficult. There are no easy professions or paths in life. Go and pick up a sword, start swinging at the pell. Your arms will ache, your back will hurt, your hands will blister, and your muscles will complain. After that you will train against others and more injuries will come your way. It will not be easy. You made the choice years ago, Kyron, to follow the path of magic. Build the construct."

Kyron took a deep breath, settling his mind and feeling for the motes of magic which streamed past him in the air and rested in the dirt below. "Yes, Master."

He gathered them together, weaving them into the shapes, twisting the strands together as the spell demanded. Holding them steady he brought his will to bear on them, forcing, cajoling, encouraging them to work together.

A circular shield, shimmering like oil on water, winked into existence in front of his face. Gritting his teeth, he added more motes and drew the strands apart, stretching them into a larger construct.

"Hold it there," his master said. "Smooth it out. I shouldn't be able to see it, not the colours, unless you wish it."

"Why would I want it seen?" Kyron whispered, his focus upon the motes, smoothing their passage along the threads and veins of the spell.

"You might want to darken it to block out a bright light, or have reflect back the light which strikes it," Padarn said, "or a thousand other uses which will occur as you practise. Good. You've got it there."

A smile formed on Kyron's face and the praise warmed him from the inside.

"Now," his master said, "draw the shield around you. Make it a cylinder which protects you from all directions."

Kyron took a deep breath and began to pull at the strands. Untying one, but holding it closed, he drew it around his body to meet the other side of the shield. Squeezing his eyes shut, feeling the motes move around him, hearing their subtle hum in his ears, and their caress as they passed close to, and in some cases through, his body. With each thread tied to another it became a little easier to maintain the flow of the motes.

"You're getting quicker, Kyron," Padarn said. "You need to be quicker still. That shield should be formed in a few seconds at most."

"I'm trying, Master," he replied, not disheartened but proud of the magic he had created.

"How strong is it?" a familiar voice asked and Kyron almost lost his grasp on the spell as the first stone struck it.

He saw the impact and the ripple of motes as they first closed on the object, throwing it back the way it had come. Another struck, and another. Soon small rocks were being scattered from the shield every heartbeat or so.

Sweat formed on his brow and a single drop trickled slowly down his cheek to drip off his chin. The rocks became larger, heavier, and were thrown with more force. Soon every impact drew a grunt of effort from Kyron as he struggled to maintain the shield.

"Can you not attack at the same time?" Emlyn asked as another object bounced from the shield.

"Certainly," his master said in a conversational tone. "Many magicians can create and hold two constructs at a time. A few masters can hold three or more."

"But Kyron cannot?" Another object, a branch this time, rebounded from the shield.

His breath was whistling between his teeth and in his ears the heavy beat of his heart almost drowned out their words. The spell continued though, and the motes whizzed about the construct, holding to their paths with a stubborn grace he found beautiful.

"Not yet," his master answered. "Though often one construct, one spell can be put to many uses. The only limiting factor is imagination and strength of will."

"Master," Kyron wheezed. "Make her stop."

"Desperation is the mother of invention, Kyron," Padarn chuckled. "You stop her."

Another branch, a twig, a stone, a pinecone, struck the shield and Kyron felt it begin to waver. The motes stuttered in their paths and the knots he had tied began to fray.

"Master," he pleaded.

"I won't always be there for you, Kyron," Padarn said. "You stop her."

"Emlyn," Kyron whined as another stone struck the shield. Cracks formed in the shield, blockages in the paths, threads, and arteries which the motes sped along. "Stop."

"Stop me," she taunted and another stone, larger and jagged, hit his construct.

The knots started to come undone and the threads unravelled as another stone struck the shield. He fought to hold them together, to ease the flow of their passage, to constrain them with his will, his power, but they refused to answer his call, to follow his demands.

Another stone and the cracks widened. His stomach twisted in desperation and anger. She was taunting him, stealing his accomplishments. To her they were nothing. His magic was nothing. He was worthless and a fire of shame burned in his gut, its flames licking at his mind.

"Enough," Padarn called. "You did well, Kyron, to stop so many missiles."

The stones stopped and his shield steadied for a moment before flickering from existence, the motes fleeing back into the world. His anger died and the flames in his mind went out.

Opening his eyes, he saw the smile on his master's face. Glancing around, he saw a similar smile on Emlyn's, but where his master's was one of pride, hers had the look of a predator sensing easy prey.

XXI

THE GENERAL

NINE YEARS AGO:

"Did Dorus really found the Empire?" the boy asked despite the talk around the table being of the foul winter coming in off the sea.

"No one really knows," he answered. "There are a few legends, some go back thousands of years. What did your Grammaticus say?"

"He said it might have been a girl," the boy replied, his face twisting in distaste.

"Bellona," he said, keeping the smile from his face. "As I say, no one really knows."

"You seem concerned, General," the High Priest said as he took his seat.

"There is much to be worried about, my friend," Bordan replied, still seeing the soldier beyond the raiment of the priest.

"Pass your worries on to me and I will cast them into the flames," Godewyn said, a gentle smile upon the large man's face.

"I wish it was so easy," Bordan said, dragging his goblet of wine across the wooden table and taking a drink.

"Is that why you are here so early?" Godewyn picked up his own goblet but did not drink.

"The council room is quiet and secluded," Bordan acknowledged, resting his hand on the leather-bound sheaf of papers in front of him.

"Until the council arrive. You needed a space to think?"

Bordan nodded. Looking down, in the deep red wine the dark reflection of his eyes stared back at him, measuring, taunting, questioning. "Some time away from my desk, the constant reports, and distractions. Finding a place to sit and gather my thoughts is becoming more difficult with each passing day."

"Age or the heir?" Godewyn said, now lifting the goblet to his lips and taking a sip.

"Both, probably," Bordan answered with his own smile. "Once the coronation is complete, I think it might be time to take a step back and let others shoulder the burden."

"Retirement? I never thought you would ever consider that," the High Priest said. "I felt sure I would be sending you to the Flame dressed in your uniform."

"I'd still want that," Bordan replied without hesitation. Priests and soldiers, the only two professions who could talk about death without getting maudlin about it.

"I'll be sure to make it happen," Godewyn said and paused before adding, "when the time has come. No need to rush these things, my friend. The new Emperor might need a little guidance from old hands such as you and I."

Bordan grunted. "He will need guidance, Godewyn. Someone he will listen to and take account of. I tutored him for a time, when he was small, and I held high hopes. You tutored him too?"

"For a time, before my ascension. I found him to be a pious boy. Belief came easy to him," Godewyn answered.

"And questions?" Bordan asked, meeting the gaze of his old friend and smiling before picking up his goblet.

"Less easily," the priest admitted. "You worry about him?"

"I worry about the Empire, Godewyn."

"You think he is not ready?"

The question caused Bordan to pause before answering, his concerns and worries encapsulated in the High Priest's words. "I think he is young, inexperienced, and untested. His father raised him, so there is that. We, along with others have tutored him, so we know his weaknesses and flaws."

"We all have flaws, Bordan," Godewyn smiled, "even you."

"True," Bordan sighed. "On the ride and in the town, I saw promise.

With the right guidance, he has potential."

"Was his father any different at his age?"

"I don't know." Bordan chuckled. "I remember his succession, but little of those years."

"Assume he was," Godewyn said. "For the sake of argument. With your guidance, and mine, Alhard could be a good Emperor."

"You're just trying to get me to reconsider my retirement," Bordan accused.

"Possibly," Godewyn acknowledged. "However, you are the famed General. He will listen to you and you can set his feet on the right path. Have hope alongside your faith in the Empire, my friend."

"There is promise," Bordan acknowledged, "and perhaps I am getting too old and too impatient. With fewer years ahead, I feel the need to see change happen quicker than nature allows."

"He will need your wisdom, Bordan," Godewyn said. "Speaking of the Prince, I have heard of his great victory over the tribes."

"You have?" Bordan looked up from his wine and back across the table to the High Priest. There was something about the tilt of the other man's chin, the way his eyes narrowed, and his lips were a little thinner than he remembered. "What have you heard?"

"An interesting tale is circulating the Church's lower orders..." Godewyn began, glancing towards the door to the imperial chambers.

"We have some time," Bordan said, resting the goblet on the table and shifting in the wooden chair to get comfortable. It also gave him a moment to focus on his heart rate and to still the expression on his face.

"The story I heard says that the legion were attacked near the border while riding to the rescue of a village. It seems, from the story, that the village had been plagued by outlaws, tribes from the nearby forest, who stole all their food and supplies, who beat their children and raped their wives." Godewyn paused to sip his wine. "The Prince had brought, I am told, a cohort of soldiers with him. Just in time, so the story goes, they spotted the villagers being herded into the forest and gave chase."

The High Priest paused once more and Bordan felt a tug in his chest, a feeling he should be saying something, correcting or adding detail to the story. It was an effort of will to hold the words within, unsaid, to hide the truth from the High Priest, though he allowed a small nod of his head.

"The Prince and the soldiers chased them into the trees. A great battle ensued, so I am informed, with the Prince leading the charge. Seeing no way out, the tribes slaughtered the villagers before the Prince could rescue them. With tears in his eyes, so they say, the Prince attacked once more. With a mighty display of skill and feats of arms beyond that of normal men, the Prince slew twenty of the tribesmen himself before they were all put down."

Godewyn's stare never strayed from his and Bordan knew he was being tested, though he did not know to pass or fail. "They say that the Prince, his sword and anger slaked by the blood of the tribes let it fall to the floor so he might cradle a dying child and aid its small soul onto the flame and the peace it promised in the next life."

Bordan did not move as the story ended but focused on keeping his breathing even and his eyes as neutral as he could manage.

"A heroic story, General," Godewyn said, "and so sad that the villagers could not be saved."

"Heroic indeed," Bordan agreed, cursing at the slight tremor in his voice. For a heartbeat he considered reaching for his wine but knew his shaking hand would betray him. "I share your anguish at the loss of the innocent villagers. War can do strange things to a person, and it is true that no one truly leaves a battle unchanged or unmarked."

"Even you?"

"I am not as young as I once was, Godewyn," Bordan admitted, using the truth to cloud the answer. "I think—I hope—that that was my last ride out with the troops. Though I'll miss it, there are many fine officers who will serve with honour. Maxentius will be an excellent General when I retire."

"I fear you are wrong, General. Not about Maxentius," the High Priest said, raising his hand in apology. "Every succession is fraught with peril and there is a change coming, I can feel it in the warmth of my soul."

"The Flame flickers?" Bordan asked, glancing at the wine once more suddenly in need of a drink.

Priests had forecast change before, and it had always come to pass. Perhaps not in the exact way they prophesied, but seeing the ever-changing future was an imprecise skill which had sent many a prophet mad. The last he could remember—a shopkeeper from the old quarter—had ended his days chained to a stone pillar in the Temple of the Flame, fed by the priests who took down his every word. Much had been gibberish, but there were kernels of truth which had come true.

"Not in my sight," Godewyn said, "but I can feel the mood of the congregation and the city."

"To be expected," Bordan replied, his heart calming, "we are in a time of uncertainty. Once Alhard is crowned, the city and Empire will calm and stabilise once more."

"You truly believe that?" The High Priest arched an eyebrow.

"I must," Bordan said, giving in and reaching for the wine, taking a deep draught and letting the taste of a fruitful summer coat his tongue. "Your guidance will keep him on the true path."

"I wish my faith in the city was as firm as yours," Godewyn said.

"A long history of service to the Empire," Bordan said, raising his goblet in salute. "It bends and flexes but never breaks."

"I hope you are right, General, though the stories I hear concern me. I fear we are heading into an age of change," Godewyn answered, raising his own goblet.

The door at the far end opened and Duke Abra stepped in. Both men at the table stopped talking and let their goblets rest on the table.

"Do not let me disturb you, gentlemen," Abra said, his tone bright and carefree as he slid into his chair. "Ah, wine. It is early, but never too early to share a fine vintage with friends."

Bordan bit his tongue, refusing to allow the words his mind conjured to be brought into existence. A sword might end a single life, but a word could lead to the death of thousands.

"You seem in a cheerful mood this morning," Godewyn said.

"I should not be?" Abra said, pouring wine into his goblet and selecting some fruit from the tray. "The Prince has returned from a victory against the tribes of the forest, gaining glory for the Empire and proving his mettle in battle. It bodes well for the future of the Empire, does it not?"

Bordan watched the other man's face, hearing the trap within the words and seeing willingness to pounce in Abra's eyes.

"No one can doubt the Prince's skill at arms," Bordan said in a soft voice.

"And a nascent rebellion has been stymied." Abra took a sip of his wine. "A good day for the Empire and so I am happy. I am grateful to you, General, for guiding the heir into battle and seeing him safely from it. The people will rejoice under a strong leader."

Before Bordan could answer, the door opened once more and Vedrix stepped in. The old man stopped and peered at the three men. He raised a nervous hand in greeting.

"Good morning," he said. "I thought I was late, you know. Seems I am not. Good. Good."

"Welcome, Vedrix," Abra said, waving towards the table. "Take a seat and a goblet of wine. We were just discussing the Prince's victory over the tribes."

"Victory?" Vedrix mumbled as he slid into his chair and took the jug of wine from Abra.

"In the forests," Abra said. "With the General here. You must have heard the stories?"

"No, um..." Vedrix said, flicking a glance towards Bordan. "I heard from some in the market square of a slaughter in the forests. A village full of people were killed?"

"Sadly," Abra said when neither the priest or General spoke up, "the General was too late to save the villagers from the tribesmen, but the Prince led a charge and killed all the tribesmen involved."

"Strange they are so far south," Vedrix said, sipping his wine, "these tribesmen, I mean. I wonder how they got there."

"They didn't come south," Abra said, looking to Bordan for assistance. The General raised his goblet to his lips and Abra shook his head. "They live in the forests already."

"In the north, I know, Duke Abra. I was referring to those in the west, where the Prince and General marched," Vedrix said. "Am I mistaking the stories? Forgive me, I wasn't listening too closely."

"No," Abra said. "They are the same stories."

"Ah," Vedrix nodded. "Forgive my lack of knowledge of the world outside the gymnasium. I do try to take an interest but there are so many things to occupy my mind. I thought that people of the western forest were of the Empire?"

"Tribal history," Abra said. "They were of the tribes once and harbour the desire to be part of them again."

"Centuries ago, I believe," Vedrix said, "before they joined the Empire, but as I say my knowledge is lacking in this area. I'm glad the Prince was able to protect the Empire from its enemies."

"As are we all, Master Vedrix," Bordan said into the quiet. Godewyn, across the table from him, grunted.

The room quietened as the rest of the Ruling Council arrived one by one, taking up their seats and whispering to each other. Bordan let his eyes close and listened to the secretive discussions, catching only snippets and single words. Enough to feel the mood of the council. All talk seemed to be of the Prince's victory over the tribes... he corrected himself, the *people*, in the forest to the west.

As they talked, the image of the blood-soaked Prince and the slaughtered villagers painted itself in the red and orange splotches on the inside of his eyelids. Trained soldiers who should know better joining in, and those who did know better standing back, unable to intervene as the villagers were shown no mercy.

At last the door to the imperial quarters opened. However instead of Prince Alhard, a member of the imperial guard stood there. He looked nervous, a sheen of sweat across his head and a flush of red around the base of his neck.

"What is it, Immunis?" Bordan spoke before anyone else could utter a word.

"General," the soldier turned his eyes to the General, grateful to be speaking to his superior, "the Empress asks that you and High Priest Godewyn join her at your earliest convenience."

"Did she say why?" Abra called along the length of the table.

"I've delivered the message as ordered, General," the soldier said, his head twitching as he fought to ignore the Duke's question.

"We will come with you now," Godewyn said, sliding his chair back and rising to his full height. "An Empress's wishes must be obeyed."

"We will wait for Prince Alhard and tell him where you've gone, if you have no objections," Abra said and Bordan watched the others nod, apart from Vedrix who was staring at him with eyes that seemed anything but confused.

"Your assistance is always gratefully received, Duke Abra," Godewyn answered.

The words were innocuous but Bordan saw the smile on Abra's face falter for a moment. There were mutters from the rest of the council as Bordan stood from his chair and followed the soldier through the door. At the sound of the solid click of the latch on the closing door, the soldier ahead sagged in relief as he turned to the General.

"What is it?" Bordan asked, noting now the pale skin and shaking hands of the guard.

"The Prince is dead, General."

XXII

THE MAGICIAN

NINE YEARS AGO:

"Your grandfather was a dirty street urchin, boy," Linus said when Flaccus strode off into the market to buy lunch.

"He's a soldier," he said, stretching to his full height and thrusting out his chest. "You wouldn't say that if he was here. It's a lie and liars get the birch."

"My father told me he was," Linus said, balling his fists and striding up to him. "And if you're calling him a liar, I'll beat you."

There was a warm trickle down his leg and the sound of laughter.

THE CRY OF warning rippled through the guard. Soldiers ahead and behind Kyron gripped shields tighter, took hold of weapons and turned to face the forest on both sides of the column. Such a smooth, practised reaction it filled him with confidence.

"What is it, Master?"

"You know as much as I do, Kyron," Padarn replied, standing up from the cart's seat and looking forward, over the heads of the soldiers. "For now, we will sit tight and stay out of the army's way."

A runner dodged past the last soldier a few moments later and slid to a stop next to the cart.

The young soldier dismissed Kyron with a glance and looked up to the man on the cart. "Master Padarn?"

"Can I help?"

"Spear Astentius has ordered your presence at the front," the soldier said.

Padarn gave the reins to the man sat next to him and smoothed down his short beard. "I will come at once." Padarn stepped down from the cart and onto the mud churned up by the passing feet of soldiers. "Kyron, bring your bag too. It will do well for you to hear what is going on."

"Actually," the soldier said, casting a sidelong glance at Kyron, "it was your apprentice the Spear wished to see."

"My apprentice?" Padarn said, his voice cold and crisp. "Whatever the Spear wishes to say to my apprentice can be said to me. I am his master, and he is my responsibility."

"I...I..." The soldier stuttered, halted, nodded. "Of course."

"Lead the way," Padarn said. "Come along, Apprentice, let us see what has halted our progress."

Following his master, his boots slipping in the mud and a hand on his bag keeping it steady against his hip, Kyron passed the soldiers and priests who stood guard around the waggon. He felt the eyes of the priests track his every step and looking up for a moment caught the hard, stone gaze of the Curate who had been assigned to watch him. She did not nod or otherwise acknowledge his presence, but every step became a little harder, his feet a little heavier.

"Do not dawdle, Kyron," Padarn turned and admonished. "The Spear awaits us."

Once past the waggon and out of sight of the priests, his tread became lighter once more. Now he noticed that there were fewer soldiers watching the forest. Instead they moved forward with his small group and filtered into new units which grouped into larger cohorts.

Ahead, the Spear stood with his staff, their horses tended by grooms, and clerks in attendance carried the tools of their trade, ink pots, stylus, and scrolls. Emlyn, the guide and his tormentor, stood to one side.

"Spear," Padarn greeted as he approached. Kyron stopped next to his master and sketched a bow, "you sent for me?"

"Ah," Astentius said, "Master Padarn. The intelligence gathered after the last attack seems to be coming true. My scouts report a large force gathered just around the bend in the trail. No doubt there are more in the forests."

"And you suspect they are hostile?" Padarn asked.

"They are armed and spread across the trail, Master Magician. Though I am told the trail widens slightly at that point, it is clearly their intention to block our path."

"We should attack," one of the other officers said.

"And I am not discounting that course of action, Cohort Borus," Astentius answered. "However, it is always prudent to gather all the information you can before you commit yourself to a course of action."

"And you think I can help?" Padarn said, drawing the conversation back.

"More precisely," Astentius said, raising a finger and pointing to Kyron, "I believe he can help."

"Me?" Kyron strangled the word as it fell from his mouth.

"With your permission, Master Padarn," Astentius continued. "I will send your apprentice along with our guide," the officer nodded towards Emlyn, "and a group of our soldiers under a flag of truce to determine what the tribespeople wish."

"Your death," Emlyn muttered.

There was a sharp intake of breath from the clerks and the gathered officers. Astentius however, laughed.

"Quite likely, young lady," the Spear said without anger, "and truth be known, I do not blame them. If the Empire was invaded, I too would want to kill those responsible." He raised his finger again, a tutor making a point, sharing wisdom. "However, our count of their number, even taking into account those in the forest whom we cannot see, suggest they do not pose a significant threat."

"Significant?" Padarn interjected before anyone else had a chance to speak. "There is a lot of room in that statement, Spear."

"Indeed," the officer agreed. "We would suffer losses, but I believe, as do my officers," there was a round of nodding from the soldiers, "that we will win any conflict here and be able to continue our mission without undue delay."

"Why my apprentice, Spear?"

"I cannot risk you," the officer answered in a matter-of-fact tone. "Your skills and abilities are too useful. I know that your apprentice can truth-tell well enough to be useful."

"Master," Kyron complained.

"And your soldiers will keep him safe?" Padarn asked, ignoring the pleading in Kyron's voice.

"Of course," the Spear nodded. "It is my intention to bring every one of them back safely with information we can use. The risk is, I believe, minimal. Is that not true, guide?"

Emlyn huffed. "A flag of truce has as much meaning for us as it does for you, probably more so. You people of the Empire are honest only when it suits you. The rest of the time the lies which reside in your heart are spoken without a care."

"Excellent," Astentius replied, and Kyron realised that the Spear had got used to dealing with Emlyn and refusing to rise to the bait she placed in the trap. "That should ease your concerns, Master Padarn. Your apprentice will be safe under the flag of truce. Our guide says so, and she does not lie."

Kyron caught the sour expression which twisted Emlyn's face for a moment. She caught his look and the expression changed into a sardonic smile.

"Then I have nothing to fear," Padarn replied, looking to the guide. "I would appreciate his safe return, Emlyn, and your own."

She nodded, a quick gesture. "Let's get this over with."

"Borus," Astentius ordered. "Gather your soldiers. No more than four, and the flag. We shall await your report."

"Yes, Spear," Borus answered. He waved to the four soldiers at the rear of the group. One of the men raised a pilum to which they had attached a white square of cloth.

"Will your people recognise the flag?" Kyron asked as he fell into step with Emlyn.

"More than yours," was her answer. She sighed, an exhalation full of sadness and regret. "We use the white flag because it is easier to see amongst the trees. Your people took it from us."

"We did?" Kyron was surprised.

"She is right, lad," Borus said. The soldiers closed in around them as they made their way down the track. "Centuries ago, before we came to the continent, we raised our shields above our head in surrender or to parlay a truce."

"It looks too much like a formation," Emlyn said, "a trick to protect you from arrows."

"So we learned," Borus agreed. "The flag is used even in the far east, in the Han lands. Though there it means something else."

"You've been to the Han lands?" Kyron's surprise kept on growing. "I didn't know anyone had really been there."

"A few merchants," Borus said, "over the centuries. The odd delegation from the southern continent, but we don't have much contact, so I understand. They prefer it that way. And to answer, no, I haven't. Doesn't mean I can't learn though."

"Well, no, I didn't mean..." Kyron said, giving up as the Cohort grinned at him.

"Don't take everything to heart, Apprentice. I'm a soldier and that means knowing your enemies. Even if conflict is unlikely, it is good to know something about people from different places," Borus said. "I find it interesting, the different ways in which people live, but I'd appreciate it if you didn't go spreading that around."

"There is nothing wrong with learning," Kyron said, his turn to be supportive and forgiving.

"Not at the top of the army, but a Cohort fights with his men, and soldiers prefer the simple life of orders, direction, and certainty."

"Then how do they rise through the ranks to become leaders?" Kyron said. "I mean, if they don't learn all they need."

"Aye, well," Borus grunted, "that's half the problem. Anyway, in the Han Lands, white symbolises death. So, the flag is really a flag of death. If we go to war, it says, you will die and so will we."

"Isn't that what ours means?" Kyron looked at the square of cloth which hung limp from the spear.

"More or less," Borus acknowledged, "but ours is more about purity of purpose, innocence and truth."

Emlyn snorted. When all turned in her direction, she changed the snort into a cough, covering her mouth with her hand.

"Cohort," one of the soldiers said as they rounded the bend and pointed down the track.

The Spear had been correct; the track widened enough at this place for four waggons to travel side by side without difficulty. If the area had not been filled with warriors of the tribes daubed in woad of blue, oval shields on their arms and a forest of spear points rising above their heads, Kyron would have described it as a clearing.

"Elvorix," Borus said to one of the soldiers, "start getting a count. Everyone else, take care what you say and guard your reactions. Let's see if we can get through this without a battle."

"Not likely," Emlyn muttered, and Kyron saw the grimace cross Borus's face.

"Even so," Borus said. The officer squared his shoulders, took a deep breath and marched forward. "Lift the flag high."

No one spoke as the small group advanced. Kyron could not help but look at the tribes arrayed against them. Each man and woman was dressed in woollen trousers and a tunic dyed into a cross-hatched pattern. However, it was the woad with which they decorated their faces and shields that drew his eyes. Splashes of blue and green across faces, more in their hair to raise it into spikes which looked sharper than the spears and swords they carried.

From the mass of warriors, insults were hurled. Though the language was one he spoke very little, the anger in the voices gave meaning enough. The Empire were not welcome and death was the only escape. He was certain, because Empire soldiers had hurled insults in the last battle, that there were also promises of much more gruesome fates.

Kyron felt trembles begin in his fingers, spread to his legs, pull at his bottom lip, and salt tears threatened to spill from his eyes. The urge to run into to forest and piss was strong, a burning sensation in his bladder. Looking right, he saw the soldiers march in step, their faces fixed and unmoving, bravery and courage earned in a thousand battles blazing from their eyes.

He blinked and saw the truth. They were scared too, they just hid it better. His fear gave way to shame. He would not, could not embarrass himself, his master, Borus, the Spear, or the Empire. He was a Magician of the Gymnasium, an apprentice to be sure, but he had passed the tests and not been found wanting. He would not be found wanting here.

Kyron echoed Borus's earlier gesture, took a deep breath and set his shoulders.

A shout went up from the tribes and silence descended on the forest. In the front line, a spear was raised with its own flag of truce hanging from it. Four warriors detached themselves and marched forward.

Unlike the regimented, rhythmic march of the Empire soldiers, the tribes came forward with an unhurried swagger.

"Be ready to truth-tell them, magician," Borus said from the side of his mouth. "Guide, you translate if needed. Remember your worth."

The last statement made little sense and Kyron was unsure if it had been directed at him, Emlyn, or the soldiers.

The delegation from the tribes stopped twenty paces from the Empire and planted the spear in the ground.

"Right," Borus muttered, "let's get this done."

XXIII

THE GENERAL

NINE YEARS AGO:

"I am not ashamed of where I come from, boy," he said, shaking his head. "I came from the streets, raised by a good man and woman of the Empire. They gave me the best start in life they could, and I joined the army. It made me who I am. There's a few of us who came from nothing and reached for the heights."

"But..." the boy said, his words faltering.

"It isn't where someone comes from, lad. It is what they do that judges their worth. Service and duty, learned that from my parents and army both."

THE EMPRESS WAITED at the door to the bedchamber. There were two guards with her and though both had faces locked into a professional expression, Bordan saw the pain in their eyes.

"Your Highness," Bordan began without knowing the words which would follow.

She turned and he saw tears tracing down her cheeks. Her eyes were hollow voids of loss, her hands shook, and her skin was pale.

"The surgeon says there is nothing that can be done," she said, her words calm and clear, at odds with her expression.

"Godewyn?" Bordan raised a questioning eyebrow.

"Perhaps if we see the Prince?" the priest offered, but Bordan heard the answer in the pause before his old friend spoke.

"In there," the Empress pointed at the door. "I can't... I can't..."

"Wait here and see to the Empress," Bordan ordered the two soldiers. They nodded, unsure of their role but grateful to be given some orders. He understood their position. In truth, there was nothing they could do, but he hoped their stoic presence would comfort the Empress.

To lose a child was a pain no one understood, not until they suffered the same wound. The emptiness, the sense of failure never left you. Every day there was a hole in your life which nothing could fill, not drink, women, or even, he confessed in the privacy of his own thoughts, work.

Godewyn nodded to him and they pushed open the thick wooden door. The scent of death was something every soldier knew. It was impossible to avoid and, once smelled, unforgettable.

The large bed, furs and blankets rucked up near the bottom of mattress, was the focus of Bordan's gaze. Upon it, the body of the Prince lay in peace. From a step inside the door he could see no wounds, no blood, and no evidence of a fight. Yet a young man, who had decades of privileged and comfortable life ahead of him, was dead.

To the side stood the court surgeon and his apprentice. The old man, wisps of grey hair about his temple, and his old-fashioned toga of white cloth wrapped tight about him, looked up as the door swung closed.

"General, High Priest," he greeted them in a sombre voice. The young man next to him did not speak but bobbed his head in acknowledgment of the newcomers.

"He is dead?" Bordan asked, but his mind was cataloguing all those who already knew of the death, thinking of strategies to contain the news until he was ready to act.

"Yes, General," the surgeon replied.

Godewyn stepped across the rugs and approached the bed, tilting his head as he did so. Bordan waited a moment for the High Priest to speak, but he remained silent.

"How did he die?" Bordan said, his eyes scanning the room. The window was closed and there would have been guards outside the door. Perhaps the Prince had not been alone. A courtesan, a paid companion for the evening, could have shared his bed. She, or he, would have information and was the chief suspect.

"I do not know," the surgeon admitted. "I can find no wounds on the body and no evidence of poison."

"Young men don't just die," Bordan said, finally moving forward towards the bed. "Alhard was young, fit and strong."

"Sometimes, sadly, General, they do," the surgeon said.

"Not a Prince," Bordan stated, ending the argument. "If there are no wounds, then it must have been a poison or an illness."

"I saw him this morning," the surgeon said, and his apprentice nodded in confirmation. "He was hale and not complaining of any illness. Bad food can kill, but it is rarely this sudden."

"So, poison?"

"If there is poison, I cannot find it," the surgeon said.

"There must be something," Bordan snapped. "He cannot have just died. Not like this. Do you know what is at stake? The whole Empire hangs on a knife edge, surgeon. If the succession does not go ahead, we'll face a civil war which could tear the Empire apart."

"I know that, but it does not change the facts," the surgeon snapped back, before taking a breath. "My apologies, General. I am as frustrated as you. I have looked after the Prince since his birth. It is like losing a son."

Bordan flinched and the temptation to correct the old man, to explain to him just how much this was not like losing one of your own flesh, was a rush of warm blood to his head. He took his own breath, letting the fresh air cool his hot blood. "It is I who should apologise. Is there anything more you can tell us?"

"Not here," the surgeon said. "There are some things I can test for, in my laboratory. There will be an investigation?"

"Of that you can be sure," Bordan answered. "However, that's not what you mean?"

"General," the surgeon spared a quick glance at his apprentice, "the outside of a body can tell us many things about life and last moments. However, a man's insides can often tell us more about the cause of death."

"You want to cut him open?" Bordan's voice rose in pitch, incredulous.

"Absolutely not," Godewyn said, speaking for the first time. "Such is forbidden."

"Of course, High Priest," the surgeon said. "However, I would be remiss if I did not make the suggestion."

Godewyn grunted and moved to the other side of the bed. Bordan noted he had not touched the body of Prince Alhard, but also that he had not stopped looking at it.

"What have you seen?" Bordan asked him.

"I'm not sure," Godewyn answered and a frown creased his brown. "However, there is..."

His next words were cut off as Princess Aelia crashed into the room. Bordan caught her by the shoulders as she tried to rush to her brother's side. The General grunted with the effort. Despite her smaller frame, there was a wiry strength to the Princess and Bordan was not a young man anymore. A moment later, Godewyn, bigger than both of them, took hold of the Princess's arm.

"He is no longer here," Godewyn said to Aelia. "His spark has joined the Holy Flame and while we sorrow, we rejoice in his everlasting life."

"Who did this?" Aelia cried, spittle flying from her mouth even as tears rolled down her face.

"We do not know yet," Bordan said. "We will find out."

"I want them found," Aelia spoke with a rasping voice that tripped over the line between rage and grief.

"We will find them," Bordan assured her.

"And then I want them crucified," Aelia spat.

Bordan almost took a step back in surprise. There was a heat rising from the young woman's skin, almost too hot to touch and Bordan could feel the heavy pulse of blood running through her arms. Grief tore at your mind, he knew that, and gave free rein to base emotions.

Some raged and spat their anger at the world. They would shout, fight, attack with words those closest to them. Eventually, they would calm, and reality would come crashing down with a hot wave of crushing sadness. Later, they would raise their heads, emotions spent, and carry on, the hole in their heart scarring over but never truly being free of the pain.

Others took the news in silence. Retreated into a world built within their own mind. A place of sanctuary and safety, a castle with thick walls to protect them from the reality which wheeled around them. Some never emerged, and those that did never healed, the open wound of loss weeping forever in their heart.

In soldiers, Bordan much preferred the former. They gained a new perspective on life, a deeper understanding of existence. Now they fought for each other, protected those alongside them, and understood the true purpose of battle was not to kill, but to live.

The latter, if they emerged, were broken and dangerous to their comrades. Spurred to feats of bravery and recklessness, they could turn the tide of battle, but too many who had yet to be tested would follow them into the fray and would die. Upon that mountain of bodies, the broken hero would stand.

Aelia was now sobbing, her rage extinguished by sorrow, the way it should be. Bordan, with Godewyn's help, guided her to the door.

"Let us investigate, Princess," Bordan said. "We will find what we can. Your mother needs you and you need her. Be strong for both your sakes and the Empire, Princess Aelia. I will tell you the moment we find anything."

"Bordan, I..." Aelia's words were choked off by another sob.

At the door, the Empress took her daughter's head in her hands and drew the young woman to her. The sobs increased in volume and Bordan saw the Princess's shoulders shake.

"Escort them to a room and get them wine," Bordan ordered the soldiers. "Find some trustworthy staff to look after their needs and return here. Speak to no one else."

"There is little you can do here, surgeon," Godewyn said, his deep voice breaking the silence which followed the imperial family's departure.

"What?" the surgeon blurted.

"You've done all you can," Bordan said, a gentle tone taking the sting from the High Priest's words. "We'll make arrangements for the body. I think it would be best if you and your apprentice went somewhere to get cleaned up and rested."

"We will go back to the hospital," the surgeon said. "There are soldiers who need treatment."

"Your other surgeons can handle that today," Bordan answered, his tone hardening. "I insist that you rest first and after write down all you can remember. We may need those records in the coming days as we investigate."

"General," the surgeon said, catching the wide-eyed look of fear his apprentice's face currently wore, "there are still some tests we can carry out."

"Not today," Bordan snapped. He took a breath. "My apologies once again. This situation has been trying on us all and it is important we act correctly from here on. I'll have some guards escort you and keep you safe while you write up your account."

He stepped to the door, swung it open and beckoned a guard over. It was a moment to issue the orders and a heartbeat later the surgeon was leading his apprentice out of the room and disappearing down the corridor with the soldier guarding their every step.

"Well?" he asked of the High Priest as he closed the door.

"You think I know something?"

"Godewyn, you were always more intelligent than any man has a right to be, and you have hinted at something," Bordan said. On the bed, the body of Alhard looked smaller in death than he had in life. The spark, the flame of life, gave presence, an indefinable sense of weight. Extinguished, the muscles and skin sagged in upon the skeletal frame.

"I'm not entirely sure," Godewyn said.

"And are you going to hedge around it for much longer?" Bordan waved around the room. "We are the only two here. Speak plainly. I would much rather listen to your guesses than another man's facts."

"All priests are," and the priest paused, his eyes flicking around the room as if searching for something he could not find, "trained to recognise certain aspects of magic. It is to keep us free of the taint and to protect others."

"Go on," Bordan answered, intrigued.

"There is something here," Godewyn said. "Something about the body, or the room. I'm not entirely sure."

"You think magic killed the Prince?"

"Yes," Godewyn said after a moment and the breath caught in Bordan's chest, "and no."

Bordan sagged, the breath rushing from his lungs. "Can you speak more clearly? If magic killed the Prince, then all at the Gymnasium are suspect."

The thought and the implications caught in his chest, a hooked dagger tugging at his innards.

"I cannot," Godewyn said. "For that you would need a magician."

"You want to bring one here?" Bordan asked.

"Much as it loathes me to admit, there are some I would trust, some whose loyalty I would not question," Godewyn said. "The most trustworthy is with the Emperor, but Master Vedrix is another in whom I would place my trust. I would rather he was not made aware of my assessment. It is important that he and I are seen as opponents across the council table."

"I will have him summoned," Bordan said, though the mention of the Emperor had stilled his heart once more.

XXIV

THE MAGICIAN

NINE YEARS AGO:
   He ran. Ducking around the stall owners, their customers, and the servants who carried the purchased goods. Shouts rang out after him, but he ignored them. The winter storm had come and gone, leaving the cobbles slippery and he struggled to turn. He had learned his only advantage over Linus and the others was speed. The rain had stolen that from him.
   A reaching hand grabbed the neck of his tunic and he was jerked off his feet.

"OFFER THEIR CHIEF my greeting," Borus said to Emlyn after the two groups had spent long moments staring at each other, waiting for the other to give way first.

   Kyron was unsure who had won the first exchange, as he had been focused on movement in the trees to his left. Flashes of bright green and blue flickered between the trunks and boughs as warriors of the tribes moved into position. He forced himself to focus, to draw upon the motes of magic which surrounded them and construct the spell Borus required.

   Emlyn spoke and her words were those of the tribes. Lilting, almost a song, but interspersed with harsh consonants which created a dissonance in the flow and melody.

   Holding the spell steady, he wound the net around the chief, the one he assumed would do most of the speaking. As before, it would be impressions rather than a direct indication of truth or lie. If the whole conversation was carried out in the language of the tribes, the task of dividing truth from lie would be much less precise.

The chief responded in the same language and Kyron let his sense roam across the net, feeling for changes which would indicate a lie. There was nothing. The net remained smooth and unruffled, which in and of itself was strange.

Words, no matter the context or meaning, came with emotions attached. Emotions which were revealed by heartbeat, by gestures, actions, sweat, facial tics, and other more subtle clues which were unseen but which the net could detect. Every word spoken should trouble the net in some manner. The skill was in reading each word, each sentence, for meaning and truth.

"He says you will find no welcome in the forests," Emlyn translated for Borus.

"Understandable," Borus nodded. "Nevertheless, we are heading home, away from his precious forest, and our journey would go quicker if his army would move aside."

Emlyn shook her head but spoke to the chief once more. This time her words were accompanied with gestures. She pointed at Borus, swept her arm to indicate the trees, and made a beckoning gesture back down the trail.

In return, the chief shook his head and a long stream of words sprung forth. Kyron looked on with worry gnawing away at his heart. The tone, the gestures, the way the chief waved his arms at the Empire soldiers, all demonstrated the man's anger yet still nothing showed in the net.

He caught Borus glance but could do nothing but shrug his shoulders in response. It earned him a scowl.

"The chief instructs me to tell you passage is denied," Emlyn said with a sigh. "He seems to think you cannot be trusted, that you will leave with the Emperor's body and return with a much larger army. At which point, the chief suggests you will set fire to the summer forest and kill everyone who dwells within."

"The thought had occurred to me," Borus mumbled in a whisper which only just reached Kyron's ears, then said to Emlyn, "Tell the chief, on my word of honour as a soldier of the Empire, that such will not be the case. We merely wish to return our leader to his family as is proper in our customs and religion. We ask him to respect that desire."

Emlyn spoke again, this time with her fist clenched to her heart and Kyron saw her pound it against her chest twice during her speech. The net did not tremble or react. Something or, Kyron realised, someone was preventing his spell from taking effect.

Now, with the truth lighting his mind, Kyron held the net with one finger of his concentration and began to quest outward with another. It was delicate and clumsy at the same time. He had no direction to aim for, no clues to follow, and the questing probe of his mind was merely prodding at empty air, seeking some aspect of a foreign magic.

He inspected the face of each man and woman who stood with the chief. None had so much as glanced at him, even though he was dressed in a tunic and cloak unlike the soldiers or Emlyn. Discounted, unimportant, not worth their time. However, if they were the person responsible for the dampening of his net there would be some link, some thread connecting their magic to the net.

Kyron took a slow, calming breath and fought down his fear. Letting the motes of magic swirl about him, he began shaping a second net. A fine weave of motes, each one joined the next by the faintest trickle of power. All the while he held onto the truth net woven about the chief.

A magician should be capable of maintaining two constructs, Padarn had told him. A good magician could hold three, and a great one could manage four. Kyron struggled. However, the nets were similar in purpose and shape, one merely an extension of the other.

His breaths became shallow and his heartbeat sped up. In the still air of the forest, sweat beaded on his forehead, but like the stones which Emlyn had thrown at him, he batted away his discomfort. Twice he almost tore the net apart, opting for speed over care and was forced to repair the threads before trying again.

The strange three-way conversation continued and when he opened his eyes, he saw the new net hanging in the air before him. Silken threads of magic, finer than any spiders, thinner than hair, but shining like a summer's sun on a morning dew. His heart swelled with pride.

"He says that should you have children with you, they are free to leave," Emlyn said to Borus, casting a glance Kyron's way.

"Kind of him, but he already knows we do not have children," Borus said. "Apprentice, anything to tell me?"

"I'm sorry, Cohort," Kyron said, and had to suppress a gasp as the very act of speaking almost tore his concentration from the two nets.

"Useful," Borus muttered. "Tell the chief that there is no need for bloodshed today. What he fears will come to pass if we are not permitted passage from the forest. Tell him the Empire will not stand for the capture of the Emperor's body. Should they try, the Empire will bring the full weight of its might to bear on the forest. Not a tree will be left standing."

"Threats?" Emlyn raised an eyebrow.

"Just tell him," Borus snapped.

Kyron let his consciousness fall back into tune with the magic, no longer just maintaining the nets, but putting his new construct to use. He lifted it into the air, where it undulated like the slow swell of the sea, and let it sink across the group of warriors who accompanied the chief.

One of them moved, raising a hand to scratch at a sudden itch on her scalp. Kyron sucked in a breath, watched, and waited. A moment later, her hand dropped and not for a moment did she look Kyron's way.

He felt for the net, letting his mind slip along the motes, feeling for the tell-tale impression of magic. If there were a magician amongst the group, the net would detect the passage of motes which were not under his control. If a foreign mote troubled the net, like a spider with a delicate foot resting on a thread, he would feel the vibration and know his prey was caught.

There was nothing and disappointment settled on his shoulders. He shook it off.

Look at it another way, he told himself. You have eliminated this group from your search, there are many more possibilities.

The army of tribes ahead were an obvious target, and there were those of the tribes in the trees to either side.

The flags of truce hung limp from the spears, and the conversation went on, solving nothing and coming to no agreements. On the edge of his awareness, he could hear the changes in tone on both sides, the deepening of the anger and resentment, and the escalation in threats.

Setting his shoulders, he lifted the gossamer net and sent it floating across the space between the negotiating groups. The front line of the tribes was perhaps fifty wide and he took the logical route to his search. Starting on the far right of the front rank, he let the net drift slowly across them. Nothing.

Gritting his teeth and narrowing his eyes, Kyron drew the net left, along the front ranks. He could see the shining threads drape themselves across each man and woman, tracing the outline of their bodies, shields and weapons in small glitters of power. Nothing.

A twitch in the net. A flicker of something. A tremble on a thread. A fly caught on a silken strand.

He wiped his sweaty palms down the side of his tunic and clenched his fists, drawing the net back along the row, feeling for another tremble. There it was, subtle, slow, and fragile.

Drawing the net in, focusing upon the magic which it had caught, it enclosed one figure who stood near the centre of the front rank. Kyron let the net settle about them, enclose them, and felt for the motes of magic which dampened his original spell.

They were there, contained, directed, a single line of motes which linked this magician to Kyron's truth-net. That line trembled and swayed, rising and falling, as it absorbed all the emotions, the tell-tales, of the chief's words.

Kyron opened his eyes. His vision swam for a moment and came back into focus upon the figure his net enclosed. She was tall, half a head above those around her, but other than that she was dressed in the same manner as all the other warriors. Oval shield, woad painted face, and spiked hair.

His heart missed a beat as he realised she was looking at him. The distance was too great to catch the expression in her eyes, but there was a connection which held him still and which chilled him.

She knows, he thought. She's a magician like me. No, better than me.

He saw her spear come up, and the faint line of her mouth twisted into a smile. The butt of her spear struck the ground and his net tore apart.

The sudden snap of his power struck his mind and he took a step back. Another crack sounded in his mind and the truth-net about the chief shattered. All the motes he had bound into the construct scattered into the air. A shimmering star-field of magic which only he and the tribal magician could see clouded the air around the group.

"Borus," Kyron gasped, even as he sought to corral the motes back into a shape, a shield with which to protect the Cohort and soldiers. His whisper was dry, a hiss, more than a word. Even so, the officer turned in his direction.

"Apprentice?"

"Magician," Kyron lifted an arm, surprised to see it shake with the effort and pointed across to the female warrior in the front line.

Borus nodded. "Guide, tell the chief I will need to take his words back to my leader. We will talk again as I am keen to avoid bloodshed if possible."

"If you do not have the power to negotiate, he will lose respect for you," Emlyn said, and Kyron saw the way her eyes narrowed as she followed the direction of Kyron's outstretched finger.

"I'm not here to get his respect," Borus snapped. "He knows I am not the leader. Their scouts have been out and about our column long enough, and do not try to deny that, Guide. We may not know this forest as well as you, but we are far from stupid."

"Whatever you say," Emlyn answered and turned back to the chief. She spoke fluidly, without anger, but there was a hint of sadness to her tone that Kyron could not place.

The chief snorted and spat on the forest floor. Without another word the warriors stepped back and, holding the flag, high walked back to their front lines.

"Let's get out of here," Borus said. "Hold the flag so they can see it. We need to tell the Spear what has occurred."

"There is going to be a battle, isn't there?" Kyron said, his legs feeling weak as he fell into step with the group.

"I don't think we can avoid it," Borus said.

"You can't," Emlyn added.

XXV

THE GENERAL

NINE YEARS AGO:

"That's the fifth day in the last two weeks he's come home covered in mud," Decima said across the table.

"It'll be the other boys," Gessius said. "There's a big one with an evil eye. I could... you know."

The boy looked up at the adults, his eyes questioning, hopeful, and his tunic torn at the shoulder.

"He has to learn to stand up for himself," he said, nodding his thanks to the old soldier. "He'll be better for it in the end."

"ALCHEMY," VEDRIX SAID, the fingers of one hand tangling in his beard.

The council chamber was sealed, and guards had been posted along the corridor. The Empress sat at the head of the table, her face a rigid mask of repressed emotion, but her eyes flashed from rage to sadness with every breath she took. Aelia sat close by and was less successful masking her emotions. Fear and loss were written clear across her face and in every movement she made.

"You are sure?" Godewyn asked, leaning both elbows on the table and looking down the bare surface at the magician.

"No doubt," Vedrix nodded.

"A poison?" Bordan asked. "The Prince was poisoned. By what or who?"

"If I may," Vedrix began, looking towards the Empress who, after a moment, nodded, "the art of alchemy can create poisons, but so can any number of skilled men and women. Even in the rural areas, especially in the rural areas, poisons are common. A plant, an animal, an insect. Some need no processing or special preparation to be effective. Alchemy is something different."

Warming to his subject, and with the room's occupants silent, Vedrix continued. "Alchemy concerns itself with rearranging, enhancing, and focusing the natural components of an object, plant, or animal. With skill, and much training, a skilled alchemist can combine ingredients into potions which can do miraculous things."

Godewyn grunted. "Miracles are the province of priests and the Flame, magician. Do not make claims to the power of the Flame, lest you feel its burn."

Vedrix stopped and swallowed. "Forgive my enthusiasm, High Priest, perhaps it made my language freer than I had intended. Nonetheless, alchemy is capable of many things which could not be accomplished without the presence of a skilled magician. The potions which your officers carry, for instance, are alchemical in nature."

"The healing flasks?" Bordan said, raising an eyebrow. "I thought they were herbal concoctions."

"There are herbs within, certainly," Vedrix said, "but they have been enhanced. The process is, I understand, laborious and often fails which is why there are so few flasks amongst the army."

"Could the flask have saved my father?" Aelia spoke in a rush.

"Without... that is... because we..." Vedrix bumbled his words and was forced to stop, to take a breath. "It is possible, Princess. However, I am certain that his staff would have administered the flask as soon as they knew the Emperor's life was in danger. Much of our supply was understandably sent with the effort in the northern forest. Flasks would have been in easy reach."

Bordan watched the light dim in the Princess's eyes once more and the young woman withdrew back into silence.

"How was Prince Alhard killed?" Bordan asked.

"Without revealing the nature of the crime, I have spoken with our alchemists and given them a sample of the substance I found," Vedrix said.

"Substance?" the Empress asked, her pale skin looking like ivory in the light of the candles.

"In his stockings, Your Highness," Vedrix said. "The assassin was most careful."

"Assassin?" Godewyn interrupted.

"Someone who kills someone else, usually for payment," Vedrix explained.

"I know what one is, Vedrix," Godewyn snapped. "I am questioning your assumption."

"I do not know how else to explain it," Vedrix answered, his own ire rising.

It would do no good for the High Priest of the Empire to argue with the Master Magician of the Gymnasium. The relationship between religion and magic was best described as tense, and it would serve no purpose to allow it to fester and erupt into sores which no potion could cure. Until the heir was crowned, the Empire needed peace and stability. The question of whether or not Aelia could bring those was one for another day.

"You are saying it was a deliberate act?" Bordan interrupted.

"Yes, General," Vedrix answered, turning his gaze gratefully onto the old General. "The substance is, I am told, only used to kill. It has no other purpose and many of the alchemists were shocked to discover it existed. It is, they tell me, famously hard to manufacture and possess, as much risk to the alchemist as to the intended victim. Skin contact is sufficient. The lightest brush against bare skin and death is almost certain."

"In his stockings?" Aelia said, her chin resting on her chest, looking down at the floor between her feet.

"It took some time to find," Vedrix nodded. "I had to follow the traces of its manufacture. The hints of magic used to enhance the properties it contains. There was a small dot of it on the inside of his left stocking and nowhere else. It must have been put there most carefully, though I could not tell you when."

"These alchemists you have," Godewyn said. "Could they make it?"

"One or two, possibly," Vedrix admitted, "though the ingredients are, I am told, very hard to come by and the cost is very high. None of my alchemists have access to the money it would cost. I've instructed our own Magisters to investigate."

"Magisters?" Bordan said, surprised. This was not a title he had heard of within the Gymnasium.

"The Emperor was clear with the Gymnasium, General. We must have those who can investigate and act against magicians who break the laws of the land. The Magisters police our work, and even I am subject to their laws."

"But they are not independent," Godewyn said. "They could cover up what they find. I insist my own Justices are permitted to investigate the production of the poison."

"Not in my Gymnasium," Vedrix snapped back. "My apologies, Your Highness. Your Justices carry their own bias with them, High Priest Godewyn. Their work in the countryside, tracking down unregistered magicians is, of course, important. However, I often note with sadness how many of these magicians die soon after discovery. With the proper training and guidance, they could have been a great asset to the Empire."

When Godewyn did not defend his priesthood, Bordan realised that it was out of respect for the magician rather than a denial of the truth.

"You can provide the Justices with the ingredient list and some guidance on what to look out for?" Bordan said. "They may be of use in the wider city and beyond."

Vedrix's eyes narrowed and he sucked in a long breath. "Of course, General. In this case, should they find the alchemist, I will not shed a tear if he is executed in a timely manner."

The ghost of a smile passed across Godewyn's face and before Bordan could ponder it further, the Empress spoke.

"General," she said, her voice flat and devoid of life, "it appears we have assassins within the castle."

"I will increase the guard about you and Princess Aelia," Bordan answered. "Men and women I can vouch for only. My soldiers have swept the castle already, however we will do so again now we are in possession of more information. Whoever killed Prince Alhard had access to his clothes. I've already questioned the guards assigned to the imperial quarters. All of them report the same thing: no one went into the Prince's quarters who was not allowed."

"Someone did," Aelia said, her voice a whisper in the room. "They must have done to plant the poison."

"I am not discounting the possibility, Princess. However, all guards work in pairs which are assigned on a random basis each day. Everyone we have interviewed reports the same thing: no suspicious activity."

"How did the poison get there then, General?" Aelia said, biting off each bitter word.

"We will question the staff who wash and prepare the imperial wardrobes. There are a lot of washers, cleaners, driers, and seamstresses to service the imperial clothes. Between the three strands of the investigation, we will find them."

"Ensure you do, General," Aelia said, suddenly rising from her chair.

The three advisers sat in silence as the young Princess stalked from the room, slamming the door behind her.

"The death of her brother has unsettled her," the Empress said and Bordan noted the way her gaze strayed to the door.

"It is to be expected, Your Highness," Godewyn said. "There is comfort that Prince Alhard's flame has gone to join the Holy Flame, but it is a comfort which comes only when grief has run its course."

"I hope such comfort arrives quickly," she said in a quiet voice before straightening in her seat and fixing them each with a stare. "However, I am more concerned with the possibility of assassins within the castle and palace."

"We will ensure your safety, Your Highness," Bordan assured her.

"More than mine, General," she replied, her tone frosty. "Aelia is now the heir. Her life is more important than anyone's now, even my own. She must be crowned, and the Empire must go on. Will your guards be enough to stop another assassin, one who uses magic to kill?"

"I can assign a Magister, Your Highness," Vedrix offered.

"A magician?" Godewyn scoffed. "So close to the imperial family and with a magician already exposed as an assassin?"

"With due respect, High Priest," Vedrix said, stiffening, "while an alchemist may have made the poison used, it is unlikely they carried out the foul act. Most prefer study to physical activity and a life spent in books, at the experiment table, does not equip them for such subterfuge as would be needed."

Godewyn grunted. "I'll assign a Justice to watch the Magister."

"If you so desire it," Vedrix agreed. "Your Highness, with Justice and Magister, plus the General's trusted guards, you and the Princess will have the best protection in the Empire."

Bordan suppressed the sinking feeling in his chest. A priest tasked with hunting magicians, and a magician with a dislike of priests, would cause a headache for the guards assigned. It was likely they would spend more time keeping the two apart than actually guarding the imperial family, and a distraction could let another assassin through.

"Godewyn, Master Vedrix, the offer is deeply appreciated," Bordan began, searching for the right words and finding them escaping the grip of his thoughts. He was saved from floundering when the Empress spoke.

"Your offers are appreciated," she said, "and we will take you up on them. Can you ensure that both Magister and Justice will be focused upon our protection, rather than their own inbred distrust of one another? I appreciate that both you and Master Vedrix are able to work together, High Priest, however there is undeniable tension between the priesthood and members of the Gymnasium."

"I assure you, Your Highness," Godewyn said in a calm voice which washed the worry from Bordan's mind, "I will select the best Justice for the role. I am sure Master Vedrix will likewise impress on his Magister the need to work together for the good of the Empire."

"Of course," Vedrix agreed. "Your safety, Your Highness, and that of Princess Aelia, will be their paramount concern."

"General?" the Empress asked.

"I will talk with the guards, Your Highness," Bordan answered, though he knew she was not asking permission. "They will be at their highest alert for any trouble."

"Your Highness," Godewyn began and for the first time Bordan saw a little uncertainty cross the man's face, "forgive me, however it is customary for the Emperor's funeral to take precedence, even that of an heir."

"What is your meaning?" she asked, her words trembling on the air.

"We have placed Alhard's body in the imperial crypt," Godewyn said, "for the present."

"And my magicians will ensure its preservation," Vedrix added smoothly, almost as if the two had discussed this before.

"Until the funeral can take place properly," Godewyn completed.

"Thank you both," the Empress said, standing. "I will check on the Princess's well-being."

Bordan stood and bowed, as did the other two men in the room as the current ruler of the Empire swept through the door her daughter had used a short time before.

"I do not want any trouble," Bordan said, after the door was shut.

"There will not be," Godewyn assured him. "I will select the right Justice for this role. I believe I have just the person in mind. Vedrix will do the same."

"And though it pains us both to admit, it will not be the first time a priest and magician have worked in concert for the betterment of the Empire," Vedrix said.

"What?" Bordan looked between the two men. "You have done something similar before?"

"We look after the spiritual health of the Empire, Bordan, and the Magicians after some of the more esoteric problems we are confronted with," Godewyn answered as Vedrix nodded. "Sometimes we must work together."

"Why did I not know?"

"Because you have enough to worry about, my old friend," Godewyn answered.

"And because there are some things you are better off not knowing," Vedrix added, and Bordan was stunned to see Godewyn nod in assent.

"When this is over and Aelia is Emperor, we are going to talk about this," Bordan promised.

"You may not like what you learn," Godewyn answered and it was Vedrix's turn to nod.

XXVI

The Magician

Eight years ago:
  Squinting through his one good eye towards the sun as it set over the walls of the city, he knew he was going to be late home. Excuses would serve him poorly, that had been a lesson well learned. Reasons mattered, and the truth: anything else was an excuse.
  He prodded at the swelling around his left eye. That would be hard to keep secret and was as good a reason as any.

"A magician amongst them?"

"Yes, Spear," Kyron said.

"How powerful, Kyron?" Padarn asked, resting a hand on Kyron's shoulder.

"She broke both of my constructs without trouble, Master," Kyron said.

"Is that difficult, Master Padarn?" Astentius asked. "Forgive my lack of knowledge surrounding your skills."

"To break Kyron's nets? Not especially," and his master gave Kyron an apologetic look before continuing. "Nets are by themselves quite fragile and the one Kyron used to find the magician was especially so. I am more concerned that she broke two in quick succession. It speaks of someone who understands their nature and can maintain constructs of her own, two very different ones at least."

"A master as powerful as you?" Kyron asked.

"Likely," Padarn agreed. "You did well to maintain two of your own, Apprentice. You're growing and learning."

"I was not aware the tribes and clans had any magicians?" Astentius said, looking to Emlyn.

She shrugged.

"How many?"

"I don't know," she replied. "I've never counted them all."

"This will complicate things somewhat," Astentius said, ignoring her answer. "Master Padarn, can you counter this magician during the battle?"

"To a degree," he answered. "I am not sure what she can or will do. Magicians tend to specialise in certain fields and areas. Those that interest them, or those they have a talent for. No two are alike. Even Kyron here has more talent in some areas than me."

Kyron felt his heart swell with pride.

"Where will she focus her powers?" Astentius asked. "Where would you if you were her?"

"At the front during the first clash of arms," Padarn said after a moment of thought. "Try to break their lines and support my own. Give them an edge."

"And after that?"

"Once battle is truly joined, I would focus on the flanks," Padarn said with a nod. "Little point in trying much along the front when it is likely the shifting line of battle would put my own troops in the firing line."

"It is just one magician," Borus said. "Give me a decent archer and a single arrow will end the trouble."

"That is also a good plan, Spear," Padarn said. "If you occupy her with arrows, she will spend a lot of power shielding herself, there will be fewer constructs attacking our troops."

"Can your apprentice help you?" Astentius said and raised a hand before Padarn could answer. "He is young, I know, and normally I would not ask. However, we cannot allow the Emperor's body to fall into the hands of these tribes. It is too important, too vital to the Empire."

Padarn's chest rose and fell, as all around soldiers drew themselves into formation. "I promised his grandfather I would keep him safe."

"Yet, you took him to war?" Astentius said. "I am not questioning that judgement. We each do what we must for the Empire."

"His grandfather did question the wisdom of that choice." Padarn smiled.

Kyron's heart fell. The old man knew war, knew its risks and rewards. He spoke all the time about service to the Empire, about honour and duty. For him to argue against Kyron's presence in the army, serving the Empire, was typical.

"However, he saw the need," Padarn continued. "Kyron would be useful, and everyone must have their first taste of battle."

"I've already seen battle, Master," Kyron protested.

"Not like this, Kyron," Padarn answered and there was a soft, sad note to the man's voice. "He will stand with me in the line, at least for the first clash."

"Good," Astentius agreed. "Kyron, serve with honour."

"Yes, Spear," Kyron said and bowed, the realisation bringing a flush of pride to his face and a worm of fear burrowing into his belly.

"Borus, they'll stand with you in the centre," the Spear said. "Make sure they are protected."

"Of course, Spear," Borus replied. "And the guide?"

"I'm not fighting my own people," she stated.

"And I am not for having you in the ranks," Borus countered.

"She can stay with the priests and guards near the Emperor's waggon," Astentius said. "It will be well protected against those in the forest, and they can guard against her."

Emlyn grunted, turned and stomped back through the gathering troops. Borus waved a soldier after her.

"We have a little time," Borus said. "Come, Kyron, let's get you some armour and a sword. I'll not have you picked out by the tribes as an easy target. Master Padarn?"

"I need no armour," his master replied, parting the robe he wore to reveal a tunic of lorica hamata. "I've my own weapons also. Though I would appreciate anything you can do for the boy."

"Come on then, Kyron," Borus said.

Kyron followed him through the troops who were settling themselves into ranks. Past the front rank, the troops carried pila, the tall javelins which they could loft over the heads of their own ranks and into the tribes.

"Here," Borus dragged a shirt of lorica hamata from the back of a cart, "put this on. This is the repair cart, so it won't be the best you could have but all the good stuff is being worn already."

Kyron huffed as he took the full weight of the armour on his outstretched arms.

"It won't feel near so heavy once you've got it on," Borus offered with a smile.

Kyron nodded, though his arms already ached with the weight. It had been years since he had worn armour, and then it had been made for him. Lighter, easier to carry and wear. His grandfather had commissioned it. Ever since he had joined the Gymnasium, he had managed to avoid wearing anything more cumbersome than a heavy cloak to protect him from the winter winds.

Bunching the metal rings as much as he could, and pushing his arms through the two arm holes, he bent his knees and pushed his head into the armour. Bending his back, taking the weight off his arms and neck, and closing his eyes he forced his head up and out through the larger opening.

The smell of oiled metal opened a window in his memories. A dusty training yard, the heat of the sun, and the sweat pouring from his forehead. He recalled hating every moment, but now, in this moment, looking back, he saw the purpose. The smile died on his lips as he straightened and the hamata fell on his shoulders. He groaned at the weight and constriction.

"Neatly done," Borus said. In the man's hand was a belt and scabbarded sword. "Now, I hope you won't be needing this. However, it is better to have one and not need it, than not have one and need it. You don't need to do anything flashy, just stick the pointy end into the one attacking you and don't get stuck with theirs. There's not a lot else I can teach you right now."

"I can use a sword, Cohort," Kyron said, accepting the belt and wrapping it around his waist. The leather was supple, but he almost ran out of belt holes when securing it. Taking the long end which dangled, he wrapped it tightly into the belt, getting it out of the way of his legs and sword.

"You've done that before," Borus accused him, though he said it with a smile.

"My grandfather taught me," Kyron said, resting his hand on the sword's grip, making sure he knew where it was.

"He was a soldier?"

"Yes."

"Did you a favour, teaching you to wear a sword," Borus said, nodding. "Your father a soldier too?"

"He's dead," Kyron replied.

"Mine too." Borus clapped his hand on Kyron's shoulder. "We'll do them honour in the battle. They'll send their own flames to warm our hearts and give strength to our sword arms. Come then. You'll stand with me and your master."

The soldiers parted to let Borus through and Kyron followed in his wake. A few soldiers cast him an odd look. True, the hamata had a section of broken links on the left side near his hip. It was, he was forced to admit, a little short and the edge was ragged where a blacksmith had been removing links to repair other armour. However, the sword on his hip looked well used and the grip felt secure in his hand.

He did his best to ignore their glances. In such a small section of the army, most would know who he was, what he was, and the sight of a magician, even an apprentice, armed for the ranks was unusual.

"In times past," Padarn said as Kyron stood beside him, "when the Empire battled on the southern continent, there were more magicians in the army. All wore armour and carried swords. When we get back to the Gymnasium, I suggest you do some reading about our history."

"I never wanted to be a soldier, Master," Kyron said.

"You're not a soldier now," Borus pointed out. "The armour and sword are a disguise to keep you safe. You said your grandfather taught you to use a sword, but I'm hoping you never have to draw it."

Kyron looked down at the sword on his hip, uncomfortable with how natural it felt there, how powerful it made him feel. He shuddered.

"Now," Borus said, "if you two would step back into the second rank so we can close up the shields, I think it is almost time we started to move."

Trumpets sounded from the back of the honour guard and the four cohorts, four hundred men and women, marched forward in step. The last cohort had been left to guard the waggon and supplies.

Kyron did his best to fall into step with the soldiers around him. No one spoke. The heavy tread of the combined force reverberated through the soil, the clank and chime of metal on metal as armour, shield, and weapon was checked and readied echoed through the trees.

Here was the might of the Empire, he thought. Not for skulking in trees or hiding in caves. A proud force which met its enemies head-on. No fear and full of conviction.

Kyron looked up, to see the standard of the army raised above all. A bronze disc engraved with the symbol of Astentius's Spear—a boar with sharp curved tusks. Below that two flags. The first, the highest, a red flag, the golden eagle of the Empire painted upon it. The second was orange with the yellow flame of the Church upon it.

Against this army, this force, no one could stand. No one had for centuries, so the histories said. Professional soldiers, trained to war, accustomed to following orders without question or delay. Each man or woman fighting for the other. The tribes who stood in their way would not know what hit them.

Kyron's heart matched the beat of the marching soldiers and the fear in his belly abated a little. He was part of this machine of war. He felt it in his bones, in his soul. His own fire heated him from within and rose as high as the flames of those around him. Here he belonged. He wanted to shout, to sing, to scream into the sky, but the soldiers marched in silence, so he did to.

They rounded the track, marching in perfect time, and went to war.

XXVII

THE GENERAL

EIGHT YEARS AGO:

"Another fight?" he said as the boy, his tunic almost too short now he was going through a spurt of growth, stumbled in through kitchen door.

The boy nodded, holding a rag up to his split lip. "I stood up to them, like you told me to. There were two of them this time."

"And one has similar wound to yours, I hope," he said, shaking his head. "Sometimes, lad, it is knowing when to fight and when to run."

"I HAVE READ the reports and it seems we are no closer to finding the assassin or their paymaster," Bordan said, steepling his fingers before his face.

"Identifying them, no," Vedrix agreed. "However, we have done well to rule many people out."

"But not all," Godewyn added. "Finding the assassin may be a game for fools. It is beginning to look more and more like a professional was hired."

"One of the gangs within the city?" Bordan asked.

"Unlikely," Godewyn answered. "They would know what the assassination of a member of the imperial family would bring down upon them."

"Even so," Bordan said. "The news is out, and the city is fearful.

We have reports of arguments and fights in the markets. Some of the traders have been complaining to the City Watch. The capture of an assassin would do much to quiet the populace. And a funeral soon after. The ceremony and rituals will calm the city."

"But we do not know who they are," Vedrix pointed out.

"It does not have to be the assassin," Borden countered. "A criminal, a gang member, someone who is known to the City Watch as violent, who is known on the streets, would be a start. It will also be good to remind the people, and the gangs, who owns the streets in the capital. I have reports of crime on the increase."

"Not unexpected," Godewyn offered. "The people are worried for the future and for their safety. They are taking steps to carve out their own little piece of safety and to set up defences. Whether that is food, valuables, or in their homes makes little difference."

"We are agreed then?" Bordan waited for the two men to nod. "I will order some raids upon the gangs. The less who know beforehand the better. I want the news to spread through the streets and quarters, though I would also like to keep the death toll down."

"But the real assassin?" Vedrix said.

"Finding the paymaster might be easier," Godewyn offered. "Greed and money will be at the root of this."

"I agree," Bordan said. "The assassin is just one person, a symbol to the people of the danger they face. The paymaster though, they are the true danger. If they can afford to procure that poison and a person skilled enough to get into the palace and out undetected, they can afford to do more."

"And how many people have such wealth?" Vedrix asked, glancing at both men.

Bordan set his wine down upon the small table they had gathered around in his office and sighed. "Too many to count."

"But who would benefit the most from a troubled succession?" Godewyn pushed. "Some of the Dukes certainly. It would give them a chance to push for more power, or should the unthinkable happen and there be no heir to the throne perhaps they consider themselves as the next Imperial Dynasty?"

"There are some who are that ambitious," Bordan agreed.

"Primal? Abra? Lady Trenis?" Vedrix offered.

"To sit on the council is to be ambitious," Godewyn said.

"We three sit on the council," Bordan pointed out.

"Not through wealth," Vedrix answered, "but from duty and long service. We each depend on the Emperor for employment and position. I cannot see any of us desiring to rule the Empire. The Gymnasium is tiring enough and that amounts to barely three hundred across the Empire."

"So few?" Bordan asked. "I thought there were many more of you."

"We are a dying breed," Vedrix said, shaking his head. "There are many more with the skills and ability, but out in the countryside they are feared, hunted, and killed. Not just, forgive me, High Priest, by the Justices, but by their own superstitious villagers."

"Religion serves the people, not the reverse," Godewyn said.

"And the army serves to protect the people at the will of the Empire," Bordan added with a smile. "So that is the three of us with reasons out of the way. Though, in truth, I never suspected any of us." A thought struck. "Vedrix, the alchemist who made the poison, is it only those of the Gymnasium who possess the skill?"

"Alchemy is one of the oldest of the arts, General," Vedrix said. "There are many in the countryside who practise herbalism, a poor cousin, but other countries who border ours or the southern continent will have alchemists with the skill."

"Which does not help to narrow down the list of suspects," Godewyn noted.

"The tribes and clans?"

"Possibly," Vedrix admitted after a moment's thought. "We know little about their way of life or their magic. Those who were subsumed as the Empire expanded added their knowledge to the Gymnasium, but so long ago, it would be hard to separate it from that which preceded."

"More suspects, and those with good reason," Bordan said, "however, unlikely. As far as we know, they lack the wealth to hire an assassin, and their knowledge of our city's ways is limited. I would be surprised if the paymaster was not someone within in the city."

"Perhaps the raid on the city's gangs would quell some of the populace with the additional bonus of causing the paymaster some concern," Godewyn pondered.

"The assassin would likely be known to the gangs?" Vedrix asked

"In the poor areas, the gangs control as much, if not more, of the streets than the City Watch," Godewyn said.

"I cannot deny it," Bordan answered after sucking in a breath, "though I might wish it was otherwise. However, we are not looking at those streets, Godewyn. We are looking for a paymaster with wealth and they are unlikely to be involved with those gangs."

"Perhaps not," Godewyn admitted. "However, the gangs are, I am led to believe, linked to each other. We would be foolish to believe that the wealthy families had no dealings with the criminal underworld of the city. The crimes may not be violent, but the outcome is always the same, people get hurt."

"You have something in mind," Bordan prompted the High Priest.

"I agree with the initial secrecy of the raid," Godewyn said slowly. "However, I would argue for a more public, more visible execution of them."

"Show the public some strength?" Bordan said.

"It would reassure them," Vedrix offered.

"It would," Godewyn agreed. "And the sight of the army marching through the streets would demonstrate the constancy of the Empire. The people are, by and large, patriots and an army marching in step is a powerful image."

"I do not want open battle on the streets," Bordan said.

"It need not come to that," Godewyn said. "However, imagery is as much a weapon as a sword. A crown, a flame, a staff, a sword; we all have our own particular symbols of power and office. Show the people those and we may calm some fears."

"You will be sending some priests with the raids?" Bordan said, shaking his head. "They are not warriors or soldiers."

"Some amongst us were," Godewyn pointed out. "It is the symbol which is important. If Vedrix offered a few magicians who would be willing to bring their own unique visibility, the symbol of the three branches of power operating together, however temporary, would bolster the populace and may cause the paymaster some worry. A worried man or woman makes mistakes."

"You have become much more cynical as a priest than you ever were as a soldier," Bordan pointed out.

"I learned from the best, General."

"I can have some magicians accompany you. They can create fire and smoke to impress the locals."

"Less fire and more smoke," Bordan said. "I do not want to set the city on fire."

"Of course not," Vedrix agreed.

"It is settled then," Bordan agreed. "I thank you both for accompanying me on the raid."

"What?" Godewyn spluttered and Vedrix's eyes widened.

"There are no greater symbols to the people than the three of us, save the Empress and Princess and we cannot put them at risk," Bordan said, a laugh bubbling up from his chest. "You did not think it completely through?"

"Caught in my own trap," Godewyn admitted.

"Two days hence," Bordan said. "I will have the City Watch suggest a few likely targets."

"Two days," Vedrix agreed with a sullen sigh.

Bordan raised his glass of wine in salute. The two men followed suit a heartbeat later.

There was a knock at the door and Bordan's secretary walked in a moment later.

"Forgive the intrusion, General," the soldier said. "However, Duke Abra wishes to speak with you."

Bordan sighed. "I thought today was going too well. Tell him I will see him in a few moments."

"Of course, General," the secretary nodded and closed the door behind him.

"Probably best if I see him alone," Bordan said. "You can leave via the other door."

"Or better that we wait in the other room and listen in," Godewyn said. "Abra remains a suspect."

"If you wish," Bordan said, indicating the door with a wave of his hand. "Take the wine in with you."

The other two men gathered up the glasses and bottle of wine before going through the door and closing it firmly. Bordan scanned his office, making sure all evidence of their presence was gone and that any confidential documents were secured away. After shifting the chairs around a little, he moved to the main door and swung it open.

"My dear Duke Abra," Bordan said. "Please, do come in and I apologise for the delay."

"Think nothing of it," Abra responded.

"Would you like some wine?"

"A glass would be welcome. Summer is coming with a pace and if the weather remains this warm, we will all be seeking shade at every opportunity," Abra said as he stepped into the office.

"I'll get the wine, General," his secretary said from the outer room.

"Thank you," Bordan said. "Please, sit, Duke. What brings you to my door on, as you say, a warm day such as this?"

"I must confess to some worry, General," Abra said as he sat down.

"These are troubled times, Duke. It would be wise to be worried, but rest assured everyone is doing all they can to ensure peace and stability in the Empire," Bordan answered as he took up the seat he had vacated only moments before.

"It is peace I am worried about, General," Abra said, pausing while the secretary entered and placed two fresh glasses upon the table along with a bottle.

"Allow me," Bordan said, accepting the duty of a host to pour the wine. "Peace concerns you, Duke?"

"Concerns us all, my dear General," Abra replied as he accepted the glass of deep, dark red wine.

Bordan watched him take a sip. "Reports suggest the expedition in the forests is going well, Duke Abra. The army continues to push north and meeting little in the way of true resistance."

"Peace in the palace, General," Abra corrected. "I understand that Alhard's death has hit Princess Aelia hard, but the stories coming from the palace concern me, and my fellow councillors."

"Stories, Duke?" Bordan took a drink of the wine to cover his concern.

"Perhaps the servants do not speak to you as they do to me, General. You surround yourself with soldiers all the time, but there are stories of the Princess's mood coming from the palace," Abra said, a sad smile upon his face which Bordan took to be false.

"The Princess is upset, my dear Duke. As you say, it is

understandable, though I must confess to not being aware of these stories you mention."

"Servants chatter, General. When work is done there is little else in their lives but to talk of their betters," Abra explained. "Excellent wine by the way. Southern?"

"Indeed," Bordan raised the glass, "expensive to acquire and transport across the ocean but worth it, I am sure you agree."

"I will have a case of southern red brought to you when next a ship docks from the continent, General. A gift to express my esteem for you."

"Most kind, Duke. When one owns the ships, I suspect the cost of travel is lower," Bordan replied. "What of these stories though?"

"Aelia is not herself, I am told. She has beaten a serving maid, they say. So badly that her family were paid off by the treasury. She may never be able to work again, the story goes," Abra said.

"Gossip only, Duke. As you say, these servants like to tell stories. I have not heard of such an event and surely the palace corridors would be alive with gossip had it happened," Bordan said, hiding the fact that he had arranged for the maid's injuries to be treated and for the family to be paid handsomely and moved to a town far to the west. The story should not have got out, not so quickly.

"There are more stories, General," Abra said, his tone conversational, but Bordan could see the hunter in his eyes homing in on his prey. "Aelia hid herself in her rooms for days. She has berated loyal servants, and many have asked to be reassigned. Even your own troops have been talking of her mood."

"I assure you, my dear Duke, my guards have said nothing of the sort," Bordan explained, which was the truth as only the most loyal and committed guards were permitted in the imperial quarters. Each and every one was trusted. "They know well the punishment for such. Perhaps some lower troops are merely repeating and embellishing the stories you are relaying here."

"A possibility." Abra waved the explanation away. "The new Emperor must be of sound mind, General. History has shown us what mad Emperors have done. Purges, pogroms, wholesale slaughter, and poverty spreading across the lands."

"You worry too much, Duke. Princess Aelia is grieving, yes. Her mood is dark and full of sadness, this is to be expected. I was the same when my own son died. She will come out of this stronger and more ready to be the Emperor than ever before. I tutored both imperial children for a time, when they were younger. Aelia has always possessed a keen mind," Bordan said, affecting an air of calm and peace.

"I hope you are right, General. There will be some who will talk of replacing the heir if her mood darkens further. The Empire needs a steady hand to guide it," Abra said.

Bordan sucked in a lungful of air before responding. "Those people talk treason, Duke Abra. Should you hear it, I expect you to inform me straight away. It would not do to get caught in such an act; the penalty is severe and excruciatingly painful."

"Of course, General, which is why I come to you now," Abra said with a smile. "The hour is getting on and I have some meetings to attend. Thank you for your time, General."

"Always a pleasure, Duke Abra," Bordan said, standing. "Please come again when you have news I may want to hear."

"Nothing would give me greater pleasure, General," Abra answered, standing. He looked down at the half-finished glass of wine on the table. "The offer was genuine, by the way. I do not always agree with everything you do, General, but please do not think I underestimate what you do for the Empire. I will have the case brought to you the moment a ship arrives."

Nonplussed for a moment it was all Bordan could do to nod as he struggled to find his voice. "That would be... most kind, Duke Abra. I will wish you a good day."

"And to you, General."

Bordan watched as the other man left the room and as soon as the door clicked shut the two eavesdroppers came back into the room.

"He knows the Prince was killed" Bordan said.

"And if he does, they all do," Godewyn said. "We need to organise the raid sooner rather than later, give the people something else to talk about."

"Most certainly," Vedrix agreed.

XXVIII

THE MAGICIAN

EIGHT YEARS AGO:

"I don't want to fight them," he tried to say, but the words bubbled up with anger and shame. "You told me to stick up for myself."

"I did," the old man said, "and you are. I am not unhappy with you, lad, but I am concerned about the number of fights you are getting into."

"All boys fight, General," Gessius said. "Some need to channel it elsewhere. He's probably ready."

He looked up into his grandfather's eyes, his legs trembling and his belly fluttering with excitement.

"We'll start tomorrow," the old man said.

"SHIELDS," BORUS SHOUTED. A trumpet took up his call and the standard bobbed up and down.

Kyron, in the second row, protected within a little bubble of soldiers, Padarn next to him, had his vision of the onrushing tribes cut out by the raised shields.

"Keep your head down," one of the soldiers to his left said.

The march halted a few paces later and the howl of the attackers broke over him. All the confidence he had felt amid the Empire soldiers faded away, his legs trembled, his lip quivered, and he needed a piss.

"Arrows," Borus roared and another blast of trumpets assailed Kyron's ears.

The soldiers to either side lifted their shields above their heads, blocking out his vision of the sky. A moment later thunder rumbled as the arrows of the tribes clattered against the shields of wood and iron.

"There'll be more," the soldier said. A prophecy which proved true a heartbeat later as more arrows descended onto the shields.

A cry came from behind him. A sound of pain followed by the shouts of the soldiers to move the wounded man out of the way.

"Forward!" Borus shouted and the army of the Empire met the charge of the tribes. If it had been thunder when the arrows struck the shields, this sounded like an avalanche and the ground shook with the force of it.

The soldier who had advised Kyron stepped into a sudden gap ahead as another fell away, clutching the ruins of his sword hand. A man from the third rank stepped into place.

"Pila," Borus called, stepping back to Padarn's side as another soldier took up his place in the front row.

A round of grunts and curses erupted from the Empire soldiers as a storm of pila sailed from the ranks to arc over the front row and descend amongst the tribes. There were shouts of agony, cries of pain, and howls of anguish as pila found their mark amongst the lightly armoured tribes.

"Padarn?" Borus said, wiping blood from his hand and checking his grip on the gladius he carried.

"I'm ready, Cohort," Padarn said.

Kyron risked a glance to the side and saw the motes of Padarn's magic gather themselves into constructs which he held steady near his chest and shoulders.

"Kyron, build a tracking net," his master ordered. "I want to know where the attacks come from."

"Master, she saw my net last time and destroyed it," Kyron said.

"In all of this," Padarn said, "she will be lucky to see anything."

Kyron gathered his own motes and strung them together as before, a tiny trickle of power binding one to another. All those threads built up quickly and the concentration to hold them together made focusing on the battle difficult.

"Push!" Borus called and the Empire began to move forward in half steps, the line no longer straight, but cresting like a wave onto a beach.

The soldiers in the second rank put their shields to the back of those ahead and added their own weight to the advance.

Underfoot the spent arrows of the tribes rolled and sought to trip Kyron as he stepped forward with the soldiers. The net he cast grew wider until it felt ready to rip under its own weight.

Another step forward and his foot came down on something soft and yielding. He looked down and the dead eyes of a tribeswoman looked back up at him. His foot was deep in her severed neck and blood welled around his boot, drowning it in red. Bile rose up his throat and his control of the net wavered. A second step, unbidden, automatic and the sight was gone.

Kyron sucked in the air, sweat scented, blood tainted, fear ridden, and death filled, into his lungs. The bile, acrid, acidic, burned his throat.

"Focus on the net, Kyron!" Padarn shouted to him and though they were next to each other Kyron struggled to hear him.

Closing his eyes for a moment, he reached out for the motes and caught the loose ends which had threatened to tear the net apart and steadied it. It was easily the largest net he had ever created, and he fanned it out across the lines of tribal warriors.

In his mind he saw them. Their beings—their flame, the priests would say, though Kyron knew telling them that his magic could let him see this would be a death sentence—glowed against the net. Unlike the disciplined Empire soldiers, the tribes attacked in pockets. Two or three fought together, coordinating their attacks in some places. In others, a single warrior swung a heavy axe at the line of Empire shields.

Soldiers fell. Either by axe or sword, by weight of numbers or by lucky arrow. Whenever one collapsed, another stepped into the line. Always forward, step by step, small increments, pushing towards the knot of warriors who protected the chief.

A tremble against the net. A flicker of power, of intention. A foreign mote caught against its threads.

"That way!" Kyron shouted, pointing forward and to the right. "I felt something."

"Take my hand!" Padarn shouted back and reached out.

Kyron grasped his master's hand and felt another presence alongside his. A subtle feather against his mind, a calm shadow which spread along his net constructed of magic.

"I have them," Padarn said. "Hold steady, Kyron."

Not a flicker this time, a disruption, a shot of power coursed down the net. "Beware."

Padarn's hand squeezed his tightly and Kyron grunted in pain. The calm presence was gone and his master called out a series of words and flung his free hand in the direction of the power.

Amongst the tribal ranks there was an explosion. Bright yellow, dull red, vibrant orange, the blue of sky and the white of clouds as smoke billowed. It slammed against the shield his master had erected in the space of a breath.

The warriors of the tribes faced the full force of their own magic which had been designed to detonate within the Empire ranks. They screamed as they burned, skin blackening and turning to ash, bodies crumbling where they stood.

Those who died quick were the lucky ones. The few that stumbled away clutched flesh which had burst apart and from which red steam erupted in fountains. Eyes had boiled in sockets, noses had melted into a horror of candlewax flesh, and lips had pulled back to reveal raw pink gums and the stumps of teeth.

"Lost them," Padarn shouted as the Empire soldiers stepped forward into the void created by the sudden wave of death. "Again, Kyron, find them."

The odour of charred flesh crept up Kyron's nostrils, coated his tongue and clung on with sharp skeletal fingers to the back of his throat. He coughed; the earlier bile, tainted now with the taste of cooked meat, swamped his mouth and he spat it onto the earth.

Another flicker against his net, a little further along the line, and he pointed once more. Padarn took his cue and launched a construct in that direction. Kyron felt it sail along the net, faster than a man could run, and drop into the mass of warriors where the flicker had come from.

Once more amongst the tribes there was a sudden gout of flame. Black smoke roiled up to the eaves of the trees and a cry went up from the warriors.

"Did you get them?" Kyron shouted.

"Keep focus on the net," Padarn snapped. "If you feel them again, the answer is no. I'll need to prepare a new construct."

"You've killed a fair number of their warriors!" Borus shouted.

"The magician," Padarn called back. "They're all that matters."

Another flicker.

"Master!" Kyron screamed and his arm pointed directly forward.

The flicker did not vanish, it steadied and then Kyron felt it begin to crawl along his net. His motes sought to catch it, but it danced from thread to thread, seeking him. His heart beat faster and despite the heat of the soldiers around him he felt chills up his spine.

"It's coming for me," he shouted, his voice shrill.

"Hold still," Padarn called to him and the grip on his hand was reassuring. "We'll do this together."

"Master, it is getting closer." Kyron trembled, holding onto the net with his concentration though every instinct told him to drop it and run away.

"Steady, Kyron," Padarn said, his mouth close to Kyron's ear. "Can you feel the thread of the seeker? Can you follow it back to its master?"

"I... I think so," Kyron answered, closing his eyes and letting the sounds of battle drift away.

"Show me," Padarn whispered into his mind and they flew along the net, past the presence of the seeker which was still picking its way towards Kyron's mind.

Kyron skipped across his own threads, Padarn holding on with the lightest of touches.

"Here." Kyron came to a halt and his mind pointed to the shape of a woman. Unlike the others, she glowed with a hint of green and brown. Glancing at Padarn, he saw similar colours swirl within his master's presence.

"Good, take us back."

They flew faster than thought and Kyron noted the seeker had leaped forward in its search for him. Another few heartbeats and it would reach him.

"Bind it with your net," Kyron felt rather than heard Padarn say. "Hold steady and I will deal with the magician. Are you ready?"

Kyron nodded as he tore the threads of his net and drew them over the seeker. Some of the threads broke apart, shattered and ripped, but enough survived the sudden destruction for him to wrap around the other magician's seeker construct.

He saw it as a spider with sharp claws, tearing at his threads. It thrashed within the net, seeking to escape, twisting and turning as he tightened his grip.

"I've got it," Kyron called.

"Hold steady," Padarn answered.

Kyron felt a sudden pulse of power which flew down the net. He felt its ripples as it travelled, burning and severing the threads it passed over.

There was the sudden feeling of cold along the threads and the seeker in his grasp shuddered and faltered. Kyron tightened his grip and the clawed spider broke apart, crumbling to glowing motes which drifted towards the earth.

"Got them!" Padarn shouted.

"Well done," Borus called. "Your work is done. Get back to the Emperor's waggon and protect it. They'll attack from the flanks soon, if they haven't already."

Kyron took a last look at the battle and without regret turned his back on it, following Padarn's passage through the ranks towards the waggon and carts.

XXIX

THE GENERAL

EIGHT YEARS AGO:

"*These were your father's,*" *he said to the boy as the morning sun crested the wall. "Gessius has set up a training post in the corner. Pick it up and let us see you hold it.*"

The boy's shaking fingers curled around the grip of the training gladius. "It's heavy."

"*It is,*" *he said. "It will help you build up the strength in your sword arm. Now, swing it against the post.*"

BORDAN SHIFTED IN the saddle, shrugged his shoulders to get the armour to sit comfortably, and checked the positioning of his sword for the third time. Beside him, Godewyn, High Priest of the Flame, rolled his eyes.

"It's all right for you," Bordan said. "You just have those robes to worry about."

"It is not like I haven't worn armour before, General," Godewyn said, "and these robes are heavy and hot. It is Master Vedrix I am in envy of."

"Me?" Vedrix looked up at the two taller men. His horse was a short, fat thing which looked as though one good canter would be too much for it. He rubbed his large belly. "I have my own labours to bear, gentlemen."

"I do not like this," Bordan said, changing the subject. It was always this way before battle. The camaraderie of people who must rely upon one another for survival, the humour and the deflection. I should be used to it by now, he said to himself.

"The other forces are in position?" Godewyn asked.

"A moment," Vedrix answered. The little man put a hand to an amulet hanging from a gold chain and closed his eyes. "Almost."

Under him, the horse's hooves clattered on the cobbled streets and the people of the city moved aside for the small army which marched ahead of him. Every man and woman had burnished their shields, polished their armour, and they shone in the midday sun. The time had been chosen so the sun was directly overhead when there would be the most people around to see, and to relay the story to others.

"I want casualties kept to a minimum," Bordan said, "especially the civilians. The last thing we need to precipitate is a riot."

"My priests have already been out, spreading the word. Sermons on the evil of crime have been shouted from every pulpit, on every street corner," Godewyn explained. "They know what we are about."

"And so do the criminals," Bordan grunted. "Many have pulled back into their territory and locked up their bases."

"We will create a gap in the territory here," Vedrix explained. "Like animals, the strongest will seek to take advantage. Little will change."

"That is not the point of today's mission, Master Vedrix," Godewyn reminded him. "We are symbols of the Empire. We are strength, peace, and the rule of law. That is what the people will remember, no matter the outcome over the next few weeks."

"I hope you are right," Vedrix said.

"I am," Godewyn said. "Have a little faith."

"I have entirely too much of that," Vedrix answered with a smile.

"Will you two stop joking and fencing with each other? Can't you see I am having a last minute panic about this whole idea," Bordan said, flicking the reins in irritation.

"Last thoughts are to be expected, General," Godewyn said. "At least that is what I say to nervous grooms and worried brides on their day of joining."

"Today is a little more than that, Godewyn," Bordan snapped back.

"Never underestimate the fear of a groom on his joining day,

General. I've seen many turn and flee the moment the fires are lit and the choir starts to sing," Godewyn said with a chuckle. "Of course, by then we have already locked the doors and there they find no escape from their fate."

"Is that where we are now?" Bordan said, squinting as he looked across the heads of the soldiers. "Locked in our course with no chance of escape."

"I fear so, General," Godewyn answered.

They rode without speaking further through the streets of the city, leaving the safety of the palace and past the homes of the wealthy, the merchants and the guild leaders. The main artery roads of the city led to the gates or the port, and the troops turned away from the wide avenue to enter the narrower streets of the poorer areas of town.

Bordan wrinkled his nose as the smell of the unwashed, of dirt, and of rotting meat and vegetables rose around him. It was not an unknown aroma. These had been his streets as a child, and he fought the memories which returned unbidden from the hidden corners of his mind.

"What is that smell?" Vedrix said, raising his hand and covering his nose with the neck of his robe.

"That is the people and the streets, Master Magician," Godewyn said. "Perhaps less time spent with your nose in your books and more acquaintance with the people of the city would provide you with a better education."

Vedrix's eyes narrowed and he cast a glance at the people who ducked back into their doorways as the army marched through. "Maybe, High Priest, but now I understand why you burn sacred herbs in your flames."

"Everything has a purpose, Master Vedrix," Godewyn answered without rancour. "As I have already said, symbols are important and not all must be visual. Also, I am sure the priests appreciate the smell of the herbs over that of the people who attend many of the temples and churches."

"I grew up on these streets," Bordan admitted, the truth drawn from him in defence of those he saw peeking out of their small windows and shadowed doorways. "It is an honest smell. One of hard work and struggle."

Vedrix looked away and mumbled an apology while Godewyn chuckled.

"You left a long time ago, General," the High Priest said. "As did I, but even so the truth is there for all to smell."

Bordan grunted and caught the glimpse of an officer waiting by the side of the road. "What is it, Spear?"

"General, the courtyard is just ahead," the Spear announced. "We've had a runner from the second force to say they are in position."

"And the third?"

"No word yet, General."

"Bring the column to a halt and prepare the troops," Bordan said, lifting his shield from the horn of his saddle and slipping his hand through the strap to catch hold of the grip. It weighed heavy on his left side and he shifted once more in the saddle. "Master Vedrix, can you find out if the other forces are in position?"

Resting his hand once more on the medallion, Vedrix closed his eyes and nodded. "They are, General."

"Then let's get ready, they already know we are coming," Bordan said, clicking his heels into the horse's flank and picking his way through the troops ahead. "Spear, block the road behind and cordon off the courtyard."

"Yes, General," the Spear said and shouted orders to the troops.

Bordan watched with pride as the troops peeled away without confusion, blockading the route they had taken and the road ahead. He knew that, on the other side of the courtyard, the exits were being blocked. No one would be able to escape without going through the troops.

The road opened into a courtyard surrounded by buildings built three stories high in Empire fashion. The ground floor was usually a business, a stall, a merchant, selling cloth, trinkets or street food. The next two floors were crowded housing, with families living cramped in one room. Night soil was collected in buckets and taken away every morning to spread upon the fields outside the city, a cheap compost and fertiliser.

Here though, the ground floor had been boarded up and the plaster walls which rose above were discoloured, rain streaked, and in disrepair. It was not unknown for buildings to collapse in the poor quarter and there would be much shaking of heads, much talk of making conditions better, of improving the lot of the people who struggled to make a living here. Nothing would come of it, but it made the wealthy feel better, salved their conscience, eased their guilt.

"Vedrix, you can make sure they all hear me?" Bordan asked as the three settled their horses in the front ranks.

"Put the stone in your mouth and talk, General," Vedrix answered handing over a small river pebble.

Cupping in in his palm, Bordan noted the small scratches on the surface and traced them with his eyes. His head swam and he was forced to blink orange sparks and yellow splotches from his vision.

"I would not do that again, General," Vedrix said with a smile. "When you have finished speaking, spit it out and I'll dispose of it later."

"And they'll all hear me?" Bordan said, unsure.

"Everyone will hear you, General," Vedrix assured him. "Did you want to me explain how and why it works?"

"No," he raised a hand, "I'll go on trust."

"I'm flattered," Vedrix said.

"You know we make good targets sat here," Godewyn observed out in a sour tone.

"This was your idea, Godewyn," Bordan pointed out.

"It sounded safer in your office," the priest grumbled.

"Foot," Bordan addressed a nearby soldier, "make sure the High Priest and Magician are protected."

"Yes, General," the soldier answered in a quavering voice.

"Let's get it over with," Bordan said, taking a deep breath and putting the stone in his mouth, using his tongue to press it into one cheek. He took a breath and walls around him vibrated, dust falling in slow clouds.

"Make it a good speech," Godewyn whispered.

Bordan glared at him for a moment. "This is General Bordan of the Imperial Army. You are ordered to lay down your weapons and surrender. For too long you have operated here, oppressing the people, lying, cheating, and stealing all they have worked hard for. No longer. For your part in the death of His Highness Prince Alhard, you are condemned. Should one amongst you wish to denounce your masters, the assassins you harbour and protect, for the foul deed they have committed, you have my word of safe passage witnessed by the High Priest of the Holy Flame and the Master of the Gymnasium of Magicians."

The words reverberated around the courtyard, echoing from the walls and rattling the cobbles embedded in the road. More plaster dust fell like a waterfall from the buildings and the troops shifted back a step.

"That is quite loud," Godewyn said, removing his hands from his ears.

"Sympathetic magic," Vedrix said, a self-satisfied smirk on his face. "Overlooked by a lot of my colleagues, as it takes a lot of planning and forethought, but it can be quite useful."

"Sir," the soldier Bordan had detailed to guard the High Priest said, "look."

At the base of one of the buildings a door had opened and a young woman was running across the courtyard towards the troops. Instinctively the soldiers raised and locked their shields, javelins were readied.

"Hold!" Bordan called, and the buildings shook once more. He spat the pebble into his hand and offered it to Vedrix who dropped it into a velvet drawstring pouch.

The woman had barely made the halfway point when the bolt from a crossbow plunged into her back. She fell, face crashing into the cobbles amid a crack of bone. She lay still, unmoving, as a dark stain of blood pooled around her broken skull.

"They are not going to surrender," Godewyn said.

"As we expected," Bordan said. "Get yourself to the back of the lines, High Priest. Vedrix, tell your fellow magicians to light up the sky, turn it purple if you can. Remember we are here as a symbol. I want the whole city to know what we are about."

"Of course, General," Vedrix said, closing his eyes and reaching for the medallion.

"You move to the back of the lines as well, Vedrix. You are too promising a target here," Bordan said, sliding from his horse and handing the reins to an attendant. "Spear, you have charge of the men, I'll be in the second rank."

"General…" the Spear began but faltered at the look Bordan directed at him. "Of course, General."

"Do not get killed, General," Godewyn said as he turned his horse and made for the rear of the troops. Bordan grunted and hefted his shield once more.

"Form a shell," the Spear called. "Form a shell."

The soldiers around Bordan closed in and those to either side lifted their shields above their heads while those on the edge locked them together in an impenetrable wall of wood and steel. With a grunt, Bordan added his own heavy shield to the roof of the shell.

On another shouted order the shells began to move forward, guided by the men at the front, towards the doors in each building. The army was built and trained to fight large battles, but tactics useful in sieges could work equally as well on a smaller scale.

Crossbow bolts, arrows, stones, pots and pans, struck the shields. Bordan grunted at each strike but held steady. Sweat was already pouring down his face and his arm ached. It had been a long time, decades, since he had stood in a shell and he silently cursed himself for a fool.

Why didn't I wait till the battle was over? he berated himself.

Because I am here as a symbol, he answered.

Light speared into the shell as the front rank reached the blockaded door and began to hack at it with the axes they had brought for this purpose.

"General," the soldier next to him shouted over the noise, "stick with us when we go in. We'll make sure you make it out in one piece."

Half-pleased, half-insulted, Bordan answered with a smile. "All in this together. It feels good to be back in the ranks again."

"Door is open," came the shout from the front. "Shields down. Swords out."

There was a clatter of wood and the silken whisper of steel on leather as swords leaped into hands.

"Flame guard old men," Bordan whispered as he grabbed his sword, feeling the grip in his hand, as warm as a loved one, familiar as a friend, and drew it from the scabbard.

Following the armoured soldier into the building was a step from sunlight into dark. Already there were the cries of the injured and shouts of fearful. A woman in a leather jerkin stepped into his path, her dagger sweeping round towards his head. It was instinctive, his free arm rose blocking the swing and his short sword punched out. There was a moment of resistance before a sudden giving way, and hot blood coated his hand. Pushing her falling body to the side, he stepped forward.

Where there was one, there would be more.

XXX

The Magician

Eight years ago:

He winced as the shock of impact ran up his arm, jarred his shoulder and rattled his teeth.

"Set your feet properly," the old man called out, "let your hips absorb the impact."

Lifting the gladius once more, he growled as he stalked the training post, dipping his shoulder and thrusting with the tip of the sword. He almost bit his tongue as the sword glanced from the rounded post.

"The flanks. The flanks!" a soldier shouted.

Kyron turned from the waggon in time to hear the whisper of the first arrows as they flew from the trees.

"Get down." A heavy hand on his shoulder and a raised shield blocked his vision. There was a hollow *thunk* as an arrow struck the shield.

"Master," Kyron called.

"Protect yourself and the priests," Padarn called back. "I'll look after the soldiers."

The afternoon light reasserted itself as the soldier drew the shield away and staggered upright to join his comrades. Kyron blinked, pressed his hands against the mud and pushed himself to his feet.

More arrows whistled from the trees. Most were blocked by the line of shields. A few arced over those and struck the waggon and carts. There were cries from the drivers and porters. More than one fell who would never rise again.

"Get down," Kyron shouted, waving his arms at the supply train. "Get down. Get under your carts."

The call was taken up and echoed along the line. Everywhere, the men and women who looked after the supplies and made sure the army were fed were taking cover beneath their vehicles. The horses who drew them were left in the open and more than one whinnied in terror.

"Oh no," Kyron muttered, seeing the future a moment before it happened.

A horse was struck by an arrow, barely thirty paces ahead. Kyron saw the metal head sink into the beast's flank. The animal raised its head to the sky and screamed in pain. Its rear legs came up, kicking at the cart it was attached to. There was a slap from the leather reins against its chest and flash of sunlight from the buckles.

Unable to free itself, the horse bolted. Even with the brake set, the cart moved, sliding on the mud as the horse bucked and dug in its hooves. Wood squealed and with a sharp snap of metal, the wheels were free. Now the cart moved with abandon, bouncing on its wheels as the horse dragged it along the supply train.

In its path, soldiers jumped aside. Two were struck, sent spinning and collapsed to the ground. Others slipped on the mud and were trampled under the hooves and wheels. Some managed to slide under their shields, but the dry snap of bone and crunch of breaking wood were loud along the track.

Other soldiers turned from the arrows and presented a bright red shield wall to the horse, clashing their short gladius swords upon the metal rims.

Kyron could only watch as the horse panicked anew. It turned from its course and ploughed into the forest, the cart's wheels becoming trapped between two trees. All the while the horse tried to pull itself free. Its whines were piteous, and Kyron wanted nothing more than to put it out of its misery.

"Form a wall!" one of the soldiers shouted. "Get up you lazy bastards. Form a wall. Protect the Emperor's waggon."

Down the track, the carters, drivers, and porters who had taken shelter beneath their carts now stood, realising the soldiers were not going to defend them from the tribes, and began to run towards the waggon.

Kyron could do nothing but watch as one after another was struck by arrows. Neck, shoulder, leg, it did not matter where the arrow hit, they all went down. Some tried to rise, a few managed to struggle back to their feet and start to run, or limp towards the waggon. They were cut down by more arrows.

"Step back, magician," a soldier said, dragging him roughly backwards into the circle around the waggon.

"The carters," Kyron said, pointing to those few who had been lucky enough to avoid the tribe's arrows.

"I'll let them through," the soldier said without turning from his watch on the forest. "If they make it."

"Arrows!" the cry went up.

The soldier ahead ducked beneath his shield and Kyron hunched next to him as another wave of arrows crashed against the barrier of the Empire.

"Here they come!"

A war cry screeched out of the trees and it was followed by warriors with blue and green painted faces, axes and swords held high. Kyron staggered back, fear controlling his legs, as weapons swung at his shield. The soldier in front, the one who had protected him, pushed his shield out to take the blow, and stepped up behind it, stabbing out with his gladius. A heartbeat later he slid back into the line and a warrior staggered away clutching his stomach.

"Watch the priests," the soldier called without turning.

Kyron spun on his heel, the slick mud under his feet making him stumble. Recovering his balance, he ran the few paces to the priests' side. None seemed happy to see him and he saw all had found weapons from somewhere. Swords, short and long, of the Empire style and others. Daggers clutched in hands and long staves held crosswise. None of them wore armour apart from their robes and symbols of flame.

"Stay out of our way," the Curate shouted, her hood pushed back to clear her vision. The Emperor's waggon was marked by arrows. Some impaled upon the side and others which had left scratches and striations, and which now lay on the floor near the wheels.

"I've come to help," Kyron said, the words sounding weak to his own ears.

"We do not need the help of a heathen magician," the Curate spat back.

He sucked in a breath to correct her, but the cry of arrows went up once more and he fell to the floor as the waggon once again became the target of the tribes. The slap and thumps of arrows ceased a moment later and Kyron clambered to his feet.

The Empire soldiers were being tested. So far, they had held their ground, but already Kyron could see injured soldiers falling from the lines and being replaced by the meagre number of reinforcements. Soon there would be none but the priests, the few carters, and him to step into the defence. A thought flashed across his mind.

"Where is Emlyn?" he called to the Curate.

"Who?" The reply came with a sneer.

"Our guide, the woman of the tribes who was with us," Kyron replied, biting his tongue to stop the curses following his words.

The Curate pointed to the waggon and then towards the ground.

Kyron knelt and looked beneath the heavy waggon. Emlyn lay on the dirt, and she gave him a brief smile, a thinning and stretching of her lips, which was gone before he could focus upon it.

"I will not fight my own people," she said.

Kyron found he had no words to argue with and settled for his own nod. "Stay safe."

There was a cry and a soldier dropped his shield, stumbling back, one hand pressed to his stomach and the other slashing his gladius back and forth. It was no match for the long spear which had punched through his armour and erupted through his back in a spray of blood.

Kyron scrambled for his own sword as a warrior stepped into the breach she had made. The woman was tall, strong, and she wrenched the spear free from the fallen soldier in another fountain of red. The smile on her face was feral, and Kyron found his hand unable to draw the sword from its scabbard.

It was not needed. The soldier on her left leaned in and rammed his gladius into her unprotected side. Her face looked both shocked and disbelieving.

As she slid from the sword, blood bubbling from her mouth, the spear fell from her grip to the dirt and she collapsed on top of it.

However, the stab had left the soldier open and before he could recover, or another soldier close the gap, an axe blade punched into his side, under his arm. He screamed in agony, his own sword falling from limp fingers.

"Either fight or get out of the way," the Curate yelled, pushing past Kyron. Her stave cracked down upon the head of the warrior trying to secure the breach in the shield wall and he fell back. The soldiers either side moved into the gap and the wall shrank a little.

Kyron shook his head and let a shuddering breath escape. Letting go of the gifted sword, he stepped forward and caught the dying soldier, dragging him back to the waggon.

"Leave him," the Curate snapped as Kyron inspected the wound. It was full of dark blood which pulsed at a regular rhythm. Shards of bone stuck out from the gash and the meat of muscles curled back from the opening. "He is dying and there's nothing you can do about it."

Kyron, words hot in his throat, turned to scream them in her uncaring face when a soft hand wrapped around his wrist.

"I'll look after him," Emlyn said. "He won't die alone."

A tear sprang to life in his eye and fell to the soldier's chest where it rested on the iron band of armour. "Thank you."

Sweeping his gaze across the line, he sought out the fiercest fighting and began to build a construct. He drew in the motes around him, some from the soil, some from the air, some from the trees, and bound them together, imprinting his will upon them all.

Within moments, a ball of contained force the size of an apple rested in his palm. A simple spell which turned all the energy inward where it was trapped and kept growing. Very soon, he knew, it would break the bonds holding the motes in place and when that happened, he wanted it far from him.

Stepping forward, he tossed the ball of magic high over the heads of the shield wall and into a knot of warriors who were advancing on the tiring soldiers. One of the tribal warriors glanced left, perhaps feeling its passage or maybe just looking for threats. Either way there was nothing he could do.

Kyron released the bonds, and the sharp crack of the explosion echoed through the trees. There was no fire, no smoke, but the warriors close by were thrown to the ground. A shower of dirt erupted where they had stood and of the five, only one staggered back to his feet, blood covering the blue and green woad.

Again and again, he tossed balls of magic into groups of warriors. Always to the same effect and the Empire cheered each time.

Inevitably, the arrows started to target him. Someone directing the attack must have sent the order around, and it was all he could do to construct a shield and deflect the arrows. Each strike drained a little more from his concentration and he was sweating behind his barrier.

The warriors rushed forward, sensing an end to the explosions, and began hammering with renewed vigour at the shield wall. Gaps began to appear with more regularity and still the arrows fell against his shield.

Two tribal warriors broke through. One, large with a braided beard and hair spiked into two horns, carried a double-bladed axe which he swept left to right, disembowelling the priest who stood in his way. The second was a wiry man with a thin beard and no hair upon his head. The blue woad was painted in streaks across his face and he carried a sword which had seen better days.

Both spotted the group of priests who stood by the waggon wheels and changed direction. In response, the priests raised their own weapons, but cowered back, tips of swords trembling as they faced their doom.

Kyron knew there was little he could do, but still ran forward, shaping his shield to protect the priests from the initial rush. The two warriors would smash through with little difficulty, but by then he might be close enough to help, or a soldier might see the danger.

He drew his sword. It flowed into his hand in a mockery of his earlier attempts, and he pointed it at the priests, guiding his shield with its tip.

"Get out of the way."

A figure pushed him aside—the Curate, he realised as he fell—and he lost his grip on the construct.

The warrior's axe clubbed aside a sword and buried itself in a priest's neck. Blood welled around the blade and when the warrior snapped it free, the priest's head lolled to the side, held to the body by a thin thread of skin. The priest next to his dead brethren screamed in terror and the axe took off his arm at the elbow.

The second warrior ducked the hasty cut of a third priest and ran his own blade through the holy man's gut. His other arm struck out in a stiff blow to the chin of the female priest who was trying to bring her sword around.

A moment later the Curate was there, her staff cracking the wrist of the swordsman's arm in a sharp blow. He howled and the other end of the staff struck him on the jaw. There was a loud snap and shards of teeth flew into the air even as the man dropped to the ground, unconscious.

Kyron saw her turn to face the axe-wielder whose grin through a blood-spattered beard was feral and welcoming. Her staff, aimed at his head, was deflected with ease and his retaliatory swipe was only avoided when she jumped back in panic.

On the next exchange she would be killed, he knew, and Kyron cursed the distance between them. Hand latching onto one of the spent arrows, a wild thought burst in his mind. Without pausing to consider, he gathered all the motes he could and stuck them to the arrow, imparting energy to the shaft and its bent metal tip.

It shook in his hand, wanting to leap free, to speed through air, to fulfil its purpose. With no time to build a guiding construct, he aimed by eye, sighting the best he could as the two combatants moved and danced around each other, and let go.

The arrow screamed as it left his hand, the fletching moving so fast it scored a bloody line across his palm and took the warrior in the neck. It punched most of the way through before snapping under the strain, the white feathers disintegrating and splinters forming a cloud in front of the wound.

The Curate swept her staff around, and with no raised axe to defend his head, it caught the warrior on the temple.

She turned to him, her staff held ready, and stalked across the ground. Kyron gave her a smile and opened his mouth to rebuff her thanks.

"You damned idiot!" she screamed. "You almost got them all killed. If you're not going to fight, get out of the way and stay there."

The Curate did not wait for a response. Instead, she turned and hurried to the shield wall.

Kyron bit down, once more on his anger and words, as he noted that silence had descended in the area surrounding the waggon. Drawing his knees under him, he stood and looked around.

Empire soldiers had flooded the area and the warriors, those that could, were fleeing back into the forest.

"Thank the Flame," Padarn said, racing into the clearing by the waggon. "You are not hurt?"

Kyron, stunned, could only raise his reddened palm which his master took in his own hand.

"Nothing serious. We'll clean and bandage it," his master said. "The battle is over. The tribes have fled."

Kyron looked up, his heart hammering in his chest, and his hands shaking as the aftermath took him. It took him a moment to find his words. "I tried to… to help, Master."

"I'm sure you did all you could," Padarn answered. "You survived and there will be soldiers alive because of that."

Kyron felt the hot tears start to spill down his face and bile rose, hot and acidic, up his throat as the sight of the priest's head, eyes open, mouth screaming, hanging by just that one patch of skin.

"Come. Come," Padarn said, patting his shoulder awkwardly. "Everyone deals with it differently. Don't be ashamed to cry. There'll be many a soldier having nightmares tonight, and they'll be thankful they're alive to have them."

Kyron lifted his gaze to meet Padarn's. "Thank you, Master, I…" A flicker of movement over his master's shoulder, above the heads of the soldiers, above their shields, and it was coming for them. Kyron screamed.

Padarn turned even as Kyron struggled to draw enough motes together build to a shield.

Too late. Too slow.

The arrow took his master in his back, just to the side of his spine. Kyron felt the shocking impact as his master fell against him, eyes open wide, shock and pain filling them.

"Master," Kyron cried, stumbling back and lowering his master to the ground. "Help. Help me."

"Kyron," Padarn's hand rested like a feather against Kyron's cheek. "Get home safe. Talk to your grandfather. He isn't what…"

A dribble of blood fell from Padarn's lips and his eyes lost their flame, their spark.

"No," Kyron whispered. "No."

XXXI

THE GENERAL

EIGHT YEARS AGO:

"It is not about anger, boy," he said, lifting the sword from the lad's hand. "It is about training, so the movement comes without thought, without emotion. It just is."

The boy wiped the sweat from his eyes. "A real person isn't made of wood."

"A real person will be wearing armour, and trying to stab you with a sword," his grandfather pointed out. "Don't mistake anger for bravery. Go and see Decima for something to drink and eat. We'll try again this afternoon."

"HOW IS THE arm, General?" Princess Aelia asked from her cushioned seat.

"It will heal," Bordan said, self-consciously turning away so the bandage was less visible. "Just a few stitches from the surgeon."

"And how is the city taking the news?"

Bordan watched the Princess take a sip of her wine. The young woman had emerged from her rooms this evening. There were dark lines around her red eyes, a sure sign of too much drink and not enough sleep.

"The last few days have been calm," Bordan reported. He reached for his own glass of wine and winced in pain. "I am told that the markets are bustling, and people are happy to have safe streets once again."

"The criminal gangs are in hiding?"

"It appears so," Bordan nodded, shifting in his seat so he could reach the wine. "It was always a possibility and a welcome one."

"Even at the cost of your injury?" Aelia said. She looked up from her contemplation of the wine and gave Bordan a smile which recalled the Princess's early years.

"I have been cut before," Bordan answered. "Some are deeper than others, but this is just a scratch. Sadly, I have no young lady to show it off to and impress."

"Did you want one?" Aelia said, her words quick in surprise. "I can make arrangements easily enough, General. It is the least you deserve."

"No, Princess," Bordan answered, considering his words, and fighting down the flush of embarrassment, "I am too old, and my dearly departed wife would not approve. I would fear the fire she would greet me with when I joined the Holy Flame."

Aelia snorted and a smile was etched upon her face for a moment. There was something in those red eyes, he thought, a woman who has seen too much for her tender years. Or likely, he corrected, a woman who had grown up coddled, protected from the realities of life and struggled to reconcile the two when faced with the loss of a father and brother in quick succession.

"I have no husband to make such objections, nor do I wish one at present," Aelia said, wiping her eyes, "so you'll forgive me if I turn in. I believe a young lady is waiting on my pleasure."

"I would not keep you from your bed, Princess," Bordan said, standing and placing his empty glass down upon the table. "It is good to see you regain some joy in life, even in these dark times. I would not seek to sadden you anymore by mentioning that, as heir, you will need to be married soon so children come quickly."

"You're trying to sour my mood, General." Aelia wagged a finger in the old man's direction. "However, nothing will dampen my ardour this evening. I find I need to experience all that life has to offer to feel truly alive at present."

"I understand," Bordan nodded. Grief took people in strange directions, but the arms of a willing woman was a good place to feel alive. "I will leave you to your pleasures. Good night, Princess Aelia."

"Until tomorrow, General," the Princess said, lifting her wine to her lips and draining the goblet in a single swallow. "Perhaps I've had sufficient wine for this evening's sport, or maybe not."

Bordan bowed and left the Princess pouring another glass of wine. As the door closed, he shook his head and turned towards his office. Tomorrow he would talk to the Empress about the Princess. She was the Emperor now in all but ceremony and the people would need to see her soon, to hear her speak. Hard as life can be, the grief must wait, and the young girl would have to take up her mantle.

As he walked, the memories of the last coronation surfaced. The Emperor, young and untried, but determined and fierce turning to face the congregation, flames rising behind him in celebration. It had been a good day and the city had rejoiced at the smooth transition of power.

A scream sounded and he stopped, turned, and listened again. It had been a woman's scream. The Princess? Not again. They could cover up one incident but nothing could stop the servants' tongues from wagging and the Princess had seemed in a better mood.

The scream sounded once more and was followed by the shout of a voice Bordan recognised. It was full of anger and alarm. A moment later, the first clash of steel on steel sounded in the corridor.

"Get the guards!" Bordan shouted down the corridor and the soldier at the end took up the call. Drawing the sword from his hip, ignoring the pain which flared in his shoulder, he sped back towards the Princess's rooms.

Under his feet the tiled floor echoed to the sound of his hard-soled boots. More screams and shouts from the Princess's room accompanied a tearing sound which sent a shiver through Bordan's heart. Ducking his shoulder, he slammed into the doors, bursting them open and drawing a stab of pain from his shoulder.

Three figures, dressed in dark robes, were attacking Aelia with spathas, a sword longer than the gladius Bordan carried in his hand. The Princess had grabbed a foot stool and was employing it as makeshift shield alongside her own gladius to fend off the assailants.

On the floor between Bordan and the assassins, the woman the Princess had chosen for the night lay covered in blood. She turned her head and gazed towards the General. Her eyes would not focus, and her mouth opened to release a flood of red. With a low moan she collapsed back to the floor, unmoving.

Bordan skirted her and advanced on the closest assassin. The man stepped away from the Princess and brought his sword around in a horizontal swipe at the General's stomach. A cut which would disembowel with only a thin tunic of cotton to put up any resistance.

Swaying back and sucking in his stomach, the sharp edge of the spatha passed Bordan by. The return sweep, following the same course but reversed was expected. A training move designed to catch out the unwary soldier and teach him to be prepared. It had been a long time since Bordan had been a novice on the training field and his gladius flicked out to catch the strike, turning it away. Stepping in as he guided the spatha out wide, he punched the assassin in the face with his free hand.

The attacker staggered back, a ragged tear in his cheek from the General's ring, and wove a shield of steel to keep the old man at bay.

A glance over the man's shoulder showed the Princess being hard pressed by the other two men. If they wanted her dead, they would have to be willing to sacrifice their own lives to get closer. The difference between a soldier and hired killer was simple. A soldier would die for the safety of others: an assassin had to live to enjoy riches earned from their dark trade.

It was enough of a distraction for the assassin to strike again. A straight thrust. With a shorter blade, like the gladius, it would have been faster, unavoidable, but the spatha was longer, slower, and Bordan slipped to the side.

The assassin had overextended. Bordan saw it in the man's eyes, in the way his shoulders dipped lower than they should, the manner in which his feet turned inward to maintain balance, a thousand little tells only an experienced soldier would note. Slamming the gladius down upon the extended blade to force the man further forward, Bordan caught his strike before it could go too far. A sudden reversal of movement, his shoulder on fire, he altered the momentum of the blade once more, slicing up and across the throat of the assassin.

It was army doctrine, with a gladius, to keep the thrusting tip sharp and leave the edges a little thicker, a little blunt to resist the damage wrought by armour and shields. However, like every soldier, Bordan had ignored that advice and sharpened the edge to cut eastern silk without tearing.

There was no sound as the blade slipped into the man's throat and resistance only came when it struck the vertebrae of the assassin's neck. It slid free as easily as it had entered and Bordan stepped to the side as the body fell.

The crash of the assassin's sword on tiled floor reverberated from the plaster walls and Aelia took advantage of the distraction to whip the stool into one of the other assassins' heads. It was a hollow sound, punctuated with a dry crack and the dark-robed assassin fell limply to the floor.

Only one remained and he backed away, casting looks over his shoulder, his sword extended before him as a warning.

"We need him alive," Bordan said, stepping forward, his own sword leading the way.

"I want them dead, General."

"Alive, Aelia," Bordan barked the order as if on the parade ground and the Princess was a new recruit. "We need answers."

The assassin remained silent but had stopped retreating, realising there was nowhere to go. The door to the corridor was blocked by the General, and Aelia guarded the route to the bedroom from where the fight had spilled into the Princess's living quarters.

Bordan slowed also, noting the assassin's grip on his sword, the way his eyes measured the distance and positions of the combatants, the set of his shoulders, and the way his balance shifted a tiny amount.

"Watch out," the General called, recognising the prelude to an attack. He brought his own sword up into a guard, not sure which way the assassin would leap, but in the end it was towards the more valuable target.

A deep, steep overhand blow with the longer sword crashed down upon Aelia's hastily thrown up guard. The Princess stumbled back, her feet and body unprepared, and cried out as she tripped over the assassin she had downed a moment ago.

The last assassin leaped forward drawing the spatha back, aligning it to stab downward at the unguarded, prone Princess on the floor. Aelia cried out once more even as she desperately tried to bring her sword around.

Bordan felt the impact through his wrist, elbow, and injured shoulder as he slammed the pommel of his sword into the side of the assassin's head and the blade aimed at the Princess went tumbling to the ground in a clatter of steel. The General fell with the assassin, letting go his own sword and wrapping his arms around the hired killer as they hit the ground. A river of fire ran up his arm and flooded his shoulder with another wave of pain.

Gritting his teeth against the tide of agony, he clenched his arms tight, grabbing the assassin's wrists and rolling the man over onto his front. The assassin was face-down and Bordan let go his grip, planting his knee in the assassin's back. Scrabbling for the small dagger at his hip, the General placed the tip against the downed man's neck.

"You move," he gasped, "you will feel the tip of the dagger. I won't kill you, but I can make sure you never walk again."

A soft hand rested on his shoulder and Bordan looked up into the Princess's face, her golden curls framed by the lantern light which suffused the room.

"He cannot hear you, General," the Princess said. "Your blow knocked him out."

Bordan looked down, noting the assassin's closed eyes and the burgeoning, growing purple and green bruise just below the man's ear. "Thank the Flame for that."

"Come on," Aelia said, offering Bordan a hand which he clasped gratefully and was pulled to his feet. The young woman was stronger than he had given her credit.

There was commotion in the door and three guards piled through, swords drawn. Behind them more soldiers appeared.

"Check the bodies," Bordan ordered, pointed down and added, "secure this one with ropes and get the surgeon to look at him."

"This one is a woman," Aelia said, turning the head of the assassin whom she had cracked with the stool.

"How did they get in?" Bordan cast a look around. The window was open, but the imperial quarters were set deep within in the palace and anyone climbing, let alone three, should be easy to spot against the white-washed walls.

"They were in my bed chamber waiting for me," Aelia said. She flicked a finger towards the woman Bordan had taken to be her bed mate for the night. "She was there too. They cut her when she started to scream."

"She's dead too," one of the guards said, looking up from his bended knee by the woman's side.

"You have," Bordan struggled for the right words, "known her a long time, Princess?"

"Only the second night, General," Aelia said without embarrassment. "She was a supple and flexible companion."

"And possibly an assassin in her own right?"

"She came highly recommended," Aelia said. "References were taken up and she was clean. Your orders, I believe."

"A wise precaution," Bordan replied. "Perhaps a period of celibacy might be in order, Princess? At least until we have found the source of the assassins."

"You're a cruel man, General," Aelia answered.

The trembles began in Bordan's hand as he slipped the dagger back into its sheath. For a moment his heart sounded loud in his ears and the warmth of the room brought him out in a sudden sweat. "I'm an old man, my Princess. Fighting and other games are for folks younger than me."

"You saved my life tonight, General. I will not forget it." Aelia said, her tone grave and level. In the room's light the dark shadows under the Princess's eyes seemed to creep down her face.

"We will have some answers soon," Bordan said with a shudder which came not just from the after-fight rush of blood. "The assassin will talk, and we will know where to strike."

"I hope you are right," Aelia said, raising her head to meet Bordan's gaze. The shadows retreated and the young woman returned.

XXXII

The Magician

*S*EVEN YEARS AGO:

The scarred soldier stepped in, shield striking out and it was all he could do to duck his shoulder behind his own shield. The impact staggered him and before he could bring his sword up, the sharp tip of Gressius's gladius was at his neck.

"Better," the old man stood to the side said.

"He is too big for me," the boy complained.

"There is always someone bigger than you," the old man said.

"His MEMORIES WILL last forever in the heart of the forest," Emlyn said as she sat down on the earth next to him.

"I want him to be here, not his memories," Kyron sobbed.

"That is not a choice we get to make," Emlyn replied in a soft voice. "None of us do. It is why every day is important. Live to the full, experience what you can, create memories which others can carry with them and continue to learn from."

"Leave me alone," Kyron snapped, much as he was desperate for her to stay.

Emlyn sighed and stood. "I'll check on you later. Get something to eat and drink. The Spear will want to talk with you. They are still looking after the wounded and counting the damage."

Kyron watched her leave through tear-misted eyes. With the back of his sleeve, he wiped the water from his eyes and blinked away the fog of sadness.

The area around the waggon had been cleared, and he had a vague recollection of helping in that task. Grass had been churned into mud and even the low bushes which had crowded the edge of the track before the forest proper began had been trampled or chopped down. Spent arrows had been collected, those embedded into the waggon had been snapped off and now there was a low, ragged forest of shafts sticking out from both sides.

Those who would no longer rise amongst the fallen had been dragged away. Professional, even in the midst of such a slaughter, the Empire soldiers had treated both soldier and warrior alike. The priests had spoken a few empty words above the corpses of the tribes, a last attempt to convert them to the true faith.

Kyron had held onto his master until the last, the priests, soldiers, and carters happy to leave him to his grief. All around the clean-up continued as his master's body cooled in his arms. He could not say who finally freed him, who lifted his master's body and carried it out of sight, the arrow still standing proud from his back. A moment of anger, fuelled by grief, and he had gathered motes to slash them across the shaft, snapping it in two.

Alone again. His parents' death had hurt, and his grandfather had tried to soften the blow over the years, but it could never truly be eased. It had poisoned their relationship and Kyron knew he had pushed the old man away, looked for an escape, a chance to start again, a chance to forget.

Now Padarn was gone. A surrogate father, a man Kyron had assumed was immortal and invincible. A single arrow had stolen a life, crushed an ideal, punctured a belief. In this ocean of trees, he was adrift.

"Come on."

The deep voice shook him from his thoughts, and he looked up to see Borus standing above him. The Cohort had a bandage around his left arm, and his eyes were tired and bloodshot.

"Where?"

"The Spear wants to see you," Borus said, offering his good hand to assist.

Kyron paused, the desire to be alone crashed against the need to be near people, and he accepted the outstretched hand.

"What about?"

"That's for him to say," Borus said, "but most likely about how we get home and how we protect the Emperor's body."

"Emlyn. She knows the way home and about the forest," Kyron replied.

"Already there."

The walk was a short one across muddy ground. Even so, the impact of the battle on the soldiers was clear enough. Many stood but were either bandaged or limping. Others were sat in small groups around cooking fires and pans full of stew bubbling away. The smell of food made Kyron's stomach grumble.

However, there were fewer soldiers than he recalled. Always before, when he had traipsed through the camp to renew the wards and spells upon the waggon, he had been forced to dodge around close packed groups of soldiers. Now the way was open and unobstructed.

Carters sat amongst the soldiers where before they would have had their own fires, their own space in the camp. On the edge of the track, Kyron could see soldiers in pairs keeping a watch on the forest.

The group of officers and soldiers ahead parted to admit Borus and Kyron. In the centre, sat on a felled log was the Spear and what remained of his officers. Two of the five Cohorts stood there and, along with Borus, that meant two had been slain. Kyron struggled to recall their names but failed. Those before him were changed: faces drawn, grey, tiredness seeping out of every bone in their body, and their uniforms—usually clean and smart—were covered in a mixture of dirt, sap, and blood.

"My sympathies for your loss," the Spear said and with a wave of his hand invited Kyron to sit on one of the other logs.

In the centre of the group a low fire burned and flatbread was being baked on heated stones around the edge. A soldier assigned to the task, sat on the dirt, poking the cooking bread with a stick.

"I am glad you could join us, Kyron," the Spear said. "You already know Cohort Borus. Allow me to introduce Cohort Rullus and Cohort Gaurus."

Both men nodded to Kyron who returned the gesture.

"You know our guide, Emlyn," Astentius said, "and our cook is

Shield Tatian. He has served in my staff for more years than I care to remember and has turned down every chance at promotion."

The cook subjected Kyron to a measuring gaze before returning his attention to the flatbreads. Emlyn was whittling a stick with her knife and spared him a fleeting glance.

"We are waiting for one more," the Spear continued, "before we get... Ah, here she is."

Kyron felt a chill as Curate Livillia entered the circle. She made the sign of the Flame before her heart which everyone around the fire copied.

"Welcome, Curate. My sympathies also for your losses," Astentius said. "Please, sit. We will eat and talk."

"Thank you, Spear," Livillia said. "The Deacon joined the Flame this morning. My brothers and sisters will stand watch over his body until we can carry out the proper rituals."

"I understand," Astentius said. "Today, we mourn and send their honoured souls to the Flame. Tomorrow, we march home."

"Spear," the Curate said, "why is the apprentice here? His sort have no place in this discussion."

"Which is where the military and Church may have a difference of opinion, Curate," Astentius said. "His master was great assistance in the battle, and I understand the apprentice played his part."

"Only in getting my friends killed," the Curate spat. "He has no place in battle nor at this council."

Astentius's face hardened and the chill Kyron felt deepened further.

"That is my decision to make, Curate," the Spear said, "not yours. Our mission remains the same, and I will use every resource under my command to ensure we complete it successfully. The magician can help, beyond the preservation of the Emperor's body, and he is here to listen and to add his thoughts. You are here for the same reason. If you feel you and the remaining priests in your charge are unable to work together to this end, you are free to leave."

Livillia hissed, a stream of air between clenched teeth and thin lips. "I will make a report to the Archdeacon."

"Which you are free to do also," Astentius snapped back. "Now, we are hurt, tired, and the last thing we need is difficulty amongst us. We must be united on our mission. Let me tell you all," and the Spear's gaze swept all of the group, lingering for longer on the Curate, Emlyn, and Kyron, "that further arguments or delays will be dealt with harshly. We operate under military law, and you will all comply with my orders."

Kyron nodded while next to him Emlyn looked sullen, her faced fixed in an expression of distaste. The Curate raised her chin and looked at the Spear, eyes full of indignation and her mouth set in a hard line.

"I'll take that as agreement," Astentius said. "Good. We lost near two hundred men during the battle, another seventy or so are walking wounded. The tribes were defeated, but we are unclear how many escaped to the trees and back to their villages. Estimates suggest?"

"Around one hundred or so, Spear," Gallus answered.

"Enough to give us serious problems on the way to the bridge," the Spear finished.

"They will not." Emlyn spoke into the quiet. She put the knife back in her sheath and tucked the stick she had been whittling into her belt.

"Explain," Astentius said.

"The villages south of here, towards your precious Empire..." Emlyn started and then paused, sighed and continued. "The villages south of here are not entirely... unsympathetic to your Empire. They have more trade with the towns along the river."

"That will not stop those hundred from hounding us every step of the way," the Spear said.

"Bread's ready," Tatian said, hooking the flatbread from the cooking stones. "There's honey in the pot, some olive oil in this one, and salt if you feel up to it. I'll not be staying for more depressing conversation, if you don't mind. My men will need feeding and my exciting company to get them through the night."

The cook did not wait for permission or a response but stood and tramped out of the circle.

"Eat," Astentius said without once commenting or looking towards the departing cook, "and explain to me why they will not be attacking again."

"We... You may be attacked," Emlyn corrected, "but it is unlikely. The army you faced was drawn from many villages. I heard some northern accents amongst them as they attacked and those from the southern forest were out to prove their manhood, or act on their hatred of the Empire. There are some in every village for whom battle is to be enjoyed, and they thrive on it."

"There could be more?" Kyron asked, waiting his turn with the flatbread that was being passed around the circle.

"Not many," she said. "Those hundred will filter back to their villages and spout a good story about how they defeated your army, but the people will know what happened."

"How?"

"Because the trees will tell them," Emlyn answered, passing the bread to him without taking any herself. "Or more likely, because my people are not as stupid as some believe."

Kyron tore a hunk from the bread and dipped it in the honey pot. Taking a bite, he remembered the meals sat around the fire with Padarn and almost choked on the sweet honey as it slid down his throat.

"If," and Astentius stressed the word, "our guide is correct, we face another problem. The attack on the supply train has left us with a shortage of horses. Even donating our own mounts," and Kyron knew there were precious few of those in the honour guard, "we do not have sufficient for all the carts we have left. Some of our supplies were taken, others were scattered upon the earth, or set on fire. Also, to compound matters, many of the carters and porters were slain in the attack. I have designated some soldiers to take over those duties."

"My estimates and counts suggest three days of food remain, five if we go to smaller rations," Cohort Gallus said.

"And with the number of wounded we have, we'll move slower than before," Rullus added.

"Thank you both," Astentius said, thumping his thigh with a clenched fist. "Borus, did you want to add your own prophecy of doom?"

"No, Spear," Borus said. "There are enough soldiers fit to guard the waggon and ensure our security." He added an apologetic shrug. "It will mean a few more watches, but I am sure some of our wounded will assist. They may not be useful in the ranks, but they can look and listen well enough."

"Emlyn," Astentius said, caution entering his tone, "you say the villages south trade with the Empire?"

"Cloth, food from the forest, meat, wood," she answered.

"They would trade with us?"

"If you bring enough money or something of value," Emlyn answered.

"And they speak the tongue of the Empire?"

"They will," she agreed.

"But the force we fought did not?"

"Most probably had a smattering. Some would have been fluent."

"The chief?" Borus asked.

"His accent was northern," Emlyn answered. "I doubt he knew much beyond simple phrases, if any."

"Did we find his body amongst the fallen?" Rullus asked.

"No," Astentius replied, shaking his head. "That worries me a little. If he was the spark which enflamed that army, he could do so again."

"There are not that many men in the forest," Emlyn said. "The southern tribes have gone soft in contact with the Empire. Money is more important than tradition or shepherding of the forest. Those that wanted to fight moved north when your army invaded."

"You make it sound like we are safe, tribeswoman," Livillia said, delicately sprinkling salt on her bread.

"Not safe," Emlyn countered, "but less at risk in the south than the north. Most trees don't like fire, priest, but the tribes and clans will happily fell as many as needed to build you a pyre big enough to send you to your god."

"A kindness, no doubt," the Curate answered without looking in Emlyn's direction and popped the bread into her mouth.

"Enough," Astentius snapped. "Emlyn, you will visit the villages as we travel. Make contact with the people, assure them of our good intentions, and secure provisions. Cohort Borus will go with you to question the locals about the route ahead. I will supply you with enough money or items of trade. Kyron, you will go too. I want you to make sure we are being told the truth about the track and any supplies we purchase."

"Spear," the Curate spoke up, "I must protest. Allowing this tribeswoman and this," her lips curled up further in disgust, "magician to determine our fate is a step too far."

"Cohort Borus will, as I said," Astentius said, biting off each word, "accompany them as will two soldiers to provide protection. Would you prefer to send a priest perhaps? You've already heard what the tribes would like to do to a priest."

"Sending soldiers is bad enough," Emlyn said, her voice tainted with venom, "but a priest also? We'll have stones and worse thrown at us the moment we appear."

"Our mission is too important," Astentius said, "to risk it based purely on your fears, Curate."

"But..." she started.

"The decision is made," Astentius said, cutting off her words with a sharp gesture. "Your role tonight, Curate, is to lead the army in prayer and ensure the fallen are honoured, respected and find a place in the Holy Flame."

"You have not heard the last of this, Spear," the Curate said.

"Probably not," he agreed, "but once the Emperor's body is safely back in the capital, I will happily listen to a list of your complaints. For now, for the sake of the Empire, and because it is your calling, you will lead the service tonight."

"I will not put the magician's body on a pyre," the Curate snapped, her eyes narrowing in challenge.

"No one is asking you to," Astentius said.

"Good," the Curate said, biting off the word. She straightened and stamped away from the fire and the discussion.

"You are dismissed," Astentius said to her retreating back and sighed. "Now, are the rest of us clear about our duties?"

"Yes, Spear," Kyron said along with the rest, happy to find his voice once more. Emlyn nodded but stayed silent.

"Don't worry, lad," Borus said. "The soldiers will honour your master with a pyre. I'll have some detailed to build it and place him upon it."

"I'll stand with you," Emlyn said.

XXXIII

The General

Seven years ago:

"*In the ranks, you'll stand with the other soldiers. You'll fight for them and they for you,*" he said, watching the boy wash the day's sweat from his face. "*You'll rely on each other. It won't matter how big the enemy is because you'll be thousands strong.*"

"*Is the army a good life?*"

"*It has always suited me, lad,*" he said.

"*But my father didn't want to be a soldier?*"

"*No,*" he answered, his good mood evaporating.

"Where is he, General?" Aelia said, her blonde curls still damp from the bath and dressed in an old cuirass of small bronze plates sewn onto a leather jerkin.

"In the cells, Princess," Bordan said, staring at the armour. "Where did you get that? I thought we stopped issuing those to the troops over a century ago. Mail is stronger, lighter, and better protection."

"My father had a room full of treasures," Aelia said, running her hand down the small fish-scales of metal. They clinked and tinkled in the quiet. "I suppose it is my room now. This was in there, and after the attempt on my life, I thought it prudent to wear something."

"It looks to be in good condition," Bordan said, leaning around the Princess and peering at the bronze plates. In the light of the lanterns the bronze took on a golden hue.

239

"Father oiled it frequently," Aelia answered and for a moment Bordan caught a glimpse of the wistful child, puzzled by grief and unsure of her next steps. "I want to question him."

"I understand your anger and need," Bordan answered, "but, forgive me, Princess, we have people trained to extract information and I would save you the... unpleasantness."

"I want to see, General. He came after me. He knows who killed my brother, who tried to kill me, and who paid them," Aelia said and the wistful child disappeared. In its place, her father's child, stubborn, imperial and imperious, ready to face the dangers.

"Of course," Bordan answered, pausing to take a breath. "Princess, I understand why you want to do this, but please, save yourself this experience."

"Did not someone say, 'Nothing happens to any man that he is not formed by nature to bear.' Perhaps I was born to suffer this."

"A philosopher," Bordan answered, dragging up a memory from decades ago. "One who lived a comfortable life under the patronage of an Emperor. He would not have seen what you now wish to."

"I have to, General." The façade of the Princess broke for a moment, giving Bordan a view of the broken soul within.

Not trusting himself to answer, the sadness choking his voice, he settled for a simple nod.

With guards in tow, they made their way past the painted plaster walls and along the tiled hallways. The intricate and expensive tessellated panels at the intersections were ignored. Busts of previous Emperors and nobles of note, draped in the black cloth of mourning, went unseen. Servants, soldiers, and clerks who carried on about their daily business were quick to move out of the way.

In a far corner of the palace, stairs led down. Regularly spaced and sized, carved from stone found in the mountains far to the west, smoothed by the tread of the years, they formed the path to the cells and prison below. Every twenty steps down there was a small landing, a flat, level piece of stone, before the stairs cut back upon their course to go down another twenty. On each of the first five landings, a door allowed access to another part of the palace used by servants, for storage, and archives.

Past those, the doors came to an end, but the stairs continued. The air cooled and there was a damp smell. Enclosed lanterns lit the way, their flames steady in the unmoving air, giving rise to harsh edges and dark shadows in which the unlucky might become lost for an age.

Despite the cool temperature, Bordan began to sweat as he descended. There was an ache in his legs and the small of his back felt like it was burning. He reached for the collar of his tunic and pulled it away from his skin, encouraging fresh air to circulate his torso.

"Come, General," Aelia said, turning and offering a smile. "I've seen you fight off assassins as well as a man half your age. A few stairs should not defeat you."

"Not the stairs, Princess, but age is an enemy I can never hope to defeat, not with clever strategy or tactics. It has chosen the battleground well and my reserves are running low. When you reach my years, you too will face this foe and I hope you bring better weapons than I."

"You shouldn't talk of death, General." Aelia stopped her descent and turned to face the older man. There was a look of sadness in her eyes which chilled Bordan to the marrow. "Not today. I've lost too much already."

"Of course, Your Highness," Bordan replied. "Today we should speak of uncovering those who have caused you and our Empire such pain. Today is the beginning of the retribution."

"A much happier topic." Aelia resumed the journey towards the cells.

The echo of each step was muted by the cool, damp air. Even the slow burning oil lamps set into hollows carved into the stone produced an apologetic light matching the maudlin mood which settled across Bordan's shoulders like a heavy winter cloak.

At the bottom, the narrow stairs opened into a small room occupied by a single guard who stood to attention as they entered.

"General," the guard saluted. "Your Highness."

"The prisoner is secured?" Bordan asked.

"As ordered, General," the guard replied.

"Has the Carnificina arrived?"

"A few moments ago," the guard said, nodding towards the door behind him. "They have not yet begun."

"Excellent," Aelia said.

"Open the door," Bordan ordered, wiping the sweat from his face. The guard took a heavy key from his belt, inserted it in the lock and gave it a twist. There was a clunk and several scratches before the guard swung the door open.

Warm air, heavy with the stink of rot and urine, gushed from the door and Bordan, accustomed to the cool air of the stairway, took a step back.

"You get used to it, General," the guard supplied helpfully.

"I sincerely hope not," Bordan replied.

Looking to the Princess for instruction, or a hint of the young woman's intentions, Bordan was surprised to see her flesh had paled and her eyes were as large as the rim of a goblet filled with dark wine. "Princess?"

He saw Aelia take a deep breath before she answered. "It is what we came here for, General. Answers."

"And justice, Princess," Bordan said.

Aelia nodded. "Of course, General."

"It is the cell at the far end, General," the guard said. "Stay in the centre of the corridor. The guards within can guide you if needed."

"Thank you," Bordan said, recognising the prompt for what it was. "I'll lead the way."

Aelia nodded, offering no other guidance or insight.

Bordan steeled himself. The cells were never pretty, and he only came down here when he must. In the last twenty years, that had been... He paused, putting the events of the last two decades in order... only three times previously. Even so, the memory was strong, and it came with a sense of sickness which burrowed into his stomach.

The main corridor was wide enough for four men to walk shoulder to shoulder and a carved channel ran down the centre. Small tributaries brought urine, shit, blood, and vomit from the cells either side into this channel where it was encouraged, either by the natural slope or more often by a guard with a bucket of water, to flow into a large trough. This was emptied every morning by dedicated night-soil workers whose sense of smell had ceased functioning.

Bordan was careful to stay away from the channel and avoid each small tributary and confluence. Low moans emanated from one of the occupied cells and he was thankful the thick wooden doors, bound with iron and scribed with symbols courtesy of the Gymnasium, prevented him from seeing in. Even so, next to him, the Princess craned her neck to try and peer through the small opening high in the door.

"Through here," Bordan said, twisting the handle on the last door.

Aelia waved him forward and they stepped into Hades. Iron braziers full of cherry red coal burned in the corners of the room, raising the temperature, and stealing the moisture from Bordan's mouth on every breath. Sweat dripped down his back, sticking his tunic to his skin. A chimney cut into the ceiling drew the smoke which clouded the ceiling where it would follow the vents which ran between the walls as part of the castle's heating system. Even so, it looked as though dark grey clouds shrouded the sky and billowed on a breeze denied to him.

The far wall drew his attention. The assassin was tied to a chair, ropes binding his arms and legs to the stout wood, a gag encircling his mouth. Two men, dressed in sleeveless tunics which fell to the mid-thigh and tied with a thick leather belt, stood close by.

Aelia was quick. Quicker than Bordan had expected, but the men in the tunics were quicker, moving to stand in the Princess's way, barring her from the prisoner.

"Get out of my way!" the Princess shouted at the two men, who stood, unarmed and impassive, in the face of imperial fury.

Bordan placed a hand on her arm, encircling her forearm, and was surprised at the heat radiating from the woman's skin. Hotter than the coals, it burned his hand, but he held on.

"We need answers," Bordan said, gritting his teeth and once more his shoulder reminded him of the wound. "They know their job. Let them do it, Your Highness."

For a moment it seemed as if Aelia would break free, but on the next breath the tension left the young woman's arm and she sagged.

"Forgive me, General," Aelia said. "I should not let my temper, my anger at the man who attempted to end my life, rule me. If I am to rule the Empire well, I must learn to conquer myself first."

The wry smile the Princess favoured him with brought hope to his heart. "Your father's words?"

"His advice to me on another matter, but I realise now he was teaching me about much more," Aelia answered.

"They have provided chairs," Bordan said, changing the subject as a thorn of loss hooked into his heart. "This will not be pleasant, Your Highness."

"I can bear this, General," Aelia replied as she settled into the chair. "The heat may force my retreat sooner than a weak stomach."

Bordan steeled himself, reciting a passage he had learned as a child. "Now stands my task accomplished, such a work, flame, fire nor sword nor the devouring ages can destroy."

"Not yet, General," Aelia whispered, "but soon."

The cutting began. With fine blades heated over the brazier the two men began to slice into the bound legs of the assassin. Behind the gag, their victim wailed and thrashed but the ropes permitted no movement. Blood began to flow, tracing its way to the floor where it puddled.

After a time, the gag was removed, and the assassin was asked a question in a sibilant whisper. There was no response, but Bordan saw sweat mat the brow on the assassin's forehead above defiant eyes.

The cutting resumed. This time the blades traced delicate paths across the man's stomach leaving a fine network of incisions which beaded with red.

After each cut, a question was asked, and the answer written down. Soon Bordan began to detect the pattern of questions. Once a fact was established, a question would be asked to test that fact. The question was always posed in such a way not to be a direct repeat of an earlier one but phrased carefully to elicit the recall of the assassin. The new answer was then written down and returned to a few questions later.

The nature of the questioning changed. Instead of cuts, substances were rubbed into the wounds and the assassin screamed. The high pitch wails pierced Bordan's skull and where he had been able to look away from the cuts, the depth of the man's anguish was impossible to ignore.

Questions were asked, repeated, checked, written down to the accompaniment of the assassin's screams. Glancing to the side, Bordan caught sight of the Princess's face as sweat dripped from beneath her golden curls. The woman's mouth moved in a silent whisper as the assassin screamed again. Aelia's eyes were wide, unable to look away from the horror before her.

Even in the oppressive heat of the room, Bordan began to feel cold and the queasy feeling in his stomach spread to his limbs. The trembling began in his hands and he clasped the arms of the chair to hide them away. Soon though, he felt them start in his arms.

The door opened and the blessing of a cool breeze swept across him, bringing a moment of clarity, followed by a spasm which wracked his frame.

"Your Highness, General." Godewyn stood in the doorway, the symbol of the Flame upon his chest appeared to waver and flicker in the heat of the room. "If I had known the questioning was to begin so soon, I would have been in attendance. How fare the answers?"

Aelia stood and gestured to the Carnificina who held the stylus.

"My lords," the man said, "we have checked and rechecked this man's," he pointed to the assassin who was shaking and heaving, each rattling breath sounded as if it was his last, "answers. He does not appear to know who hired him and his colleagues to assassinate the Princess. He is aware of the previous death of Prince Alhard but does not know who carried out that contract. It appears that is not the way his group operate."

"What do we have that is useful?" Aelia asked, glancing at the assassin before looking away.

"Not much, Your Highness," the Carnificina said, shaking his head a little. Small droplets of sweat arced through the air to land with a sizzle upon the stone floor.

"Perhaps," Godewyn's deep voice cut through the heat, "I can assist. This is Justice Zonara, one of the most experienced inquisitors in the Church."

"And she will get more from the assassin than the General's Carnificina?" the Princess demanded.

Bordan squinted into the shadows cast by the braziers and flames but could only see the outline of the woman in the doorway.

"With all due deference to the talents of the General's men, yes," Godewyn said, ushering the woman into the room. "With your permission, my Princess?"

"Go ahead, High Priest," Aelia said, turning her back on the assassin with an expression which Bordan would have said was regret. "I will be interested to see how the techniques of the Church of the Holy Flame differ from those of the military."

"We have a great deal of experience of extracting confessions from those who would rather hide their sins from the light of the Flame," Godewyn answered, beckoning the inquisitor forward into the room.

She was smaller than the Princess, but it was not her height which drew Bordan's attention. There was a livid scar covering the right side of her face. It looked as though the skin had melted into ripples which had slowly drooped down her face, pulling the skin of her forehead down and obscuring her eye with a fold of reddened flesh. Bordan shivered once more.

"Sadly, Your Highness," Godewyn continued, "her work and that of the Church is sacrosanct. Only I will remain in the room while she puts the assassin to the question."

"Unacceptable," Aelia snapped. "I am the heir to the Empire and it was my brother they killed, and me they tried to kill. I will be here when he names the bastard behind it all."

"Your Highness," Bordan spoke up, "forgive me, but perhaps it is better to let the Church keep its secrets and for us to learn those the assassin keeps hidden from my own Carnificina."

"Bordan," the Princess accused, "you side with the High Priest over the heir?"

"Your Highness, I side with a tradition which has kept the Empire safe for centuries," Bordan explained, choosing his words with care. "The High Priest is a man I have placed my trust in for more years than I care to remember. He would not demand this of us were it not required."

Aelia looked between the assassin whose head was sagging on his chest as he heaved in great gasps of hot air and the newcomer whose expression did not change. For a moment, Bordan wondered if the inquisitor's expression was fixed by the burn mark which disfigured her when she blinked both eyes and spoke.

"Your Highness," her voice was smooth, rich, deep and alluring, at odds with her appearance, "I can guarantee the assassin will tell me all he knows. He will suffer in doing so, more than you can imagine."

Bordan spotted the moment the woman's words convinced the heir and shivered once more. The bronze plates of the Princess's armour had turned as red as the blood which dribbled from the assassin's many wounds.

"Come, Bordan," Aelia said, half a smile playing on her lips, "we will wait outside. I'll have chilled wine brought down. You look positively exhausted."

XXXIV

THE MAGICIAN

SEVEN YEARS AGO:
The wooden pew made his bum numb and the back dug into his
spine. He squirmed, trying to find some comfort.
"Sit still," the old man said in a harsh whisper.
"I'm not comfortable," he complained.
"You're not supposed to be comfortable, you are supposed to listen
to the priest's words."
He settled and strained his ears to pick out the words of the tall
man, dressed in white, who stood near the altar at the front of the
church.

HE SLEPT FITFULLY. The cloud of smoke which rose from the pyres in
the clearing joined with the low clouds and blocked the moon from
view. Axes and saws wielded by soldiers had been busy all afternoon
cutting down trees for the monstrous number of pyres, and the
clearing had grown in size.

"The trees will grow back," Emlyn had said. "The ash of your
soldiers will provide new nutrients to the soil."

"That's a callous way to look at it," Kyron had mumbled, his
thoughts dwelling upon his master. He turned over the key and chain
he had taken from Padarn's body, the fire giving the iron key a subtle
orange tint. Motes of magic, an enchantment, swirled slowly in the
metal of chain and key, a last remnant of Padarn's power.

"You think so?" She turned her head to look at him. "I find it quite reassuring. Even from death there can come life. There is a cycle to things. Perhaps, in your cities, you have forgotten this?"

"I know the science behind it," Kyron snapped back, lifting the chain over his neck and tucking the key inside his tunic.

"Science is cold," she replied without anger. "This is a truth. We bury our dead so that their souls and body may become part of the forest, part of our future. You burn yours, yet here the outcome will be the same."

"Their souls will not lie in your forest, they will join with the Holy Flame," Kyron answered, though his heart was not in the argument.

"Their ash won't, and that's enough," Emlyn said with a smile that sent a rush of blood through Kyron's heart and made his fists clench in sudden fury.

Ahead, in the light of the pyres, the Curate climbed the platform built by the soldiers to begin her speech, benediction, and prayers. All around, Astentius included, bowed their heads and made the sign of the Flame.

"Come," Emlyn said. "Let's go see to your master."

With a last look at the conflagration, smoke, and curate with her arms raised to the sky, Kyron turned his back and slunk back into the shadows. The soldiers, at Borus's direction, had made a pyre just off the track at the back of the column. Livillia had stamped her feet and called down all manner ills upon the Spear's head if Padarn had been allowed to burn with the regular soldiers. Infection, curse, and unclean were some of the more moderate words she chose to employ.

It was a low tower of wood. Freshly cut and unseasoned, Kyron knew it would take a strong fire to get it burning and the sap would spit and sizzle. The gesture, by Borus, had been a good one, a gentle one, and maintaining the fiction cost Kyron a sliver of guilt.

"Normally," he said into the dark, "there would be others to help. A magician's passing is mourned by the Gymnasium and we gather to honour their deeds, to recite their teachings, in the courtyard."

"We can do that," Emlyn said, "the two of us, here and now. Borus gave me a flask of oil to get the pyre started."

"In a moment," Kyron said, taking a deep breath. "I need to tell you something and ask a favour."

"A favour? Of the tribes?" She sounded shocked, but he recognised the false drama she coated her words with. "What do you need? I've no love of the Empire, nor your priests, but Padarn treated me well, and it wasn't the first time he had traversed the forests."

"We..." he began and stopped to re-evaluate his words. "That is, magicians do not cremate their dead."

"You would have had him on a pyre with the soldiers," she pointed out.

"I was angry. Upset and angry," he admitted. "However, given the choice, magicians are not cremated, they are buried."

"For the same reason we bury our dead," Emlyn said. "To rejoin with the forest, with the land of our ancestors and be part of it forever."

"Something like that," Kyron said, caution entering his thoughts. Don't tell her too much, one voice whispered in his ear. She already knows more than you know, another voice whispered in the other ear. Padarn had trusted her, and found her intriguing, though the conversation they were going to have had never happened.

"You know I prefer burial, and I am sure the forest will accept your master into the forever," Emlyn said, her voice soft and measured. "I will help you dig a grave."

"It isn't that." Kyron's voices argued once more, but he silenced them with a shake of his head, decision made. "Magic comes from the little particles of life, the bits that make up our bodies, the air, the trees. If you burn it, you destroy it. Though, some believe they eventually return to us over thousands of years." He paused, shaking off the desire to avoid the conversation by lecturing and explaining. "With burial, the body is decomposed naturally and all the motes, the particles, return more quickly to the world. It propagates the magic, sustains its presence in the world."

"Cremation destroys your magic?"

"Something like that, yes," he said. "I can dig the grave quickly enough, I spent some time creating a spell this afternoon. But I need help laying him in it and covering it."

"You tell me what you need, and I will do it, Kyron," she said, and he wondered if that was the first time she had used his name. "We bury our dead near a favourite tree, or in a sacred grove."

"Padarn wouldn't mind where he was buried," Kyron said, thinking back over his years with his master. The first meeting after the testing, leaving the only home he had known, and putting his trust in a man he had barely met. "I spent years with him in the city, learning and practising. I never realised, I never stopped to think what he had given up to take me on as an apprentice."

"It is a big commitment, to teach another."

"In the Gymnasium there are classes taught to children who would be magicians. There are rooms to board in, to stay in, and timetables of lessons. You can see a different teacher every day, or even one before lunch and a different one after," Kyron said, his gaze fixed on the body of his master. "He never subscribed to that process. Stifled learning and brought everyone to the same level whether they were gifted or not is what he used to say. Experience, practice and creativity. Read all you can. Learn what you can from others but be prepared to try something. If it works, practise and hone it. Advance your skills that way, he said, you can be greater than any magician who has attended a class."

"He sounds wise," Emlyn said. "Our children learn by experience and from everyone as they grow. Each adult has skills different from the other. We encourage our children to take risks, but we watch them all the time, keep them safe."

Kyron nodded. "It wasn't just magic he taught me."

"What else? Tell me," Emlyn encouraged and for a moment he felt her hand grip his before it let go.

"To think." Kyron continued after a moment, hearing the words his master had spoken, in his voice, his cadence and manner. "He always said the skill to think was the most important one, and anyone could learn it. Take the evidence, he said, and inspect it from every angle. Test it, if you can. Form your own opinion but listen to others. Determine your own truth, but rely on the facts, not the bias of your elders."

"Not everyone learns that lesson," Emlyn agreed.

Kyron allowed himself a small, quiet chuckle. "I am still learning."

"The grave?" Emlyn prompted. "Let me pick the location. I know the forests, and it is the least I can do for him."

Kyron felt a lump swell in his throat and could only nod.

"This way." She stepped off the track, ducking under the boughs of a tree coming into bloom. The pines of a few days ago had begun to thin and more of the trees he was used to seeing were appearing. Also, the forest floor had gone from a carpet of sharp needles to an undergrowth of ferns and flowering bushes.

The covering of cloud and lack of moon made following Emlyn difficult. She made little noise as she moved through the leaves, thorns, and vines which tangled his legs and trapped his feet.

Fortunately, she did not travel far and stopped beneath a tree with silver-white bark which rose branchless to a crown which spread wide to encompass the sky above.

"Here," she said. "This tree flowers in the summer and is one you'll find the furthest north and furthest south. It grows anywhere the soil is good enough and the climate fair enough. Its type has seen everything and been everywhere. We call it the First Tree because you can find it most anywhere, even amongst the pines of the north, though there it is shorter. We believe its like was here before all other trees. They grew from it and took over the earth before we arrived."

Kyron put his hand against the tree, feeling the smooth bark and the rough places where it was peeling, and where knots marked branches that had fallen off as it grew.

"Padarn reminds me of this tree," she said. "Not just the silver in his hair, but his view of the world, his love of travel, and finding new knowledge, new experiences."

Kyron smiled, a sad, wan smile. That she had come to know his master so well in such a short pace of time was, he thought, so like him. Anywhere they had been, Padarn had found a way to fit in, to make peace with people and to understand them. Always by his side, Kyron had felt awkward, ungainly, unsure, nervous, and lacking.

"Its roots are deep and spread in all directions, but it does not fight with other trees as some do. No poison in its sap or near its roots," she said pointing to a spot on the ground. "Here."

He nodded once more. "Stand back. I've never tried this before."

"You make him proud once more," she said, stepping away and into the darkness.

Kyron focused on the earth, noting the new growth, the old leaves, and the undulation of the dirt. Taking the marker he had spent some time that afternoon creating, the symbols clear and defined upon its surface, glowing slightly in the darkness, he drew the motes to him. They came from the earth and trees, from the sky, from Emlyn who he felt a few paces away and from himself.

Binding them and shaping them, he linked the motes together with a whisper of words. The shape he held in his mind was simple, uncomplicated, but the release of the spell would change it, contort and twist it in just the right way, he hoped, to accomplish the task. Each mote had to be carefully placed, its connection to another balanced, and the construct held steady until its potential was released.

For a seeming age he moved each mote into position, drew energy from one to another, held the power in check, however only a few heartbeats of time passed. The afternoon spent creating the marker, visualising the construct, and experimenting with aspects of its build had not been time wasted.

He drew a last breath, held it, and pointed the marker at the earth. Speaking a single word, he released the power of the spell and dirt flew into the air. It was no explosion, no demonstration of raw power, no fire directed against the earth. The dark sod rose into the air and sank gently to either side of the dark hole his magic had created.

When it was done, the grave was deep, and each face was sheer, pristine. The most accomplished, most practiced gravedigger could never have produced such a hole.

Without speaking, Emlyn and Kyron recovered Padarn's body from the pyre, laying him on a large square of cloth to be carried to the grave. Taking two corners each, they carefully lowered him until he rested at the bottom.

Kyron stared down at his master and in the grainy vision of the night he would swear the man still breathed. An illusion built from desire, from grief, and one easily dismissed much as he wished it was the truth.

Taking a clump of earth in his hand, he bound more motes to it, activating those that already resided there, commanding them to a purpose and sprinkled them the length of his master's body.

"It is done, Master," he said. "I will try to live up to your teachings, but I am afraid."

"He would not want you to live up to him, but to be your own man," Emlyn said, coming to stand beside him. She bent and picked up her own handful of soil, scattering it over his body. "Keep your wisdom, Padarn, the forest will learn from you and be stronger for it. Life is suffering and death the escape. The memories you leave with us will live forever in the heart of the forest."

Kyron sighed and released the last of the spell. Dirt began tumbling into the hole, covering his master's body in a slowly rising tide of earth.

Within twenty heartbeats it was done and all which remained was a raised area of earth in front of the tree. Kyron found his legs rooted to the dirt, unable to move.

Emlyn however began to walk around the grave, kicking leaves and detritus over it. "To disguise it from others and return the forest to is natural state. He will become part of it."

"He will become part of the magic," Kyron corrected.

"One and the same perhaps," she answered without rancour. "Now, we need to burn the pyre. They expect to see it go up in flames and the embers will answer any questions they might have."

XXXV

The General

Seven years ago:
"What did you think?" he asked of the boy.
"The priest, he spoke a lot about sin and holiness."
"The Holy Flame will cleanse our sins, lad," he explained.
"It sounds painful," the boy said, "and what if I haven't sinned, and what is a sin, and why does the priest get to decide that?"
"Questions are good," he said. "I don't have all the answers."

"You are not the only target," Godewyn said, as he emerged from the cells two hours later.

In the torch light, Aelia's skin paled.

"Who else?" Bordan asked, feeling the weight of the answer in the pit of his stomach.

"The Empress," Godewyn replied in a subdued tone.

"Where is she now?" Bordan snapped at the two guards who had brought the chilled wine. Both looked at him with blank, uncomprehending expressions. "Don't just stand there. You, go and warn her guards. You," pointing to the other guard, "go and find the Spear of the Guard. I want the palace locked down and every door guarded within the hour."

Both men saluted, turned, and raced up the stairs.

"Her rooms," Aelia said into the sudden quiet. "She told me she was going for a rest. That is where she'll be."

Before Bordan could respond, she had leapt from her chair, drawn her sword and clattered up the stairs, following the guards.

Bordan heaved himself from the chair, the wound in his shoulder complaining at the movement, and with Godewyn following, climbed as fast as he could after the Princess.

The first flight of stairs was simple, and Bordan felt younger by decades as he took the second in his stride. The cool air outside the cells had revitalised him, the wine had dulled the pain in his shoulder, and the thought of assassins stalking the Empress gifted him urgency.

Echoes of frantic feet filtered down from above and Bordan pushed his newfound stamina to greater speed. Three, then four flights of stairs passed in a blur. One hand on the wall for balance, he leaned forward into the stairs, keeping one eye on his route and the other on his feet to ensure he did not trip.

Sweat began to bead on his face and the cool air did little to evaporate the moisture which stuck his tunic once more to his back. The air, so refreshing a few flights ago, now burned in his lungs and his knees began to jolt on every step. The vibrations pounded his hips, shook their way up his spine, and made his lungs feel as if they were dangling by a single thread which would snap on the next step.

His toe caught a step and Bordan fell forward. Both hands shot forward and his callused palms protected his face from the worst of the impact. Even so, pain shot up his arms as the stone stairs bit into the flesh and bone.

"Get up," Godewyn's voice called from a lower step.

Bordan looked down and saw the former soldier frowning at him. "I am getting too old for this."

"Very true," Godewyn acknowledged without softening the blow. "This is why you're a General and no longer a soldier. You have men to do this for you."

Bordan huffed and lifted himself from the cold stone, his arms and legs aching. "Go past. I'll catch up at the top."

The last sight of the High Priest was a swish of white robe and the bottom of a leather sandal as he turned at the next landing.

No longer running, Bordan tramped up the steps, stopping on each little landing to catch his breath, while his mind worried at the events occurring above. The Empress would be fine, she had to be. There was so much still to do to secure the throne for her daughter. The palace was considered safe and well-guarded, but if so how did the assassins get in to attack Aelia and kill Alhard? They had to have had help. And he had ordered a doubling of the guard, trusted men only. There was no way any more could get in and certainly not to the Empress.

But what if they did?

The thought set him running again. Each breath a burning poker shoved down his throat into his lungs. He hawked and spat out the boiling phlegm which threatened to clog his airways. Another flight done, another quick rest, and he climbed once more.

Broaching the last stair, stumbling out of the door, he found the palace in a state of confusion. Guards stood with drawn swords and spears readied crowding the corridors he stumbled along. Servants, fearful of getting in the way, hunched in doorways and alcoves. Whispers crept along the hallways, following in his footsteps. Shouted orders drowned out his footsteps and the number of guards increased as he closed in on the imperial quarters.

He noted the change in their expression and slowed. Here, near the centre of the Empire's power, there was quiet and those around spoke in hushed tones. The door to the Empress's chambers was open and voices wafted out, but the blood still pounding in his ears rendered them unintelligible. One hand on the frame, Bordan turned into the room and froze.

In the centre sat Aelia, golden curls covering her face as she looked down into the face cradled upon her lap. To the side was her bloodied gladius and beyond that the dark-clothed body of the assassin. Just behind Aelia lay another body, that of a guard, one Bordan knew and had entrusted the safety of the imperial family to. Godewyn stood, unmoving, and he too looked down at the Empress's pale face.

Her gown, one of deep purple, was rent and torn. The front of it was soaked in blood and the hilt of the assassin's knife jutted from it.

"No," Bordan breathed.

Godewyn looked away from daughter and mother, a gaze filled with sadness. "I arrived too late, General."

"What..." Bordan faltered because the answer was obvious. The lay of the bodies, the bloodied sword, knife, and stench of death told him everything. The assassin had somehow gained entrance to the Empress's room, killing the guard and then, as the Empress came out of her bedroom—the door was open to his right—stabbed her. Aelia had arrived then, or very soon after, and the assassin had been unable to retrieve his knife and fled for the window which looked down the sheer wall of the palace. Before he could reach it, Aelia had cut him down and returned to her mother. A thought struck him. "One of Vedrix's potions?"

Godewyn pointed to the vial by the fallen Empress. "I tried, but it was too late. Death is a kingdom from which no magician may reclaim a soul."

"How many more are there?" Bordan pointed towards the assassin laying near the window. The curtains were thrown back, light spilling across the dark robes from the window.

"The assassin in the cells does not know," Godewyn said. "There could be many more of the Circulus Sicariorum in the castle."

"Are you sure the circle is involved?"

"I can only vouch for the one in the cells, but yes, I believe so," Godewyn replied.

Bordan turned to one of the soldiers by the door. "Seal the palace. No one gets in or out without being vouched for by two people, one of which must be known to a guard. If anyone starts to fuss, send for me, and I will put them right, or into the cells."

"Yes, General," the soldier said.

"And get the Spear of the Guard here now," Bordan snapped.

"The story will get out before the guard reaches the doors," Godewyn pointed out.

"Likely," Bordan agreed, "but I want to sift through every man, woman, and child still in the palace. I want to know they are all our people and we have no one unknown here. After that, I am going to seal the palace. Only those trusted, those with authorisation, will be permitted to enter or leave."

"And the servants?"

"Can sleep here," Bordan grated out between clenched teeth. "Do not go inventing problems now, Godewyn." He began to pace. "We must protect the Princess beyond all others' comfort and position. When it is sealed and safe, I am going to hunt down every last member of the Circulus Sicariorum even if I have to take the city apart stone by stone."

"You may not have to," Godewyn said, but was interrupted by the appearance of a Spear.

"Sir," the Spear said, "you sent for me?"

"I want the palace staff questioned. Every single one from the clerks down to the kitchen scrubbers. I want to know where they were, who they saw, what they did since the Princess and I went to the cells. The moment anything rings untrue, the heartbeat you feel something wrong, lock them up until you can verify their account."

"Sir, that will take an age," the Spear said.

"I do not care," Bordan snapped. "Do as ordered or I will find someone who can, and you can go back to the training ground."

"Yes, sir." The Spear snapped to attention. "You and you," he picked out two soldiers stood on guard in the corridor, "come with me. We are starting with the clerks. Find one who can write a legible hand and we can verify quickly."

The three hurried off, the sound of their sandals and boots fading away.

"What were you going to say?" Bordan said, turning back to the High Priest and the Princess. The young woman had not moved or spoken, just cradled the head of her mother in her lap and let the tears fall across the dead Empress's brow.

Godewyn looked down upon the grief-stricken Princess and nodded towards the corner of the room. Bordan followed him there.

"What else do you know?" Bordan whispered.

"We will have to watch the Princess most carefully," Godewyn replied, whispering also. "So much tragedy in such a short time will be difficult for her."

"It was already difficult, but she is the heir to the Empire," Bordan said. "She will survive and be stronger for it. Power weighs heavy on young shoulders, but she has the strength to bear the grief alongside it."

"I hope you are correct," Godewyn said. "However, the assassin knew his employer."

"What?" Bordan blurted out, the single word a shout in the quiet room. He glanced at Aelia who had not moved in response or given any indication she had heard. Bordan lowered his voice once more. "He said he had never met his employer or knew of him."

"He lied to your man," Godewyn said. "My inquisitor was very thorough. Our assassin did not lie when he said that he had never met the man who took out the contracts. However, he was a cautious assassin, cheated by employers before he said, so he asked around, sought out answers, and put gossip together. I see no reason to doubt his final conclusions. As I say, Zonara was very thorough."

"Who paid them?"

"Duke Abra."

"Abra?" Again the word came out as a shout.

This time Aelia did turn and look up at the General. Her eyes were hollow, and the madness of grief swirled in them. Tears fell, tracking down her cheeks and dripped from her chin. "What of Abra?"

Bordan swallowed, biting down his own bubbling anger and rage. "It appears it is he who hired the assassins, Your Highness?"

"Abra?" The Princess's voice shook, disbelief, grief, and now a sharp barb of anger.

"Cohort!" Bordan called across the room and another soldier entered, saluting smartly even as his face paled at the sight before him. "Send troops to secure Duke Abra. His home, office, business, street. I don't care where he is, I want him in chains before the sun sets tonight. Sweep the city for him if you need and there is no need to be gentle."

"Sir?"

"Now, Cohort," Bordan barked.

"You cannot just arrest a Duke of the Empire, Bordan," Godewyn pointed out in an infuriatingly calm manner.

"Watch me," Bordan replied.

"Bring me the warrant, General. I'll sign it," Aelia spat as anger won the battle for her voice. "And I'll see him hung on a cross before the city gates so everyone can see, then I'll personally tear him down, cut open his belly and set a cage of starving rats upon him. The whole city will hear his cries for the mercy of death."

XXXVI

The Magician

Six years ago:

The new tunic was rough around his neck, scratching and irritating his skin.

"I don't understand why I have to wear this," he complained.

"Because we have an important guest for dinner," the old man said, his own tunic freshly cleaned. "Now, stop fussing with it and, please, tonight, try to be polite."

"I DEMAND TO accompany them." The Curate's shrill voice pierced the chill air of morning. Overnight, as the pyres burned down, a wind had come from the north bringing cold air and the promise of rain. The trees rustled and branches creaked, but they protected the army from the worst of the weather.

Kyron sat around the command fire, huddled in his cloak, still wearing the gladius on his hip, although the lorica hamata had been handed back to the armourer for repair. He cupped the warm tea in his hands and sipped at it without tasting. The cook, Tatian, sat on his haunches stirring a pot of porridge.

Astentius peered at the priest over the rim of his own cup. "You demand?"

"I am the ranking priest," she said, puffing out her chest and straightening her shoulders, "and I do not trust a magician or our guide to work in our best interests."

"And Borus will go with them, as will two soldiers," Astentius explained. "It really is too early in the morning for a repeat of such arguments, Curate Livillia."

"The tribes are heathens, pagans," she continued. "It is the duty of the priesthood to convert all such to the true Flame."

"They don't want converting," Emlyn pointed out.

"It is not their choice to make, guide," Livillia spat.

"It should be," Emlyn responded. In her hands, her knife flicked another sliver of wood from the piece she was whittling. It sailed through the air and landed on the Curate's lap.

"Spear," Livillia complained, pointing towards Emlyn, "why is the tribeswoman allowed a weapon in camp? I demand she be stripped of all weapons and armour."

Kyron shrank in his seat and sipped once more at the tasteless tea.

"There you go again, Curate, demanding. This is not how the army operates. We have a strict hierarchy and I sit at the top of it," Astentius said, his earlier friendly tone developing a layer of frost. "The decision has been made and you will not be going into the village. You heard, I'm sure, our guide's summation of the situation regarding priests and the tribes. Were I to send you in, I would be sending you to your death, and worse still, ensuring that we could do no trade with the tribes hereabouts. We need supplies. We need food."

Livillia drew herself up even higher, a pose Kyron thought must have been painful. "I will complain to your superiors."

"When we get back safely," Astentius replied, turning and looking down the trail for a moment before rolling his eyes, "feel free to do so. However, for the last time, while you are in this camp, with this army, you will cease demanding things of me and comport yourself as the ranking priest. Look after my soldier's immortal flames but stay out of my decisions. You are here as a courtesy and to ensure the safe return of the Emperor to the capital."

"I will not stand for this treatment of the Church," Livillia said.

"You will," Astentius replied, looking into the fire, "or I will find a priest amongst those few left and promote them. It is a wide forest, Curate, with many dangers, and you would do well to remember that the army protects you at all times. Now, Tatian, is that porridge ready?"

"Yes, Spear," the cook replied, spooning the thick white paste of oats and water into a clay bowl and handing it to the Spear. "Be careful. It is hot."

"Thank you," Astentius said. "Please, the rest of you, eat. It has been a busy few days and you need food. If Borus cannot negotiate a deal with the village, we will all go hungry soon enough."

"You threatened me," Livillia finally managed to splutter.

"I offered you some porridge, Curate," Astentius answered. "I am always alert to the needs of the Church, and to that of those under my command."

Kyron accepted the bowl from Tatian and noted the smirk upon the cook's face. It vanished when Tatian noticed him watching.

"Good fortune today, magician," Tatian said. "We need supplies. I'd best go see to my men. With your leave, Spear."

"How far would you say the village is from here?" Astentius asked, as the cook stood and left the circle.

"Half a day's walk," Emlyn answered. "My pace of walking that is, not the army. We will likely spend the night there. It is customary."

"And we will be there in the morning?" Astentius asked.

"If you keep to your current pace," Emlyn replied.

"All the wards and other magic," Astentius continued, turning to Kyron and raising an eyebrow, "are in place and secure?"

"Yes, Spear," Kyron replied. "I renewed the markers this morning. They will last a tenday at least."

"And this village had no part in the attack on us?" Astentius asked, his gaze flicking to Emlyn.

"A warrior or two perhaps," she replied, "but no more than that. Likely none."

"And the track will be safe?"

"I cannot guarantee anything. However, it should be," she answered. "I've no wish to starve alongside your army."

"Why not just run away?" Curate Livillia chimed in, her voice full of poison.

"Because I cannot just 'run away'," Emlyn said. "I made a bargain with your Legion, and unlike priests, my word means something."

Kyron saw Livillia draw in a breath to retort, but a cold look from the Spear stilled the words in her throat.

"Excellent," Astentius said. "I have provided Borus with a sample of our trade goods, and enough coin to be taken seriously. We need that food. I cannot impress upon any of you the importance of this. We still have a distance to travel and we are slower than before. Though we have fewer to feed, the amount of supplies we lost in the battle is serious. Make the best deal you can, but do not be afraid to lose out on the bargain. Money and possessions are not as important as completing the mission."

When no one responded, the Spear nodded. "Good. Eat your fill and set out as soon as you are ready. Borus, you've selected your soldiers?"

"Yes, Spear," Borus answered. "Two trustworthy men, good fighters."

"I do not want any fights, Cohort." Astentius raised a warning finger. "However, I would like you back safe and with a bargain sealed."

"It will be done, Spear," Borus assured.

Kyron gulped down another spoonful of hot porridge. The walk did not thrill him, but the chance to be away from the priests, Livillia especially, was a welcome one.

Across the fire, Emlyn whittled another sliver of wood.

IT FELT STRANGE to be walking the forest tracks in such a small group. Every shadow, every rustle of leaves in the wind was a tribesman with a bow.

"How can you stand it?" he whispered to Emlyn as they walked. Borus and the two soldiers followed behind, all three dressed in lorica segmata, armed with a gladius, but their shields left behind with the remains of the army.

"What?" She stepped around a bramble which had grown onto the trail.

"All of this." He waved at the trees which towered over him, shading the light from the cloud covered sky.

"Your buildings, in your city, are high and block out the light?"

"Well, yes, I suppose so, but we have streets we can walk down without having to step around plants and puddles full of mud."

"Your streets are empty?" She paused to pick up a small fallen branch, inspect it from all sides and discard it once more.

"Of course not," he scoffed.

"Then how different are the forest tracks?" she said. "I've never been to your city, but I've listened to your soldiers talk in camp. They make it sound dirty, with rubbish piled in corners, loud with thousands of people talking and shouting all at once, and dangerous. You have to employ people to patrol the streets to keep people safe?"

He felt the sting of her words and struggled to find the answer to her question. "We have theatres, the Colosseum where the games take place, restaurants to eat in, shops to buy clothes, squares to meet in on hot summer days."

"And everywhere you go, you're being watched by those guards?" She reached over her shoulder, gathering her hair and tying it into a ponytail. "There is none of that here. Here, there is freedom. Pick a direction and go that way, nothing and no one will stop you."

"Borus and the soldiers will," he pointed out, regretting the words as they left his mouth.

She turned a sour look upon him and drew one of the whittling sticks from her belt. "I know."

"I'm sorry," he offered.

"It isn't your fault." She unsheathed her knife and began stripping the bark from the stick.

"Why did you come with us?"

"You heard the Legion, he has assurances."

He recognised the venom in her low voice and winced a little, glad it was not aimed at him. "But what does that mean?"

"You don't know?" A sliver of bark flew from the stick, spiralling through the cool air to come to rest on the leaves of a fern which peeked out onto the trail.

"No," he said. "I never asked. Should I have?"

"I did wonder." Her knife flicked again. "I did consider that you were just being polite by not asking or talking about it. But now you've asked, I realise it was just ignorance."

"That's not fair," he protested.

"Fair?" A thick chunk of the stick went flying and she grunted in frustration. "What about this is fair, Kyron? Is it fair that I am taken away from my people? Fair that your people have decided you need to rule the world, own more land and take that from people that have lived here forever?"

"We're bringing peace and civilisation," he answered, though visions of death and smoking pyres clouded his mind.

"Civilisation just means a way of living," she replied, her knife moving smoothly along the wood, "and we have that. One of our own, not yours. And how do you bring peace? At the tip of a sword or javelin."

"But the Empire has culture."

"Theatres to tell your stories in?"

"Yes, and plays written by the best playwrights in the world," he said, some pride entering his voice and a memory of being taken to see a drama where all the players wore masks. He could not remember the story, but the majesty of the event, of the building, had awed him.

"We have our own stories," she answered. "The Colosseum where your precious games take place?"

"I've been to the chariot racing there," he said. "It was incredible, exciting."

"And the other games?" Her knife gouged into the wood, freeing a triangular sliver which she discarded. "The gladiators? The fights against animals and the slaughter of those who disagree with your Emperor or Church."

"There have not been those for decades," he said.

"Gladiators?"

"Well, there are still those fights, but they are trained and know what they are getting into," he answered.

"They fight to be free," she answered. "A lot of them are slaves, are they not?"

"Slavery was outlawed a long time ago," he shot back.

"Then they are prisoners?"

"Some of them," he admitted, "but most are professionals. It is their job."

"To end up dead, gutted and bleeding out on the sand for the amusement of others," she answered before he could continue. "You call that civilisation? It is barbarism."

Kyron could find no words, no answer to the accusation. In truth, his one visit to the games, with his grandfather, had been enough. He could see little from the stall they sat in, but his imagination filled in the gaps with more than enough blood. The gladiator, wearing greaves and a manica to protect his sword arm, who lay dead on the floor looked so small and it brought back memories of the raid on his village, the death of his parents.

"Why did you come, agree to guide the Empire you dislike so much?"

"I told you, your Legion had assurances," she said, glancing over her shoulder to see the three soldiers trailing them.

Kyron followed her gaze before turning back to her. "That is not an answer."

"What do you want me to tell you, Kyron?" Another sliver of wood flew from the stick in her hands. "You believe your Empire to be just and good, to be the right way to live, to be based upon peace, a fair society. What will you listen to?"

"My master..." he started, but was forced to stop and swallow the sudden ball of grief which blocked his throat. "My master taught me to listen to everyone, but to make up my own mind."

"I can see that he would, but teaching and learning are two different things," Emlyn said, stepping across a depression full of muddy water.

"Is all this a long-winded way to say you are not going to tell me?"

He heard her sigh and the knife stopped moving against the wood in her hand.

"Your Legion has my parents," she said in a quiet whisper which he had to strain to hear. "If the honour guard reaches the Empire safely, they will be released. If not, they will be executed."

"Why didn't you tell me?" Kyron hurried a step or two to bring himself alongside her.

"You didn't ask. Padarn knew. He asked me one evening while you were recharging the magic on the Emperor's funeral waggon," she said, resuming the whittling of the stick. "Borus knows, as does Astentius, and I'm sure any number of soldiers. You've never asked, listened or looked further than the end of your nose.

"The world is changing, Kyron, your world especially. So now that you are on your own, start to see how it really is, not how you childishly wish it to be."

XXXVII

THE GENERAL

Six years ago:

"It is good to see you, my old friend," he said as the newly raised High Priest stepped down from his carriage.

"A wet night," the High Priest said, glancing up at the dark clouds.

"Come in, I have food and wine," he said. "You can relax this evening, we both can. The troubles of the Empire can wait till tomorrow."

"That would be very welcome," the High Priest replied with a smile. "And who is the strapping lad next to you?"

"Reports from the west quarter, General," the clerk said, handing over the bound scroll and retreating from the room.

Bordan unfurled the scroll. His eyes scanned the lines of neat script written in the way only a true soldier could. It was short, to the point, and frustrating. Bordan found his hands crushing the scroll and forced himself to calm.

It was to be expected, and the expected was to be cherished by a wise commander as only the unexpected could ever lead to defeat. The saying, from an old manual on military tactics he had once read, had served him well down the years. Re-rolling the scroll and tying the ribbon about it, he placed it to the side.

After dipping the stylus into the pot of ink which sat upon the desk far enough away from his elbows that he had to stretch to reach

271

it and holding the writing implement carefully above the map on his desk, he paused, looking at the roads, streets, and lanes which marked out the different quarters of the city. In the centre was the palace, and from it a spider's web of threads connecting it to every part of its domain. There should have been some trembles along those narrow strands, something to indicate where Abra had gone to ground. Nothing.

With a sigh, he marked off the roads and buildings searched as detailed in the scroll. Each mark he added whittled down the potential hiding spots of the treasonous Duke. The city was in lockdown, the gates guarded most closely, and everyone and everything going in and out of them was searched thoroughly.

A boat, or rather a ship, he corrected, was a likely mode of exit for the Duke of the water, but those too were searched and only three had left the city in the past two days. The sailors were unhappy, and the City Watch had called upon soldiers to assist in policing the dock's inns and taverns during the nights. The cells were overflowing by sunrise and the morning tide of sailors returning to their impounded ships was rising every day.

"You have to be somewhere," Bordan muttered at the map as he finished his marks. "You could not get out on your own, and whenever you rely on others there is always a weak link in the chain."

Pushing his chair back, Bordan crossed his office to the low table upon which refreshments had been laid by his secretary. How long ago he could not say. Condensation still beaded on the terra sigillata jug and pot. A small tower of cut fruit rested on a low, wide platter and there was only a touch of brown on the white flesh.

Lifting the jug of wine, he poured a measure into a goblet and added water to it. Swirling the goblet in his hand he mixed the liquid and gazing down into the mirrored surface, saw the lines which spread like bird's feet from the corner of his eyes come into focus. His hair was grey and the stare which transfixed him was one of exhaustion and fear.

He shook his head, dispelling the image of age and defeat, lifted the goblet and drank it all down in a few large gulps.

Picking the least spoiled piece of fruit, he held it up to his eyes. The flesh was firm, strong, and pure white, an echo of the Empire around him. On the edges though, where the Empire met the other lands, brown spots of corruption had set in and were slowly expanding their influence across the fruit, the land.

"Immunis!" he shouted, dropping the fruit back to the table where it bounced from one cut slice to another before cartwheeling off the surface and onto the floor.

"Sir?" His secretary opened the door and stepped in.

"He had help," Bordan said. "He must have done."

"Duke Abra, sir?"

"Of course, Duke Abra," the General said, stomping back over to the map. "Who helped him?"

"I do not know, General," the Immunis answered, stepping into the room and closing the door. "You believe the answer to be on the map?"

"Staring us in the face," Bordan said, slapping his hand down upon the desk. The strike hurt his palm, little needles of pain ricocheting up his arm bone and spiking into his skull. It was inconsequential, a moment of punishment thoroughly deserved. "We assumed it was the gangs and criminals, or the merchants who would help him. All are well-versed in smuggling, in hiding people, bypassing our customs agents. Who better?"

"Indeed, General," the Immunis said, a hesitant cautious cadence to his words. "That does make a good deal of sense."

"We were wrong," Bordan said. "Corruption in plain sight is often a distraction, or a sign that you have acted too late. It is the hidden decay that rots from the inside which we miss and holds more danger."

"General?"

"The other Dukes and nobles, Immunis," Bordan looked up from the map. "They have the wealth, the people, and the resources to hide him or get him out of the city."

"Who though, General?" the Immunis ventured. "Forgive me, but it would not be wise to antagonise them all by casting allegations without evidence."

Bordan caught the rush of swear words, phrases learned on the training yard and left in the ranks, before they fell from his mouth like molten rock from the fire mountains which dripped into the sea raising a screen of mist and the hiss of a thousand furious snakes. "I want to stir the hornet's nest until the one I am looking for tries to fly away. Find Legion Maxentius. Tell him I need to see him right away."

"Yes, General." The secretary was through the door before the last syllable had dropped from his mouth.

Bordan stared at the map again, tracing his finger across the homes, streets, docks, and businesses, fighting the urge to ball it in his fists and throw it against the wall. "Stupid. So stupid."

He paced. The walls of his office had never seemed so close, so restrictive. Lost in his thoughts, the knock at the door and its subsequent opening was almost lost on him.

"General."

"Maxentius," Bordan greeted, choking down his anger. "I've been stupid and missed what was before our face since this began."

"Your secretary informed me you wished to see me?" the Legion said, his voice calm as he moved across the room to look down at the map.

"We have a problem which will need a quick solution," Bordan said, taking a breath and meeting the other man's eyes. "I suspect other members of the Ruling Council will be assisting Abra to leave the city."

"The Ruling Council?" Maxentius's eyes widened.

"Suspect only. Though proof will not be hard to find now that we know where to look."

"What do you want to do, General?"

Now Bordan paused, glancing once more at the map. "Draw back half the forces searching in each area. Form four cohorts and ensure they are ready for deployment tomorrow morning at the latest. Who is the most senior officer we have as yet unassigned?"

"Spear Ecdicius," Maxentius said without a pause. "He was wounded in the recent action against the criminal gangs."

"He is fit again?"

"Fit to command, if not fight, General," the Legion said, his eyes looking up to the ceiling for a moment before he added, "a broken arm, if I recall."

"Draft orders, put him in command of the new cohorts," Bordan said. "I will give him the target list and order of arrest in the morning."

"I'll get that done, General," Maxentius agreed. "What are you thinking?"

"That we need more wine and fresh fruit," Bordan said, his gaze sliding to the platter, "but do not have it peeled. I want it be whole and unsullied."

"YOU'VE GONE TOO far, General," Aelia shouted as she entered the council, slamming the door behind her.

Bordan caught a quick glimpse of the two guards he had assigned to protect the Princess before the carved wood cut them off from their charge.

"You are unhappy, Your Highness?" Bordan said as he stood and bowed. The other occupants—Godewyn, a nervous-looking Master Vedrix, Duke Flaccus, a man of few words and fewer thoughts, and Duke Gellius, from an old merchant family who were raised to nobility by the Princess's father—stood also, but held their tongues.

"Unhappy?" Aelia scoffed, dragging her heavy chair back with one hand. "More than that, General. I've had petition after petition sent to me this past day. A queue of nobles, landowners, and merchants demanding to see me. All of them to complain about you."

"I understand," Bordan nodded, clasping his hands behind his back to keep them still.

"Understand?" Aelia stopped in the act of sitting down. "You *understand*? And yet you have sent troops into their homes. Asked questions of their loyalty. Interrogated their servants. Searched their belongings. Demanded information of their spending and savings."

"I have done those things," Bordan said, remaining upright, as did all in the room.

"You counselled my mother about arresting the nobles," Aelia accused. "Said they would cause problems for the army, for our security."

"Yes, Your Highness," Bordan nodded.

"I believe I signed an order for Abra's arrest only. Well?" the Princess snapped, finally falling into the waiting chair, the one her father had sat in last. It was a gesture not lost on Bordan, and a gasp sounded from his right. Aelia's gaze moved languidly from Bordan's to the source of the sound. "You disapprove of my seat, Duke Flaccus?"

"No, Your Highness," Flaccus stuttered.

"You think someone else should be sat here?" Aelia leaned forward, her eyes taking on the aspect of a hawk, narrow, piercing, hunting.

"No... no, Your Highness," Flaccus answered, hurried and unsure.

"There's your traitor, General." Aelia pointed to the elderly Duke who began to shake. "All of your investigations, your assaults on the nobility, and I unmask him in moments."

"Your Highness," Flaccus said, stumbling over his words and putting out a frail hand to the table to support him on suddenly weak knees.

"Sit down, Flaccus," Aelia snapped, pushing herself back into the Emperor's chair. "You're too useless, too old, too scared to be a traitor."

"And too loyal," Bordan added, as the old Duke's legs gave way and he fell into his chair.

"That too," Aelia allowed, waving her hand in a gesture of dismissal. The red flush of anger which had warmed the Princess's face faded and Bordan watched her take a long, slow breath. "So, General, explain yourself. What have you done? Tell me why I should not give into the demands of the nobles to have you crucified on the hill outside the gates."

"We found Duke Abra."

The words fell into the silence of the chamber and triumph, anger, and eagerness rippled across the Princess's face.

"You have him?" Aelia shot upright in her chair, one hand stretched across the table, palm up, fingers clawed, grasping towards Bordan.

"With regret, no," Bordan admitted. "However, we know where he is, where he is going, and who aided him."

"How? Who? Where?" The questions dripped from Aelia's mouth like acid and burned their way across the air to Bordan's ears.

"With your permission," Bordan asked and Aelia nodded with something like lust swimming in her eyes. The General took a breath and called, "Bring him in."

The doors to the chamber opened and two guards carried in a broken man. It was clear from the way in which they grasped his arms, the blood which crusted his face, the black bruises which surrounded his eyes, and his hunched shoulders which struggled to support the weight of his head, what he had been subjected to.

"Who is this... creature?" Aelia asked, puzzled.

"Duke Primal, Your Highness," Bordan answered to a shocked hush from the other members of the council sat at the table.

"He knows where Abra is?"

"Your Highness," Bordan began, letting some confidence fill his heart and voice, "Primal was instrumental in assisting the Duke with his escape from the city."

"Traitor!" Aelia roared, her hand slamming down upon the table, rattling the cups and jugs which lay atop, spilling wine from more than one goblet.

"Lady Trenis is with Abra, Princess Aelia," Bordan added. "I believe we have identified the major players in the plot which has led to the death of your mother and brother."

Aelia rose from the Emperor's chair, her bronze armour golden in the light spilling in through the window, and, her hand on her sword, stalked up to Primal and the guards.

"Where are the traitors, Primal?" the Princess snarled.

"I didn't..." the Duke tried to say. When the man's mouth opened, Bordan could see the broken teeth and the gaps where others had been yanked from the man's jaw. "Didn't know."

"Liar!" Aelia screamed into the man's face, her voice cracking as she drew the word out.

"He may be telling the truth," Godewyn said, his voice quiet but carrying the length of the table. "He may not be aware of Abra's actions towards your family, Your Highness."

"He helped him escape," Aelia said, rounding on the High Priest, flecks of white spit arcing from her mouth.

"Of that there is no doubt, Your Highness," Godewyn acknowledged with a bow of his head. "However, both the Carnificina and my own Inquisitors put him to the question. We have checked and rechecked his story. He was aware that Abra was in trouble, but not the precise nature."

"He helped him escape from my justice," Aelia growled. "That is treason, and there can be no excuse."

"I merely point out that he was unaware of the crime which Abra had committed, not that Primal is innocent of his own crimes," Godewyn said.

"Priests," Aelia said, her lip curling, "always correcting, always lecturing."

"As you say, Princess Aelia," Godewyn allowed. "However, in this case the distinction is important. Primal assisted Abra escaping the city. He has confessed to that. Abra himself told Primal that his life was in danger from assassins."

"Now you jest," Aelia replied.

"No, Your Highness," Bordan answered, sharing a glance with Godewyn. "Abra had been speaking to Primal over some weeks, telling him that his life was in danger. Indeed, Abra has borrowed a large sum, on the surety of the merchant fleet, from Duke Primal."

"What for?" Aelia rounded on the broken Duke. "What did he want the money for? To hire more assassins? You paid those creatures to kill my brother and mother?"

"No... Pr... protection," Primal stuttered, still hanging between the guards, and broke off into a coughing fit.

"Primal believes his money was spent hiring guards to protect Abra's holdings in the city, around the ports and in the north," Bordan said, looking away from the wreck of a man who had once sat on the council.

"You haven't finished, General," Aelia realised, her eyes narrowing.

"No, Your Highness." Bordan nodded and took a deep breath. "We believe, the clerks having reviewed Abra's and Primal's accounts, that the money has been spent hiring mercenaries."

"Is that not what Primal said?" Aelia's face wore a puzzled expression.

"Somewhat," Bordan replied. "However, tracking the payments and collating information from my own resources, the Church, and Master Vedrix's more esoteric avenues, we believe that the hired troops are concentrated on the northern plains, even as far as the city of Cesena on the border."

"Seal the city off," Aelia demanded without a pause. "Have our soldiers take Abra into custody and drag him back here."

"I have issued orders," Bordan said carefully. "However, Vedrix's sources report that the garrison which protects the bridge across the river there is outnumbered."

"What?" Aelia turned on Bordan. "Why? Is not Cesena our most northern outpost? Our guard against the tribes of the north?"

"And with our army in the far north," Bordan said, "those left behind to guard the bridge are the very young or the very old. The militia have bolstered their number, per your father's orders as he left on campaign, with retired soldiers. Even so, the garrison is weakened and less numerous."

"They cannot take Abra into custody," Godewyn added. "Not without entering into conflict with Abra's own troops."

"And that may lead to widespread alarm and destruction in the city itself," Bordan added.

"Cesena," Aelia muttered. "I know the name. I know that place. You have mentioned it before. Where is the map? I need a map."

"We will have one brought," Bordan said, nodding to one of the guards who held Primal. "However, Cesena is the crossing over the River Abhainn."

"Is that on the route my father's body will take?"

"It is, Princess," Bordan agreed. "We had planned to bolster those numbers with troops from the Third Army. The trouble in the countryside and our concerns in the city delayed those plans."

"Get word to them, to the honour guard," Aelia ordered. "We cannot lose my father's body to Abra. I must be Emperor."

"We are commandeering ships, though the fleet is depleted. It appears Abra had ordered many to the southern continent on trade missions, to take the message," Bordan replied. "Messengers will ride with all speed to find the honour guard. Though, I must warn you, Your Highness, it may not be in time."

"Send more riders. Give them orders to be resupplied with fresh horses on every stop," Aelia said, a pleading look entering her eyes.

"They will likely be stopped at Cesena or picked up by Abra's troops," Godewyn said. "It is likely, and appears from the records, that Abra has been building up mercenaries and others in the north ever since your father's untimely passing."

"However, we have already sent riders with such orders," Bordan replied. "We will not let your father's body fall into Abra's hands."

"And you didn't know? The General with all his talk of spies in households," Aelia accused. "Where was the information when we needed it."

Bordan took a breath, stilling his heart and dampening his own anger. "I failed there, Your Highness. Every precaution was taken, but Abra appears to have been much cleverer than I gave him credit for."

"I do not think it is prudent to lay the blame at anyone's feet. Princess Aelia," Godewyn said, stepping forward. "What matters now is your father's body and whatever Abra has planned."

"I'll not forget," Aelia said, her voice sullen but untouched by anger. The Princess leaned forward, placing her hands flat upon the table and bowed her head before jerking up and turning a gaze filled with hope towards the magician. "Vedrix, you can contact the magicians with the honour guard? We don't need the riders and the ships. This is why my father protected your Gymnasium, to serve the Empire."

"Ah, well, Your Highness," Vedrix bumbled for a moment, "we have tried to contact Master Padarn—he is the magician accompanying the honour guard."

"Tried means failed," Aelia snapped.

"Yes, Your Highness," Vedrix answered. "The last contact we had mentioned some of the tribes were intending to attack the guard. A small number only, not enough to pose a risk to the guard itself. Since then, we have heard nothing and cannot re-establish contact. We believe, that is to say, our best information is, that Master Padarn is no longer with us."

"He has become a traitor?" Aelia's body went stiff, and Bordan saw the young woman's hands clench into fists.

"He is dead," the General said. "Killed in the skirmish. There is, I understand," Bordan swallowed, "an apprentice with the honour guard."

Vedrix nodded. "There is, a young man named Kyron. However, whilst we believe him to be alive, he has not had the training necessary to speak to us across such distance."

"Mobilise our troops, General," Aelia said, swinging her gaze back to the old soldier. "We are riding for Cesena and the bridge. I will not allow a city to fall to mercenaries or my father's body to be desecrated by Abra."

"They are gathering as we speak, Your Highness. Provisions are being sought, and ships commandeered," Bordan answered. "We will be ready to leave in two days."

"One day, General," Aelia snapped.

"If we leave the supplies behind," Bordan replied, "however, I would not advise such an action. We may face a siege or a protracted battle."

"I do not care," Aelia commanded, her tone cold and final. "We leave tomorrow. The supplies can be brought up to us the day after. We cannot allow my father's body to fall to Abra."

Bordan swallowed his reply and settled for a bow. "Of course, Your Highness. And what of Duke Primal?"

Aelia turned slowly to face the Duke. "Crucify him on the hill. I want the people to see what becomes of those who stand against me. I want them to see his tears and witness the fate of all traitors."

"No..." Primal wheezed. "My Princess... I did not know... I..."

"Take him away," Aelia waved to the guard and focused upon Bordan. "One day, General. No longer. We ride to save the city and the Empire."

"Yes, Your Highness," Bordan said, his shoulders feeling the weight of every year, of every battle ever fought, and every death. Now even more would contribute to the bowing of his back, the pain he felt upon rising, to the guilt which encircled his heart.

XXXVIII

THE MAGICIAN

Six years ago:

"He doesn't seem to be like the other priests," he said, watching the carriage vanish into the rain and dark.

"The Church is in good hands there," the old man said. "He was a soldier once, one of my best officers."

"Why did he leave?"

"The Holy Flame called him to service, lad," the old man said, looking down at him. "Service and duty are the bedrock of the Empire. Never forget that."

THEY HAD LEFT the main track south long ago, and without the sun to gauge the time, Kyron was worried they had walked forever. Perhaps Emlyn was taking them to a place they could be ambushed, captured, tortured, and killed. He shook off the sour mood and bitter thoughts. She had her parents to consider and had shown no desire to betray them before.

"How much further?"

"Not too far," she answered. "The markers have been consistent, and the track is well used."

"Markers?" Borus asked from behind.

"The signs the tribes use to give directions," Emlyn replied, not turning. "As you've no doubt realised, you can't see very far in the forest and unless you know the tricks of surviving out here it is easy to get lost. So, we use markers to help us navigate."

"I've not seen any signs," Kyron said, scanning the trees around him.

"And you won't," she said. "That's the point. They are for us, not you."

"Can you teach us to read them?"

"No. Even if I could, even if I wanted to, it wouldn't help," she answered.

"Why not? If I could read them, I would know where I was going and how to get there?"

"Because you would have to learn a new language," Emlyn replied, following the trail around a corner, "and some of them are lies."

"Lies?"

"In case someone who wasn't of the tribes ever learned the language, we put in traps to catch them out." There was a matter of factness about her tone which made him believe the traps were a more serious threat than just being sent in the wrong direction. "Borus, keep your men's hands away from their weapons from now on."

"Why?"

Kyron looked back to see the three soldiers looking confused.

"Because we are being watched and you are from the Empire. I suspect a few of the watchers would like an excuse to put an arrow through one of them," she answered. There was a loud chuckle from amongst the trees and a startled gasp from the soldiers. "You too, Kyron. Don't even think of drawing that sword."

"I won't," he promised, peering intently into the shadows beneath the trees.

"You won't see them unless they want you to," she said without pausing in her steps. "You'll just strain your eyes."

Sweat trickled down Kyron's back as he followed her down the trail. Every second he expected an arrow to sail out of the leaves and strike him down, just as one had Padarn. The cold wind which had picked up just yesterday had grown in strength and even sheltered by the trees, it chilled him.

"Just ahead," Emlyn said, pointing to a gate that Kyron would have sworn was not there a moment ago, so carefully constructed and camouflaged against the trees that it had seemed part of the forest.

"Borus, it will be better if you let me do the greetings. They'll know who you are and why you're here, but there are some formalities."

"Will this village have contributed to the army that faced us?" Borus said.

"One or two, maybe," she replied. "If you don't want to come in, you can stay by the gate. However, if you are permitted entrance you are safe. We have traditions and rules about how we treat guests."

"Murder them in their sleep?" Borus asked.

"Only those who insult us," Emlyn answered. "The village isn't one the Empire merchants visit often, but trade is still important. You'll be safe as long as you don't do anything stupid and insulting."

"We can be polite," Borus said.

"Good."

The gate grew as they walked until it towered over Kyron, forcing him to crane his neck to see the top. He looked left and right, noting the fence and palisade of sharpened logs that vanished into the trees.

"Well protected," Borus said.

"It isn't just the Empire we fight," Emlyn said, stopping a few paces from the gate.

"Oh," Borus asked. "Who else?"

"Other tribes, mostly," she answered with a shrug.

The gates swung open to reveal three warriors dressed in the same clothing Kyron had seen at the battle, though the blue woad was missing from their faces. Just behind stood three more people, two men and a tall woman with red hair caught up in a ponytail.

Emlyn raised an open palm and called out in the language of the tribes. Kyron held his breath, hoping that she was greeting them and not asking for them all to be killed so she could escape, head back north and free her parents.

He stayed silent as the conversation continued, aware of the weight of the sword on his hip. As precaution he began to draw in the motes of magic from his surroundings, unsure of the most appropriate construct but holding them close just in case.

Emlyn glanced over her shoulder and narrowed her eyes before turning back and speaking loudly to the villagers. There was a laugh from the group behind the warriors and the tension eased from the confrontation.

Kyron sagged, releasing the magic, as the warriors parted and the unarmed villagers behind beckoned Emlyn and Kyron's party into the village.

"They've named you guests," Emlyn said, turning on them all with a sudden vehemence in her voice. "Don't do anything to ruin that, I've vouched for you all and it would be my duty to mete out the punishment if you mess up. You carry your own lives and those of my parents on your good behaviour from this moment until we leave. You had best believe I will not do anything to risk their lives."

Kyron gulped at the fire in her eyes and the determination in her words. His feet felt like heavy lumps of stone as he stepped forward to greet the villagers.

"Chief Doirean," Emlyn spoke with the tall woman in the centre of the three, "may I present, Cohort Borus, Foot Noster and Foot Esdras, of the Empire's army."

"You are welcome in the village as our guests," the chief said in a voice deeper and warmer than Kyron had expected. "And this young man?"

"Apprentice Magician Kyron," Emlyn said.

"You have our welcome too, young man," the chief said. "We have met a few of your magicians before. They come to study the tribes, our ways, and have always been gracious in the past. I trust that will not change."

"No, your..." He looked to Emlyn for assistance.

"Chief Doirean," she supplied.

"No, Chief Doirean," Kyron said. "My master told me he had travelled the forests to learn of them."

"A wise man, your master, for life is about learning. The moment we no longer seek new knowledge, we stop living and contributing to our communities," Doirean replied with a smile. "Perhaps, Emlyn will take you to meet our priests and you can continue your master's lessons."

"I would like that, Chief Doirean," he replied, sketching a small bow to cover the disappointment on his face. Spending the afternoon talking to old men and women about religion was the last thing he wanted, but then again discussing the price of flour and meat would not be the most exciting way to spend his time.

"Excellent," she said, clapping her hands. "Cohort Borus, if you and your men would follow me. I speak your tongue well enough to discuss trade, as do some others in the village."

"You speak it much better than I speak the language of the tribes," Borus replied.

"We felt it an advantage to learn. It prevented any misunderstandings on the price of certain goods." She smiled again. "Some merchants were not, we discovered, as entirely honest as we first thought them to be."

"It is a skill and a fault they learn all too easily, Chief Doirean."

"Indeed. Emlyn, take young Kyron to the priests. I fear you will need to stay and translate some of what they speak of," Doirean said. "You may also find their counsel reassuring given your predicament."

"Thank you," Emlyn said. "Come on, Kyron."

He stood still for a moment as Doirean led Borus and the soldiers away to a large hall built amongst the trees. With a last glance, he turned and followed Emlyn along the tracks between small homes which were often built around the trunks of trees. Here and there he spotted ladders and ropes leading up to platforms built amongst the branches.

"What are those?" he asked, pointing upwards.

"Food stores for the most part," Emlyn answered. "Wolves, bears, and other animals are not good climbers and it keeps our stores safe. They also make good platforms for archers if the village is ever attacked."

"Was your village ever attacked?"

"Twice while I was growing up," she acknowledged.

Kyron ran four sentences through his head to try to offer his sympathy, but all sounded weak, so he settled on silence. The path she followed led them through small clearings where children, dressed in shorter versions of their parent's clothes, sat on the earth grinding seeds, or tending fires. A few played, throwing stones in the air and catching them on their knuckles or palms, giggling when one fell to the ground. The adults watched him with guarded expressions as they passed, but though many had knives in their hands or close by he did not feel threatened.

"Through here," Emlyn said after they had walked a little while, pointing to an arch made of branches and decorated with blooming flowers. On the other side, he could see a wide area of grass lit with bright sunshine. He glanced up, through the boughs of the trees and saw little but grey cloud.

She went first, leaving him in the village and for a heartbeat he was on his own for the first time in months. The rustle of leaves in the cold wind, the sound of village life, and a calm sense of age and timelessness swept through him. He took a deep breath, tasting the life on the air around him, the sweetness of new growth, and the earthy richness of the old trees.

"Are you coming or not?" Emlyn said, and he glanced around to see her stood in the archway. "The priests are waiting."

"Sorry," Kyron mumbled and stepped through the arch.

The air here was calm and cool, and the grass carefully maintained in the clearing. Around its edge, Kyron could see a series of small huts, not too different in shape to his tent but made of branches covered with turf from which sprouted wildflowers.

She led him off to the side where four people sat around a low fire, heating a soup or stew in a pot hung above it.

"Welcome." One of the men stood and called to them in the Empire tongue. "You eat?"

Emlyn replied in her own language, her voice bright and clear in the quiet of the clearing. The man nodded and spoke to the three still seated. They all moved around creating room for Emlyn and Kyron to sit.

"I speak not much Empire," the man said. "Emlyn, honoured, speak for us."

Kyron nodded, puzzled, as he folded his legs beneath him to sit cross-legged on the grass by the fire.

"I'll translate what they say," Emlyn said. "The same for you. In-between all that, I'll try to eat."

"Thank you," Kyron said.

"Here, eat. Eat." The man ladled the contents of the pot into a clay bowl and passed it around the fire to Kyron who took it and looked around for a spoon to eat it with.

"Emlyn," he said, unsure.

"Drink it," she answered, taking her own bowl. "All the vegetables and meat have been chopped up small enough. Priests prefer simple food, and some haven't got many teeth left."

"Washing up less," the man chuckled.

Kyron allowed himself to laugh alongside the man's infectious giggle and open smile. "I hate that bit too."

The priest nodded his head, three times in rapid succession, like a bird plucking seed from the dirt, and then drank deeply from his bowl.

Kyron lifted the bowl to his lips and gave it a cautious sniff. Steam rose and the smell of home filled his nose. A strange sensation, and the tickle of a memory from his early years. The bustle of a woman about a small kitchen, the rhythmic chopping of vegetables, the heat from the cooking fire, her quick movements as each ingredient went into the pot. He struggled to see her face, but it was gone, locked away behind the passing years. Still, he knew her, remembered her, and the warmth of her embrace for just a moment. Mother.

And then the memory was gone. He took another breath of steam, trying to recapture it, but the only scents now were of the vegetables, the charred wood in the fire, the heated clay of the bowl.

"He asks if you are enjoying the soup?" Emlyn translated.

"I am. Very tasty," Kyron said, opening his eyes and offering a smile of thanks to the priest. A warmth spread through him, up from his stomach and into his chest and arms.

"His name is Gwri," Emlyn said. "The others are Aiden, Brite, and Elsha, though they have some duties to perform this afternoon. Gwri will stay with us."

"He called you honoured?" Kyron said, thinking back to the greeting and his puzzlement. He took another sip of the soup, enjoying the heat on his tongue and the vague hint of herbs and spices.

"Yes," Emlyn replied.

"What does it mean? I mean, I know what it means, but why did he call you that?"

"I am a guest in the village and in the glade," she answered after a moment. "The translation is not exact."

"Oh," he sighed and felt a stab of disappointment. "Chief Doirean knew about your parents."

"Yes," Emlyn said again.

"How?" Kyron felt the warmth of the food spread to his legs, a feeling of relaxation and time which had been absent ever since he had joined the army's march north.

"Word spreads through the forest faster than your army marches," she answered. "Finish your soup. Gwri is going to try and teach you something about the tribes. Listen better than you normally do."

XXXIX

THE GENERAL

Six years ago:

"Don't you go forgetting he's the High Priest," Gressius said as he closed the door.

"He was a good officer, Gressius," he replied, "dragged you out of the ranks when you took a wound once, I recall."

He watched as a yawn creased the boy's face and smiled.

"Even so," Gressius continued, "he's got other people to worry about."

"Once a soldier, always a soldier," he replied, "and a discussion for another day. I think it is time this lad went to bed."

THE SHIPS SET sail on the evening tide as the sun sank towards the horizon. Bordan's last view of the city was the faint flickers of the torches which lined the top of the palace walls. The dark shapes of the buildings against the stars faded out of sight and the captain turned the ship to shadow the coastline.

"You look pensive," Godewyn said, coming up to the rail, resting a hand upon the worn wood. The creak and splash of the oars dipping into the sea and powering the ship forward was rhythmic, almost hypnotic. "You are worried about her?"

"Like you," Bordan answered, not taking his gaze from the dark sea, "she should have stayed in the capital where it was safer."

"I did not mean the Princess."

Bordan grunted in answer, not trusting himself to speak.

"However, the city is not safe. Recent events have proven that to be true," Godewyn continued.

"We have found the paymaster," Bordan replied. "There will be no more assassins, no more attempts on Aelia's life. Here though, anything can happen. The ship could sink. Abra's forces could be too great for us. Illness can strike a camp. An army may march on its stomach, but too often they march in spite of their stomachs."

"The same can happen in the city," Godewyn pointed out.

"But there we have more control," Bordan answered, leaving words unspoken.

"She is spreading her wings, Bordan," Godewyn answered after a pause. "Aelia will be Emperor soon."

Bordan glanced around, checking his surrounding and timing his speech with the slap of oars against waves. "She is not ready."

"No one is truly ready," Godewyn pointed out, lowering his voice. "She will learn. We, you and I, can guide her."

"She has yet to come to terms with the death of her family," Bordan whispered. "She has lost them all in short order. That changes a person."

"Changes everyone, General. For a time, we were worried about you," the priest said, resting a hand on the older man's shoulder. "Yet, here you stand, stronger than before."

"Older, Godewyn, not stronger."

"Then you do not understand the truth of strength, my friend. It is not in your sword arm, nor in your knowledge, but in your heart. The Flame warms us, and we are tempered in its heat. You have never warped or broken, Bordan," and the General felt the hand on his shoulder squeeze him briefly before it let go, "and that is true strength."

"You think the Princess is strong enough," Bordan said, a statement, not a question.

"I think she will be Emperor," Godewyn said.

"If we can recover the amulet and her father's body," Bordan pointed out.

"We have the utmost faith in you," the priest answered. "However, it is time I found my bed and I suggest you do the same."

* * *

LIFE ON SHIP was one of boredom interspersed with nausea. Two days of progress against the winds—which had unseasonably decided to stream down from the northern continent—had been cold and chill. The waves had grown in strength and the soldiers on the lower deck had been press-ganged into service as oarsmen to keep any headway.

In his cabin, a small room on the exposed upper deck which he shared with Godewyn and Vedrix, Bordan had spent the night holding his belly and trying desperately not to vomit the meal the ship's cook had prepared into the wooden bucket at his feet.

Godewyn had sat with him a while, placid and reassuring, before he finally gave in to sleep. Vedrix had started snoring the moment his head rested against the hammock. That left the General all alone with his worries and the roll of the vessel as it cut a slow path towards Cesena.

Aelia had a cabin to herself, forcing the repurposed merchant vessel's captain to sleep on deck with his officers and crew. The man had taken it with grace, and for the privilege of having the Princess on board had been promised wealth. Merchants scored their lives by the coin they earned and soldiers by the battles they survived. To serve was its own reward, Bordan knew. One hard-earned, not granted on a whim.

As the grey light of a cloud-ridden dawn crested the horizon, Bordan stumbled on to the deck and sucked in a lungful of the cool sea air. Immediately his stomach turned over and he staggered to the rail, turning his face downwind and heaved what was left in his stomach over the rail.

"Better to get it out than hold it in, General," one of the crew called. "Get yourself some dry bread and just a sip of water. It'll settle your stomach soon enough."

Bordan waved his thanks, not trusting himself to open his mouth in case more bile rose in his throat. He glanced at the cresting waves, picking out the clouds against the dark water. In instinct, he had turned right to reach the rail, a direction which faced the open sea, so he turned and leaned against the wooden side of the ship.

There, a slightly different grey smudge between wave and sky, was land. Too far to swim but comforting all the same.

"How fare the soldiers?" Bordan asked as one of the Shields passed by. Bordan struggled to remember the woman's name, but lack of sleep, sea sickness, and, he was forced to admit, age kept it from him.

"Shield Vacia," the woman said, tapping her chest with her fist. Her armour jingled in the early morning air, a sound which brought, like the sight of land, a strange comfort to Bordan's heart. "They are well. Shoulders a little tender from rowing yesterday, but it will build up their strength for the fight. Good to get exercise even when confined to a ship."

"Make sure they are well fed, Vacia," Bordan answered. "We will all need our strength soon enough."

"You also, General. If I may, I grew up on the coast, in a fishing village, and was always out on the water in my family's boat," Vacia said. "Don't listen to the sailor over there. Eat your fill and drink good wine. Until you've got your sea legs, it won't matter a damn what you put in your belly, it'll all come back up. Might as well eat the good stuff in that case. Leastways, that's what my mother and father said."

Bordan chuckled, warmed by her concern. "Wise people, your parents. I trust they are still well?"

"Drowned at sea, General," Vacia said in a tone in which he could detect no sadness or anger. "The dangers of a fisherman's life. Sword in the guts for us, drowning for them. We each struggle to keep the fear at bay. At least with a sword, I've got a fighting chance, but no one ever beats the waves."

"Is that why you joined the army?" Bordan asked as his stomach rolled with the ship.

"That and I couldn't face being pregnant and tied down before I'd seen more than the fishing village. For me, the army was a better way of becoming a full citizen than being left with a handful of children and husband dead to the waves," Vacia replied.

With no words to say, Bordan settled for a nod and Vacia offered a smile. Both knew death and had kept the silent goddess at bay while others succumbed to her embrace. He watched the soldier walk to the steps to the lower deck, hearing her calls and shouts as she greeted her soldiers.

*   *   *

"WELL?" AELIA SAID, hands gripping either side of the tiny table around which they sat. The benches were fixed to the floor and each of the four had a steaming bowl of meat and vegetables set in holes cut into the table for that purpose before them.

"The sea makes things difficult, Your Highness," Vedrix said with a stutter. "I am unable to make contact with the honour guard for the reasons we have already discussed." The magician offered Bordan a small, apologetic smile. "There is a Master of sufficient skill in Cesena, however. I made contact before we set sail."

"And what did they tell you?" Godewyn prompted.

"Abra was, as far as she knew, not in the city," Vedrix said. "She did mention an influx of mercenaries. They had set up a camp half a day's ride from the city, in a wooded area, but were coming in to buy supplies. The local governor was concerned enough to add to the wall guards."

"And they have not done anything?" Aelia asked.

"As far as she is aware, they have not marched on the city or made moves to go anywhere," Vedrix replied. "Communication is less exact across open water. The sea water has some strange resonances with the magic."

"While the exact nature of the magical problems are no doubt interesting, Master Vedrix," Bordan interrupted before the magician could get truly started on a lecture, "perhaps you could give us any updates you have managed to glean?"

"Well, quite," Vedrix said, shifting in his seat. "Master Junila suggests that the mercenaries appear to be waiting for someone or something and doing their best not to antagonise the locals. Those that come to buy supplies pay a good price, are polite, and stay out of trouble."

"Can she speak to one of them? Ask some questions?" Aelia chimed in.

"I'm not sure," Vedrix admitted. "I will try to get a message through to ask."

"Any information is useful," Bordan said. "We have two more days at sea, and can assume that Abra is, at the least, three days ahead of us."

"And what will he do with his forces?" Aelia asked.

"Most likely, he will march across the bridge as soon as he has word the honour guard are close. Scouts will be out, riding the countryside north of the bridge," Bordan answered. "It is the only route into the Empire for a good distance. It is also where the campaign departed from."

"But the bridge will be guarded," Godewyn pointed out.

"By a small force only," Bordan admitted with a shake of his head. "There has not been a serious attack or trouble within two days' journey north of the bridge for decades. The city garrison has pacified the tribes thereabouts. An extra layer of security for the crossing."

"But the garrison is gone," Godewyn countered.

"Its main strength, yes," Bordan answered. "However, the city militia guard the gate for the most part. The garrison were concerned with the tribes and only provided support for the bridge."

"So it is still guarded," Aelia said. "The mercenaries have no way across. Abra will be trapped. We have him."

Bordan paused and exchanged looks with Godewyn, then choosing his words with care said, "Your Highness, it is likely that Abra has planned a way across. Either he has bribed the militia, has enough forces for the militia to be inconsequential in his plans, or has another stratagem in place. Nothing about this has the feel of being hurried or ill thought out."

He looked to the other two at the table for support and both nodded.

"It is possible that they will be across the bridge before we arrive," Bordan continued.

"I told you we should have left more quickly," Aelia snapped, lifting and slamming her palm down upon the table. The bowls jumped in their sockets and Vedrix gasped. "Now we will lose it all before I have even been crowned. If we had set sail the moment you had news of Abra's location we could have stopped him, but you wanted to gather the force and wait for supplies. If I had not insisted, General, we would be even further behind the traitor. My father's body will fall into his hands and I am lost."

Bordan schooled his expression and fixed his eyes upon the Princess. "He will not venture far into the forest, Your Highness. The tribes are fearful of the garrison and soldiers of the Empire. They know what can befall them if they interfere or attack. Mercenaries will not be afforded the same discretion."

"And if Abra is working with the tribes? What if it is all some plan of the clans and tribes? They killed my father, and you have already said there has been a battle on the journey back," Aelia shouted. The Princess's eyes darted between the three men and Bordan saw the young woman's hands clench and unclench.

"He will not be," Bordan assured him. "Abra is a traitor, but he wants the crown. Colluding with the tribes would turn the military against him. Remember there is an army in the north and he knows Maxentius of the Third would never bow to him if he brought an army of our enemies to the city."

"And once he has my father's body and the amulet?"

"We will stop him before that happens. Our best information is that we have time," Bordan said. "He will not advance far across the bridge. My greatest fear is that he will try to hold the bridge, preventing us attacking with our full force."

"A siege?" Godewyn said.

"Across a bridge, with few supplies," Bordan said, regretting the words and hurrying to complete the sentence, "though the city can aid us until ours arrive."

"We will have more men," Aelia said, some of the flush leaving her cheeks. "We can march across the bridge and battle Abra's mercenaries."

"They will have the advantage," Godewyn said before Bordan could speak. "We would lose a lot of men trying to cross under arrows."

"However," Bordan added, "he does not know we are coming. He will suspect, but even so will not expect us as quickly as we will arrive." He nodded to the Princess and saw a smile of pride flash across Aelia's face. "We may well catch them by surprise."

"Two days," Godewyn said.

"Two days," Bordan agreed.

"Two days to victory," Aelia cried, erupting from her chair, holding her goblet of wine high as some sloshed over the side.

"Victory, Your Highness," Bordan agreed as the other men rose in salute.

XL

THE MAGICIAN

FIVE YEARS AGO:

He woke with a scream. It echoed around his room and the oil lamp on the shelf flickered in response.

Blinking away the sudden swirl of stars, blobs of orange and yellow afterimages, he sat up. His legs trembled and he could feel the fear welling up his throat. With a determined swallow, he fought it back down.

Wiping the sweat from his forehead, he settled back onto the mattress and rested his head on the pillow. His eyes would not close.

"DOES EVERY VILLAGE have a place like this?" Kyron gazed around the clearing, enjoying the moment of peace.

"Not all of them," Emlyn said, handing her bowl to one of the priests. "This one isn't the largest I've seen nor the smallest. Some villages, the really small ones far from the travelled tracks, won't have a glade or a priest."

"But here does," Kyron nodded. "I didn't know that the tribes had a formal religion."

"There are a lot of things you don't know, Kyron," Emlyn said, as three of the priests stood and collected the bowls, heading off about their chores.

"That's not fair," he complained, but the words came attached to a smile.

"But true nonetheless," Emlyn answered. "I know what the Empire thinks of the tribes. Backward people who still live in mud huts. Dirty people who rarely bathe. No culture or sophistication, uncivilised barbarians."

"That's not true," Kyron protested though his words fell flat, even to his ears.

"I could tell you that it is all a front. We let the Empire see what it needs to see, that there are, deep in the forests, towns of surpassing beauty and grace which are the true heart of our lives."

Kyron sat forward, intrigued, the cobwebs in his thoughts parting for a moment. "Are there?"

"No," she laughed and Gwri copied her, though how much the priest had understood Kyron could not be sure. "We are what you see. A people that live in the forests, fall in love, have children, and die here. We look out for one another, we trade with each other, and we war with one another at times. What did you expect?"

Kyron let his thoughts wander slowly through his memories, collecting his impressions, his biases, preconceptions, and all the stories he had been told over his youth. "My mother and father grew up in the capital," he began, his words slow and lips strangely numb, "but against my grandfather's wishes, they moved north to a village near the forest. Further west than here. Near the hills and mountains. There were stories of gold and gems being found in the foothills, and my father saw a chance to start a new life."

"A new life? Why?"

"He didn't want to join the army," Kyron said. "It was what was expected of him, but he was really a carpenter. He enjoyed, so I was told, making and building things with his hands. So they left."

"And?"

"They were killed," Kyron said. Memories tried to surface, but they never broached into his conscious thoughts. "Killed by people from the mountains and the forests."

"Well, you got your own back, didn't you?" Emlyn said, the sad smile on her face softening the words.

"It wasn't my decision to come with the army," Kyron answered. "My master made that decision for me."

"But you support the army in its invasion?"

"Yes," he said without thinking and, a moment later, added, "No. I don't know. My grandfather wanted me to join the army, but instead I became a magician."

"To avoid the army?"

"No," he said, a truth falling from his lips without thought. "It is who... what I am."

"You thought us all to be raiders who strike from forest and mountain and kill peaceful villagers?"

"When I started out with the army, yes," he admitted. "Now, I am not so sure. Padarn was right. I need to learn and to do that I need to travel and find things out for myself."

"Good," Emlyn nodded. "Here is a good place to start. Religion in your Empire is one thing. I've seen your priests and listened to them. Here, it is something else. Gwri?"

The priest began to speak in his own language, then paused.

"As he understands it," Emlyn said, "your religion, the Flame, requires everyone to believe the same thing in the same manner. Is that correct?"

"We all worship in the same churches, if that's what you mean," Kyron answered, wiping the sweat from his forehead.

"Here there are no churches," Gwri said, through Emlyn. "Even this glade is not really what you would call holy ground. It is just a site for priests to live, to work, to keep out of the way of others. The holy ground, as you would know it, is the whole of the forest."

"My priests would say every person was holy because they carry a part of the Flame in them." There was a strange feeling, not pain, but of emptiness in his stomach as he defended the Church and Empire.

Gwri just nodded as Emlyn translated and something like a smile split his face. "Yes. Yes. You see that too. We believe that everyone is holy because they are alive. Each person is equal in that regard."

"But you have a chieftain who rules your village, and you are priests," Kyron said, looking down at his fingers, which seemed somehow both larger and smaller than he remembered.

"Doirean is chief because she is best suited to the role, the people decided this," Emlyn said, not waiting for Gwri. "Priests are only special in that they work to understand the forest more. Everyone in the village, in all our villages, contributes in some manner to the life and success of the settlement."

Gwri looked between them, lost. Emlyn sighed and translated what she had just said to accompanying nods from the priest.

"You say this place is not special, but I've not seen that type of tree before." Kyron pointed to the other end of the clearing, surprised his heavy arms obeyed his command.

"A rare tree in the forest," Gwri answered after Emlyn translated. "Come."

The priest stood and beckoned, leading them over to the large tree with its broad canopy. In its shade the air was cool and still.

"The village tree," Gwri said, reaching out and patting the broad trunk. "It was here before the village. It is why the village is here, it is our heart."

"You built your village around a tree?"

"Yes," Gwri said with a smile and fond look at the tree. "They are rare and precious to us. Emlyn says you are a magician?"

"Yes," Kyron answered cautiously.

"You can feel the life in the world?"

"The what?" Kyron puzzled, turned his gaze away from the tree.

"The life," Gwri said. "All the little pieces of being, of life."

"Ah," Kyron replied, realising what the priest was getting at. It took a long moment for the words he wanted to say to fall into order in his mind. "We call them motes, and they are not alive, but are the things that make up everything, give it form, and energy. We think, that is the master magicians think, they were created by others, a lost people, a very long time ago. Magicians, people who can feel and see the motes, are descendants from those lost people."

"Truly?" Gwri cocked his head to one side.

"That is what the Masters who have studied it all have taught us," Kyron said, feeling a little less sure of himself.

"A strange belief," Gwri answered. "Why cannot life create life? Mothers give birth to children, do they not? Why should there be a lost race who created these little bits of life? And if there were, who created them?"

As Emlyn translated, Gwri chuckled to himself.

"I don't know," Kyron answered after he searched his memory for the lesson on motes and creation. "The priests say the Flame washed the world clean many thousands of years ago. Magicians think that this meant the end of the lost people."

"I could show you trees that are tens of thousands of years old," Gwri said, his brow furrowed in thought. "Some trees need fire to seed and regrow, but they live much further south where the weather can cause such fires."

"I might have got the years wrong."

"It does not matter," Gwri said. "Reach out and touch the tree, feel its life."

Kyron stretched out a numb hand, silently cursing at the way his fingers trembled. Within a few fingertips of touching the tree he stopped, a thought occurring. "You can feel the life, the motes?"

"Of course," Gwri nodded, his smile widening. "Many in the tribes can, and we become priests, or are given other duties which contribute to the well-being and safety of the villages."

"When someone is found who can feel the life," Emlyn added to her translation, "it is a moment of great joy in the village. A feast is held, and the parents are blessed, the child looked after and raised amongst us all. Is that not the same for the Empire?"

"You've seen the way the priests treated me," Kyron said.

"I thought that was just you," Emlyn said. "You can be a difficult person to like."

"Thanks," Kyron muttered, the sting of her words softened by the glint of mischief in her eyes. "When a magician is found, someone who can see and command the motes, they can be trained in the Gymnasium. If their magic is wild, they have taught themselves and not registered in the Gymnasium, the priests hunt them down."

"And bring them to your place of learning?" Gwri asked.

"No. They kill them."

Gwri's face curled up in shock and an expression of deep sadness followed Emlyn's translation. "Is that not a waste of lives and potential?"

"Yes," Kyron nodded: it was the only word he could find.

"So sad," Gwri said. "Touch the village tree. Feel its life. Let it feel yours."

"It can sense magic," Kyron blurted, his hand stilling once more.

The bark of the tree seemed to shimmer in his vision, like the haze of heat over a cornfield.

"Of course," Gwri nodded. "Touch. Touch. It will not harm you. It is just a tree."

Kyron swallowed, his mouth dry, lips and tongue numb, held his breath, brushed his fingers against the tree and fell.

Wind rushed past his ears, sounding like an ocean storm, waves crashing against the harbour walls of the city. There was darkness and though he could feel his eyes move, twitch, and look in new directions, he saw nothing. His stomach dropped, making him feel lighter, floating for a moment before the plummeting began again.

There was a light ahead, not the yellow of the sun, but green haloed by a pale blue. It was towards this he fell. He tried to scream but no sound came from his throat. Kyron put his hands out, an instinctive gesture of protection.

He reached for the motes, a desperate attempt to weave a shield. The roaring in his ears intensified as millions of motes answered his call. He was falling through them, drowning in them. Kyron fought to breathe, and the motes swamped his throat and filled his lungs. He coughed, choked, hands clawing his throat as he fell.

When he did not die, when the expected darkness did not envelope him and as the light ahead steadied, his panic began to subside. Kyron exhaled and the motes flew from his mouth, dancing and cavorting in twisting patterns as more were drawn in on the next breath.

Reaching out, Kyron drew the motes around him into a shield, a bubble of magic, and found he was no longer falling but stood on a sward of green grass beneath the village tree. Looking up he saw the shining sun and clear blue skies.

"What was that?" Kyron turned to question Gwri and Emlyn. However, neither stood there. He was alone.

The priests' homes were empty and the flowers on their roofs in the full bloom of summer. Past them he could see the arch through which he had entered.

"Where is everyone?" he muttered and after a few heartbeats spent looking for signs of life, he walked with a stiff, nervous gait through the arch and into the village.

Here were people. Between the homes, the tracks were full of folk going about their business. A few looked up without recognition in their eyes as he passed them by. Which was no surprise, he had not been long in the village though he suspected his clothing gave away the fact that he was not of the tribes.

Where would Doirean have taken Borus and the soldiers? Perhaps Emlyn would be with them. How long had he stood at the tree? Maybe she had got bored waiting... though it had seemed only a few seconds, Kyron was aware that he could sometimes lose track of time - but not this much, surely?

"Excuse me," he said, putting out a hand to stop one villager in their tracks, "where is the chief's house?"

"There are no chiefs here," the villager said, an elderly man with wisps of grey beard upon his chin. "You will not find what you are looking for if that is your question."

Before Kyron could say another word, the old man stepped sprightly to the side and moved on.

A hand gripped his wrist and Kyron jerked in shock, but the fingers were strong and held him steady.

"He won't help you," said a young woman, red hair tied up in a style he had never seen and wearing a long simple dress which reached to the grass beneath her feet.

"I was looking for Chief Doirean," Kyron said, breathing quickly and trying to calm the rapid beating of his heart.

"I don't think she is here," the woman said. "Not yet, at least."

He was lost at sea, waves crashing all about him, swells obscuring his view of land, salt water washing away his thoughts and certainty.

"Emlyn? Gwri?" he gasped. "Borus?"

"Gwri?" the woman said and there was a spark of recognition in her green flecked eyes. For moment, under his feet he felt solid rock, stability, and a glimpse of the shore of understanding. "He visits from time to time."

"Is he here now?"

She nodded. "He doesn't stay long."

"Can you take me to him?" Kyron gasped, the rock under his feet becoming a path.

"This way," she giggled and, taking him by the hand, drew him along the pathway. They passed by houses and homes from which the sound of domestic activity came. Her feet danced through the knots of people and he did his best to follow, apologising when he bumped into someone.

"I know you," the man said, his voice gruff and angry.

Kyron stopped, tugging the young woman back. "You do? Thank the Flame. Do you know where Emlyn is, or Doirean, or the people I came in with?"

"You can never come here with anyone," the man said. "I know Emlyn, though. The guide who saw me on my path here. I know you too. Kyron, the magician."

"Yes," Kyron said, smiling. At last he was on more certain ground and there was a chance his path would lead back to some semblance of clarity and normality.

"You watched as they questioned me. Told them if I was lying or not," the man accused, and heart thumping loudly in his ears Kyron recognised him.

"But... but... I saw you killed," Kyron stuttered, the image of the knife plunging into the man's flesh and his life dimming in his eyes.

"You didn't stop it," the warrior reproached.

"I couldn't," Kyron said, heat rising in his face and bile burning his throat.

"Maybe not," the warrior allowed, "but here you are, in our Heart. You are not of the forest. Who let you in?"

"I didn't... I mean, what? I touched a tree... the village tree." Kyron fumbled for the words, feeling the path beneath his feet begin to crumble. He pointed back the way he had come.

"Kyron." His name called out, clearly and with purpose, in a voice he knew.

The apprentice turned and almost fell. Striding along the trail towards him were Padarn and two others, their faces familiar yet vague, like mist over the sea obscuring the masts of the sailing ships.

"I—" he choked. "Mother?"

XLI

The General

Five years ago:

"*You look ill, boy,*" *he said as the lad slumped at the kitchen table.* "*Decima, do you think we should get a medicus in to see to him?*"

"*I didn't sleep very well,*" *the boy said.*

"*I can see that,*" *he answered, noting the red-rimmed eyes and dull stare.*

"*I'll fix him a tonic,*" *Decima said,* "*and put him back to bed.*"

"*Probably for the best.*"

"The army is camped, and provisions have been drawn from the town stores," Bordan said, tapping the scroll he carried against his palm.

"And no sight of Abra's mercenaries?" Godewyn asked from his position near the table they had set up in the Governor's office.

"The scouts we sent have returned," Bordan answered, striding to the table and unfurling the scroll. On it was a crude map of the area, the town, the bridge, and the land to the north and south of the River Abhainn.

Aelia leaned forward in her seat while Godewyn and Vedrix shuffled a little closer to see. The governor, a fat, sweaty man with only wisps of dark black hair oiled to his head, stood from his chair, the legs scraping across the tessellated floor.

"We found their camp here," Bordan pointed to an area west of the town. "They are gone. However, the scouts counted the fire pits, the pitches, and any other information they could gather to determine the possible numbers."

"And?" Aelia snapped. "Whether you've forgotten or not, General, we are here to secure my father's body, not to play games more fit for the theatre. How many were there and where did they go?"

"Forgive me, Your Highness," Bordan said, bowing in respect. "The scouts estimate a force of between six hundred and a thousand warriors. Some mounted, but it was impossible to be sure how many."

"And?" Aelia looked up from the map. "I am not my father, Bordan. I do not like to guess."

"The scouts to the north were prevented from crossing the bridge," Bordan started.

"Governor," Aelia snarled, rounding on the fat man who backed away, shaking his head. "If your guards are preventing my soldiers from carrying out their duties, it will be you hung from the cross, not them."

"My... my... Princess... I—"

"It was not his guards that stopped the scout, Princess Aelia," Bordan interrupted. "The northern end of the bridge is guarded by mercenaries. They stopped my... our scouts from crossing. From the tracks that others found and this information, we are sure the mercenary army has crossed the bridge."

"You let a thousand mercenaries cross the bridge, Governor." Aelia's voice was a cold whisper in the room.

"We had no reason to not stop them, my Princess," the governor explained, clutching at his clothes and bunching the material. "Mercenaries often accompany trade caravans or have other business in the forests to the north."

"A thousand men is not a trade caravan," Aelia roared, "it is an army."

"We should be able to see them," Bordan said into the quiet that followed, "when the rain clears. If not, I would suggest they have gone into the forest. The governor's staff say there are barely three leagues of farmland between the river and forest."

"And those on the bridge?" Godewyn asked.

"Left to dissuade us from following," Bordan answered, grateful to have someone other than the Princess asking the needed questions.

"Were it me and knowing the honour guard is five hundred strong, I would comfortably leave a hundred men to hold the bridge."

"A hundred." Aelia stopped her pacing. "Is that all?"

"The bridge is not wide," Bordan said, pointing to his map. "Two, maybe three carts wide. Twenty men, stood shoulder to shoulder, would block it."

"And they would have put up blockages and barriers," Vedrix ventured.

"They have, so the scouts tell me."

"But we can take the bridge," Aelia said, coming back to the table and stabbing her finger at the map. "Twenty men, even a hundred, can be swept aside by our forces."

"It would be a bloody battle, Your Highness," Bordan said. "They will have set up enough blocks to funnel us into smaller numbers, preventing us from bringing the full weight of our army to bear on them."

"You seem to know a lot about what they will do," Aelia stated, her tone bordering on accusation.

"I know what I would do, and mercenaries are often led by those who know the price of a life and would make anyone pay dearly," Bordan answered.

"But we can get across?" Godewyn asked.

"We can," Bordan answered. "I do have one concern."

"General..." Aelia growled as Bordan paused.

"Once we clear the bridge, we will only be able to bring across as many soldiers as the bridge is wide," Bordan explained, drawing a finger from one side of the bridge to the other on his map. "We will be vulnerable on the northern bank until we can bring enough troops over. If Abra's mercenaries attack us at that moment, we face losing a lot of soldiers, perhaps the bridge."

"How many?" Godewyn asked.

"Half, maybe more," Bordan said. "If not all dead, then captured or injured beyond the ability to fight."

"So how can we stop that happening?" Godewyn asked.

"We need information from the other side of the river," Bordan said. "Has Abra marched into the forest, or is he camped on its edge waiting for the honour guard to emerge? If it is the latter, we will need to find another way across."

"There is not another crossing within a day's ride in either direction," the governor said. "At least, not large enough for an army."

"There are smaller bridges?" Bordan asked. "Where? Mark them on the map."

"Um…" The governor took the stylus and dipped into the ink, brushing the excess off on the lip of the pot. He began to draw lines across the river to the west. "Here and here, within a day's ride, but they are old. Built centuries ago, when the land up here was wild and untamed. Most are in disrepair and only a few farmers use them, and then only in the winter when the river freezes. The ice holds the supports steady."

"But I could get a small troop across, a few scouts to determine what was happening across the river," Bordan said. "Have you seen the bridges with your own eyes?"

"Only this one," the governor pointed. "It isn't sturdy enough for a horse. It may even have collapsed this spring when the floods came."

"But you don't know," Bordan pressed.

"I don't," the governor admitted.

"Half a day's ride?" Bordan peered at the map, trying to gauge distance when there was no scale and only the memory of a man who had not visited the site recently.

"On a fast horse."

"So, we could have information by tomorrow," Bordan said, clapping his hands. "At that point we can plan our attack and see if there is merit in sending a force across here," he pointed to the first bridge the governor had marked and then the second, "or here if we send riders with spare horses."

"General," Aelia said, and all eyes turned to her. "We all know my education was more philosophical than my brother's, but it seems we are intending to spend a lot of time waiting?"

"Information is a weapon as much as a sword, Princess Aelia," Bordan said, welcoming the chance to guide the Princess's anger and frustration. "To strike at the bridge and lands beyond, we need the knowledge that will enable us to get across in one go. Better to wait a night and win our way across in a day, than rush to attack and be bogged down on this side for three days."

"It may..." the governor began and stopped, before an angry glare from the Princess made him continue. "That is, I have some information from the tribes. A bird arrived from one of my people in the tribes, just as you arrived. I haven't had the opportunity to—"

"You have people in the tribes?" Aelia snapped, cutting the governor off with a sharp chopping motion of her hand. "You talk to the tribes, have dealings with them? Traitor."

"I, that is, as Governor of Cesena it my duty to be aware of the activity on the other side of the river," the governor said, looking towards Bordan for support. All the General could offer was a slight nod.

"I will judge your duties and how you carry them out, Governor, not you." Aelia bit the words off, turned on her heel and stamped over the window which looked out across the rain shrouded city.

Into the silence, Bordan asked, "And what did your messenger tell you?"

"The honour guard fought a battle, General, with the last of the holdouts from the tribes. Many were from the northern parts of the forest. By the account I received, it was a slaughter on both sides."

"Your Highness," Bordan said, trying to bring the young woman back from the brink of losing her temper, "this will be the battle Master Vedrix told us they were preparing for."

"Carry on, Governor," Aelia said, waving a hand but not turning from the window where the rain struck the thick glass obscuring the view of the city. "Who does your... messenger say emerged victorious?"

"Well," the governor said, casting a glance at the seething Princess, "taking into account the tribe's natural tendency to paint their accomplishments in the best light possible, I would say the Empire. The message says they have lost a lot of supplies, but their journey and the large waggon they accompany continues on its path to the bridge."

"Did they give you an estimate for its arrival at the bridge?"

Bordan watched as the governor took a deep breath and cast one more fearful glance at the Princess.

"If the message is true," the man said, his voice quavering, "and accounting for its age and time it takes to travel the forest..."

"Get on with it," Aelia shouted, her voice cracking against the stone of the tower.

Bordan exchanged a glance with Godewyn who inclined his head, moved over to the Princess and began to whisper in her ear. The young woman's shoulders sank a little, and some of the tension drained from her frame, if not the room.

"Well, yes, Your Highness," the governor replied, shrinking upon himself, "I would expect it tomorrow or the day after. Three days at the latest."

"Tomorrow?" Bordan whispered. "Governor, we have spent time sending out scouts, discussing strategy, how to gather information, and you had this sitting in the back of your mind."

"Tomorrow?" Aelia cried, shaking off Godewyn's hand upon her shoulder. "Governor, you have served me poorly. This information should have been your first utterance when we arrived."

"Your Highness, I didn't think... that is, I did not get the chance, you were—"

"You. Blame. Me." Spittle flew from the Princess's mouth and the young woman stamped back to the table gathered up the drawn map and waved it in the governor's face. "All of this. All of this wasted time. While scouts rode out, while the old General worried about crossing the bridge and scared us with what-ifs, and you knew that my father's body was close."

"But, I—"

Aelia cut off the governor's excuse by grabbing the back of the man's head and shoving the crumpled map into his open mouth. "Now tell me your excuses. Now tell me you haven't cost me the throne."

"Your Highness," Bordan began but caught the fire of rage in Aelia's eye.

"Do not ask for forgiveness for this one, General," Aelia growled out, pushing the map further and further into the governor's mouth, ignoring the choking noises coming from the man. "One day, Bordan. One day, and you wanted us to wait for supplies to be loaded on the ships."

"Your Highness," Godewyn said, his voice calm and controlled, "you have been ill-served here. However, there are other ways of dealing with this."

The governor's face was turning red and his hands were grabbing at Aelia's, nails digging into the gloves the Princess wore along with her armour.

"Not now, High Priest. I've no need of your counsel and wise words. This piece of shit," Aelia rose in anger as she shook the man's head from side to side, "waited to tell me. He waited for half a day. We should be across that bridge by now, tackling Abra's forces."

"I agree, Your Highness," Bordan said, glancing at Godewyn whose face was calm but resigned and Vedrix, who turned away and walked to the window overlooking the town.

The governor's struggles were weakening and his face had turned purple. Even as Bordan watched, the man's eyes rolled up in their sockets and his arms fell limp at his side.

"I told you, General. I told you," Aelia's rage cresting as she allowed the unconscious man to fall to the floor, and her voice now carried the heavy burden of guilt. "We should have been quicker. Damn the supplies, damn the boats, and damn you. I will *not* lose my father's body to Abra and his mercenaries. Get my army across that bridge, whatever it takes, whatever the cost."

"As you command," Bordan answered, struggling to keep his voice level. He bowed, clasping his hands together to stop them from shaking, a mixture of fear and anger coursing through his veins. "We will attack at dusk."

"Not dusk, General, now," Aelia shouted, looking down as if seeing the governor for the first time. "Have someone sent in to look after him, would you, Godewyn? And once he is awake, lock him in a cell."

"Of course, Your Highness," Godewyn answered, catching Bordan's eye. "I will see to that immediately."

"I AM," BORDAN paused, choosing his next word carefully, "concerned."

"About taking the bridge," the High Priest said, arching an eyebrow.

"Partially," Bordan acknowledged. "Driving rain is never a good time to assault a fortified position. They know we will be coming, whether that is today, tomorrow, or a day later. Abra's a fool, but he's schemed enough to make plans for every contingency."

"You don't think you can take the bridge?"

"The army can take the bridge," the General replied. "Of that there is no doubt. I'd rather not lose more soldiers than I must. Her father," Bordan glanced over his shoulder towards the room they had just left, "would have cautioned patience before action."

"Half the battle is won before a sword is drawn," Godewyn quoted. "One of yours, I believe."

"I may have said it, but the source is much older than me. However, that doesn't make it any less true. We need information before we attack."

"But the Princess has ordered the attack," Godewyn pointed out.

"And I have no choice but to obey," Bordan said, disappointment souring his tone. "I will order the soldiers forward as soon as we are ready. We should have spent more time tutoring Aelia in strategy and history, rather than poetry, discourse and philosophy."

"A second child, and a daughter at that," Godewyn answered with a shrug. "No one expected her to take the throne, at least not without some time to prepare."

"And now time is our enemy," Bordan wiped the rain from his face.

"How long can you delay?"

"Late afternoon," Bordan answered.

"Around dusk?"

"Just before, I hope. Mind you, I pray the rain stops and we can see who we are fighting and what we face," Bordan replied. "Night fighting is never pleasant, and I can't imagine Abra's mercenaries will oblige by lighting enough lamps and torches to assist us."

"You've been through a thousand battles, Bordan, and many of them in circumstances less than ideal," Godewyn pointed out.

"Circumstances are never ideal, I just prefer them to be more in our favour," the General answered as they continued down the steps.

"So what has you more worried now than before?"

Bordan stopped on the next landing, glanced around to ensure they would not be overheard. Satisfied, he grunted and steeling his mind said, "She does. Our Princess and heir."

"She is young, General." Godewyn smiled. "Don't let that concern you overly. Once she is crowned, there will be time to grow into the role."

"Perhaps," Bordan agreed, "I remember stories of her father being a little rash when he came to the throne, but he listened to advice. You know what Alhard did in the village?"

"I am aware," the High Priest said, lowering his voice.

"You didn't see him though," Bordan whispered. "Stubborn and unwilling to listen, he let his fears overwhelm him. In the ranks, he would have been a danger to everyone around him."

"Such people were victims of a wayward sword or arrow from their comrades," Godewyn said. "It wasn't common, I know, but I heard of such incidents when I was in the ranks."

"In the ranks, Alhard would have been unlikely to make it through the next battle. You know how it works. Each man relies on those either side, to protect and fight for them. He would have put everyone at risk and the soldiers would have seen that, and taken action," Bordan whispered and gripped the priest's forearm. "I don't agree with it, but I know it happens. The Empire is the same. It needs to be guided on its purpose by a strong Emperor. One who can listen, learn, knows their faults and surrounds themselves with good advisors. Everyone working together. Aelia needs to listen to advice, to be guided, and to guide. She is lashing out at all the wrong people at the moment."

"Heirs and Emperors, especially young ones, don't have to act the same way a soldier does, General. Their ascension has been brought by the Flame and has a purpose. Once the amulet is transferred, once the memories and souls of the Emperors are passed across, she will understand," Godewyn replied, placing his own hand over the General's. "Aelia has a better mind than Alhard possessed. We may find that an education in poetry and philosophy is more suited to govern than a military one. She is operating from grief and anger. Aelia will find peace, General. You worry too much."

"The curse of getting old, Godewyn," Bordan said. "My time is coming to an end, but she listens to you still. Guide her, Godewyn, be the calming influence she needs."

"I will do my best, General." The priest smiled and clapped Bordan on the shoulder. "Now, I had best let you see to the army so you can please the Princess with an attack before dusk."

"I live to serve," Bordan agreed.

"I know, old friend. Believe me, I know."

XLII

THE MAGICIAN

FIVE YEARS AGO:

He screamed, sitting bolt upright in his bed. The oil lamp flickered, and he could see sparks trailing from the small flame. They arced into the air and cascaded down upon the stone floor like a waterfall. No fire began though, and catching his breath, he reached out for the sparks as they fell, but they twisted away from his fingers.

KYRON SAT ON a wooden bench in the wattle and daub hut. There were no corners to catch his eyes and he had no place to look but into the faces of his parents.

"You're dead," he said, struggling to find the right words.

"Most here are," his mother said, her voice gentle and teasing out memories he had long since lost touch with. "The priests visit from time to time, bringing news of the world and changes."

"Why are you here?" Kyron's breath was shallow and dark spots were beginning to fill his vision.

"Be calm, son," his father said, the deep voice, the calm tone and surety within it an echo of an older man. "Breathe easy. That's it. You know why we're here."

"But," Kyron said, fighting down the lump in his throat, "why here? Why not in the Flame?"

Both his mother and father smiled at him, a soft, sad smile which broke the dam he had built to hold back his emotions. Kyron lunged forward and fell into their arms, sobbing, crushing them to him, breathing deeply of their scent, so familiar, so lost to time, so needed, so safe. He felt small hands stroke his hair while his father's hand patted him awkwardly.

"Let him cry, Ryce." It was his master's voice. "We have time and he has been holding this in since I met him."

"He shouldn't have," his mother said. "His grandfather should have let him have his tears."

"It isn't my father's way, Aedre," Kyron's father said. "You know that, but he raised him, gave him safety, and let him choose his own path."

"Learned from his mistakes, you mean." His mother's voice was like steel, cold and unbending.

"He did the best he could," Padarn said. "He let him go, let him join the Gymnasium though he knew the risks and troubles it would cause."

"And you brought him to the forest," his mother said.

"As I came when I was young," Padarn answered. "I could see it in him. The desire to wander, to learn, but it was shrouded from him. Too used to hierarchy and certainty."

"With an army though?" his father asked, as Kyron's tears began to ease.

"It was an opportunity," Padarn said, "and service and duty run in his bones."

He heard his father grunt in acknowledgment.

"I'm sorry," Kyron said, sitting back and wiping the tears away with the edge of his tunic.

"Don't apologise for crying, Kyron," his father said, "there's usually a good reason for it. We cried," Kyron saw his father take his mother's hand and squeeze, "when we lost you."

"I lost you," Kyron corrected.

"It depends on how you look at it," his father said with a smile.

"Why are you here?" Kyron tried again, rebuilding the dam and holding back the grief, sadness, loneliness, and joy which threatened to overwhelm him.

"Where should we be, Kyron?" his mother asked.

"The priests tell us that we are all together again in the Flame," Kyron said, recalling words heard in Church.

"Not our priests, son," his father said. "We belong to the Heart of the Forest. The Flame is just a story. All fire does is burn and destroy."

"It warms us," Kyron said, recalling the lessons from the priests when he was younger, "and cooks our food."

"It consumes, Kyron," his father corrected, "look at the wood beneath your cooking pot and you'll see embers, dust which will be blown away on the wind. All the life which was in it is lost to us, carried away to other lands, other shores."

"The tribes use fire to cook," Kyron pointing to the low fire which burned in the centre of the home.

"And the ash is contained, dug back into the soil and earth, returning it to the forest," his father replied.

"The soldiers were cremated," Kyron said. "Why are they not here?"

"There are not, in my limited experience, any of the Empire here," Padarn said.

"There are," his mother countered. "At least those, like us, who were part of the Empire and knew of their heritage. Those that understood and made the arrangements."

"We are from the Empire," Kyron pointed out, gazing at the three faces which looked back at him in silence for a long time.

His father was the first to speak. "How much of the Empire history do you know and understand, Kyron?"

"I know what Grandfather taught me, and what Padarn has told me over the years," Kyron answered.

"He listens," Padarn shrugged, "but it never sticks unless he finds out for himself. I had to take him out of the lessons at the Gymnasium and teach him differently. His teachers called him stubborn and I would not disagree with their assessment. However, I think it is also that he finds trusting hard. His grandfather could certainly attest to both aspects of his personality."

"Your grandfather's grandfather," his father said in the patient manner a parent talks to a difficult child, "was not of the Empire. He was born and raised in the forest which once covered much of the eastern half of the continent."

"He was one of the tribes?" Kyron said, looking at the three faces who stared back at him.

"When the Empire arrived, they invaded the forests. Cut it down to make their ships, towns, and cities. Began farming, cultivating the land for crops and preventing the forest from returning. They marched north, bit by bit, year by year, taking control of the land. Some tribes saw the end coming and chose to join the Empire," his father explained.

"It has happened before," Padarn added. "The southern continent of the Empire is just the same. A history of conquered lands and conquered people who were absorbed into the Empire."

"Where did it begin? The Empire, I mean."

"Much further south, in a single city over a thousand years ago," Padarn said. "The history is there in the Gymnasium should you wish to read it, though the scribes did become bogged down by every tiny detail."

"The point is, Kyron," his mother said, "that you are of the tribes, just as we are, your grandfather is, and Padarn. For you it has been many generations since your ancestors lived in the forests."

"Barely three generations for me," Padarn interjected.

"When I... When we," his father said, glancing at his wife, "found out the truth we wanted to connect with our past, to find out more, and," his father shrugged, "I was never going to join the army as my father wanted."

"But the tribes killed you," Kyron said.

"Outlaws killed us, Kyron," his mother said in a voice filled with sadness. "It was all we could do to hide you."

"Outlaws from the tribes."

"Some may have been, but a lot spoke the language of the Empire," his father said. "There was a lot of gold in the hills and the village we lived in was not big enough to afford a militia. The Empire soldiers were stretched thin, and we had been given warnings."

"I think they were hungry," his mother said.

"I think they were greedy," his father countered. "It doesn't matter. The key is to understand that it wasn't the tribes, at least, not only people of the tribes."

"Why am I here?" Kyron said, shaking his head and trying to clear his thoughts, looking for certainty.

"You're not dead," his mother said. "If that were the case, we would be crying also."

"Then why?"

"Because we had the chance to see you," his father said.

"Because Gwri and Emlyn made it possible," Padarn answered.

"Emlyn?"

"She and I had a talk in the camp, when you were maintaining the wards, after I collapsed in the first raid," Padarn confessed. "I asked her to look out for you if anything happened to me. Explained a little of your history to her."

A thought struck Kyron and he blurted it out before he could think it through. "You killed people of the tribes, Master. You fought against them. Killed your own people."

"I protected us," Padarn countered. "I protected the soldiers. The tribes chose to attack, I chose to defend. I was raised in the Empire, Kyron, just as you were. If you look though, if you read, you'll find our history in the library of the Gymnasium.. I am still loyal to the Gymnasium, if not the Empire entirely. Unlike others," he made a vague gesture to encompass the area outside of the hut, "I can see some of the good the Empire brings to places, and I know the bad also. There is always conflict, Kyron. Some of it large, politics and marching armies, and many will die during those times. Between people who care for one another there is conflict, though tempered with love. In here and here," he tapped his skull and heart in turn, "there is conflict. You resolve each as you will, as dictated by knowledge, reason, morals, and ethics. More than that you cannot ask."

"Which still doesn't explain why I am here," Kyron snapped, standing and pacing. "Going on is hard enough without you, Master. I don't know what to do, what to say, and what is right. Now, you've turned my world upside down and shaken it so hard I don't know where to stand, on which side I should stand, or even who I am."

"You are who you've always been," his mother said, stepping around the fire and running her fingers through his hair. "My son, there is no right and wrong, no black and white. Life is not such a simple thing. You cannot look at each decision you make and bind yourself in chains of worry. Trust who you are. Trust the person you've grown into. Your father and I set your feet on a path. Your grandfather, though I disagreed with him often, has guided your feet with best intentions. Master Padarn, and we have talked a lot about you since he came here, has given you chances to take the paths you felt were right for you, and helped you learn to walk on your own. Now, the path is yours alone to tread upon."

His father stood and placed a hand on Kyron's shoulder. "Decide who you want to be and what is right for you. The choices are yours to make. Even your grandfather would admit to that."

"But I don't know," Kyron complained.

Padarn stood in front of him and took his free hand. "You've always learned best by experience, Kyron. Go and find out."

Kyron fell.

XLIII

The General

Five years ago:

"*I'm worried about him,*" *Decima said across the table.* "*He hasn't slept well for a month or so.*"

"*I know that, Decima. His mood is worsening every day and nothing I say is right,*" *the old man answered, lifting the watered wine to his lips and taking a drink.*

"*He had nightmares when he first came,*" *Gressius said,* "*not that he remembers now, but this is something else.*"

"*Maybe we should ask the medicus to look at him?*"

"You have failed, General."

Bordan swallowed as the Princess slammed the shutters on the driving rain and fires which burned across the stone bridge in the distance.

"A simple bridge," Aelia continued. "That is all I asked you to do. Take the bridge and march our army across. What my father saw in you has long since faded, General."

"They expected us, Your Highness." Bordan stood stiff, forcing his hands to stay relaxed by his side and his tone to remain even. "The bridge is littered with barriers and obstacles. The men cannot form a rank and, in the dark, they are easier targets for the mercenaries we face."

"General, the amulet and my father's body could be here tomorrow."

The Princess stormed to the table, grabbed the goblet, took a deep swallow and her expression soured further. Glancing to the lone servant in the room, she snapped, "Fresh wine."

"We will take the bridge, my Princess," Bordan said, shifting his gaze to Godewyn for a moment. He received a shrug in return. "The rain is making the task much more difficult. When it clears, we will have much more luck."

"Luck. Luck, he says," Aelia called out, casting the empty goblet onto the table where it rolled to a halt on the map, the last dribble of red wine staining the drawings. "I don't want luck, General. I want Abra dead."

"As do I, Your Highness," Bordan assured her.

Aelia stared at him for a long moment and sighed. "One would hope so, General. When do you expect to take the bridge?"

"If the rain lets up, by dawn. If not, then mid-morning at the latest. We will take the bridge, Your Highness. My soldiers will fight and die for you."

"*My* soldiers, General, and well they should. Master Magician?"

Vedrix, sat in the far corner nursing his own goblet of wine, had contributed little to each discussion, answering only when asked, stirred back to life. "Hrm... Yes, Princess?"

"Can you not make this rain disappear so our brave General can take the bridge?"

"That is not within my power. Not with a thousand magicians could I make that happen," Vedrix answered.

"Then what use are you?" Aelia huffed, falling into her chair. Vedrix did not answer, merely focused his gaze upon the goblet of wine.

"My High Priest," Aelia turned her gaze to Godewyn. "Perhaps you could press upon the Angels of the Holy Flame to stop the rain."

"I have prayed for that to be so, Your Highness," Godewyn said in his smooth, warmest voice. "I am sure they are at work on your behalf even as we speak."

"At least one of my advisors has some use," Aelia crowed, standing from her seat as if being still was somehow a crime, and moved around the desk to stand next to the High Priest. "General, go to your forces and do not return until the bridge is taken. Let us see if you can serve as well as my High Priest."

Bordan swallowed once again, his jaw tense, teeth grinding and bowed. "Of course, my Princess."

"I've stood in the ranks, Your Highness," Godewyn said. "The General is doing all he can, as are the troops. The Flame is on our side, we will be victorious here."

"We must be," Aelia said. "General, go with my good wishes for a speedy victory."

"YOU SHOULDN'T BE in the ranks, General," Spear Sarimarcus said.

"Perhaps not, Spear," Bordan agreed as the rain dripped from his helmet and chilled the exposed flesh of his hands, "but we need to take that bridge as quick as we can. Down here I can make decisions and have them acted on quicker."

"You put yourself at too much risk."

"I'll be safe enough amongst the ranks, Spear," Bordan said with a wry smile, ignoring the quizzical look he earned in return. He glanced east and saw the hazy light of the hidden sun progress in its rise. "I think we've got the best light we're going to get. Order the men forward, Spear. Let us bring our Princess her first victory."

He looked left and right along the front rank of the Empire's army and the warmth of pride swept through him. They were his army, inherited from the General before, but honed and sharpened, moulded into the most formidable force he could imagine and led by officers of virtue.

Gripping the worn hilt of his gladius, Bordan nodded to the Aenator ahead. "Let's make this one a proper attack. We are taking that bridge and marching for the Emperor. Sound the advance. Raise the banner high."

The Aenator raised the bugle to his lips and blew out the call for advance and beside him the banner was raised high by another warrior. A cheer rose from the lines and, despite the rain, the cold, and the disquiet which had settled in his heart, Bordan raised his voice alongside his men.

When the call faded, and as well as any troop fresh off the parade ground, the front rank stepped forward as one. Behind them came the second and third. Though the army was smaller than that which had gone north with the Emperor, their feet still caused the earth to reverberate with every step. The clank and jingle of harness, shield, sword and armour was sweet counterpoint to the bass thrum of the march.

When the Empire marched, other nations quaked. So the saying went and nothing in his experience suggested that not to be the truth.

The rain fell and the wind flung it into his face as the bridge came into focus, smoke still rising from its span adding yet more grey to the sky.

"That'll be the carts," Sarimarcus said. "The mercenaries set some on fire. They're laden with amphorae of oil, so they exploded and killed quite a few of our soldiers in the first assault."

Bordan winced once more. Even though he had read the reports, the memory of visiting the burned troops this morning was yet another memory he would carry to his grave. Faces melted like candle wax, weeping puss and blood, smothered in honey, and very few able to do more than groan in pain despite the distillate of poppy they were fed by the medicus who attended them.

"After two went up in great balls of fire, the mercenaries started using flaming arrows and fire-pots thrown from as far as they could," Sarimarcus continued as they marched closer.

"There are more on the bridge?" Bordan asked, more to keep the conversation going and his mind off the incipient bloodshed.

"Reports say they cleared half the bridge last night," the Spear answered. "We've still got scouts near the bridge reporting back. The latest information is that more have appeared near the rear of the bridge. Two scouts tried to get a closer look but were attacked by archers. Both made it back alive, but one will likely lose the use of his arm."

"And the river itself?"

"In spate, General," Sarimarcus said. "We sent some of our best swimmers to look last evening and again this morning. It is too fast and too full to cross. Even a small boat would not get very far, and likely come under attack by archers. They've filled both towers at the far end."

"And those at the town end of the bridge?" Bordan pointed to the two round towers with their crenulations peeking out of the rain.

"Are ours now," Sarimarcus said. "I've got archers stationed in them, but it is something of a stalemate. Given the rain and wind, our arrows cannot reach them, nor theirs reach us."

"But the threat has kept them back?"

"Most assuredly," Sarimarcus nodded. "They tried a few times to send troops across, but soon retreated from our arrows."

"So," Bordan sighed, "it still comes down to us marching across that bridge and clearing it."

"I'm afraid so, General."

"Well," Bordan looked up at the sky, hoping the rain would clear but lacking faith in the outcome of Godewyn's prayers, "let us get it done. We will halt near the bridge. I want the latest reports brought to me. If there are more carts on the bridge, send the strongest archers up to the towers with orders to set them alight, if they can. I'd rather they had already exploded before I send the men in."

"As you command," Sarimarcus said, saluting, and breaking ranks to issue orders to his runners and officers.

THE GROUND SHOOK as another cart went up in flames and even the rain gave way for the barest beat of a heart.

"That's all the carts they could reach with their arrows," Sarimarcus announced.

"Send in the troops, testudo formation, to get the rest of the carts," Bordan ordered and a moment later, after a flag was waved and bugle call sounded, the first troops mounted the bridge encased in their shields. "Get the second and third groups ready to advance and support."

"Yes, General," Sarimarcus acknowledged.

"As soon as the third group advances, I want the front ranks to start marching," Bordan said. "We need to keep the pressure on the mercenaries holding the bridge. They fight for money, not the Empire, and they know the exact price of their lives. They'll flee once we make some headway and they see what is coming at them."

"I hope so."

"And I'll be in the front rank," Bordan said, settling the belt and gladius on his hip into a more comfortable position.

"General, I don't think—" Sarimarcus started.

"I need to be across the bridge at the start, Spear," Bordan cut him off. "We need to establish a bridgehead and bring the rest of the army across as quickly as we can, and I need to be able to see to make decisions, not wait for reports. Assign some quick runners."

"Yes, General," Sarimarcus said, "and if you're not insulted, I'll have a few of my best men on your right and left."

Bordan chuckled, a grim sound in the cold rain. "No insult taken, Spear."

"General." The call came from behind and Bordan turned to see Master Vedrix, dressed in his usual robes with the hood pulled up, bushy beard protruding past its edge.

"Master Vedrix, what brings you out this early and to a battlefront?" Bordan called back.

"Well, now, General, I am used to being up early in the morning," Vedrix said, his words trying to overtake each other, "or is that late at night. I suppose it doesn't really matter either way, does it?"

"No, Master Magician," Bordan answered with a smile, "I suppose it does not. However, this close to a battle is not where I would place you."

"Oh, really, bless the Flame, why not?" Vedrix stopped a few paces away and peered over Bordan's shoulder towards the bridge. "I heard the cart go up. Nice explosion, by the way, though I wouldn't want to be anywhere near it. Did my own stint in the ranks as a youth, you know. Not many years, but I travelled with the army west to pacify the tribes that way. Did my bit for the Empire."

"Can you destroy the other carts blocking the bridge?"

"With magic? Not without getting a lot closer than I am here. Magic loses efficiency and power over distance, General. Sending a thought, a dream, a word or sentence, communication between magicians is possible, you've seen it happen, but that is not too complicated," Vedrix answered.

"I wouldn't think setting fire to something to be that difficult either."

"It is all about energy, General," Vedrix started, losing his bumbling demeanour now he was on safer ground. "Fire is really just an expression of energy, in this case heat and light. Now, to get combustion you need to increase the heat of a fuel source. Some have quite low combustion temperatures, oil for instance. Others, much, much higher. Stone, for instance, can be made to burn, but the energy required to do so is incredibly high. There was a fellow, or was he a she, I can't remember, but they investigated that once. Quite an incredible piece of research—"

"Vedrix," Bordan interrupted as the magician took a breath, "I'll take your word for it. How close would you need to be?"

The magician went silent and Bordan could see the man's eyes flickering back and forth to the bridge, calculating and considering.

"A bow shot's distance, if the cart was covered in oil," Vedrix concluded. "Closer if it wasn't and you wanted an immediate burn. Further if you have time to wait."

Disappointed, Bordan sighed, but did his best to keep the smile on his face. "That is good to know. I'll keep it in mind. Now, why did you come down here? I'm about to send the first troops across."

"Two reasons, my good General," Vedrix said, looking anything but disappointed in the answer he had given. "I wonder if I might speak with you out of earshot for a moment?"

"It really is not the time, Master Vedrix," Bordan replied.

"Oh, really? I think now is the perfect time, General. Perfect time. I promise not to take up too much of it. A few moments only." The magician clamped Bordan's arm in a surprisingly strong grip. "Over there, perhaps. Council business. I am sure you'll find it interesting and useful in the upcoming battle."

"Sarimarcus," Bordan called, "I want to know the moment the second group starts across the bridge. You have till then, Master Magician."

"Of course, General," the Spear said, hurrying away.

"What is it, Master Vedrix?" Bordan said as they stepped away from the soldiers.

"First, a gift." Vedrix reached into his robes and brought out a small, smooth disc of wood. "I made this last night."

"Thank you," Bordan said, holding it up and inspecting both sides. "It is very... nice."

"What? Oh? Well, I suppose it is," Vedrix answered. "It was just a piece of wood I had in my things."

"Why have you given it to me then?" Bordan squinted at it and tilted it to encourage the water to run off.

"It is a shield token," Vedrix said. "Wear it close to your skin and it will last all day. Should protect you from at least one or two blows. You're not as young as you were and last time you went into a battle you came out with a wound. This should help."

"Magic?"

"On its own the wood wouldn't stop much," Vedrix laughed. "Yes, magic."

"I'm not entirely sure..." Bordan hesitated.

"A moment ago, you were happy for me to set fire to things, but magic which stops you getting hurt you have a problem with?" Vedrix said, brushing the water from his beard.

"You're right," Bordan said after a moment, tucking the thin token beneath the neck of his lorica segmata. "Thank you. And the other matter?"

Vedrix's face lost its smile and the spark which seemed to reside permanently in his eyes dimmed. "Aelia."

"What about her?" Bordan asked, glancing around. The closest soldiers were all facing the bridge and the noise of the rain striking armour and shield was loud enough to drown out the whispers.

"She seems... angry," Vedrix observed.

"Worried," Bordan answered. "Her father's body is close and the amulet also. Plus, Abra, the man who organised the assassination of her mother and brother is just across the bridge."

"Possibly the death of the Emperor too," Vedrix added. "I have considered that possibility. The same man may be responsible for all three."

"The thought had occurred to me also, but with no proof it is only a thought," Bordan replied. "If that is the only concern you have, I must get back to my soldiers."

"General," Vedrix paused and Bordan saw him take a deep breath, "I know I seem confused, and I do not always make myself clear, nor do I speak up in council. I am happy to nod and answer direct questions only. However, please do not mistake me for an idiot. I am Master of the Gymnasium of Magicians, a place where almost every person is learned, a researcher, and a thinker. If they are not, they tend to die quite early on in their careers. I watch and I listen. The signs are there if you know where to look and none of them take magic to see."

"Signs of what, Master Vedrix?" Bordan asked, his stomach felt heavy and he felt his heart rate quicken. "In case you haven't seen, I have a battle to win."

"You are out of favour, Bordan," Vedrix snapped, all trace of the bumbling, genial magician gone, as the man straightened to his full height and pulled back his shoulders.

Bordan took a step back, realising for the first time that the magician was taller than him. In every council meeting, on the journey here, Vedrix had appeared unsure, smaller, rounder, and if Bordan was being honest, ineffectual. No threat, he realised.

"Aelia has turned away from you and looks to others for assurance and guidance," Vedrix continued stepping forward and speaking in a harsh whisper. "Win this battle and that may change, but I think not. The Princess has a madness in her eyes, a hunger for power. Whether this is because of the sudden deaths of her family or was there before I cannot say. It is there now, and you have seen it."

"Master Vedrix," Bordan gasped out, "this is treason."

"This is honesty, Bordan," Vedrix whispered. "This is respect, mine for you. The Gymnasium dwindles, and even under the last Emperor our numbers have fallen. The Church hunts magicians in the countryside and we are a dying people in the Empire. Yet, we cling on and provide our services. Change is coming, General. I see it, feel it, and know it. Decide what is most important to you, General, and look to that."

Bordan gaped, his mouth dry and no words came to mind.

"You will do your duty, and you will serve, but family is important," Vedrix continued, his shoulders slumping and a spark of mirth returned to his eyes as he shrank back into the appearance Bordan recognised. "He is alive and he is coming. Choose wisely, my old friend."

"I've got a battle to win," he managed to utter.

"Keep the token close, General," Vedrix said, nodding. An absent-minded gesture, Bordan would have described it as before, now he was not so sure.

"Sarimarcus," Bordan shouted as the old magician vanished into the rain. "Have the third group gone onto the bridge yet?"

His question was punctuated by an explosion of flame from the bridge and the shouts of warriors.

XLIV

THE MAGICIAN

FIVE YEARS AGO:
The market was crowded, and the sun was warm upon his head. Grammaticus Flaccus was speaking, but he found it hard to concentrate on the discussion of poetry and legend. All around him the fruit, herbs, and spices were giving off the most wonderful scents. His eyes were drawn to the bright yellows, dull oranges, vibrant reds of the fruits and in his vision they merged into ocean waves of colour which rolled towards him.

He stood, wonder and awe, fear and trepidation, coursing through him as the waves crashed over him.

KYRON LOOKED OVER his shoulder. The Emperor's waggon was struggling through the mud, pulled by those few horses which had the strength to do so. The driver would change them soon, to preserve their strength, but already seven horses had been injured so badly that they had been slaughtered over the past three days. The meat had been welcomed by those troops fortunate enough to be chosen, but it surprised him how few a horse fed.

The three remaining priests, with Livillia at their head, tramped through the mud, sloshed through puddles, using their staffs to keep themselves upright. A tight smile flitted across his face as he caught sight of their robes, sodden, dirt smudged, and torn. The Curate looked up, caught his eye and sneered.

Behind the waggon came the injured, guarded on the perimeter by those still able to wield a gladius. Astentius and his staff had gathered the supplies Borus had secured from the village—not as much as they had hoped—and distributed it as fairly as possible. Kyron had heard some grumbling from the soldiers, but Borus had told him that was a good sign. The injured were fed, as were the soldiers. However, the rations were less than before and their pace had slowed further.

The remaining soldiers carried their food, but more and more they were laden down with the injured who could no longer walk. Only the horses seemed to find enough to eat in the new spring grass and shrubs by the side of the track. They were given time to eat as the column staggered forward. If the horses could pull no more, the carts would have to be left behind with those too hurt to walk. Everyone knew, and it weighed heavily on over-burdened shoulders.

"How many more days?" Borus asked as he slogged through another puddle.

"At this pace, we will be there by tomorrow afternoon," Emlyn answered. "If we slow much more, we'll be spending another night under the trees. If the rain keeps up, that might not be a bad thing."

Kyron stepped around the lake of liquid mud in his path. "It isn't far from the edge of the forest to the bridge, and it's farmland with proper roads."

"Why does the Empire have such a fascination with roads? You build them, I'm told, everywhere," she replied, drawing her cloak tighter about her.

"To enable the army to move swiftly about the Empire. Merchants also like them. They can get produce to market more quickly and command a higher price," Borus explained.

"It is not about stamping your presence on the land?"

"Probably a bit of that," Borus replied. He looked up into the sky. "Can't see the rain stopping."

"No fires tonight," Emlyn agreed. "All the wood will be sodden."

"There is some dry under cover on a cart," Kyron said. The Spear had ordered wood gathered when the cold wind gave way to rain.

"Not enough," Borus answered. "We'll be having a cold meal tonight. Unless?"

Kyron caught the questioning glance from the corner of his eye and turned to Borus. His eyes off his path, his foot splashed into the large puddle, cold water spraying up his legs. "I can dry some wood or heat up stones. Enough for a few groups, but not everyone."

"I'd settle for dry boots," Borus laughed, lifting his own mud-caked boot from the dirt and shaking it. Water flew from the leather and clumps of mud fell away.

"Halt." The cry came from the front of the column. "Rest."

The creak of the waggon's wheels, a sound Kyron had come to take as part of the forest soundscape, stopped and a great sigh went up from the bedraggled army.

"Let's move under the trees," Emlyn said. "The leaves will keep a lot of the rain off our shoulders."

He followed her off the trail with Borus and a few soldiers into the shelter of a large tree. All along the column soldiers, the healthy helping the injured, did the same until only the waggon and covered carts marked their presence on the trail.

Kyron dipped into his satchel and pulled out a hard biscuit. Their ration of flour and wheat had been ground up, mixed with a little water and baked upon flat stones on the edge of the fire the first night. It had been Borus's suggestion and Emlyn had agreed. Better to use the flour and wheat rather than risk it turning mouldy as they travelled. Since the rain had started, that advice had become worth more than all the gold in the Empire.

Crunching down on the tasteless food, careful to catch every crumb, he watched the rain pummel the ground and fill every footprint and rut with water. The horses, left in the rain, pulled their carts to the side of the trail and began searching for things to eat.

A call came down the line. "Cohort Borus."

"Here," Borus called back.

"Spear Astentius requires your presence."

"Great." Borus heaved himself up. "Stay here."

"I'm not going anywhere," Emlyn replied.

Borus grunted and took two steps before turning back. "I don't suppose you've remembered another village close by?"

"There isn't one," Emlyn answered. "At least, not one that has any signs out. From what I can see, the next village is close to the edge of the forest."

Borus nodded and resumed his walk to the front. The other soldiers who had come with him moved away a little to other trees to seek shelter and conversation with their comrades.

And to be away from me and her, Kyron thought, his eyes tracking to Emlyn.

"The magician and pagan."

Kyron's head snapped up as an acidic voice burned away his train of thought. He swallowed, noting who had stepped into the sheltered area around the tree. Curate Livillia and the two remaining priests.

"Curate," Kyron greeted her, cursing the quaver he heard in his voice. "How can I assist you?"

"You can't," Livillia answered. "You never could."

"The wards on the waggon are not due for renewal for another two days," Kyron said, ignoring her words.

"They were never important, Apprentice," the priest said. "Preserving a body which should have been given to the Flame weeks ago. Worse still, defiling it with your magic and preventing him from joining with the Holy Flame is a sacrilege."

"I only do what the Legion required of my master and I," Kyron replied, keeping his voice level and calm.

"You may have cremated him, but he'll never join the Flame. Nor will you," the Curate said, stepping in closer.

"And count themselves bloody lucky they didn't," Emlyn said, pushing off the tree where she had been leaning. "Who wants to spend eternity being burned to ash again and again? Sounds hideous. Cruel, too."

"You dare insult the Holy Flame?" Livillia snarled, rounding on the guide.

"You don't like my words? My pagan voice damages your faith, cuts your truth to pieces?"

Kyron took a breath, noting the way Emlyn's hand was hooked in her belt, close to her knife and those sharp sticks she whittled continuously. "I don't think that Emlyn meant to insult the Holy Flame, Curate."

"Don't tell me what I mean, Kyron," Emlyn said, her voice cold and her eyes never leaving Livillia's.

"You've got yourself a pet," the Curate said.

"You've got an evil mouth and the mind behind it is a festering hole," Emlyn replied with a smile.

"You can't talk to me that way," Livillia screeched and Kyron noted the other two priests exchange a look before stepping forward.

"I can talk to you any way I wish, Livillia," Emlyn answered with a broad smile. "I am not a brainwashed boy and I've seen the truth of your religion. Invasion. Forced conversion. Bloodshed. Cruelty. All knowledge contained, corralled, and put into neat little boxes."

Kyron's hand dropped to his own belt, not far from the hilt of the gladius Borus had given him. Under the boughs of the trees, the priest's hands strayed to their own weapons.

"This you can know. This you can't. Don't question this, but you can ask this. Here is an answer to a question you didn't ask. Take it as the truth because a priest said it," Emlyn continued. "If you're representative of your whole religion, it is one based on fear and ignorance. Kyron's magic, and Padarn's, saved you and the soldiers. He has preserved your Emperor's body so his wife and children can see him one last time and remember him for who he was. Do you thank or acknowledge?"

Livillia's face had whitened, her hands were clenched at her side, and she had frozen in place. With a stiff gust of wind, Kyron was sure she would tip over.

"Of course you don't," Emlyn continued. "You mock. You speak against him and his master. You try to control the thoughts of others who have seen the benefits he brings to this, to them. It scares you, and he scares you."

"I am not frightened of magic, him, or you." The Curate's words were thinned by her compressed lips.

"You keep telling yourself that, Livillia," Emlyn said. "You keep believing in everything you were taught by those above. Don't ever start thinking yourself, Curate, or your faith will be snuffed out like the last guttering flames of a campfire."

"You cannot."

"I did," Emlyn snapped back, anger entering her voice for the first time. "Now, is there something you actually wanted?"

"Is everything all right?" The shouted question came from Borus as he strode back into the shelter of the tree.

"The Curate just came to... to..." Kyron floundered.

"She," Livillia said, her voice ice and finger pointed into Emlyn's face, "cannot speak to a Curate of the Holy Flame like that. I demand you do something about it."

"I didn't hear your discussion, Curate," Borus said, nodding towards the two priests who stood with raised staffs. "You'll be wanting to put those down, lads."

"I demand you punish her," Livillia screeched. "Put her in ropes. Whip her."

"Burn her?" Emlyn added, a smile of innocence upon her face.

"Insolent bitch," Livillia snapped.

"I didn't hear your discussion, Curate," Borus said, "and Emlyn is here to guide us to safety. She has already assisted in gathering the food you and your priests have been eating these past days. If you've a complaint, take it up with Spear Astentius. I follow his orders."

"You will not have heard the last of this, Cohort," Livillia snapped, turning on her heel and stomping past her two startled priests out into the rain which fell upon the trail.

"One day," Borus said, heaving a sigh and reaching out one hand to rest again the trunk of the tree. "And before you tell me the story, I don't want to know."

KYRON DID NOT sleep well. The rain hammered against the waxed canvas of his lonely tent and even buried amongst the blankets he shivered.

Emlyn had not made any attempt to talk to him about his experience with the village tree. When he had come back to the world, all she did was smile. Three times yesterday he had tried to broach the subject, searched for the words that would explain what he had seen, who he had talked to.

"Was it real?" he had asked the last time.

"Did it seem real to you?"

"Yes, but..." he admitted, and the words dried on his tongue.

"You experienced what you experienced, Kyron," she said. "That is as real as anything gets to be."

"It can't have been."

"You are that learned and wise to know all that can be and cannot be?" She favoured him with a wry smile.

"Well, no, obviously not," he answered.

"The trees show us realities in their roots which reach across the world," Emlyn said. "However, your reality is not mine to know."

"There was something in the food," he accused.

"Yes," she said, matching his stare with one of her own, "and we all drank from the same pot. Don't go looking for answers when there are none, Kyron. Accept things as they are when you must, question when you must, but know you will not always get the answer you like."

"Now you sound like Padarn," he said.

"He was a very wise man," she answered, turned and walked away before he could say anymore.

His thoughts dwelled on his parents, on their explanation, and on his grandfather and his own version of events. Perhaps all were telling the truth, from their own perspective. Padarn had been little help and had kept things from him. His ancestry being the most vital.

Though, he considered, it may be that he should have opened his eyes sooner, seen the world for what it was. Upon rejoining the army, talking to Astentius about the supplies they had procured, the difference in names struck him. Each hinted, though blurred by choice and generation, at their heritage. Kyron was so much closer to Emlyn than Astentius. Though heritage seemed no barrier to progress in the Empire, his grandfather being an example.

He staggered out of his tent when he heard the rest of the soldiers begin to move, as the shouts of officers roused those who would much rather stay in their beds. The tent was simple to deconstruct, a few wooden poles and waxed fabric kept taut with ropes and carved wooden pegs.

He joined Emlyn and Borus near the front of the column as they began to move once more. The mud sucked at his feet or slipped out from under his boots. More than once, Borus caught him by the arm and set him back on his feet.

"Best to stay clear of the priests for today," Borus said as they stopped for a mid-morning rest. "I heard Livillia screaming at Astentius last eve. He hasn't given way, but if she starts on the men, speaking against you, he may have no choice."

"She's been doing that the whole way," Kyron said.

"Maybe," Borus acknowledged, "but now she has more reason and more poison to inject them with."

"We'll be out of the forest by this afternoon," Emlyn said. "After that, it won't matter what she says. Many of your men will just be grateful to be alive."

"And she'll take credit," Borus cautioned. "For the Flame, of course, but I've seen priests like her before."

"We will avoid her," Kyron agreed.

The rest of the morning was wet and tiring. Twice the waggon got stuck in soft ground, brown water welling up beside the sinking wheels. Soldiers had gone back to drag it out and the whole column had to stop while it was freed.

During the midday break Borus took the report that three more soldiers had died on the carts. It was not clear whether that was due to their injuries, which were severe, or the weather. The biscuits they all forced themselves to chew were especially dry and tasteless. Not even the water from their skins could help them swallow.

"I can see a break in the trees," one of the soldiers at the front called after they had been moving for a time.

Kyron squinted through the rain, lifting a hand to prevent water from dripping into his eyes. The track did indeed seem lighter ahead, the browns and greens of the trees coming to an end. His heart rose, some burden lifted, but it was accompanied by bitter sadness which he could taste on his tongue.

"What will you do?" he asked Emlyn as the trees thinned. "Go back to your parents?"

"I don't know," she said. "Not yet."

They tramped on in silence, Kyron's gaze fixed on the gap in the trees ahead. "I think the rain is lessening."

Next to him, Emlyn looked up. "End of the storm. I wouldn't have wanted to be out in the open during this one."

"Form up," came the orders. Borus marched along the front row. "Spear Astentius wants us to look our best as we march to the bridge. Remember, we are soldiers of the Empire. We are the honour guard to the Empire. We were chosen as the best and we will look it as we march."

"There is a town ahead," Kyron said. "Cesena, just over the bridge. We will be dry once we get there."

The last of the rain passed over their heads as the trees thinned and the track turned into something which more closely resembled an Empire road: wide, with a subtle curve to either side which encouraged the rain to dribble into deep gullies cut into the soil. The mud became gravel and stones before giving way to close-set cobbles which announced civilisation to the soldiers.

"Form up," Borus continued to call. "Get your uniforms sorted out, neat as you can. Retrieve capes and attach. Let's look like the Empire."

Kyron watched as there was a rustle of packs and fabric. Each soldier retrieved the short red capes which they had last worn on their march across the bridge and into the forest. Once out of sight of the town, they had changed into battle dress, and the cape which an enemy might find a sturdy handhold had been the first item to go into their packs. Different belts and clasps, less ornamented, more rugged and durable had replaced the decoration of rank and purpose. Now they were returning to the Empire, certain things were expected of them.

"What's that?" Emlyn took Kyron's shoulder and turned him in the direction of the town.

"What?"

The clearing rain revealed the smudge of figures ahead. More than Kyron would have expected for the farmers he knew lived and worked the land on the edge of the forest.

"Borus," he called, pointing towards the figures. "I think the town sent a guard to meet us."

Borus came striding back to the front and focused his gaze on the figures which, through the fading mist of rain, were getting clearer.

"Shit," he said, spinning on his heel and running, armour clanking, towards the Spear.

"What's the problem?" Emlyn asked.

"I don't..." Kyron's sentence trailed off as he saw what Borus had seen. "Those are not Empire soldiers."

XLV

THE GENERAL

FIVE YEARS AGO:
"You should have called me sooner," the medicus said.

"It was just nightmares," he explained. The boy lay on the bed, his eyes closed, skin cold and pale, with a blood spotted bandage around his head. "What is wrong with him?"

"His humours are out of alignment," the medicus said. "His blood and bile are too hot."

"What can we do?"

"I'll bleed him a little," the medicus said, drawing a sharp scalpel from his bag, "and leave you with some leeches."

THE BRIDGE WAS clogged with smoke and soldiers. Already there was a steady stream of the wounded being helped towards the rear, to be bandaged, treated and sent back to battle if possible, or given the gift of poppy if the injury was too severe.

"Down!" Sarimarcus shouted.

Bordan looked up as the Spear's hand pushed his shoulder and he stumbled to the side behind the ruins of the cart. The soldier's shield came up and the arrow bounced from it, clattering to the floor where it tumbled away.

"Send in another group," Bordan ordered, clambering back to his feet. His own shield was heavy on his arm and his lungs were scorched by hot smoke.

A moment later, after orders were shouted, five ranks soldiers marched past, their shields interlocked around the sides and those in the middle holding their own above their heads.

"The last carts aren't filled with oil," Sarimarcus said, peeking over the rim of his shield.

"Mercenaries aren't stupid enough to have them explode when they are using them to funnel us into their killing ground," Bordan said. "How is the leg?"

Sarimarcus looked down and checked the tight wrapped bandage. "Barely feel it. Only a scratch."

"We need to push," Bordan said, gritting his teeth, knowing he was sending men to their deaths. "Get the ranks formed."

The Spear swallowed and nodded, waving the Aenator forward and issuing the orders. The clarion call to battle sang over the bridge, cutting through the smoke and rain, overwhelming the roar of the water beneath. Men appeared through the downpour, from behind ruined carts and broken masonry, with tall wicker shields, wider than three men and braced to stand up on their own, pushed before them. The closer they had come to the two towers at the far end of the bridge the more the arrows had come from the mercenaries on top, and those stationed to the side of the bridge who loosed blind into the rain.

"The longer we stay here, the more time Abra has to reinforce his troops at the end of the bridge, and the more soldiers we will lose to unlucky arrows," Bordan said, slapping the Spear on the shoulder. "Let's go. Second rank."

Sarimarcus grimaced as he stood, lifting his shield to cover his body. Bordan gave the man a grim smile and stood next to him, his own shield raised to protect them both.

They wove their way into the ranks of soldiers, finding a place in the centre of the second rank. The soldiers displaced did not grumble or complain but moved back into the third rank. Bordan had a clear view of the obstacles blocking the bridge and the third group of soldiers he had sent into to clear space to march.

"Forward!" he shouted, and the bugle took up the call.

There was a wave of noise, shouts from the men, shields being raised and locked into place, weapons readied, and they started forward at a measured pace. Bordan lifted his sword and beat his shield with it in time with his steps. All around the soldiers took up the beat and every step was echoed by a thousand swords against a thousand shields.

"Let's put the fear of the Empire in them, Spear," Bordan called between steps. "On my command, form the arrow aimed at the gap in the mercenary's barriers and let the barritus ring out across the lands."

The commands went out to the ranks. The experienced and well-armoured at the front would take the initial brunt of the attack, but the second rank, including Bordan, would support them.

Arrows struck shields and ranks reacted with practised efficiency, every soldier knowing their role, raising shields and protecting one another. Even so, some found a path through, many having rebounded or been caught by a shield and tumbling through gaps. Any injured soldier would halt, and another would take their place. In this manner they advanced through the smoke and rain.

Over the shoulders of the front rank, Bordan got his first glimpse of the mercenaries. Some wore Empire armour, the chain links of the hamata or the banded steel of the segmata, but many others had covered themselves in padded tunics which would cushion blows and might just stop a weak sword thrust.

"Give the order, Spear," Bordan said as the energy of battle began to run in his blood, sharpening vision and hearing, a roaring tide in his ears and exultation sweeping away his fears.

The bugle called out and the barritus, a single great cheer rang out from the troops. It shook Bordan in his armour even as his own voice rose in the war cry.

The front rank raced forward, shrinking to a single point which swept out to either side forming a sharp arrow with which to pierce the mercenaries' protection. Bordan kept up with the second rank, running forward to fill in the gaps and support as the tip of the arrow slid through the gap in the overturned and stone weighted carts the mercenaries had used as a blockade and funnel.

A shock ran through the army as the point of the arrow met the mercenary line. Bordan set his shoulder to his shield and pushed forward, even as those behind did the same to him. Forward progress slowed for a heartbeat as the cries of soldiers and sound of weapon on armour rang out.

Bordan was being crushed, his breath coming in short, dirty gasps and sweat stuck his tunic to his flesh. The rim of his helmet dug into his forehead and sweat misted his vision. His shield hand, gloved to protect his knuckles, was cramping and his arm was a mass of aches, tiredness already seeping into his limbs. In his other hand, his gladius, one he'd carried since he had scooped it off a battlefield decades ago, was a comfort.

He glanced across at Sarimarcus and grinned. "Push."

The bugle cry went up once more and was followed by the barritus. This cry was drawn from the pit of the stomach, not a word so much as a feeling of rage and pride, a dismissal of fear and a welcoming of death in service to something greater. It was everything he saw and loved in the Empire.

To his left, the cart of the final barricade slipped by as the ranks lunged forward. Now there was room, a sense of space opening up, and ranks, funnelled and channelled by the blockade, could expand across the battlefield. The true power of the Empire ranks could be unleashed upon the mercenaries.

General Bordan, most excellent leader of the Empire's army, slotted into the front rank as a soldier staggered back, arm dripping bright red blood.

A mercenary stepped forward, his large axe already swinging towards Bordan's head. The blow would likely break his shield arm if he lifted it to protect himself. Instead, the General dropped his hips and let the bottom of his large, heavy shield rest upon the ground. Ducking his head at the last moment, the axe stuck the metal rim of the wooden shield and Bordan felt the shock travel up his arm and rattle his teeth.

Bordan had been wounded more times than he wanted to remember, and killed more than he could recall. Old warriors were old because they had killed and lived. Experience was the only true gift of age, its one compensation for the loss of strength, the slowness of limb, and shallow well of energy.

His gladius stabbed out, slicing into the flesh of the mercenary's inner thigh. A killing strike, and even as Bordan stood up, the axe fell from the warrior's weak hands and he stumbled back. Bordan punched out with his shield, pushing the dying warrior onto those behind.

A second mercenary swung a sword at him and this time he raised his shield to meet it, careful to keep his head out of the way in case the sword slipped off the wood. The soldier on his left took a half step forward and slid his gladius between the mercenary's ribs, and Bordan moved up next to him, feeling the soldier on his right do the same. Moving as one, fighting as one, protecting each other as they went.

"Sarimarcus," he shouted stepping back into the ranks and allowing another to take his place, "get soldiers in those towers and kill the archers. Replace them with our own."

The bridge was theirs and now the task of securing this bank of the river consumed his mind. Recognising another soldier, he waved the woman over.

"Cohort," he said, coughing the smoke from his lungs and spitting it onto the bridge stones, "get a gang together and clear the carts. Tip them over the side if you need to, I don't care. I want that bridge clear and open as soon as possible."

She saluted. "Yes, General."

Turning back to the battle, Bordan surveyed the scene. The stone bridge and cobbled road were strewn with the detritus of war: blood, bodies, and weapons. Following the path of the road as far as the rain would allow, Bordan saw it rise up the hill to the north and along it, mercenaries were fleeing the battle. His own troops, he was happy to see, did not follow and were focused on ensuring that no enemy warriors were faking their own deaths by the simple expedient of stabbing them. It was gruesome work, but they did not have time to take prisoners and these mercenaries were traitors to the Empire. There was only one punishment and it was much worse than a clean sword through the neck.

"General," Sarimarcus called as he trotted up, the wound on his leg not seeming to slow him down, "the archers say the rain is clearing from the north."

"Not now. Not now," Bordan muttered. "For once, I wanted it to rain, to give us cover as we brought the army across. How many do we have this side?"

Both men looked around, estimating and counting those soldiers they could see.

"A quarter to a third?" Sarimarcus guessed.

"Closer to a third, I think," Bordan agreed. "Abra, if he has any sense, will attack as soon as he can. Break us against the bridge. He'll know those coming across can do little if we cannot push forward."

"We need to clear the bridge," the Spear said.

"I've got a Cohort on that," Bordan said, "and soldiers are coming across as fast as they can. I think it is time to be bold, Sarimarcus. Abra isn't a soldier and the mercenaries that return to his line will tell him what is coming. Better still, they'll treble the count of our force and even if their commander halves that, Abra will be worried. We need to use that time of indecision."

"Yes, General," Sarimarcus said, waving the Aenator over to his side. "Your orders?"

"We form up to attack," Bordan said, squinting at the land around him, "and give ourselves room to bring the troops across. Three ranks, veterans at the front, and let's stagger the maniples, create some gaps the mercenaries are likely to head towards. If they fall for it, we can close up and deal with them in pieces."

"You think they will?"

"If it was a practised leader, no. Abra, though, I am not so sure," Bordan shrugged. "Either way it gives us a little more time while they decide upon their own tactics. Keep archers in the tower. We will set the ranks just back from their bow range."

"It will leave our flanks exposed," Sarimarcus pointed out, "and the mercenaries may be able to get around us to the bridge during the battle."

"To be met by more of our soldiers coming across," the General answered. "We set up to attack, but don't advance until we have to. Let's use the fact that we are getting constant reinforcements from the other bank to our advantage. Keep them guessing and worried."

"As you order," Sarimarcus said, issuing his own orders to the Aenator who blew the signals from his bugle.

"General," a familiar voice called from behind. "You promised to take the bridge and you have done so."

Bordan sighed as fresh soldiers began to stream past him, taking up positions at the base of the towers. "Godewyn, what are you doing here? It isn't safe."

"Safe enough for the Empire's General," the priest said with a smile as he stepped alongside Bordan. "And I am not so naïve as to come without some protection."

The priest parted his robs and the grey metal rings of a hamata shirt appeared.

"You know that won't stop an arrow," Bordan said. "Why are you here? Why does everyone seem to want to put themselves at risk?"

"Better me than Aelia," Godewyn said, peering past Bordan towards the rise ahead. "It took a lot of convincing for me to stop her coming."

"But you did?" Bordan glanced over his shoulder to make sure none of the soldiers were the Princess.

"I did, but she is not happy about it," Godewyn smiled. "I promised to bring her back news of your victory."

"Godewyn," Bordan said, "is that a sword at your waist?"

"My old gladius," the High Priest replied, patting the leather-bound grip. "I've not worn this in over a decade."

"And you couldn't resist belting it on while you came down to determine the fate of the battle?"

"I choose to call it prudent," Godewyn said with no trace of guilt. "You won, Bordan. You should be happy and relieved. I know Aelia will."

"It isn't over yet," Bordan grunted.

As if to punctuate his words, a call rose from the top of the eastern tower, and Bordan squinted into the rain to see an archer stabbing his hand towards the north. Moments later, the dark smudge of an army appeared at the top of the rise.

"Now we know where they are," Bordan said and at his side it was Godewyn's turn to grunt.

"They're flying the flag." Sarimarcus pointed up the slope.

"You've better eyes than me," the General grunted. "I haven't got a clue what he wants to say, but if it buys us a little time. Raise the white flag and get me that Cohort and five soldiers. I'll go meet him."

"General," Sarimarcus began, "better for me to go."

"No," Bordan answered, waving away the concerns he knew were coming. "I know Abra and he knows me."

"And I'll join you," Godewyn answered, untying his robes and slipping them from his shoulders. He handed the garment to a passing soldier who stood in awe of the cloth he held. "I would dearly like to see Abra's face now he knows what judgement his traitorous ways have brought upon his head."

"Godewyn," Bordan began, then became more formal, noting the presence of soldiers who had gathered around. "High Priest, it is not prudent to join this meeting. Two of the Empire's Ruling Council would be a great prize for Abra."

"It is a flag of truce, General," Godewyn said, nodding towards the ridge. "He will not break it. Certainly, the mercenaries would not—it is their usual means for avoiding conflict and saving their own lives."

Bordan looked into the High Priest's eyes, saw the younger man who had stood the ranks with him, and exhaled a long, slow breath. "If this goes wrong, she'll have us crucified."

"Have faith, Bordan," Godewyn said, tightening the buckle on his sword. "Can someone lend me a shield?"

He waited in the front rank for the soldiers to assemble, nodding to the Cohort who carried the white flag when she arrived.

Cohort Cypria nodded towards the approaching mercenary group. "They're coming."

"We had best go meet them," Bordan said, striding forward, Godewyn and the soldiers following.

Stepping away from the front ranks was an exercise in trust. The white flag of truce had a long history and not all of it good. War had rules, but rules were often made to be broken. Desperate people do desperate things.

Cypria stepped up beside Bordan and the five soldiers, swords sheathed but shields ready, followed them into the dead land between the two armies.

"Do you want me to kill him, General?" Cypria asked as they walked.

Bordan glanced to the side to see a grin split the woman's face. "Tempting, but I think this will be a short conference and as our esteemed guest has pointed out, they will not break the truce of the flag."

"And the longer it goes on, the more troops you can bring across," Godewyn added.

"Then why the parlay?" Cypria asked. "To kill you?"

"Possibly, though unlikely." Bordan pondered. It was customary, before a battle, to have a conference of opposing leaders. A setting of rules, a show of respect. Abra was a traditionalist in many ways, but the mercenary leader would have—should have—counselled against wasting this time. Although, Bordan conceded Godewyn's point, the mercenaries might be looking for a way out. When you fight for money, you know your life's exact worth. "Something else is going on. Keep your ears open and swords loose in their sheaths."

Bordan arrived first and Cypria stabbed the earth with the pole to which the flag was attached. Bordan looked at the square of white cloth, sodden and hanging limp in the rain, and smiled. The Cohort had chosen a spear to tie the flag to and the sharp point pierced the clouds above. Trust, the flag said. Only so far, the spear point cautioned.

"My dear General," Abra said, sketching a bow as his own group stopped a short distance away.

"Abra," Bordan nodded.

"Ah," Abra replied. "Well, to be expected. Allow me to introduce Princess Hanno. She leads the army you see gathered upon the ridge."

"Princess Hanno," Bordan favoured the mercenary with a nod. "I confess, your fame has yet to reach my ears."

Hanno spat on the floor at Bordan's feet. "I've heard of you, General."

"From Abra? All very flattering, I am sure," Bordan replied, hooking his thumbs into his sword belt. "You are not from the Empire?"

"This one?" Hanno gazed around, her dark eyes swallowing the landscape. "It is too wet for me. I prefer the warmer lands of the south."

"Perhaps it is time you returned there?"

"Once my coffers are full, General," Hanno answered.

"Of course," Bordan replied, ignoring the expression on Abra's face. "Perhaps I could assist you with that. I'm sure I could match Abra's offer and save you the trouble of dying for it."

"Money not to fight?" Hanno laughed. "That would ruin my reputation, General."

"What reputation, Hanno?" Bordan replied, his voice as cold as the rain that fell. "I've never heard of you, and when you die here, no one ever will."

"You insult me," Hanno's voice rose into a shout.

"I tell you honestly," Bordan countered. "If you chose it to be an insult, that is more on you than me." He turned from the fuming mercenary to the treacherous noble. "Now, Abra, what is it you wanted with this meeting?"

"I'd hoped we could talk," Abra said. "Like the old days?"

Bordan raised an eyebrow. "We fenced in council, Abra, and we are fencing here though with more men, more swords, and more chance of death. Your mercenaries are outnumbered and will run rather than die. Money is their master, Abra, not you."

"It was not supposed to be like this," Abra said, though to whom Bordan was unsure.

"Battles are always like this. I've fought in too many, and hoped never to fight another, but here we are, and I lay that at your feet," Bordan said. "You turned traitor, Abra. You desired the throne and made your choices. When your blood is soaking the ground beneath your feet, I hope that's small comfort."

"I was forced into this," Abra suddenly spat. "You have no idea, General. Too blind. Too consumed with duty and service to see what is really going on."

"Abra," Godewyn interrupted stepping forward, "talking to you is like holding an eel. Your words are slippery and coil around the truth until it is strangled."

The moment of shock on Abra's face was almost worth risking the High Priest's life just to see. A man who thought himself better than others, more intelligent and cunning, had been outmanoeuvred once again.

"You—" Abra began.

"You killed a Prince," Bordan interrupted, intending to keep the former Duke off balance and himself in charge of this conversation. "Your assassins killed the Empress. You brought this on yourself."

"Me?" Abra's voice was strangled by disbelief and the man glanced at the High Priest who stood in the rain with his hand on his sword, hair plastered to his head, and beatific smile upon his face. As Bordan watched, something changed in Abra's eyes. A finality, a darkness, and a cold choice entered them. "Whatever you believe is wrong, but I can't change that or you, General. We are where we are, and all I need for you to refer to me as Emperor is the amulet and a priest to perform the transfer. Luckily for me, you brought a priest with you. It's always good to have a spare. The next time we meet, General, you will bow to me. And Godewyn," Abra's smile was that of snake, full of venom, "don't get killed in the battle. You would be the perfect choice to perform the ceremony."

"The next time we meet, Abra," Bordan spat, raising his hand to prevent anyone else from speaking, "you will die like all traitors. Princess Hanno, a pleasure to make your acquaintance; do you wish to accept my offer of payment?"

"General," Hanno nodded, chewing her lip, "I made the bargain with Duke Abra and will see it through. My reputation, such as it is, is built on trust and promises."

"I understand," Bordan answered. "I think, Cohort Cypria, Godewyn, we are done here. Farewell, Abra, I do not think we will speak again."

"I do not think you would listen if we did, Bordan," Abra answered.

There was little point continuing the conversation so Bordan spun on his heel and marched back to the Empire lines. As he went, the rain lessened and the wind picked up, chilling him.

"We have a problem," Bordan muttered when he was sure Abra and Hanno were out of earshot.

"I think it went quite well, Bordan," Godewyn chuckled. "His face is one I'll remember for many years."

As they rejoined Sarimarcus in the lines Bordan said, "The parley isn't the problem, Godewyn. I think the honour guard is about to arrive or has arrived at the edge of the forest. That is why he was happy to talk and risk us bringing more troops over."

"And he will get the amulet?" Cypria asked.

"If he does, he will have a hold over us," Sarimarcus said, a grimace on his face.

"He said he has a priest too. The rest was just posturing and delaying. He could become Emperor. We need to attack now," Bordan said. "Sound the advance."

The bugles blew.

XLVI

THE MAGICIAN

FOUR YEARS AGO:
"Don't, please," he said as the old man lifted the jar of fresh leeches from his bag. "It isn't helping."

"I don't know what else to do," the old man said, sitting with a sigh on the edge of his bed. "The medicus does not know either, but you keep having the nightmares and the fits. I just want to help."

"I..." he started to say and trailed off.

"You what, lad? Tell me, I want to help."

"I see things in the night, not bad dreams, but colours, sparks, and stars."

"FORM UP. BATTLE dress. Form up. Battle dress." The cry flew like a falcon along the column, screeching into the ears of all who tramped wearily from the forest. There were cries as the wounded were set down, carts came to a halt, and capes were ripped from shoulder to be left on the earth or thrown into a nearby cart.

Kyron followed Borus as the Cohort raced to Astentius and the gathering of officers. He felt rather than saw Emlyn in his shadow. The clatter of shields and swords echoed in his wake.

"Get the soldiers into a rank, Borus," Astentius said, wiping the last of the rain from his forehead. "Those look like mercenaries. They'll be practised soldiers and they know what they're facing."

Kyron heard the false confidence in the Spear's voice, an attempt to raise spirits. Glancing over his shoulder, the tired soldiers, some of whom had been pulling carts of wounded for the past day, and all who had not eaten properly in the past three days, were drawing up into their ranks.

"Why haven't they attacked?" Kyron asked, looking forward to the line of mercenaries, their mismatched shields and weapons clear to see as clouds gave way to sunshine.

"They were waiting for us to come further from the forest," Astentius said. "If the rain hadn't stopped, we would be out on the plain and an easier target."

"And what do you intend to do now, Spear Astentius?" Livillia's shrill voice cut through the conversation and Kyron felt his stomach sink even as Astentius's face became fixed.

"I intend to carry out my mission, Curate," Astentius said.

She changed tack and pointed at Kyron. "Why is he here? And her?"

"This is a military conversation, Curate," Astentius growled, "and they are here to offer advice. Kyron is a military magician and the guide is in my charge. If you have something particular to add, please do so. If not, can I suggest that you repair to the Emperor's waggon and pray to the Holy Flame for our deliverance."

"Spear," Livillia said, her voice lowering, "you had best pray to the Flame for our deliverance or I will see you crucified and buried, never to join the Flame."

"I am always praying, Curate," Astentius answered. "However, I thank you for your concern."

Kyron held his breath, hearing the unspoken words in his answers and preparing for the Curate's response. None came and when he looked he saw that her cheeks were flushed red and her eyes reflected the Flame she so fervently worshiped. After a silent moment, during which Spear and Priest stared at each other, the Curate finally turned her head away in disgust and retreated to the forest.

"You'll be paying for that soon enough," Borus said as he rejoined the group.

"She is the least of my worries, Cohort," Astentius said. "Have you seen how many face us?"

Kyron peered once more at the mercenary army which waited less than a league away. There was no doubt in his mind that they were outnumbered. He recalled the lessons his grandfather had tried to impress upon him and knew the battle would be short, bloody, and they were unlikely to win.

"Appear weak when you are strong, and strong when you are weak," he whispered, one of his grandfather's sayings.

"An old quote," Astentius said, a small smile passing across his face, "but possibly the only card we have to play."

"I'm sorry, my lord," Kyron stuttered. "I did not mean to speak."

"Don't apologise for good advice, Kyron," Astentius said, "though that you know that quote is intriguing. Not many study the old manuals of war."

"Just something I heard one day, amongst the soldiers," Kyron lied.

"Possibly," Astentius said. "However, it is as good an idea as any I had considered."

"There are near five hundred soldiers facing us, Spear," Borus pointed out. "Likely more we can't see."

"And we have two hundred fit and another hundred or so walking wounded who can lift a sword," Astentius said. "Staggered ranks, Borus. Cover the track and the route to the waggon."

Borus called to the troops and they moved smoothly into maniples, three ranks deep, red painted shields, battle scars still evident upon them, at the front. A gap, maybe ten paces wide, appeared between each maniple and through those, set back a little, Kyron could see another maniple of soldiers. Those were, he knew, the walking wounded, placed for a show of strength and to hide the desperation of the situation.

"Well, Kyron," Astentius said, "what can you offer?"

"I'll do what I can, Spear," Kyron said, his mind racing to find spells, ideas, or constructs which would make a difference, but coming up with little. "I am not my master."

"Do what you can." Astentius gave him a warm smile. "Everything will count in this battle. Guide? Emlyn?"

"I'll happily kill to protect myself," Emlyn answered, "but I want little part in your war."

"Stay with Kyron," Astentius ordered. "Remember, the message still needs to be sent."

"I'll stay with him," Emlyn answered, resting her hand on her knife.

"I've no wish to see any harm befall your parents, Emlyn," Astentius offered.

"The soldiers are ready, Spear," Borus said as he returned to the small group.

"Let's take our places," Astentius said, turning to the ranks of Empire soldiers who stood without moving in perfect ranks. The Spear raised his voice. "Soldiers of the Empire. Honour guard. Every challenge which has been placed in our way, every test we have faced on our journey, you have overcome. You are the pride of the Empire, honoured above all to escort our beloved Emperor home. One last battle awaits us. One more opportunity to show our mettle, to demonstrate the invincibility of the Empire."

Astentius paused, looking along the ranks of his soldiers and Kyron followed his gaze. Every man and woman dressed in the armour of the Empire, every face looking his way, and not a trace of fear on any of them.

"Mercenaries fight for money. Their hearts are bronze pennies. Easy to bend and break. Easily damaged and lost. Ours are Empire gold. Worth a thousand each of theirs. Eternal. Never to be tarnished by fear or cowardice."

The Spear drew his gladius and held it high.

"Our swords are strong, built to fight alongside one another, forged of good Empire steel. Theirs are base metals. They fight alone. Look to your right. That man will shield you with his life. Look left and see the soldier who will kill your enemy even as you protect them."

Along the ranks, swords sang from sheathes and were raised to the sky. A forest of bright metal in the now shining sun.

"Through our long history, we have never been defeated and today is no different. Those mercenaries will break against our shields and we will break their hearts with our swords and our bravery. You fight for the Empire. Let your blood sing. Let the Flame give you energy. Let your sword swing true."

Astentius's voice rose to a harsh cry on the last words and a great cheer echoed his final cry.

"Tell them," Astentius shouted as the cry subsided and he spun on his heel pointing his sword at the now advancing mercenaries, "we have never been defeated."

The soldiers took up the cry of 'Never Defeated' punctuating each word with a clash of sword against shield. Three hundred voices rang out across the battlefield and Kyron's was amongst them.

"Forward," Astentius cried and the army, as one, stepped forward. Two steps only, but two symbols of intent, of will, and determination. "Set shields."

The front rank bent at the knees, setting the rim of their shields into the rain-soaked earth.

"Heavy pila."

The triangular points of the long spears emerged through the front ranks, over the shoulders of the kneeling soldiers, and extending a good two arm lengths beyond the shields.

"You should retreat into the forest," Emlyn suggest.

"And give up the one advantage we have," Borus glanced across at her. "Every soldier here fights for his brother and sister, as one. All those mercenaries fight alone. They'll break against us."

"And if they break your ranks?"

"Not on the first attack," Borus said. "We've done this before, Emlyn."

"Shields." The shouted order was met by the second and third rank lifting their shields above their heads to provide cover from the hail of arrows which descended from the sky.

Kyron ducked out of instinct as the missiles clattered from the Empire shields. He closed his eyes, shutting out the sounds of the advance, and reached for the motes of magic. They were all about him, in the air, the dirt, the trampled grass and shrubs, in the trees behind him. So many more than he had sensed before. A constant torrent streamed from the sky, burning motes of blue and yellow which scattered from leaves and dirt like a million drops of rain. He gasped.

"Can you see the life of the world, Kyron?"

He heard the whisper, but the voice was both familiar and unfamiliar. His grandfather's dry voice, his master's tone of instruction, Emlyn's superior smirk, Gwri's stilted sentences, Borus's harsh whisper, his mother's soft hushed tones.

Kyron drew the motes to him and bound them in a shield which he extended in front of the first rank, anchoring it to the ground, tying knots of motes with those in the air and earth. With a sigh, he let the motes go and for the first time felt sure they would hold.

"Close the lines and brace," Astentius's voice rang out along the lines.

Behind him, Kyron heard the movement of soldiers as they thinned the ranks and filled in the gaps between each maniple of soldiers.

The clash of mercenaries against Empire shields was like a thunderstorm and earthquake combined, but the line ahead of Kyron did not bow or break, his shield taking the brunt of the attack. With a shout, he shattered his construct, and each fragment or shard which had absorbed the impact of the swords, axes and arrows now struck back. Shouts and screams of pain erupted alongside the rip and chop of metal through flesh and bone.

Spears were pushed forward, stabbing into the mercenaries who attacked with a chaotic energy the Empire lines could not match. Axes fell on shields and more than one was ripped from a soldier's grasp. The ranks stepped forward to close the gaps as the enemy tried to barge into the space they had created.

"Pila," Astentius's order was loud above the battle and was met with the whisper of wood and metal as they sailed over Kyron's head.

He saw them pass over his shield and pierce the armour of the mercenaries. A swathe of enemy were cut down or injured by the first flight and a moment later the second arced overhead.

"Push," the order came the moment the second pila landed amongst the mercenaries.

Every soldier on the front rank took a step forward, pushing shields into the faces of their attackers, driving swords into groins and soft stomachs. All of it accompanied by a great shout from the ranks.

The mercenaries broke and shouts of retreat could be heard amongst their forces. Through the line of shields Kyron saw the mercenaries in mismatched armour and weapons turn and begin running back to their own lines.

"Hold," Astentius ordered.

There was a moment when Kyron hated that order. Here were the backs of their enemies, easy targets for gladius, pila, arrow, or magic. Here was a chance to break them and win freedom, win the open space that had been denied amongst the trees. The very tops of the bridge towers were a grey smudge against the clearing sky. The lands of the Empire, of home, were just beyond that bridge and home meant safety. All they had, all he had to do was destroy the mercenaries before them.

"Hold, Kyron," Emlyn said, grabbing his arm.

"Do as she says," one of the soldiers next to him said. "I've seen it before. They retreat, drag us out of formation and round on us before there's anything to be done."

Kyron drew a deep breath, laden with fear and sweat, into his lungs and told his heart to steady. He forced his hand to let go its stranglehold on his sword and the tension eased out of his muscles.

"Good lad," the soldier said. "Don't you worry. They'll be back soon enough. Take a sip of water, if you don't mind the advice. Being in the ranks will parch your throat and dry you out."

The apprentice nodded, not trusting himself to words and lifted his water skin to his lips and took a sip, moving the water about his mouth, and swallowed.

"Shields." The cry sounded out as the mercenaries advanced again. This time was different, there was no headlong rush into battle as the first attackers had done. These warriors came on at a slow pace, shields of all sizes locked together in a crude imitation of the Empire ranks.

"One step back."

The rank retreated one step and Kyron craned his neck for the reason behind the order.

"The dead and the spears will hamper them," the soldier said, nodding towards the injured and dying ahead of the ranks.

Kyron swallowed and reached for the motes once more. As before, they came flooding to him, more than he could count and more than he knew what to do with. The original shield which had slowed the attackers' weapons and buttressed the shields of the Empire was undone and its magic swirled back into that around him.

What constructs did he know that would be of use in battle? The shield certainly. Preservation markers would be of little use. Starting a fire. Keeping warm. Discovering the truth. All little magics, little tasks which no soldier would find a use for. Except, those had been created and cast with fewer motes than he could summon now and while intricacy may still elude his understanding, brute strength was an easy concept to grasp.

Kyron drew his sword from the sheath, already scratching the markers on the grip and across the revealed steel with the tips of his fingers, a preservative spell to keep it untouched, unblemished.

"What are you doing?" Emlyn asked, trying to edge around him to see.

"Step away," Kyron said, holding onto the motes and drawing them to the blade in a second construct, one that sent the magic dancing and spinning around the blade faster and faster. Tying off the flow of magic, sealing it around the preserved blade, he whispered a single word. "Ignis."

Flames wreathed his sword, and the heat was strong enough to draw exclamations of surprise and fear from those around him. Kyron caught their surprised look and broke the construct apart in a gust of hot air.

"No," Borus said as he appeared amongst the ranks. "We don't need flames amongst the ranks. Nice trick though."

"I must be able to do something to help," Kyron pleaded.

"Shield the men who need it," Borus said, "just as your master did."

"But he sent flames and fireballs too," Kyron replied.

"Can you do that?"

"Well," Kyron admitted, "some."

"Just do what you can, Kyron," Borus said, clapping him on the shoulder, "and don't startle the soldiers."

The Cohort looked away from Kyron's face and across the battlefield. "Here they come. Fight hard. Pila, ready."

The rank behind Kyron lifted their wooden shafted spears with thin metal stalks which ended in a polished sharp point.

"Set shields," Borus called, as he stepped back alongside Kyron, giving the first rank room.

The mercenaries ahead began beating their shields with their weapons as they came on and sound drowned out Borus's shout. Even so, the wave of his hand and the expression on his face was enough for the third rank, and pila sailed overheard.

Many clattered from raised shields, others stuck upright from the ground proving an impediment to the mercenaries, and some found their mark.

Kyron picked one which had not made it to the enemy's ranks and drew the motes to it as fast as he could call them. He whispered, "Ignis."

The upright pila burst into flame and cries erupted from the mercenaries who were closest. Those behind followed their lead and were forced to divert around it. Along the line, where the mercenaries came close to the pila they gave them guarded looks and space.

"It is something," Kyron said.

"Can you set fire to the men instead?" Borus asked.

Kyron shook his head. "They are too large and moving all the time."

The lines came together once more in a gigantic crash of steel, wood and bone. A more measured battle, where swords and axes took lives on both sides. Borus called orders and sent men into gaps which formed in the lines.

Ahead of Kyron, the soldier who had stood next to him fell to an axe which his heavy shield was too slow to block. The mercenary stepped forward and swung at Kyron, a slash from shoulder to hip. The sword in the magician's hand did not move, but the shield he had erected took the blow and the mercenary stumbled forward, surprise and pain on his face. Borus's sword took him in the neck and the man fell onto the Empire soldier he had killed.

The line was bowing and the ranks thinning as the mercenaries pushed forward. Amongst the second rank, Kyron wiped the sweat from his face with a trembling hand. His legs were heavy and he had not yet swung his sword in anger. The shields he had constructed and tied off were depleting and many had shattered under the axe and sword of the mercenaries.

"Step back," Astentius called and Borus took up the shout. The ranks stepped back, but the mercenaries came on. The call went out again and again. Step by step the forest track was coming closer and the line of the front rank, bolstered by those behind, was becoming narrow.

Kyron backed away, seeing soldiers falter and the line of shields begin to fragment. He looked left and right, seeing blood running from wounds hastily bandaged as soldiers were forced back into the line. The trees began to invade the horizon and conquer the sky around them with the sole advantage, if the slaughter going on around him could be said to have one, of compressing the front line and deepening the ranks.

It would not be enough. The mercenaries were pushing forward, losing as many, if not more than the Empire. Some fell, more staggered away clutching wounds which leaked or sprayed blood, which exposed red flesh turning purple.

Kyron's heart raced and his hands shook as blades rose and fell. At the last, as they fell back, they were going to lose, to die. The Emperor's body would never reach the capital and Padarn's death would be for nothing. He reached for the magic, drawing the motes to him, but they fell from his grasp, slipping through his fingers like sand.

The soldier before him stumbled back, his shield falling from limp fingers, the gladius coming up to deflect the long sword which sliced down at him. The ring of metal on metal was the only sound to reach Kyron's ears and then the soldier fell on him.

They both fell, Kyron's arms coming around the soldier as the air exploded from his lungs under the heavy weight of man and armour. Above him the mercenary raised his sword once more and in his eyes Kyron saw the end.

The sword fell and Borus's shield struck the mercenary a heavy blow from the side. Kyron watched it happen as a slow movement between one breath and the next. His life had been ending on the tip of a mercenary's sword and was saved by a shield of the Empire.

Borus drove his own sword into the side of the mercenary. "Get up, boy. We need to pull back."

Kyron struggled from under the wounded soldier while Borus helped the man to his feet. His chest hurt and he gasped for breath. Wiping his mouth with the back of his hand it came away bloody.

"Borus?" he stammered, holding up his red-stained hand.

"Yours?" Borus said, dragging Kyron and the wounded soldier back through the closing ranks.

"Yes," Kyron coughed and the taste of iron filled his mouth.

"They're pulling back," Emlyn said, her voice far away and hollow.

"What?" Borus said. Through blurry eyes, Kyron saw him turn away for moment as a cry of joy went up from the remaining soldiers. "Why? They almost had us."

"I can't see," Kyron mumbled, hearing nothing but a swift wind.

XLVII

THE GENERAL

FOUR YEARS AGO:
Colours, sparks, and stars. It isn't normal. Maybe the boy is seriously ill, or something is wrong in his head.

Godewyn? He pondered. A priest will know what this is about. Sparks are like the Flame.

No, he corrected. Vedrix of the Gymnasium. They have a lot of knowledge and herbalists, alchemists. They'll know something.

Someone must. I can't lose him.

BORDAN WATCHED THE ranks begin their advance up the hill, shields forming a solid line at the front and those behind raised their own to give cover from the expected arrows. The army standard remained at the base to the hill, guarded by a small group of soldiers and the Aquilifer. Those climbing the hill knew if they turned and ran they would have to pass this symbol of their courage and purpose with their heads held low in shame.

"This will be a battle of attrition," Sarimarcus said.

"We have more troops," Bordan pointed out.

"And they have the high ground," Sarimarcus replied. "That slope is sodden with rain, and underfoot it will turn to mud far too soon."

"Cohort Cypria's troops will draw some away from the front line," Bordan answered, looking east where the Cohort was leading a hundred soldiers away. "The mercenaries will be keeping a close watch on her movements. Once they start up the slope, they'll be forced to divert some from their own ranks to protect their flanks."

"If only we had cavalry," Sarimarcus said.

"Or even enough horses to mount some infantry," Bordan added. "We don't, and Cypria seems to know her task well enough."

"We have two more cohorts of soldiers forming up by the bridge," Sarimarcus said.

"Send them up after the first arrow storm is over," Bordan ordered. "Keep the next two across in reserve."

As his sentence ended the promised hail of arrows fell from the sky upon the Empire soldiers marching into battle. Most struck shield or earth, but a few found their mark and soldiers fell with cries of pain.

The climb up the hill, arrows falling constantly, took forever and Bordan's grip on the reins of his horse tightened with every gap that appeared in the ranks. In the soldiers' wake, silver bodies and red shields dotted the hill. Some were still while others staggered or crawled down the hill.

True to his order the new cohorts were fighting their own way up the slope now turned from grass to slippery mud. Their advantage was the lack of arrows aimed their way; however, the line was anything but Empire straight.

"Order a cohort west," Bordan said. "They are to clear the lines and start up the hill. If they come under attack, have them retreat out of range and try again. That should occupy more of those mercenaries."

"Yes, General," Sarimarcus said, turning away.

"I want two cohorts in reserve here all the time. However, when more are across and formed, send them east and west, alternate. If they meet no resistance, they are to crest the hill and attack from the flanks."

"Of course, General," Sarimarcus nodded and strode towards the bridge and waiting troops.

Bordan watched the battle ahead. The front ranks are for the young and fit, not the old and grey, but blood was blood and his was surging. One hand on the reins of his horse and the other on his sword, the frustration built.

At the crest of the hill the two lines met, and the clash of steel was as if a thousand blacksmiths had gone to work at their forges all at once. Unable to see the details, his imagination brought scenarios to mind, snippets of battle, memories of his own time in the ranks conjoined with the sight before him.

An axe rising into the air, the sun's light scattering from its chipped edge. A whisper of air and a cry of effort as a shield met the blow and shattered. Splinters pinwheeling through the air and sudden lack of weight on his arm. Gladius stabbing forward, driven by training and instinct. A gap opening in the line ahead. A soldier falling and stumbling over the injured man, desperate to keep his shield high and sword in tight. Moving into the gap and slamming the shield forward to create room, peering over the top, wary of an attack. Heavy armour and biting pain at the base of your neck where the helmet's rim met flesh. Sweat pouring down your face, under the cheek guards, and hot breath burning lungs as each precious gasp powered you forward.

"You want to be up there, General?" Godewyn's voice came from low on Bordan's right.

"Too old, too slow," Bordan replied as he looked down to the High Priest. "And I thought I ordered you to the rear of the ranks."

"I am not sure you can order me anywhere," Godewyn answered. "How goes the advance?"

"You can see as well as I," Bordan answered.

"We've had a messenger from Cohort Cypria," Sarimarcus said. "She crested the hill and met resistance but is pushing towards the eastern flank."

"And those to the west?"

"Nothing yet, General," Sarimarcus answered.

"Send a runner," Bordan ordered, lifting himself in his saddle to look west. The soldiers were climbing the hill, though he could not see what was happening at the top.

Water was brought and Bordan took a drink, watching as the lines at the top of the hill ebbed back and forth. A constant stream of injured soldiers came down the slope and staggered, stumbled to the medicus. The litters were full, and the poppy was doing the rounds. Battlefield surgery was unpleasant and though soldiers appreciated the surgeons and staff, they were justly scared of them too. Stitches to close wounds were common, but amputation was often a death sentence for the injured soldier. The sweet aroma of burning pitch mingled with the smoke of charred flesh which hung above the field hospital.

Bordan caught the moment the battle changed. The Empire line at the top of the hill convulsed, a wave spreading out like a ripple on a pond. His breath caught in his throat and the water he had just swallowed went down the wrong way. He coughed, spluttered, his ribs aching and his stomach muscles spasming to clear the water from his lungs.

"Throw in a cohort of reserves," he choked out, pointing to the hill.

"Aenator," Sarimarcus shouted and the call sounded out.

A cry went up from the cohort of soldiers to the rear and the rumble of feet shook the ground.

"Are you all right, General?" Godewyn asked, his hand on Bordan's shoulder.

"Fine," he coughed, wiping his mouth with his gloved hand. "Push. We need to push. They're breaking."

"General," a messenger ran up, panting and face red.

"Speak."

"Cohorts to the west have engaged the mercenaries on their flanks," the messenger said between gasps.

"Sarimarcus," Bordan said, his throat raw from coughing, "order the last cohort to secure the bridge. We're heading up the hill. Godewyn, join the cohort on the bridge and make sure they stay there."

"General," the High Priest said, and Bordan drew in a breath to argue, "I think that is a very good idea."

Bordan itched to move, the temptation to drive his heels into the flanks of his horse was speeding his pulse. Bordan took a breath and coughed once more to clear the water from his lungs. Glancing over his shoulder, he slipped from his saddle and nodded as Sarimarcus returned.

"Let's join the advance, Spear," Bordan called over the noise of the cohort of soldiers as they passed by. The two officers joined the last rank and headed for the hill.

Underfoot, the mud was slippery and made worse by the blades of compacted grass. The lorica segmata slowed him and progress was only made possible by digging the toe of his boots into the earth to grab some purchase. Halfway to the top, his legs burned, but the sound of battle came clearer, the ring of swords on armour sounded brighter and the whimpers of the dying were a constant murmur on the breeze.

At the top, Bordan took his first sight of the plateau leading to the forest. The road passed under the battling soldiers and into the distance where the forest was only an indistinct brown smudge. Between the battle and forest, and further to the east and west, the land was farmed, and the shoots of the new crops were breaking the surface.

Homes and farm buildings, now a part of the battle landscape, were dotted along tracks leading from the main road. Smoke rose from a few, evidence of habitation and life going on despite the bloodshed taking place. Around some Bordan could just make out the people, families he supposed, standing and watching the battle. Ready to pick over the remains, he knew. There was money to be made from death if you were not too squeamish or simply poor and starving. An empty belly robs a man of many of his morals.

General Bordan paused to draw in air and give his legs a chance to recover from the climb. The cohort of soldiers parted and with a smile and sigh he marched forward aware of the looks the soldiers on either side gave him. He held his head high and face impassive, one hand on his sword and his other with its thumb tucked in his belt, the very image of a victorious general.

"Cohort Acaunus, General." Sarimarcus introduced the officer of the one hundred men who saluted.

"Cohort," Bordan returned the salute. "It looks as though the battle is almost over."

"Yes, General," the Cohort agreed.

The ranks of the Empire surrounded the mercenaries on three sides, leaving the route of a retreat open. It was always best, and been Empire doctrine for centuries, to allow a defeated army the room to retreat. Better to give a man the chance to live than have his sons return ten years later looking for revenge.

"Your soldiers are fit and ready?"

"Yes, General."

"Spear," Bordan ordered, "sound the advance. I want the ranks in front to clear a channel. We are ending this battle by striking at its heart."

The bugle calls sounded out and the cohort marched, Bordan in the centre of the second rank, Sarimarcus by his side. As they approached the rear of the battle, the troops parted and the line narrowed, drawing into an arrow aimed at the small farmhouse around which the mercenaries fought and defended. Bordan was forced further back in the ranks yet even so he felt the moment the point met the enemy's flesh.

The joy of a wedge formation was the power it brought to one particular point of an enemy line; however the attendant downside was the fragility of that point. To either side, mercenaries hacked and slashed at soldiers no longer in their accustomed joined shield wall. The shields were there but the gaps between were larger and each was less protected than before.

As they drove forward, his soldiers began to pay the price. As each fell, staggered, or was dragged into the mercenaries' lines to be butchered, Bordan found himself closer and closer to the edge. Bending, he scooped up a fallen soldier's shield, feeling the comforting weight on his arm and drew his gladius.

Bordan threw his body behind the shield and a mercenary's heavy mace, a polished wooden branch bound with iron rings, crashed against it. His teeth rattled and his body shook with the impact. The gladius, his sword which had not seen true battle for over a decade, was an extension of his arm as he stabbed out. A feral smile split his face as he felt the blade bite into flesh.

There was no time to see the damage as another warrior stepped up ahead, the short spear in his hand lashing out at the General. The heavy shield was too slow to bring to guard and Bordan swayed aside as the spear point slid from the metal of his neck guard. His gladius stabbed again, its sharp polished edge driving into the warrior's gut and out in less than the beat of a heart.

Bordan stepped forward, keeping the edge of the arrow moving and relying on the soldiers ahead and behind to do the same. This type of fighting, like most in the front ranks, was less about skill and more about the rote muscle memory of shield and sword. Keep the stout wood close and absorb the blows, deflect by tilting down or rolling to the side a little, stab with the sword from the concealment of the shield.

Block, absorb, tilt, stab. It was repetitious and all those drills on the parade ground to keep in time with your fellow soldiers, all the time at the pell swinging the lead weighted wooden swords to build up memory and strength, was the strength of the Empire's army.

In the games, a gladiator fought with skill and daring. Duels between those who favoured the trident and net and those who wielded the swords of the Empire were for entertainment only. It was not real. The blood was real, and death was sometimes the outcome, but rarely was such a contest taken so far.

Here there were no such niceties. No such rules and traditions. This was the Empire army as it was meant to be, a machine which ground down its opponents by constant repetition and overwhelming strength. Enemies were the wheat beneath the millstone of the Empire's great windmills.

He pressed on and the men to his rear stepped up to his side as they broke through the mercenary line and linked with the other cohorts who pushed in from the flanks.

There he was. Through those warriors still standing, Abra waited. His Empire armour gleamed and reflected the sunlight, the shield on his arm looked well used, but his drawn gladius was still virginal.

"Sarimarcus," Bordan called over the clash of swords and shields, "I want that man. Push on. Push on."

The soldiers took up the call and soon it echoed down the lines. "Push on. Push on."

Another warrior, a youth barely bearded and likely in his first battle came swinging at Bordan. Block, stab, and the boy would never see another sunrise. No older than my grandson, Bordan thought for a moment before pushing the distraction aside.

"Abra," he shouted, his voice hoarse and dry from battle, as he and his soldiers burst through the line.

The Duke, a merchant, a man born to wealth who had likely held a sword only at ceremonies, blanched. Even so, the man stepped forward, and called out. "Come on then, old man."

They met shield against shield, swords stabbing but not finding flesh. Abra backed off a step and Bordan moved forward thrusting with his heavy shield, catching the Duke's and forcing the other man to turn, unbalanced.

As the Duke stumbled and struggled to gain his balance, Bordan stepped forward again, always forward, and brought his sword out to drive it deep into the other man's lower back, just where metal met leather at the base of the lorica segmata.

Bordan was slower than in his youth and Abra had the luck of the amateur, the scared, as he wheeled around slicing out with the edge of his gladius with intent but without aim. The intended stab was halted and Bordan flinched backward trying to escape that sharp polished blade. Too slow. Too old.

It scored a line across his forearm, just above the leather gloves he wore. Not deep and the pain would come after the battle was over. He saw the blood flicked from the wound by the passing of the sword as a warning, a reminder. Luck was a fickle mistress on the battlefield and many a skilled soldier had been felled by an untried boy.

He shouted, though what words he could not say, and moved forward once more. Abra was still unbalanced, recovering from the wild slice and tried to reverse the path of his sword, cutting from left to right. Bordan tucked the shield in tight to his body and let Abra's sword rebound from the painted wood and steel. Stab.

A trained, practised soldier would have backed away rather than reverse the strike. Sword arm blocked shield and armour was only good for the areas it covered. Bordan's gladius slid into the man's groin, cutting through flesh like water.

He saw it in the Duke's eyes. The reality of death, the exquisite fire of a sword slicing flesh, the warmth of your own life's blood fleeing your body. Abra crumbled to the earth before the farmhouse, sword spilling from his hand and the shield discarded by fingers no longer strong enough to grip.

Bordan heaved a breath, glancing around to see the soldiers of the Empire form a ring of shields and steel around him. He knelt, stabbing his sword into the soft earth and unbuckling his helmet.

"Bordan," Abra wheezed. The man's face was pale, and his eyes were wide as if staring into the dark at a low flickering flame far away.

"Your rebellion ends here, Abra," Bordan said. "You've been given a better death than your assassins gave Alhard or his mother."

Abra's only reply was a dry chuckle as his face slackened and all life left his body.

"General," Sarimarcus said as Bordan sat back on his heels. "The mercenary leader has surrendered. The battle is over."

"The honour guard? Has anyone seen them?" Bordan looked away from the sightless eyes which stared up to the infinite sky above.

"There are soldiers in the trees, north along the track and I've had Cypria send messengers. However, there are also many bodies lying on the earth before the forest."

"Take the mercenaries' surrender, Spear, and detail enough soldiers to watch them. They will not earn any money for further fighting today."

"Duke Abra?" Sarimarcus asked.

"Dead," Bordan answered, heaving a sigh and grunting as he stood on tired legs which trembled at the strain. "A better death than a traitor deserves. See if you can find Cohort Acaunus. His soldiers fought well, and I'll need an escort to meet the honour guard. See to the dead and living. And send a messenger to High Priest Godewyn, I am sure he would like to convey the news to the Princess. The battle is over. We will have the Emperor's body across the bridge before nightfall."

"Yes, General."

XLVIII

THE MAGICIAN

FOUR YEARS AGO:

He sat in his room, alone. The few toys he had played with, his father's chariot among them, were safe on the shelf and his scrolls were neatly packed into the chest. Summer's heat barged in through the open window and the sound of people on the street outside filtered into his consciousness.

The room, this house, had become his world. Too frightened to go out, to visit the market with friends, to play, to live. Gressius took him to the Grammaticus and brought him home, and he saw fear on the other boys' faces.

HE WAS AWARE of the voices first as sounds within a dream. Tall trees of spreading boughs and swirling bark surrounded him. Each track he took, little more than a narrow band of mud and encroaching shrubs led him to another clearing and more trees. The arrangement was different each time, the shape of the clearing varied, and size of the open sky above grew larger or smaller.

It was progress, he thought in his fuzzy dream. He was going somewhere.

The destination escaped his understanding, only the imperative to get somewhere made his feet move.

In one clearing he found a small, clear stream which flowed from between the trees, crossed one corner of the open grass and passed back into the shadows. Kyron staggered to it, his legs tired and heavy, and he sagged down upon the gentle bank. Cupping his hands beneath the surface he drew cool water up to his lips and took a sip. Sweet and clean it moistened his dry lips and soothed the raw scrape in his throat.

It was tempting to follow the river, but beneath the trees there was only dark shadow. Little light reached the forest floor, and as he squinted all he could make out were small puddles of light which illuminated tangles of brambles and thorns. He sighed and pushed himself back to his feet, grunting at the tightness in his chest.

Kyron probed the ache with light fingers and winced at every stab of pain which followed.

"Bruised, maybe cracked," he thought in a voice which was not his. Kyron looked around, but only the trees stared back. He did notice another path leading from the clearing and set off in that direction.

The trunks hemmed him in and he was forced to duck under low branches which reached out to block his path. Little air moved beneath the trees and it was warm in his lungs. Sweat began to bead on his forehead, trickle into his eyes, and his clothes were sticking to damp skin.

He reached up to wipe his hand across his forehead and sighed at the slight relief it afforded. A heartbeat later he stopped, realising his hand had not moved and yet the sweat was gone.

"Too warm," his thoughts said in another voice and a cool breeze picked up beneath the leaves, cooling his face and causing a shiver to run up his spine, shaking his body.

"Too much," his thoughts said in a third voice.

There was a light ahead, another clearing. It was bright and he blinked away the tears in his eyes. The light brightened as he moved closer and the trees thinned. Brighter still and he wanted to raise his hand to shield his eyes, but it refused to move. His legs kept moving, feet rising and skimming across the leaves towards the light.

His heart beat faster and now the light was no friend. It was a threat. A yellow burning flame which would consume him. Cremate him. He was dead and about to be cremated, his thoughts, in his own voice said.

"Almost," said the first voice.

Kyron blinked and for moment, less than a moment, the trees vanished, and dark shapes moved around him. He blinked again, a reflex, and the trees reappeared. The light still burned and despite his efforts his legs carried him towards it. A burning heat and the lick of flame caught the leaves dripping from branches near the end of the path. So close he could feel his hair begin to curl and melt.

Gritting his teeth, he fought to stop his forward progress. His breath came in shallow gasps, each one a stab of pain in his chest. The thought struck him that he was not moving but being dragged. Kyron held his breath, stopping the pain in his chest and allowing him clear focus. He reached for the motes and, between blinks of forest flames and dark shapes of twisting smoke, they came to him. A rainbow of life, every colour, every spark of energy dancing and cavorting his thoughts.

"What's he doing?" he heard a voice say from ahead, from the light.

"Stop him," a panicked voice replied.

"I can't," the third voice answered. "Too strong."

Water filled his mouth, his eyes, splashed from his forehead, soaked his hair, found its way up his nose. He coughed, spluttered and lost his grip on the magic.

Kyron blinked. The edge of the forest path was no longer lined with trees but were the flaps of a tent pulled back to let in the light of day not the yellow of flame. He gasped, filling his lungs with cool air and pain flared along his side.

The shapes made of smoke resolved themselves into faces. Master Vedrix was sat to his right, dark eyes brimming with concern. Cohort Borus stood at the end of his bed in full armour. Above Kyron, looking down and carrying an empty pail of water was Emlyn.

"So," she said, "you're not dead."

"How long?" he managed to croak out.

"Three days," Borus answered.

"What happened?" Kyron looked to each in turn, waiting for an answer.

"Mostly exhaustion, but the soldier who fell on you crushed your ribs," Borus said.

"You were bruised internally," Vedrix said. "The weight on your ribs caused some bleeding around your lungs and the muscles beneath. Nothing too serious. It was actually quite interesting. In the Gymnasium we do not often get to see such injuries. The alchemists have some tinctures, unguents and potions which would be very effective in such cases. I must make a note for them."

"They healed me?" His voice was a dry whisper.

"What?" Vedrix answered, and above him Emlyn rolled her eyes. "No. Of course not. No alchemists here. However, I did some reading when I was younger. A scroll by Galen I remember as being particularly fascinating."

"He kept you unconscious so you wouldn't move and make it worse," Emlyn said.

"Well, yes," Vedrix admitted. "There was that. Also, I made use of the medici's poppy along with a little magic to encourage the blood to go elsewhere."

"Thank you, Master," Kyron whispered.

"No thanks needed, young Kyron," Vedrix answered with a beaming smile. "Least we could do for someone who helped escort the Emperor to safety."

Kyron caught Borus's raised eyebrow and wondered if the soldiers were having the same amount of care and attention.

"I am not really a healer," Vedrix admitted with a shrug and a glance towards the Cohort, "however, it was felt that a magician should oversee your treatment."

"Not a priest?" Kyron coughed and his ribs reminded him not to do that again.

"The priests were all," Borus paused, "looking after the soldiers. There were none to spare and the medici who attended you said you would heal."

"We just sped it along," Vedrix said.

"You did scare us, though," Emlyn said.

"Sorry," Kyron managed to say, the lump in his throat at her confession making speech difficult.

"You started to fight us just now," she continued. "Your master over there was struggling to contain your magic and Borus had to sit on your legs."

The lump melted and the reason for the bucket of water was clear.

"Sorry," he repeated because nothing better came to mind. He looked towards the open tent flaps. "What time of day is it?"

"Late afternoon," Emlyn said, putting the empty bucket down.

"We've been marching for the past two days," Borus said. "Princess Aelia did not want to wait. We left most of the injured at Cesena."

"Not me?"

"Had orders to fix a cart for you and one or two others," Borus answered. "Spear Astentius rode with you most of yesterday and today."

Kyron looked left to the empty bed, the only other piece of furniture in the tent. "He is not in here?"

"Died of wounds this afternoon, just before we stopped," Borus said, his voice grey and quiet.

"Oh," was all Kyron could manage.

"He was a good man, and a good soldier," Borus said. "He brought us this far. It's a shame he won't get to see the Emperor get home."

"Livillia?" Kyron asked, trying to keep the hope from his voice and failing.

"Alive and well," Emlyn answered and Kyron saw her face screw up in disgust. "She can't even get herself killed properly."

"She was wounded," Borus explained. "A cut on her arm. A few stitches is all it needed. She travels with the High Priest."

"The High Priest is here?" Kyron started. "Hold on, why is Princess Aelia here? Surely Prince Alhard would come for his father's body and escort it home."

Vedrix sighed. "Cohort, why don't you go and see to your men? Now, Kyron is awake there are some things I'll need to talk to him about."

"If you are sure?" Borus looked uncomfortable.

"I am," Vedrix replied. "I do thank you for looking after Apprentice Kyron during the journey. I am sure it could not have been easy."

Emlyn, still by his side, snorted.

"He is a boy with many questions," Borus replied, the ghost of a smile on his face.

"His master often said the same," Vedrix said.

"I'll see you later, boy," Borus said. "I've still got a few of my command who can walk and talk. I'd best go and make sure their tall stories of the journey through the forest aren't too tall, and that they give me place of honour in them all."

Kyron's laugh was cut off by a cough and then a groan of pain. Borus tapped him on the leg and ducked out of the tent.

"I take it you are staying?" Vedrix looked across him at Emlyn who sat on the empty bed.

"Looks like it," she said, slipping her knife from its sheath and selecting a stick from those in her belt. The whisk of blade on wood was strangely comforting.

Vedrix grunted. "A stubborn young lady."

"Yes," Kyron answered.

"Now, Apprentice," Vedrix began, drawing himself up straight on his stool. "I am sorry to tell you that Prince Alhard and the Empress were killed in the capital. Princess Aelia is now the heir to the Empire."

Kyron sucked in a breath, ignoring the complaint from his bruised ribs, and tried to sit up.

"Don't move," Emlyn said, not stopping carving. "We didn't look after you this long just for you to hurt yourself again."

"I didn't hurt myself," he protested.

"Same as," Emlyn answered. "There's a mug of water on the floor."

"I can't reach it," he said, to which she sighed and helped him take a sip. "How were they killed, Master?"

"Alchemy and assassins, Apprentice," Vedrix answered. "It would not be too much to say that the Gymnasium of Magicians is in a difficult position."

"It wasn't us though," Kyron said, suddenly unsure. "Was it?"

"No," Vedrix answered with a firm shake of his head. "Duke Abra, one of the council members, appears to have hired the assassins in order to claim the throne. It was his army who attacked you when you left the forest."

"And the alchemy?"

"A poison, a rare one, expensive," Vedrix said. "We are sure the assassins sourced it from an alchemist outside of the Gymnasium."

"Why does it matter?" Emlyn asked. "Dead is dead."

"The Gymnasium is supported by the throne, young lady," Vedrix said. "I understand from Borus that the priests, Livillia in particular, were less than happy about Master Padarn and Apprentice Kyron's presence."

Emlyn nodded and Kyron grunted.

"That is true for most priests, and the Empire as a whole, I am sad to say. They do not understand magic and so they fear it," Vedrix explained. "The Gymnasium was set up centuries earlier to give the Empire control of magicians and it is a valuable resource. It also gave magicians a place to study, to experiment, to be safe and to thrive."

"I know your priests hunt magicians," Emlyn said.

"Those who are not in the Gymnasium," Vedrix answered. "A wild magician, one without training, is dangerous."

"It is not just that though, is it?" Kyron whispered.

"No, Kyron," Vedrix's voice was low and sad. "We do what we can to find magicians before the priests do, but we are not always successful." The Master Magician sighed and continued, "Princess Aelia may well wish to see you, to thank you for your service. Be aware of how you act and try not to say too much, or anything. There is anger in the city about the role of alchemy in the deaths and Aelia is not her father."

"My master died to bring the Emperor's body this far," Kyron complained.

"And that may be our saving grace at the moment," Vedrix replied. "I have spoken about Padarn's sacrifice. Spear Astentius's records also speak of his bravery and service. Try not to do anything that risks that."

"No, Master," Kyron gulped.

"You served well, Apprentice," Vedrix said after a moment's pause and a smile found its way to his face. "Padarn would be proud of you."

"I hope so," Kyron replied, finding tears welling in his eyes once more.

"I had best leave you to rest," Vedrix said, his fingers fluttering and twisting with each other as if uncomfortable.

"Thank you for looking after me," Kyron said as the older man stood from the stool.

"Your friend here," Vedrix nodded towards Emlyn, "did much of the actual caring. I just popped in from time to time to do what I could."

"Thank you anyway, Master."

Vedrix moved to the tent flaps in small careful steps, stopped and turned. "I almost forgot, getting old, you know. General Bordan will likely visit later. He has seen all the surviving troops and offered his thanks for their service. You were not conscious. I am sure when he learns of your recovery, he will want to offer his thanks to you."

Kyron glanced at Emlyn who had not stopped carving the stick in her hands.

"He does not need to, Master," Kyron said, trying to keep his voice from quavering.

"I'd imagine he knows that, Apprentice," Vedrix said, his eyes flicking to Emlyn and back to Kyron's. "However, it would be remiss of him not to. It is also a signal to the Princess of the value of the Gymnasium."

"If you say so, Master," Kyron nodded from his lying position.

"Try not to antagonise him, Apprentice," Vedrix warned.

Kyron swallowed. "Of course not, Master."

XLIX

The General

Four years ago:
The magician bumbled about the room, his bushy beard moving as he spoke. In the centre of his office, the boy sat on a chair, unmoving, and confusion plain across his face.

"I'm very glad you saw me. Very glad indeed."

"If you can help me, us, Master Vedrix, then I will be glad also," he said. *"I didn't know where else to go, who else to turn to. The medicus said there was nothing more they could do."*

"Oh, most assuredly there was not, is not. I think he has it. Quite rare these days, getting rarer. Of course, we will need to be sure."

"Seven days more." Aelia slapped the arm of the chair to punctuate her words.

"We are constrained by the speed of the waggon, Your Highness," Bordan replied.

"I don't want excuses, General," Aelia snapped back.

Bordan schooled his face. "My apologies, Your Highness. The Empire roads are enabling us to make good time. Messengers have been sent ahead to secure supplies in the towns and villages along our route."

"Supplies, General. Always you talk of supplies. If we had waited for your supplies to be loaded on the ships, Abra would have possession of my father's body and the amulet." Aelia lifted her goblet of wine, sloshing a measure over the top and across her hand. With a growl of frustration, she threw the cup across the tent where it splashed up the white canvas walls and stained the rugs which covered the floor. "You would now be bowing to a different Emperor, General Bordan."

In the corner of the room, catching the last light of late afternoon, Vedrix shifted in his chair, turning the page in the book he was reading.

"We are making good pace, Your Highness. The General is correct that we need supplies as we march. An army, even a small one, needs a lot of food," High Priest Godewyn offered. "The Flame will see you crowned Emperor before the next ten days are done."

Aelia's eyes focused on the High Priest and some of the wildness faded. "You are right, Godewyn. Thank you. My apologies, General. The delay does not sit well upon me."

"Abra's army is finished, Your Highness," Bordan said. "Between here and the capital are only loyal citizens who wish to see you carry on your father's good work."

"Loyal citizens? So loyal that one of my own Dukes had my brother and mother assassinated. So loyal that an army was raised against me," Aelia's voice trembled as she spoke. "By what measure is that loyalty, General?"

"Your Highness, I…" Bordan began but Aelia turned and stomped from the tent. There was silence inside the canvas walls and none of the three men moved for a long, drawn-out moment.

Bordan held the cup of wine in his hands, staring into the reflection on the dark red surface of the liquid. For two days since they had recovered the Emperor's waggon, the Princess had seen only Godewyn, preferring to spend her time with her father's body. This morning she had reappeared, dark circles under her eyes, hair matted, unwashed, and her clothes dishevelled.

Servants had, on Bordan's waved order, taken the Princess in hand, bathing her, rubbing sweet, scented oils into her skin and laying out fresh clothes. The morning march had been delayed, but once Aelia was ready she mounted a large, white horse and led the army south towards the capital.

This afternoon they had stopped early and pitched the camp.

According to the map, there was a large town just south which they would reach tomorrow and resupply. An army ate a lot of food each day and Cesena had supplied them well enough for a few days. Sadly, the supply ships had not reached the town when Aelia had ordered the march south just the day after the battle was won.

My fault. Bordan's thoughts had been a mixture of concern and sour realisation since Abra's death. It took no great political genius to know he was out of favour with the Princess. His time as General was over and, he admitted, that was something of a relief. A new General would lead the army once Aelia was made Emperor. A small estate, somewhere in the west, where he could farm and make wine would be a well-deserved retirement.

"Her mood will improve," Godewyn said into the quiet, "as we get closer to the capital."

"It will have to," Bordan said, keeping his voice low. "There is an Empire to run."

"Aelia is still young, General," Godewyn replied. "She has not come to terms with the death of her family. When she has, I am sure the Empire will flourish under her rule."

"Perhaps confronting her father's body is the beginning," Vedrix said, closing his book. "It was the one death which had not yet been made real. Now she has seen, the healing can begin."

"Perhaps," Bordan mused.

"She has seen her father and held the amulet," Godewyn said. "I feel you are right, Vedrix. Suddenly, everything has become very real and there is no urgency, no crisis to divert her attention on the march. It gives us all time to think. That can be a blessing and a curse to those grieving."

"Can we occupy her time on the march south?" Bordan asked. "She has read the reports of the battle but has never stood the ranks and faced an enemy, even in training."

"What are you thinking?" Godewyn asked, his eyes narrowing.

"There are excellent officers in our ranks," Bordan mused. "We could have them report in person to the Princess. Have them tell of the battle and their part? Let her ask questions so she can begin to learn the realities of battle and army life."

"Aelia won't ask," Vedrix's voice drifted across the tent from the comfort of his chair. "I mean no disrespect to the Princess, but she is a young woman thrust into ultimate power. To ask questions, she will see as a sign of weakness."

"I can sit at her side," Godewyn offered. "I'll ask the questions."

Bordan nodded. "That would be kind and reassure my officers."

"Then that is settled. Now, the crowning ceremony?" Vedrix asked.

"We have sent messengers to the capital," Bordan answered after a glance at Godewyn. "The priests and palace staff will be ready for the day after we arrive. I think it is best if we do not delay."

"I agree," Godewyn said. "It is best if we secure the succession and give Aelia a purpose as soon as we can."

"There is still an army in the far north," Bordan added.

Vedrix nodded. "I have communicated with Master Elouera. They are a tenday or so from the clan lands."

"We should be concerned with their progress," Bordan replied. "Better to have Aelia crowned on our return so decisions can be made, and our focus can be upon the campaign."

"Stand aside." The shrill voice came through the tent's walls like a sharp knife.

"My apologies," the soldier on guard duty could be heard to say, "however, you are not allowed in."

"I am a priest of the Holy Flame," the high-pitched voice continued, rising in volume, "you will not put your hands upon me."

"One of yours, Godewyn?" Vedrix said from his chair.

"I fear so," the High Priest answered, chewing his bottom lip. "A fervent believer."

"To be praised then," Vedrix replied.

"Most of the time," Godewyn answered, and raised his voice. "Let her pass, please."

The tent flap was thrown aside and a sharp-faced priest stalked in. She stopped three paces inside and bowed, making the sign of the Flame to the High Priest.

"You wished to see me, Curate Livillia?" Godewyn said, his voice deep, calm and soothing.

"High Priest, may the Flame always warm you," Livillia said, bowing once more.

"And you," Godewyn answered.

Bordan saw the look of suffering which flickered across the High Priest's face. In every institution were those with zeal and passion, and a vision so narrow it always amazed him they could turn a street corner. Watching from his seat, Vedrix rested both hands on the book he had been reading.

"High Priest," Livillia began, her voice still piercing even at a lower volume, "I have come to make a complaint."

"Have I done something to upset you?" Godewyn asked, folding his arms across his chest.

"No," she stammered, flustered, "not you, High Priest. Never you."

"That is good to know. However someone has?"

"The army, High Priest," Livillia said.

Bordan raised an eyebrow but kept his own counsel and waited to see where this would lead.

"Really? I know soldiers can sometimes be a little coarse of manner, but, like all in the Empire, they are ours to care for. Perhaps you could explain a little further, Curate Livillia?"

"They have the magician taking up a tent all by himself," she spat the words out as if they burned her tongue.

"And you think he should not?" Godewyn asked.

"I think his heathen carcass should have been left on the battlefield, High Priest," she said.

In the corner Bordan saw Vedrix turn his head slowly in his direction and catch his eye. Bordan shook his head, a small motion which the Master Magician saw and nodded in return.

"He has committed some heresy?"

"He is a magician," Livillia said as if that explained everything.

"Who, I am given to understand, preserved the Emperor's body as was his role, and participated usefully in the battles fought on your way here," Godewyn said.

"He is too close to that tribesgirl," Livillia replied. "And Astentius gave them too much time, listened to them too often. I counselled him against it. His flame was in peril. Consorting with magicians is an abomination to the Holy Flame."

"The Emperor maintains the Gymnasium," Godewyn pointed out, his gaze locked on the junior priest's.

"It is wrong," Livillia said. "The Flame speaks out against them."

"I believe I am aware of the teachings of the Holy Flame, Curate Livillia," Godewyn snapped, his voice cold and harsh.

"For... Forgive me, High Priest," Livillia stammered, bowing and making the sign of the Flame once more. "However, a tent to himself is too much honour for a lowly magician whose existence is against our teachings."

"The tent is mine," Vedrix spoke, his voice gentle and warm.

Livillia started, her head twitching around to see the old man with the bushy beard sat in his comfortable chair as if he had suddenly appeared from nowhere.

"You should know better then, my lord," she answered after a moment during which she looked around the room and caught Bordan's hard gaze.

"The boy was unconscious and needed specialist care," Vedrix continued, his voice unchanged. "And the tent was mine to give up."

"Before you speak again, Curate, allow me to introduce Master Vedrix, the Master of the Gymnasium of Magic," Godewyn said. "I believe that he was best qualified to care for the apprentice. Surely you would not want the boy to be cared for amongst the soldiers. Keeping him apart seems to meet at least some of your objections."

Livillia looked to Vedrix and back at the High Priest, opened her mouth and closed it once more.

"And this is General Bordan, Commander of the Empire's forces," Godewyn said. "If you had burst in a little earlier, you would have had the good fortune to embarrass me in front of Princess Aelia also."

"Your... High Priest... I am..." she said, her words cut off when he raised a hand.

"I think you have said all that you could wish to, Curate," Godewyn said. "You and I will continue this discussion later this evening. Thank you for bringing your concern to my ears. You are dismissed."

A red flush raced up the young woman's cheeks and much of her grace fled the bow she offered the High Priest before she turned and walked with stiff legs out of the tent.

"My apologies," Godewyn said, heaving a great sigh. "The young have all the passion and none of the wisdom."

"We all have them amongst our ranks," Bordan said, lifting the jug of wine and offering it to Godewyn.

"It worries me that we may once have been them," Vedrix said. "However, it is time for me to retire. The boy did awake this afternoon. I may just drop in and see him before I sleep. I am sure he will appreciate the company."

"I know who he is, Vedrix," Godewyn said. "So, please, you can stop hedging your words."

"You do?"

"He does," Bordan answered. "Godewyn has known my family a long time, since before the boy was born and before…"

"Ah," Vedrix replied.

"And probably best to keep the knowledge between the three of us," Bordan said.

"Certainly," Vedrix answered.

"Of course," Godewyn said. "I am a little surprised you have not been to see him."

"I will," Bordan replied.

"Family." Godewyn offered the single word, imbuing it with more meanings than Bordan could fathom.

"I will," he repeated. "I need to hear his side of the battles, and I understand the girl was quite useful in her own way."

"Considering the Legion had her parents as hostage?" Godewyn said, half an accusation, half empathy.

"A time-honoured custom," Bordan answered, "though not one that makes me comfortable. I've had a message sent to ensure their safe release."

"Master Elouera has given the message to the Legion, including the passphrase," Vedrix said, tucking his book under one arm and ambling over to the exit. "I may sound like your father, but don't stay up drinking too late tonight. You're both far too old to cope with the morning after."

Bordan smiled, a sad affirmation of the truth, while Godewyn let go a throaty chuckle.

"I can't afford to drink, I've an over-reaching Curate to deal with," the High Priest said when his laughter died away. "Go see the boy, Bordan. Best to get it over with. Old wounds fester and sometimes the poison needs to be drawn out."

L

THE MAGICIAN

FOUR YEARS AGO:
"You don't have to do anything," the woman said, walking around his chair and into view. "Just stare at the other wall or close your eyes."

"I don't need to do anything?" his voice shook, and he cursed his nerves.

"Just tell me what you see or feel," she said.

TWO DAYS AFTER waking, after suffering the bumps and thumps from the cart as it clattered over the cobbles which provided the hard-wearing surface of the Empire road, Kyron was glad to have the chance to stand on his own two feet.

Vedrix and his appointed nursemaid, Emlyn, had spoken with one another and declared him fit enough to walk. Despite straining his ears to catch their conversation he managed to hear only a few words, and those were less than complimentary. When they had returned and told him the news he had jumped from the cart and onto the surface, slipping a little and having to hold onto the wooden side of the vehicle to regain his balance.

Stretching his legs had been a wonderful freedom. No longer at the mercy of the driver and his unerring accuracy for every missing cobble, Kyron could enjoy the beginning of summer and the warm breeze against his face.

To his left the land fell in a gentle slope towards the sea, and on his right the low hills, the only highland on the northern plains, broke the constant horizon of villages and farmland. Here grew the wheat and corn which was milled into flour, baked into bread, and sold in the cities and towns. People came out of the homes to watch the army pass, bowing as the Emperor's waggon clattered down the road.

"Used to be a hill fort," Emlyn said as she stepped up beside him.

"Where?" he asked.

"In those hills," she pointed to the west, "and forest all around."

"Really?"

"A few centuries ago," she said, "before your Empire clawed its way this far north."

"Bringing civilisation, farming, food, roads, and a better life," he said, surprised at his reaction.

"Your civilisation," she answered, not looking away from the hills.

It was true, he still thought of himself as of the Empire. Raised, trained, educated in its institutions. His parents had sought their heritage, their history, and it led to their deaths. His grandfather had immersed himself in the Empire's ways and was still alive. Perhaps there was a lesson there.

"South is the great river," Emlyn said. "The tribes lived south of that too."

"Before the Empire."

She nodded. "Before the Empire came. The land has changed under the Empire's wheels, hooves, and tools."

"My master used to say that change happens," Kyron said, swallowing the lump in his throat. "You can either adapt or be crushed beneath its weight."

"Change should be slow," Emlyn replied, glancing at him. "It should allow those who live through it to change alongside. That is the natural way of things. Trees change by the seasons, adapting to the weather, to the rain, sun and snow. Plants bloom, flower, and the bees come to carry pollen from one to another. A sudden, late frost will kill the plants and the bees lose their source of food, dying days later. On and on the ripples of that are felt throughout the land and forest. The Empire was, and still is, that frost."

"It has been hundreds of years," he complained.

"Over six hundred," Emlyn agreed. "And like the seasons, there are years when the pattern remains the same, when summer follows spring and autumn leads into winter. But then there are years like this, when you send armies to conquer land, to destroy cultures which have existed for thousands of years. What shores those ripples end upon and who is drowned in the waves no one can know."

Kyron looked towards the hills, imagining the land around covered by forest, and found the words to rebut her accusations were beyond him. They walked in silence for a time and slowly the hills faded into the distance as afternoon crept towards dusk.

When the army was called to a halt, there was just time to help Vedrix and the few soldiers who had been tasked to assist to pitch the tent. Emlyn had her own cot within and Vedrix had proved to be an excellent host, if a somewhat loud snorer later at night. Exhausted, his ribs still aching, Kyron found sleep easy.

It was a soft hand that awoke him, and the bright yellow flame of the lantern brought tears to his eyes. He blinked them away, looking towards the tent's entrance to see that it was still dark, and the camp was quiet.

"What? Who?" he mumbled as he struggled to rise.

"Forgive me, Kyron," Vedrix said, his voice low and serious. "Your grandfather is here to see you."

Kyron sucked in a breath and sat upright with a gasp of pain escaping his lips.

"You've only slept a short while," Vedrix explained.

"It is my fault," a voice beyond the lantern flame said, so recognisable and familiar that the years fell away and the cold water of reality crashed in upon his sleep muddled thoughts.

Kyron coughed, clearing his throat and summoning moisture to his mouth. "General," he said.

"Come and sit at the table, Kyron," his grandfather, General of the Empire's Army, said. "I've brought wine and some food."

Kyron looked to Emlyn's cot and saw it empty.

"I sent her on some errands a while ago," Vedrix confessed. "Enough to keep her busy for a time and listening to you snuffle in your sleep is not that interesting."

Kyron swung his legs from the bed and dragged the blanket around his shoulders as he stood. He grunted at the ache in his ribs, less painful and yet more annoying than yesterday, and lurched over to the table drawing the blanket close against the cool summer air.

Drawing on the motes about him, he willed the oil lamp sat upon the table to flame and a soft light filled the interior. A construct he could not have managed a few weeks ago, but now was, if not simple, at least easier.

"You've grown," his grandfather said.

Sitting drew another grunt of pain from his lips, but he refused to keep his discomfort to himself. Across the wooden table, lamp light illuminating his face, Kyron saw the man who had raised him.

"You've aged," Kyron answered, stating the obvious. Grey hair had been edging in when Kyron had left for the Gymnasium and lines which had once given the General an air of rugged strength had stretched into those which told the story of a long life.

"We've both changed, Kyron," his grandfather said, shifting a leather bound book to one side and pouring three cups of wine and handing one to Kyron. Vedrix took the other as he sat in the remaining chair.

Kyron felt a brush of motes across his skin and gasped, drawing more to him and beginning the construction of a shield.

"My apologies," Vedrix said, patting Kyron's arm. "I've merely made it more difficult for our voices to leave the tent."

"Merely," Kyron said in wonder. Sound was made of air and air was a nebulous medium at best, hard to hold onto, harder still to control for more than a heartbeat. He sighed and reached out with his own small net of motes, touching, feeling and seeing the construct which Vedrix had created with a moment's thought.

"Trace the knots," Vedrix said, "and you'll note they are connected to the tent fabric itself. Good magic is all about the planning and the use of as little effort as possible."

"You've built the construct into the tent," Kyron said, letting go of his net and seeing only the canvas walls once more.

"A few years ago," Vedrix confessed. "However, that is enough learning for today. I'm not sure how long you have until Emlyn returns. I suggest you both use your time wisely."

There was silence at the table and Kyron picked up his goblet of wine for something to do. He took a sip, enjoying the notes of summer's end upon his tongue. Wine had been part of most meals, watered down when he was young, when he lived with the old man, and Padarn had introduced him to more as they travelled.

"Taste the wine and you will understand the people and land upon which it grew," he whispered.

"Very true. Who said that?" his grandfather said.

"Padarn, my master," Kyron said, looking up from his drink feeling the sadness of autumn settle about him.

"In wine, there is truth," Vedrix said, his voice deep and rumbling, lost for a moment in the tent before he glanced at the two sat silent, "so drink up."

His grandfather's smile was a fleeting memory of years ago and for a heartbeat Kyron was back in the old man's house, listening to his lessons and dreaming of the day he would carry a sword in the Empire's Army. The vision faded into mist and was blown away by his sigh.

"How have you been?" his grandfather asked.

"Well," Kyron said. "I've been well."

"I am sorry about Master Padarn," his grandfather said. "He was a good man. I liked him."

"You didn't know him." The words spilled from his mouth like poison.

"I did," his grandfather said. "I met him a few times when he took over your training, and he kept me up to date on your progress. I even spoke with him before you left on campaign."

"You were checking up on me?" Kyron clenched his jaw as he uttered the words, strangling the words which he wanted to say, knowing they were those of a child, not a magician.

"You are still my family," the old man snapped back before taking a calming breath. "My only family, Kyron. You know me well enough. Until I die, you are my responsibility, and one I carry with care and joy."

Kyron grunted. "I cannot believe I've brought you much joy."

His grandfather smiled and this time it reached his eyes. Kyron was surprised to see actual happiness in the old man's eyes, too used to sadness and disappointment.

"Ever since you were born," his grandfather said. "Before. The day your father came to tell me. We were never a large family, Kyron. My brothers did not make it out of the crib and my sister died during a plague. All my parents could do was send me off to the army."

"Were they from the tribes?" The thought struck him, and it was spoken before he could stop himself.

"What? No," his grandfather said. "My parents were from the city."

"And their parents?" Vedrix spoke into the quiet while the older man took a swallow of wine and Kyron tried to get his thoughts into order. "Each of us have ancestors amongst the tribes who used to own the land, if you look back far enough."

"I don't think they owned the land," Kyron said, trying to untangle why the thought of possession made him uncomfortable. "At least, I don't think that is how they think, or thought."

It was Master Vedrix's turn to smile. "Perhaps not, Apprentice. However, my point remains true. The Empire conquers and absorbs. It is like the lava from a volcano spreading across the land, swamping all before it but building upon it."

"Lava burns and destroys," Kyron pointed out and the only response from Master Vedrix was a slight shrug.

"It is no secret," his grandfather said, resting his hand on the book. "Much of the Empire's people are from different lands, the far south, some even from the east. My ancestors were from here, from Sudrim."

"What was it called before it became Sudrim?" Vedrix said in quiet voice. "Even so, our ancestors all came from what we now call the tribes."

"I do not deny that," his grandfather said. "Though I am not comfortable with your description of the Empire."

"I've heard it called worse," Kyron said, "and with better analogies. Sorry, Master."

"No need to apologies, Apprentice, words were never my strongest skill," Vedrix answered with a small chuckle.

"My parents went back to where our family began," Kyron said, a statement rather than a question.

"I don't remember telling you that," his grandfather said, squinting across the table at Kyron.

For half a moment Kyron considered telling his grandfather where the information came from, but the old man had never had much faith in magic and he was aware that the story stretched the limits of anyone's belief.

"I think I put it together from your stories of my father and your time in the army. Also, my time with Padarn opened my eyes a little. He taught me to see more than was there and I've spent some time with Emlyn, listening to her talk about the tribes," he explained, and though the lie came easy, in his grandfather's eyes there was a hint of disbelief. The old man had not made it to be General of the Empire's Army without being shrewd.

"Padarn always said you had more brains than you seemed to use. More magic too if you ever managed to unlock it," Vedrix said. "Bordan, he deserves to know. It will affect him too. He should be prepared."

"What?" Kyron looked between the two men. Both had given the other a hard stare and then taken a drink from their wine.

"Once we reach the capital and the Princess is crowned Emperor, I will be retiring," his grandfather said. "I am too old, and the Empire needs younger blood in charge."

"There's more," Kyron said, judging the other man's words and noting the way his grandfather's hands clasped his cup.

"I've told you what happened in the palace," Master Vedrix said when his grandfather remained silent. "It has caused some tension between the council and the Princess."

"Me and the Princess," his grandfather grunted.

"Well, yes," Vedrix acknowledged. "Your grandfather is concerned, though he does not say it, that you will be tainted by this tension."

"I want you to be safe," his grandfather said. "It was one reason I supported your entry into the Gymnasium."

"Supported?" Kyron spat. "We argued every day for weeks. You tried to talk me out of it over every meal."

"I had to make sure it was what you wanted and..." His grandfather's words trailed off.

"And what?"

"And you were more likely to do the exact opposite of whatever I said." His grandfather sighed. "It is what young men do. I recall your father doing the same."

"When?"

"When they moved west," his grandfather admitted. "When they moved away from the capital to start their own lives, to be their own people, not the General's son. My life comes with risks, and I wanted you all to be safe."

"And now?"

"Now is the same," his grandfather said. "I will retire, and I had hoped to keep you free from any problems that resulted."

"Retiring is not a problem. You've served the Empire all your life with honour and distinction," Kyron pointed out.

"Things change," his grandfather replied, "sometimes too quickly to make adequate plans."

Kyron's thoughts returned to an earlier conversation. "Someone else told me something similar."

"They are right, listen to them," Vedrix added.

"Anyway, you are a magician of the Gymnasium," his grandfather said. "You should be safe there. I hope you'll visit."

"You are not telling me everything," Kyron said, leaning forward and putting his cup on the table. "All this trouble to speak to me in private, the ward, getting rid of Emlyn."

"There is always more, Kyron, but to know would put you at risk. Whatever happens, Master Vedrix can assist. Only he knows who you are," his grandfather said.

"And Godewyn," Vedrix pointed out.

"I cannot rely upon him, though it pains me to say so. A High Priest cannot protect a magician. The stakes would be too high," Bordan replied and Vedrix nodded.

"You are starting to worry me," Kyron admitted.

"Good," his grandfather said. "That will keep you alert. It may come to nothing, but it is best to be prepared."

"What are you all talking about?" Emlyn's voice cut through their quiet conversation as she entered the tent.

"About the honour guard and the journey," his grandfather said, "And now we must let the apprentice rest. Good night to you both."

As the magician and General left the tent, he caught the questioning look which Emlyn directed at him. He shrugged, echoing Vedrix's answer of earlier.

LI

The General

Four years ago:

He paced the corridor of the Gymnasium. Ever since the boy had been ushered into the room, the worry had gnawed at his belly.

"It will be some time, General," Master Vedrix said. "Some take only a short while, but many take much longer. They will tell us when they are done. Come, I've had some chilled wine set aside."

"They won't hurt him?"

Master Vedrix laughed, an honest, deep chuckle which seemed to shake the walls. "Of course not, General. We're magicians, not barbarians."

"We will reach the capital tomorrow," General Bordan said. He shifted his weight from one foot to the other, a trick learned on the parade ground to ease the ache in his legs and back.

"It has taken far too long," Aelia said, not looking up from her plate of food. Thin slices of steaming meat, vegetables covered in bright red sauce, and dark olives swimming in clear, golden oil.

"An Emperor must arrive with all due pomp and ceremony. It takes time, Your Highness," Godewyn said from his seat at the table.

"I need to look impressive at the head of the army, when we bring my father's body home," Aelia said, spearing a slice of meat with her knife and chewing on it slowly. "The grooms must prepare my horse and armour. I want them both to shine, to be seen from the walls as we crest the horizon. The people need to know who brings their beloved Emperor home and who will now sit on the throne."

"I will ensure the grooms do their jobs properly," Bordan said, a niggle of pain in his lower back.

"Excellent." Aelia said, cutting another sliver of meat.

"Messengers from the capital report that all preparations are proceeding on time," Bordan said. "The populace have been notified and we expect them to line the streets upon our arrival."

"Keep them back a little. There may still be assassins," Aelia said.

"The army will secure the route, Your Highness," Bordan said with a nod.

"Master Vedrix, it will be a fine day tomorrow?" Aelia asked, pushing her plate away.

"I expect so, Your Highness," Vedrix answered from his customary seat in the corner, not far from the exit to the tent.

"What use is magic if you cannot tell me a simple thing? What will the weather be like tomorrow, magician? I want the skies clear and the sun to beam down upon us as we reach the city," Aelia said.

"The weather does as the weather does, Your Highness. Many magicians have sought to understand and exercise some control over it. All failed," Vedrix said, sitting up in his seat as if a thought had struck him. "There was a magician, what was her name? I forget. Anyway, she claimed to be able to make it rain whenever and wherever she was."

"And?" Aelia said. "Was she telling the truth? If you can make it rain, you can make it stop, surely."

"No one knows, Your Highness. The last record of her is of her stood on a high cliff commanding the wind to blow," Vedrix said. "I do wish I could remember her name. Fascinating life history and quite the experimenter."

"What happened to her?" Godewyn asked.

"We believe a gust of wind caught her robes and she fell from the cliff," Vedrix answered. "Either way, the weather is too big for magic. Only the Holy Flame has that much power over the world, Your Highness."

"It is good of you to recognise such, Master Vedrix," Godewyn said, inclining his head in the magician's direction.

"One must always know where one stands and the limit of their power," Vedrix replied.

"Just so," Aelia agreed. "I am sure the General agrees with you. Don't you, Bordan?"

"Of course, Your Highness," Bordan answered, gritting his teeth. "I understand perfectly."

"Have the army in full battle dress," Aelia said, her knife hovering over the plate of vegetables before stabbing a morsel of choice.

"Formal dress," Bordan said, "cloaks, shields and armour polished."

"That is what I said." Aelia rolled her eyes as she spoke.

"As you say, Your Highness," Bordan answered, biting down the words, knowing that to argue the point would serve no purpose.

"General," Aelia said in the tone of a much younger child, reticent and unsure. "The plot to kill me, to steal my throne. It is over, isn't it?"

"From everything that we," and Bordan waved a hand to encompass the High Priest and the Master Magician, "know, yes. However, it is best to proceed with caution and security."

"Did you enjoy killing Abra?" The question was sudden and Bordan almost stepped back, catching himself at the last moment.

"I've never enjoyed killing, Your Highness," Bordan answered, struggling to find the right words as the Princess stared at him with wide eyes. In them the General could recognise the need for reassurance and the fear that swam just beneath the surface.

"You are a soldier," Aelia pointed out. "Killing is what you do."

"No true soldier wants to kill, Your Highness, they want to live to an old age, have children, and retire in comfort," Bordan replied, measuring his words as if embarking on the most delicate of recipes.

"But you did kill Abra," Aelia stated, though Bordan recognised it as a plea.

"I did," Bordan agreed. "Abra is dead."

"What did it feel like?"

"Feel like?" Bordan repeated, sharing a glance with the High Priest, as he searched for the right words, realising he would have to settle for half a lie. "Justice and an ending, Your Highness."

"He killed my brother, and my mother," Aelia said, and Bordan could see the young woman's eyes were elsewhere.

"He is dead, Your Highness," Bordan said, treading carefully. "You will be Emperor in just a few days, and you can honour your family."

"I wanted to kill him, Bordan," Aelia shouted, her eyes snapping back to the present and she slammed a clenched fist down upon the table. "I wanted him to suffer. I wanted him to die slowly, to feel every drop of his life drip from his wrecked body. I wanted him crucified where I could watch the pain in his eyes as his fate consumed him. I wanted crows to peck at his wounds, flies to lay eggs and maggots to erupt from the rotting tears in his flesh. I wanted him to beg, Bordan. I wanted him to cry out for death and do you know what I'd do?"

Bordan stood motionless, but from the corner of his eye caught Vedrix's movement, the simple act of closing the book he was reading and, in that gesture, he glimpsed the future. It scared him.

"I'd tell him no, General," Aelia continued, her voice calming and lowering almost to a whisper. "I wanted him to suffer, General. Just as I have. I wanted him to know what it is like to have everything taken from you."

"Believe me when I say this, Your Highness, it would not have helped," Bordan croaked and was forced to work his jaws to bring moisture to his dry mouth. "The desire for revenge can destroy a person or fuel them for a time, but revenge fulfilled is an empty thing. In the end, it is how we deal with our losses that defines and guides our futures."

"You've lost people?" Aelia said, her voice losing its anger, replaced by a deep sadness.

"Comrades, friends, my brothers and sisters, my parents," Bordan said, feeling the familiar lump in his throat and tightness around his eyes. "My own children."

"And you carried on?" Aelia looked up from her seat into Bordan's eyes for the first time.

"We all have to," Bordan answered. "Killing Abra would have done little to assuage the grief, Your Highness. I am sorry."

"I don't blame you, General. You did what I'd ordered and secured my father's body."

"Thank you," Bordan answered, bowing to cover nascent tears in his eyes, wiping a sleeve across them as he stood straight once more.

"What did he say?" Aelia said after a moment's silence.

"Say, Your Highness?"

"Abra, when you killed him? Those officers you had report to me all told me of the duel," Aelia said, the smile still creasing her face. "It is famous in the camp already. The Old General kills the traitor."

"It was not much of a duel, Your Highness," Bordan replied, rubbing the bandaged cut on his forearm.

"You do yourself a disservice, General," Aelia said, smiling up at the old man. "They tell me it was a great duel. How you fended off his attacks with your shield, protecting the men around you. How you were wounded by a coward's trick and drove your sword, despite your grievous wound, into the traitor's body."

"I fear they have embellished the events somewhat, Your Highness," Bordan said. "It is a tendency of stories and battles. He was not much of a swordsman and I am too old for battles."

"Yet, you killed the traitor, General?"

"Yes, Your Highness."

"And you spoke to him as he died," Aelia continued, leading forward.

"A few words only," Bordan agreed.

"What did the traitor have to say for himself?"

"He begged for forgiveness, Your Highness," Bordan answered, finding the lie coming easy to his lips. "Dying soldiers often ask for forgiveness. They fear the judgement of the Holy Flame."

"As they should, General," Godewyn said. "Abra will burn forever in the Flame. His agony will last a thousand lifetimes and more."

"Thank you, General," Aelia said, pushing her seat back. "I think I needed to hear of his death. I will go and sleep. Make sure the soldiers are looking their best in their formal dress," a faint smile crossed the Princess's lips, "when we approach the city."

Bordan bowed, as did Godewyn and Vedrix, the magician rising from his chair to do so.

"I will, Your Highness," Bordan said. "They will shine in a reflection of your glory."

The Princess paused for a moment and nodded. "I like that, General."

"I did not know you had such a gift with words," Godewyn said after the Princess had left.

"She still has a long way to go, Godewyn," Bordan said, sighing and taking a seat at the table. The Princess's half-eaten food before him, but any appetite had long since fled.

"She speaks with the wisdom of youth, Bordan," Godewyn assured him.

"I hope you can guide her," he said, reaching for the wine and pouring a measure into a clean cup. "My advice will be rarely heeded I fear."

"She still looks up to you, Bordan. She appreciated your words tonight. They brought some comfort I think." The High Priest took the other free chair at the table. "Aelia knows you served her father honestly and dutifully. I think, like all young people, she is scared and worried."

Bordan grunted as he took a sip of wine. "It has been a long time since I was a young man."

"But you raised two of your own, Bordan," Godewyn answered. "Both a credit to you. The boy cannot be much younger than the Princess."

"Not much," Bordan said, sipping from his wine. "How fare the preparations from your side?"

"The church is being prepared for the coronation," Godewyn said. "The ceremony can be held the day after we arrive."

"Good. The sooner, the better."

"We need to secure the throne, General," Godewyn said. "Princess Aelia is insistent she is ready to build on her father's legacy and bring safety to the Empire. For the Church and the Emperor, we desire the old Emperor's flame be freed to join the everlasting Flame and the paradise which awaits him. He has waited far too long."

"On that we agree."

"Will your staff be ready?"

"Maxentius has it in hand," Bordan said, tilting his cup from side to side, watching the rise and fall of the wine never letting any spill. "The city is secure and there will be no trouble. I've been told the route from palace to church is being cleared and decorated. We will have everything in readiness."

"Master Vedrix?" Godewyn said.

"Hmm... what's that?" Vedrix rubbed at his face and sat up in the chair. "My apologies. I am really not used to this much fresh air and travel."

"Are your preparations ready for the coronation?" Bordan asked.

"Of course," Vedrix said. "I've been in communication with the Gymnasium and preparations, such as we can make, are complete. Some fireworks and displays to celebrate. They will look spectacular."

"In that case," Godewyn said, finishing the last of his wine in one swallow and placing the empty cup upon the table, "I think I will retire also. Tomorrow is looking to be a busy day."

"And then there were two," Vedrix said after the tall priest had left the tent. "Have you made some decisions?"

"About?"

"Your future," Vedrix asked.

"Retirement," Bordan answered.

"And Kyron?"

"He will remain a magician, will he not?"

"He can," Vedrix agreed. "We can find a new master for him, though in truth he is not far from completing his training. Padarn did an excellent job of unlocking his abilities. Travel was just the thing, it seems. It is a shame he is not around to finish Kyron's training. He would be proud of what the boy's become."

"You are suggesting he might decide to do something else?"

"Would you invite him to come with you?"

"Into retirement?" Bordan pondered the idea for a moment, a sad smile crossing his face. "No. He has his own life to lead."

"Good," Vedrix nodded. "He would go with you if you asked."

"I doubt that," Bordan replied, dismissing the thought.

"Then you misjudge him, General," the Master Magician replied. "It is time for me to retire also, I feel. I will leave you to your thoughts, though I'd recommend you turn in soon. As the High Priest has said, tomorrow is likely to be a busy day."

Left alone, with only wine and the illusion of silence for company, Bordan sighed. The oil lamps and torches flickered in their sconces and pots, casting dancing shadows against the tent. Outside, the sounds of an army camp were muted by the late hour, but it was never truly quiet. Over the years of campaigning, those sounds had been a comfort, an aid to sleep. Tonight, the whispers sounded harsh, the noise of armour being cleaned with sand and oil was discordant to his ears. It was wrong, though he could not say why.

From his pack, he drew out sheaves of bound paper and a small pot of ink. Turning to the next blank page, he dipped the stylus into the black ink and began to write. The familiar lines of his handwriting appeared on the rough surface of the paper. His own coded language, his own thoughts, for him alone.

LII

THE MAGICIAN

FOUR YEARS AGO:

"I can see colours," he said, though his eyes were closed.

"Good," the woman replied. "Now, I want you think about one of those colours."

"They are all mixed up, like little bits of sand or chalk dust, but different colours," he said, trying to explain.

"Just pick one of the bits of coloured sand," she said. "Concentrate on it."

"I've picked one."

"Now try to move it into your hand," she said. "Just think about moving it and keep your hand still."

"NOT LONG NOW, lad," Borus said, coming up beside him as the soldiers marched past the stone columns which rose either side of the road. On each was a carved inscription detailing a victorious battle or extolling the virtues of a hero from myth, a past Emperor, or soldier who won glory for the Empire. "My favourite bit of road."

Underfoot the cobbles were smooth and the camber of the road led in a soft arc to the rain gutters at the edges. Beyond the road the farmland began to give way to villages and inns, trading posts and barns which would fill with produce as the summer progressed to autumn.

"Why?" Kyron asked, looking around for something which stood out and finding only those things he had always seen.

"Home, Kyron. It means we are almost home," Borus answered, waving his hands around to indicate the clarity of his vision. "Not just the farms and buildings, but the columns, lad. Look at them. The whole history of brave deeds and battles. They'll build one to us, one day."

"To us?"

"The honour guard," Borus clarified, "I doubt we will actually get a mention, but my descendants will know I was part of it."

"What did we do that's worth one of these?" Kyron asked, and next to him Emlyn grunted. He ignored her as a thought occurred. "When was the last one erected?"

Emlyn stifled a laugh.

"We passed it a while ago, it was still pristine and sharp. All these," Borus pointed to a column on his left, "are old and worn down by the rain and wind."

"But when was it," Kyron paused, glanced at Emlyn who responded with an impish grin, "built."

"Not entirely sure," Borus confessed, biting his lower lip. "I think it commemorates one of the Emperor's first victories over the tribes."

"Is that what we do?" Kyron asked, puzzled. "Is every column to do with war?"

"I think so," Borus answered, looking back over his shoulder. "They tell us of our past and the road leads away from the capital into the future. All those soldiers who gave their lives for the Empire. Even if a column is dedicated to just one hero, it stands for every soldier who fought."

"Do you have any statues or columns to which celebrates something other than killing?" Emlyn asked, leaning forward to look past Kyron and catch Borus's gaze.

"What?" Borus grunted. "Well, we've got the Colosseum."

"Where you play games?" Emlyn said, stepping over a pile of horse dung which steamed in the late morning sun. "Isn't that what you said before, Kyron?"

"Battles," Borus said. "Duels between gladiators."

"Gladiators?"

"People trained to fight and who make their living on the floor of the arena," Kyron explained.

"It glories in violence again," she stated and the certainty in her voice grated on Kyron's sense of national pride.

"No one is killed," Kyron pointed out.

"Not often, anyway," Borus added.

"But your crowds go to watch it," Emlyn said. "They enjoy the spectacle of men dealing violence upon one another. The blood and sweat."

"It's honest," Borus said with no hint of anger or shame in his voice. "The gladiators choose that life, train for it, and can earn a fortune if they are successful."

"And if they're not?"

Borus shrugged. "I don't know. I don't follow the losers. I suspect a few join the army and put their skills to some use."

"And some probably spend their lives crippled and in pain?" Emlyn said.

Kyron spared her a glance and tried to read the expression on her face but as always she confounded him. Hating himself, but unable to give up the opportunity to show off his learning, he said, "It used to be slaves."

"What did?" Borus asked.

"Who fought in the arena," Kyron said. "Used to be captured slaves or those sold into slavery. They could earn their freedom if they survived twenty-five fights."

"You said you had no slavery," Emlyn asked, shocked.

"Not for centuries," Kyron said. "Longer, maybe, but my tutors in history at the Gymnasium did talk about it."

"At least they had a chance," Borus said, "to earn their freedom. Though I bet not many of them did. Skill will get you so far, but you need luck to."

"I don't know how many were freed," Kyron agreed. "I do know there was a rebellion led by a slave-gladiator on the southern continent, back when the capital of the Empire was there."

"Is that your capital?" Emlyn pointed and changed the subject.

They looked forward as the horizon south was broken by a hill topped by a grey smudge of walls.

"Sudrim," Kyron said. "Home."

"Not mine," Emlyn said.

"You could have gone back," Borus pointed out.

"My parents will be freed," Emlyn said. "I may not like your legion, but I wanted to see your city. We are taught to travel, to experience new things and bring the knowledge back to the forest."

"Padarn travelled," Kyron said, remembering the fire and conversation.

"It must be in the blood," Emlyn answered.

"What's blood got to do with it?" Borus asked, his brow furrowing.

"Wanderlust," Kyron replied before Emlyn could open her mouth and give anything away. "It is in the blood. Some people are born to wander. Perhaps that's why you stayed in the army, to see the world."

"I stayed because the pay was good, better than being a porter at the docks like my father," Borus explained.

"What will happen when we get there?" Emlyn asked, staring at the city.

Kyron turned away from the sight of home and looked at her once more. There was a hint of something in her eye, sadness, loss, or something else. He cursed himself for not understanding and not knowing what to say.

"The army will escort the Emperor's waggon to the palace before heading to the barracks," Kyron said.

"The Princess?"

"She will go too," Kyron nodded. "To get ready for the coronation which Vedrix says will be tomorrow."

"So soon?"

"An Empire needs an Emperor," Borus said. "There'll be a parade through the streets first. When we get there, I mean."

"And the funerals of the Prince and Empress?"

"After the coronation," Borus answered.

Before Kyron could add anything, the order came through the lines and the army stopped, every soldier retrieving their red cloaks and swinging them around their shoulders.

"We have to look our best," Borus explained as the army resumed its march. "Can't imagine we'll stop for food before we reach the capital. It is going to be a long day."

True to the prediction, the army marched through the morning and afternoon. The hill upon which the city sat rose before them and they climbed the road to the main gates. Atop the walls Kyron saw the populace and heard their cheers and whistles.

"What are they throwing?" Emlyn asked as the gate came closer.

"Flowers and petals," Borus answered. "It is custom. I don't understand it much myself. I'd prefer coins."

"They smell sweet," Kyron said with a sigh. "It is supposed to mask the scent of blood and battle."

"Really?" Borus asked.

"Yes. Men returning from battle did not always stop to bathe before seeking their wives or," he felt his cheeks aflame, "the company of other women. The petals symbolise a perfumed bath which those women would make the men take before they... well... you know."

"Had sex," Emlyn said. "Makes sense. As strange as anything else in your Empire, but it has some sense to it. I wouldn't want to lie with a man stinking of blood, guts, and sweat."

Borus laughed while Kyron's eyes widened, and he was uncomfortably aware of just how warm it had just become. Emlyn smiled and bent down to pick up one of the petals, bringing it to her nose and inhaling the scent.

Inside the walls, the cheering was cacophonous and echoed from the tall buildings as people leaned from windows to shout and scream. The petals soon stopped falling, but nothing could drown out the noise. It was almost a shock to realise how little breeze there was coming down the street and how often they walked in shadow. It was a forest of stone, full of baying and howling animals. For the first time Kyron could recall, he felt uncomfortable in the city.

Moving along the crowded streets, following in the wake of the Emperor's waggon, hemmed in by the soldiers' perfect marching and the buildings, he was lost. The roads he knew, and the cobbles beneath his feet were as familiar as the soles of his boots. Shops, restaurants, merchants and markets were recognisable and sparked memories which cascaded through his mind, but as though they belonged to someone else.

The bath house, the communal facilities provided, at a cost, to the people of the city passed by in a half-seen daze. A hazy memory of visiting, of sweating in the caldarium, before plunging into icy water. On his arm, small goosebumps rose, and he felt the chill of the frigidarium in his bones.

"You all right, lad?" Borus asked, laying a hand on Kyron's shoulder. "You look a little pale."

"Fine," he stammered, his stomach queasy and a shiver running through him.

"No, you're not," Borus said, dragging him to one side out of the main flow of soldiers. "You've been through a lot, especially as you're not a trained soldier. Even the novices get sick of the fighting and death. It's when you get back home you feel it the most."

"I'll be fine," Kyron protested.

"What's the matter?" Emlyn asked, struggling free of the parade.

"Young Kyron's not well," Borus said. "I've seen it hit a lot of soldiers over the years. Overcome by it all. Recognition of home does it. Suddenly realising it is over and you survived, that kind of thing. He needs a stiff drink and good rest."

"Where?" she said, ignoring Kyron's looks and words of protestation.

"Probably the Gymnasium," Borus said, bending down and looking into Kyron's eyes. "Is that where you're staying, lad?"

Kyron tried to swallow and speak, but when no words came, he settled for a nod.

"I can't leave the parade," Borus said, glancing towards Emlyn and then at the soldiers passing by, "at least not for long. You think you can walk that far?"

Kyron nodded once more and Borus smiled.

"I'll make sure he gets there," Emlyn said.

"I was going to have you put up in one of the army rooms, least till you decided what you were going to do," Borus said to her, "but I suppose the magicians can put you up just as well. You're used to their company."

"Where is this Gymnasium?"

Kyron pointed in the general direction.

"He'll get you there," Borus said. "Might even find his voice on the way. If you get lost, just ask. Most folks will point you in the right direction."

"Right," Emlyn nodded. "You'll tell Vedrix where I've taken him. Not sure I want a whole building of magicians after me."

"They don't run fast," Borus chuckled. "Most are as fat as Vedrix. Padarn and the boy here are almost the exceptions. Look after him, he's been a good companion on the road. I'll try to check in later."

"Thank you," Kyron croaked.

"Don't even think on it, lad," Borus answered and Kyron saw the concern in his eyes.

"I'll send word if I can," Emlyn said.

"Get some rest," Borus replied. "Coronation is tomorrow and you'll need your energy for the celebrations."

With a last nod, the soldier slipped back into the parade, the troops making room for him without a complaint.

"Which way?" Emlyn asked.

Kyron pointed at a side street just ahead.

"Come on then. Sooner we're off this main street and with a bit of room to breathe, the better you'll feel." Emlyn caught him by the arm and began to half-drag, half-support him down the road, turning the corner on the side street and pushing her way through the cheering crowds. A few city folks complained, but one look in her eyes or at the pale, shaking Kyron next to her, and they moved aside.

They made their way through the streets, the crowds thinning as they put distance between themselves and the parade. Some gave them strange looks, but most paid them no heed at all. The scent of food wafting from the thermopolia, the shops offering the city dweller a choice of hot food from across the Empire, made his stomach rumble even as another shudder raced through him.

"Stop," he said, leaning against the low wall of one of the many fountains and pools fed by the river and aqueducts which brought water from the far away mountains to the west. The white stone was carved to depict a great battle.

"Left," he mumbled. "Not far. Big building. You'll see it."

To the right, he could see the Colosseum and as they stumbled along yet another street Kyron recognised the large blue doors which marked the entrance to the Gymnasium at the far end. The houses here were occupied by magicians and those who worked for them. In any other city, in any other place, the building would have been imposing and its majesty would have shone for all to see. It would be whitewashed to a shine and bright Empire red would have competed with gold paint which ran in strips around the building. Towers would have leapt to the sky from the roofs and there would be a bustle of learned people going to and fro on important business.

That was the image in his mind, constructed from reading scrolls in the library and hearing stories from Padarn's encyclopaedic knowledge of the Gymnasium's history. It was clear, just looking at the building which now seemed to squat, hoping not to be noticed, amongst homes and businesses, that its best days were far behind.

Kyron limped up to the door, Emlyn holding him upright, and knocked three times. A small window opened, and two suspicious eyes peeked out.

"Kyron, Apprentice Magician," he said, trying not to mumble his words.

"And she is?" the voice which belonged to the eyes said.

"A guide, a friend," Kyron struggled to find the right words. "Master Vedrix sent her with me."

He felt the construct of a truth net flitter against his skin, and knew it read his words as true. Defeating the net by being selectively honest was a lesson every apprentice learned quickly or spent too many evenings in the kitchens scrubbing the pots.

The door creaked open, sticking a little at its base and only giving way on a great heave.

"Looks like the preservation charm is weakening," the man who stood revealed in the late afternoon sun said. "I'll have to get an apprentice to renew them, and then he can clean out the stables for letting them get this bad."

Kyron tried a weak smile, a memory of his own time at this task. Time well spent given the last few weeks, but never enjoyable.

"I'd tell you to do it, but you don't look well," the man said. "Where is your master, Apprentice?"

"Dead," Kyron answered, a chill sweeping through his body and he shook, unable to control his muscles.

"Oh," the man said, leaning closer and examining him, "you're Padarn's apprentice. A good man, good magician too. You want me to get someone to look you over?"

"He just needs rest," Emlyn said. "Got a little hurt in the battle, and it has been a long walk."

"Aye," the man said, "can see he isn't right. Take him to his rooms, but don't go wandering off, young lady. Most of the corridors are safe, but there are things here which might be dangerous if you go into the wrong place, at the wrong time."

"I'll stay with him," Emlyn said. "He needs rest and good food."

"More than likely," the man agreed. "I'll have an apprentice bring up some food and drink for you both."

"I can make it to the refectory," Kyron protested.

"Not if you're asleep," the man said, "which you will be soon as your head hits the pillow I'd wager."

"Stop talking, Kyron," Emlyn told him.

"Take him to Padarn's room," the man said. "There's a spare bed if you need it."

"Thank you," he heard Emlyn say. "Which way?"

They followed the route, though in truth Kyron could have walked the path with his eyes closed. Magicians, apprentices and novices, wide-eyed and hurrying with quick steps, flitted about the corridors. The scent of magic drifted on the air, a heady mix of sulphur, pine, and ozone which tickled his nose. He sneezed and groaned as a stab of pain ran through his chest.

"Just here," he said, nodding to a plain door on the right side of the corridor.

"It won't open," Emlyn complained as she grabbed the handle and pushed.

"Locked," Kyron said. "We locked it on the morning we left."

"You lock your doors?" she said, jiggling the handle once more.

"Here," he said, reaching into his tunic and lifting the chain with its attached key he had taken from his master and kept safe for the entire journey.

The inside of Padarn's rooms were tidy and warm. Light fell through a window high in the facing wall and splashed across the floor picking out the dust which floated and swirled in the air.

A tall bookcase stood next to the door, full of scrolls and precious books. Kyron recalled paging through these tomes, marvelling at illuminated manuscripts, poring over plain and simple texts, and staring at drawings which detailed everything from the internal workings of the human body to the circling of the stars in the sky.

Much of it was beyond his understanding, but knowledge was a narcotic to which he was addicted, and his curiosity was an appetite which could never be sated.

A bench ran along the wall beneath the window and a bed, his bed, rested in the far corner. In the other wall was the door to Padarn's room.

He stopped halfway to both, torn.

"I don't need sleep," Emlyn said, "and we'll leave Padarn's room as it was for a while longer. Get some rest, I'll take the chair by the fireplace."

Kyron looked over his shoulder at her and smiled. "Thank you."

"Means I'll hear the door when that apprentice gets here with the food," she answered as she strode across the room and threw herself into the chair, stretching out her legs before her. He watched for a moment as she took one of the sticks from her belt, unsheathed her knife and began to carve.

The memory of his own bed was as nothing compared to climbing back into it after all the time away. Pillows sank beneath his head, rising like soft snow drifts around his ears, muting the noise from outside. His mattress was his mother's arms enfolding him in the warmest embrace of youth.

A contented sigh and sleep took him.

LIII

THE GENERAL

Four years ago:
  He watched Master Vedrix unfurl the scroll, read a little and nod.
  "Do you know what is wrong with him? Can it be cured?"
  The large magician collapsed into his cushioned chair with a deep sigh. "We know what is wrong, and no it cannot be cured."
  "He is going to die?" The goblet of chilled wine shook in his hand, little ripples sloshing against the side.
  "No," Master Vedrix said, shuffling forward. "The boy can see magic, General. He needs training, to learn control, or the Church will come after him."

"THIS ARMOUR WAS never comfortable," Bordan complained as the red cape was fixed to the shoulders and he fastened the sword belt. The sheathed gladius would rest in his office today, but the pugio in its ornate, decorated scabbard would remain. A soldier never went anywhere unarmed, a lesson drilled into him through far too many inspections during his early years in the army.

So many friends, and so few still living today. Old age had taken some, illness others, but many had fallen to the blades of enemies on campaigns which were now part of history. In the blurred reflection of the silvered mirror, he saw the armour of the Empire and the face of an old man who had lived for duty and service. Hard lines around the mouth, wrinkles creasing his forehead, and eyes of dark pride and sorrow.

"You made your choice a long time ago," he muttered to the reflection.

"Sorry, General?" Cohort Cypria said, stepping into view.

"Talking to myself," Bordan said. "Getting into bad habits."

"We've all got those, General," Cypria said with a smile.

"A lifetime of practice," Bordan smiled. "Are the troops ready?"

"Yes, sir."

"Then we'd best get to it," Bordan said, straightening his back and settling the armour on his shoulders.

Hand on the pommel of his pugio, Bordan swept from the room, keeping his pace measured and face calm. Yet his heart beat faster with each step and his mind raced behind his eyes. Soldiers and staff saluted as he passed, and he returned the honour as a reflex.

The last time a day like this had happened, the old Emperor had been a young man and Bordan had possessed a spring in his step. Today was different: the elation he had felt as he marched as part of the General's staff, a newly raised Legion in the Empire's army, was absent.

Outside the sun shone down upon the palace and city. From the wall, the church, its symbol of the Flame and its towers built tall to accentuate the power of religion, was bright and clear to see. A simple march down the avenue which connected the martial power of the Empire to its religious heart. The crowds were growing, kept back by fences erected over the days since the battle at the bridge, and the noise of their chatter carried to his ears without pause. A thousand voices, two thousand, an army of civilians who had gathered to see the new Emperor crowned.

At the opposite end of the avenue, the barracks and yards of the army. There, he knew, rested the Emperor's waggon. A decorated, more ornate, open waggon had replaced the one which had carried his body without complaint or falter from the north. Its labour was complete, and it would be retired with honour, or more likely chopped into firewood ready to stave off the bite of winter.

Resting a hand on the sun-warmed stone of the wall, he took a deep breath, drinking in the sight of the Empire's heart. Is this how the old General had felt before he had descended the steps to lead the funeral guard to the church? An ending to one chapter and the opening of another, hoping it would be a lighter, better, happier story, and fearing it would not.

He shook the thoughts away and put his feet on the first smooth step, forcing himself down them one at a time. No rush, he told himself. Calm and steady. Service and duty.

"They are ready," Sarimarcus said as Bordan joined him at the head of the guard.

"Thank you, Prefect," Bordan replied. "The new rank suits you."

"Thank you, General," Prefect Sarimarcus replied.

"You'll be a Legion before too long," Bordan said. "Duty and service, if you can balance both there won't be anyone to stop you."

"The higher you go, the more responsibility," Sarimarcus said. "I am in no rush."

"You are wise too," Bordan said, glancing at the ranks of soldiers behind him, and in their centre the Emperor's funeral waggon. Pageant and ceremony were the symbols and strength of the Empire. The passing of power today would be cemented in the heart of the populace by the rituals conducted. "I think it is about time. Issue the order."

"Yes, General," Sarimarcus said and wiped the sweat which dripped from beneath his plumed helm from his face.

Trumpets sang out across the avenue, echoing from the walls and the sounds swelled in his heart. Everyone fell silent in their wake, the city stilled, and the soldiers took their first step.

They marched past the crowds on either side. No one cheered, none shouted, and no banners were waved. Only the feet of the soldiers against the stones and the creak of the waggon's wheels broke the silence. Overhead a single raven fluttered from the church tower, crossing the cloudless sky and vanishing behind the palace walls.

Every face turned as they passed, following their progress along the avenue, and Bordan felt the weight of each gaze. History walked beside him, and he felt her presence, heard her subtle whispers in his ear and knew she saw everything in his heart. His fingers itched for his diary and stylus. Someone, somewhere, would document this day and get everything wrong, miss every subtlety, and read the wrong portents in each action. She would know the truth. It was small comfort.

At the base of the church steps, the procession halted, and the ranks widened, spreading out to protect the entrance. Everyone important, all those invited, would already be inside, sat, waiting.

"Prefect," Bordan instructed and with whispered orders the Emperor's pallet, carved from southern oak, was slipped with exquisite care from the waggon.

Flowers surrounded his body and as the bearers drew level with the General, he noted the makeup which had been applied to give the man a semblance of life and cover the wound a borrowed arrow had made in his face. Nothing could disguise the sunken skin, the stillness, the lack of an inner fire. The man he had called a friend, his Emperor, was no longer present.

The dark red gem on the corpse's chest absorbed the sunlight and appeared, to Bordan's eyes, to ripple with each step as if it contained a liquid which sloshed against either side. All for this, a holy object which Emperors had worn for thousands of years and which owed as much, he suspected, to magic as to religion. If the legends and stories were true, that was, if the memories really were stored within and it was not just another ceremony, another symbol which helped glue the Empire together.

He led the bearers up the steps and into the church. They passed the mass of nobles, influential civilians, rich merchants, their husbands and wives. The aisle from the door to the altar which looked down upon the fire at the far end was clear. Priests in white, the symbol of the flame upon their chests, walked along the rows swinging censers which gave off a sweet-smelling smoke of sea dew and jasmine. Tendrils drifted towards the high vaulted ceiling.

General Bordan paused in the door for moment, knowing the next step would mark the beginning of the end. His life, almost as much as the Emperor's was over, finished, and incomplete. It must be the same for everyone, he thought, to have lofty ambitions which are kept out of reach by the infinite power of time.

He took the first step, marching in a measured pace towards the sanctuary, its altar, and an ending. Prefect Sarimarcus was a step behind and the bearers carried the dead Emperor into the church.

At the far end, Godewyn stood waiting, dressed in his long robes, golden staff in hand atop which a candle burned. Princess Aelia, in fine robes and with a circlet taming her golden curls, looked down the aisle towards them.

She looked regal, powerful, Bordan thought as he drew closer. The imperial purple spoke of power and command, but only by hiding the truth behind fine embroidery and rich furs. Few would look further, and fewer still would meet the heir's eyes. The girl, the young woman, had lost her family to murder and ill-fortune. All present today and those in the city would share her grief. Yet worry gnawed at Bordan's belly with little teeth and scurrying claws.

"Your Highness," Bordan bowed as he stopped in front of the Princess. "A sad day and one I thought never to experience."

"General Bordan," Aelia replied, "thank you for bringing him back to us."

Bordan saluted and stepped aside, sliding into the seat which had been saved for him. Vedrix, looking uncomfortable in his own robes shifted across slightly to give him room. Sarimarcus directed the bearers to place the Emperor upon the altar. They slid the wooden pallet across the polished metal surface.

The soldiers turned as one and Sarimarcus led them in silence to the rear of the church.

"Today," Godewyn's voice was rich, warm and comforting, reaching all aspects of the church and congregation, "we come together to give the Emperor to the Holy Flame. We should feel grief and sorrow at his passing, but joy that he goes to join the Holy Flame, becoming part of it once more as we all were before the world was formed."

The silence hung in the air as Godewyn paused and scanned the seated audience. Bordan felt uncomfortable on the wooden seat as the moment stretched to breaking point. It was an oppressive quiet, one that forced all present to look around the church, note the icons, stained windows, its height and the heat from the pit just beyond the altar. Flickers of flame rose like the beaks of hungry chicks, snapping and snipping at the air, casting shadows against the wall as they waited, impatiently, for a meal.

"An Emperor," Godewyn resumed, "is the heart of the Empire just as the Holy Flame is its soul. Each needs the other to thrive. We have lost our heart today, but the soul is eternal. It can be reborn into the heart of another and so the Empire endures."

Bordan watched as Aelia stood and stepped up to the altar. Godewyn took the young Princess's hand, covering its shaking with his own firm grip and placed it down upon her father's chest.

"From father to daughter, the Flame will pass, and the Empire will rise once more. Renewed. Reborn. And the memories of the past, the wisdom of ages imbued by the beating heart of each Emperor since the founding will stay with us forever."

Around the body of the Emperor, a yellow light grew to encompass the three at the altar. Bordan sat straighter and next to him Vedrix twitched in his seat as the light brightened into a halo.

"We are the Flame, a part of the whole, ready to be reclaimed," Godewyn intoned in his sonorous voice and the light darkened, turning red like the gemstone in the amulet, pulsing like a heart. "What once we were, we will be again."

A bell tolled in the tower. A single note which rang out across the city, its echoes amplified by the thick stone walls of the church.

"To the Flame we give his body," Godewyn continued as the echoes died and pulled upon the lever embedded in the altar. The metal rose at the end nearest the congregation forming a slope down which the wooden pallet slipped.

Bordan's last sight of the man he had served and followed was of his body falling into the flame. There was a hollow crash, the crackle of wood and fire, and dark smoke began to rise from the pit drawn by the chimney above.

Aelia stood silent and still, looking down into the pit where her father's body burned. No one moved or spoke.

Bordan focused upon the Princess as she slowly turned away from her father and held up the blood red amulet for all to see. It pulsed in time with the General's heart and he swore he could hear the beat, feel it through the church floor.

"The Emperor has joined the Holy Flame," Godewyn called out, his voice rising as the flames behind him surged. "Long live the Emperor."

He took the amulet from Aelia's hands and lowered it over her head. Godewyn stepped back and Bordan had a clear view of the new Emperor.

Aelia's eyes burned with an inner flame and her body shook. Her hands curled into fists and the cords upon her neck stood proud, etched as if on a marble statue. Her lips were pressed tight and Bordan noted the slow trickle of blood which bloomed in one corner of her mouth and dripped down her chin.

From the fire pit there was snap and hiss as once more the flames surged higher, driving dark smoke before them, pushing it higher into the vaults of the church roof.

"Long live the Emperor!" Godewyn shouted above the roar of the flames and the congregation took up the chant. Vedrix, next to him, flashed a concerned look at Bordan even as he called out the chant in time with everyone else.

No words would come. His mind knew what to say, could read the rhythm as well as anyone, but the sounds died in his throat, his tongue was still, and only his eyes moved as he watched the new Emperor raise her clenched fists to the ceiling.

Fear. Vedrix's eyes had radiated fear.

The chant hit a crescendo and died altogether on the next breath. A silence heavier than iron settled about the church.

"My people," Aelia spoke and her voice was deeper, darker, colder than before. Age now altered the pitch, years passing dropped the timbre, slowed the cadence, and took on a masculine tone. "My people, people of the Empire, a new age has dawned with the passing of my father. A new Emperor, Aelia, is crowned and the wisdom of ages past is mine to guide us."

The Emperor paused, coughed, and shook her head.

"A new age," the Emperor continued though now the voice was her own, but the newly gained confidence remained, "of glory and wealth. The Empire will grow beyond its borders. Those tribes who killed my father will pay the price in blood and fire. Those who, through mendacious means and traitorous plans, killed my mother and brother will be brought to such justice as will be spoken of for centuries to come."

Somewhere, at the back of the congregation, there came a cheer. It was awkward, mistimed, and misunderstood. No one followed and if the Emperor noticed she did not react.

"My father's wisdom, and that of Emperors past is mine. Their memories I see as my own, and the truth of all is finally revealed.

Plans within plans, my people, strategy and masterful tactics of misdirection, precision strikes and measured actions are those weapons which stole my family from me."

Bordan shivered despite the heat from the still roaring and surging fire. The High Priest's gaze was focused upon the Emperor's and his expression had frozen halfway between elation and concern. General Bordan flicked a gaze at Vedrix, scared to miss any movement in the tableau before him, and saw the fear once more bloom in the magician's eyes.

"Duke Abra," Aelia shouted and her voice echoed from the walls of the church, "is dead, but he was a stone upon the latrones board. Moved and pushed about to deceive and fool us all. I see it all now. I recognise the hand of our opponent."

Another pause and Aelia pressed a thumb into her temples, massaging some pain there, but the anger in her eyes was plain to see in the dancing flames. Godewyn reached out a hand towards the Emperor, taking half a step closer. Vedrix moved on his seat, beginning to rise and his mouth opening to speak.

"Arrest that man!" Aelia shouted before any could reach him or call out. "Arrest General Bordan!"

LIV

THE MAGICIAN

THREE YEARS AGO:
His whole world was squeezed into a soldier's backpack. His clothes, his favourite scrolls, his father's chariot wrapped in a tunic, and a spare pair of sandals. The room which he had called home for seven of his fourteen years carried his imprint, and that of his father, but was no longer his home.

He sighed, took a last look around, and closed the door.

HE HAD PROTESTED when they woke him in the morning, complained bitterly as they forced him to eat breakfast, and given the clothes they had laid out for him a sour look.

None of it had made the slightest bit of difference to Emlyn or Master Vedrix. The Coronation was to take place today and he was going as an honoured guest, as were many members of the guard who had seen the Emperor's body safely back to the capital.

The streets were busy and their party had taken a carriage from the Gymnasium to the steps of the church, avoiding the indignity of struggling through the crowds. Peering through the windows, Kyron saw the people of the city surging towards the avenue which joined the three branches of the Empire into a whole. It was not lost on him that the Gymnasium was set far away from that place.

From the base of the church steps Emlyn and he had been escorted to their seats near the rear of the building where injured soldiers from the guard sat along one row. Vedrix favoured him with a smile and moved to the front where, Kyron assumed, the council members would be sat.

Already the seats were filling up with the great, the good, and the wealthy. All of them sitting closer to the front and chatting with each other with an easy familiarity which escaped him.

Over the tops of their heads, he saw the High Priest and Princess Aelia enter the church from a side door and walk to the altar. Both moved slow with heads bowed. Neither acknowledged the people sat and after a moment of quiet the hushed whispers picked up once more.

Kyron watched as the High Priest stopped by the altar, a large block of marble with a metal casing upon the top. He seemed to be speaking to Aelia, pointing at the altar which was orientated along the length of the church and indicating with small hand gestures the procedures for its operation.

From the other cremations he had attended, he knew the metal would lift forming a slope down which the body would slip into the fire. In the poorer churches, a priest to either side, or a family member, would lift the top of the altar consigning their loved one to the flame.

It was the smell which he would never forget. Even the sweet smoke of the herbs burned in the lamps did little to mask the acrid scent of cloth and the bitter stench of hair at first, giving way to the sweeter aroma of cooking flesh. It set off reactions he could not reconcile, revulsion and hunger. His mouth flooding with saliva which he was loathed to admit and never spoke of. He shuddered at the memory.

Burial was simpler, nobler, and there was a finality to it, a returning of flesh, energy to the soil. Still unpleasant, still with an ache of loss and stab of grief, but more, he struggled for the right words, suitable, appropriate.

The song of trumpets pierced the conversation and a silence fell inside the church. Every head turned to the doorway through which the glare of sunlight brought tears to eyes used to the dim interior. Priests began to filter down the side of the aisles, burning censers in their hand spilling smoke into the air. One of them looked his way and sneered down her nose at him. Livillia, it seemed, had found her own place amongst the ceremony.

Kyron felt the wisps of smoke tickle his nose. The scent of jasmine and sea dew lightening the air and he breathed it in. It would mask the odour of cremation, but it also brought calm, slowing his pulse and freeing his mind of worry.

He saw the General lead the procession into the church, the pallet upon which the Emperor rested borne to the altar and placed there. No glance or exchange of gesture passed between them as his grandfather took his seat at the front.

The High Priest spoke, his voice carrying to Kyron's ears without trouble. He heard the words, but felt the sentiment, the dull twist of loss combined with the sacred joy of rejoining the Flame in eternal life.

Another breath of jasmine tickled his nose and he shook his head to clear his thoughts. He looked around, everyone's attention was focused upon the High Priest and his words.

"Is it always like this?" The whisper from Emlyn at his side was pitched for him only.

"What?"

"Your church services and funerals?" she asked. "Why is everyone so quiet?"

"It is a funeral, and for the Emperor. You think they should be jovial?"

"No," Emlyn whispered, "but this doesn't feel right."

Kyron felt the shift, the sudden sense of worry blossom in his heart, however there was nothing he could say for certain. "It is just different to your ways."

The Emperor's body slipped into the fire pit, the flames surged, and Kyron could just make out the Amulet of Emperors being lowered over Aelia's head.

"Long live the Emperor," the High Priest called out and the crowd took up the chant.

At his side, Emlyn was quiet, and Kyron noticed her hands were playing with the ever-present sticks she had carved on the journey. He should be chanting too. He knew he should, but the words would not come.

The new Emperor began to speak and the crowd quieted. Kyron stretched in his seat, trying to see better as the Emperor continued in a darker tone.

"Do you think she really possesses all of her father's memories?" Emlyn said, also straining her neck to see over the top of the crowd.

"I don't know," Kyron admitted.

"Duke Abra," Aelia shouted from the front of the church and if anything, the silence deepened further so every word was as clear as a trumpet's note, "is dead, but he was a stone upon the latrones board. Moved and pushed about to deceive and fool us all. I see it all now. I recognise the hand of our opponent."

Kyron strained his neck further. Abra had tried to steal the Emperor's body and it was his actions that had caused the death of Astentius.

"Arrest that man!" Aelia shouted. "Arrest General Bordan!"

The commotion was instant. Kyron shot from his seat and all those in front and around did the same. A rattle of armour and swords in the church, a sound the magician had come to associate with battle, and confusion reigned.

"Arrest him!" the Emperor screamed once more.

Kyron looked behind him and then to the aisle. There were soldiers stationed there to protect the ceremony and the people, but they had not moved. Each one glanced at their closest companion and Kyron saw the consternation on their faces. It would not be, he knew, an easy matter to arrest their General.

His grandfather was a stubborn man, a difficult man to live with, opinionated, confident and so sure of himself that few could encourage him to change his mind. He was not, Kyron knew, a murderer and certainly not of an Emperor and his family. It went against everything he knew of the man. Service and duty were not just words to him, they were a code to live by, as dear to him as anything could be, as much a part of him as his heart.

This was not right.

Kyron looked to the end of the row and began to shuffle in that direction. The soldiers of the honour guard who occupied the seats there looked up at him as he moved. Their whispers were full of concern and disbelief.

"Not a chance," one said.

"No way," said another.

"He could have done it," a third uttered, and Kyron made sure he stood hard on that man's feet as he passed.

"Kyron," Emlyn called and he heard the scrabble behind him as the soldiers tried to get out of the way.

He did not stop, and broke free of the pews, turning towards the front of the church. However, he was far from alone. Others in the congregation had stood and were beginning to crowd the aisle. The volume inside the church rose as everyone began speaking at once.

Kyron forced his way through the rich and wealthy, his elbows digging into the backs and stomachs of those too slow to move.

"Now see here, boy," a fat man with drooping jowls grabbed him by the wrist. "Don't go pushing through your betters."

Kyron drew on the motes and found they would not heed his call. They were there, he could feel them but they were distant and obscured by a faint mist in his mind. Instead, he wrenched his arm free and pushed forward once more.

"Kyron," Emlyn called again, "what are you doing?"

There was confusion in the church. The crowded aisle was becoming impassable, and the thought of summoning more magic to clear the path sped across his mind. It was brought to a stop by the understanding that such an act, even if the motes would obey him, would likely condemn him to a slow death upon a cross.

An arm grabbed his shoulder and he turned ready to defend himself.

"Come with me, lad," Borus said, tugging him back into the crowd and down the aisle.

"Let me go," Kyron called, his voice lost amongst the escalating shouts from the crowd.

Ahead, in the wrong direction, he saw soldiers begin to clear the aisle, pushing the wealthy back into their seats. The military were taking control, he thought, they won't let Grandfather be arrested. A moment later the thought of rebellion and civil war doused his enthusiasm. Service and duty.

"Borus," Kyron called, "we have to save him."

"Who?" Emlyn said appearing at his elbow.

"The General," Kyron answered.

"There's nothing you can do," Borus said, waving the soldiers out of his way as the trio made it to the back of the church.

"They'll arrest him," Kyron complained struggling to get free of Borus's iron grip.

"Unless he orders them not to," Borus said. "Look."

They turned, following Borus's pointed finger. The church had fallen silent once more and Kyron could see a ring of soldiers surrounding his grandfather. Swords were drawn, yet none were pointed at the General. Each sharp tip was aimed at the floor and between the High Priest, the Emperor and his grandfather the air seemed to crackle. No one moved and no one spoke.

Kyron took a breath, trying once more to draw upon the motes in the air around him, to ready himself to do something, but still they would not come. At the far end of the church, the flames rose higher and he saw within them the swirl and play of power. It would be so easy, they seemed to say.

"Arrest him!" the Emperor shouted, her voice high and nasal. "I am your Emperor and you will obey me."

Kyron's hand rose trying to draw on the magic once again. Instead it was the flames which answered, swelling in the funeral pit and he could feel himself getting warmer.

"It would be so easy," he whispered.

"Kyron," Emlyn's hand gripped his wrist and pulled him around. The draw of the flames dissipated at her touch. "What is happening?"

"He won't start a war," Kyron said.

"I would," Borus said. "The punishment for treason is unpleasant to say the least."

"He won't," Kyron reaffirmed.

Near the altar, the Emperor raised her hand much as Kyron had done, a gesture of power, of command, and called out. "You will arrest that man. I command it."

Kyron's eyes were drawn to his grandfather who turned in his direction for just one moment before nodding.

"Do as you are commanded by your Emperor," the General's strong voice rang out through the church clear and unwavering.

There was a pause and mass of indrawn breaths as the soldiers turned to their General, saluted, and put their hands upon him. Without waiting for another command, they turned the General and marched him down the aisle.

Kyron, stood to the side, tried to catch the old man's eyes but he marched head down staring only at the floor. As they passed through the open door to the church the noise within grew once more.

"How did you know?" Borus asked.

"He is my grandfather," Kyron answered without turning, and felt a tear fall from his eye to the stone floor below.

"Ah, Kyron, Emlyn, and Borus, isn't it," Vedrix said as he stomped up. "Get the boy to the Gymnasium and make sure he doesn't leave."

"I want to help," Kyron said, adding, as an afterthought, "Master."

"You will do as you are told," Vedrix snapped. "I felt what you tried to do, and I know how you feel, but you can't help him right now. Certainly not that way. If he is to live through the next few days, and you are too, it is best if you let me do what I can."

"Master..." Kyron began and was cut off with a wave of the older man's hand.

"Get him out of here," Vedrix ordered, all pretence of the bumbling magician gone. "Talk to no one and stay in the Gymnasium. I'll join you there as soon as I have found out where he has been taken and what is going on."

"Come on, Kyron," Emlyn said.

"Do as the man says," Borus added, waving to two soldiers. "Escort these two to the Gymnasium. Don't delay and don't let them wander. Guard the gates and make sure they don't leave until Master Vedrix gives permission."

LV

The General

THREE YEARS AGO:

They stood outside the double doors of the Gymnasium, looking up at a building which, anywhere else in the city, would have drawn the eye, but here, cramped amongst the homes and businesses just looked out of place.

"Are you sure about this?" he asked, looking across at the boy who was now almost his equal in height. "You can still join the army. We can find a way."

"I think this is the right place for me," the boy said. "We both know I would not make a good soldier."

"No one is born a good soldier, they are made by the army," he answered.

At LEAST THEY had left him an oil lamp, he thought as he completed his latest circuit of the cell. There was little room to walk, but even so his legs ached, and his feet were sore. He turned his back and slumped against the cold, damp wall. There was enough light to see by and what he saw did little to lift his spirits.

No furniture, just a pile of damp straw to sleep upon. Walls of heavy stone blocks sealed with crumbling mortar down which rivulets of water constantly ran. Moss and lichen grew between the blocks and, in the corner near the thick wooden door, it had begun to spread from the relative safety of the wall. The oil lamp had been placed upon the floor in the other corner and it was a small mercy, likely the only one they could give.

In the prison, below the palace, he knew his rank meant little. Former rank, he corrected. However, a soldier's respect was hard won and harder lost. Time in the ranks bred a loyalty which became an integral part of a soldier's being.

He had felt it during that long, impossible moment at the coronation. It had beat in his heart, lifted his head and straightened his shoulders. The look in the eyes of each soldier, the way they stood, ready to follow his command had been, he reflected, one of the proudest moments of his life.

On his word, in that moment, the fate of the Empire balanced.

In his cell there was no way to mark time, no way to measure its passage. For a soldier raised in a routine, it was strange to have the freedom of time, though there was nothing to do but think.

The claw and itch of his own thoughts could not be ignored and in the silence, the empty time of the cell they scratched at his guilt, conjuring up images of missed chances, fleeting opportunities in which the right word might have turned this path onto a happier road.

Footsteps broke the solitude and a key turned in a door, his door. General Bordan struggled to his feet, pride pushing him upright.

"You may leave," the figure outlined in the doorway said.

"Yes, Your Holiness," the guard said.

"Godewyn?" Bordan said, surprised.

"I've seen you look better," High Priest Godewyn said as he stepped into the cell. "I trust I can leave the door open?"

"I am not going to run," Bordan said, half a smile dying on his face. "I'm old, my friend, and my running days are far behind me. How fares the city?"

"Mostly in confusion at the moment," Godewyn answered as he drew a pack from his shoulder and began slipping the buckles open. "The militia is out on the streets, keeping the calm, but the celebrations are, perhaps the best word is, muted."

"The army?"

"In their barracks," Godewyn said, lifting a thick blanket from the pack and spreading it on the floor. "I'll leave you the blanket when I go. I don't expect the guards will risk offering you such comfort, but none will argue with me."

"Thank you," Bordan said, as they both sat on the blanket, the action drawing a grunt of effort from his lips.

"Here," Godewyn said, lifting a skin of wine from the pack and passing it over. "Might help you sleep tonight."

"What time is it?"

"A little past dusk and evening is settling on the sky," the High Priest said, unwrapping a wedge of cheese, some bread, and meat. "The guards checked the bag as I came in so there is no escape equipment."

"Just a last meal?" Bordan said, taking a pull on the wine.

"Something like that," Godewyn acknowledged. "There seems little point in lying."

"This is insane," Bordan said, leaning back and resting his head against the stone. "Aelia is not in her right mind. Like you, I see little point in lying."

"She is stressed and on edge," Godewyn replied.

"It is more than that," Bordan said. "She is hurt and striking out without thought."

"With a little more time, I am sure she will come to terms with her losses and her mood will improve," Godewyn pointed out.

Bordan grunted. "You said you saw little point in lying, Godewyn, and as one soldier to another, don't treat me like an idiot. I deserve better. We both know I don't have that time."

"I am sorry, my friend," the High Priest said after a moment and the mask of rank fell away. "No one could have foreseen this."

"I didn't kill her family."

"I know. I've known you for a long time, Bordan. The thought never crossed my mind."

"But the Emperor does not see it that way?"

Godewyn took a drink from the wine. "She does not. I have tried to talk to her, however she is convinced and nothing I say will dissuade her. She claims your constant arguments for a delay were to give Abra time to gather his mercenaries, that you did not want to cross the bridge, that you killed Abra to keep him quiet. Aelia believes that you wanted to be Emperor. With the army behind you, it is not difficult to see that you could accomplish that."

"I wouldn't. I've never sought power and been content to serve," Bordan complained, accepting the wine skin. "The joining with the amulet pushed her over the edge. All those souls, all those memories have her seeing shadows where there are only candles."

"I've read the histories a little," Godewyn replied, chewing on some fresh bread. "A few mention the process and talk of its effects. Usually, however, it sinks the new Emperor into a depression for a few weeks. They seek solitude and see few except to give orders. I would imagine the task of reconciling the memories of previous Emperors, including your own father, would be a great challenge."

"Are you saying we should have waited to crown her? You know what that would do to the Empire. It needs continuity, not chaos," Bordan answered. For a time there was silence between them. "I was going to retire, you know. I've a small estate. Out of the way and unknown, I'd have seen my remaining years out growing grapes and making wine."

"You'll never be the General again, but perhaps I can convince her to let you retire quietly to your estates."

"Where, no doubt, she will believe I will be plotting against her. Raising an army to bring her down," Bordan replied, his voice dulled by the stone walls.

"I will keep trying," Godewyn said.

"And how long have I got?"

"A day," the High Priest answered, "maybe two."

"This isn't how I wanted to end my service."

"It was the conversation with Abra," Godewyn said with deep sigh. "All the Emperor talked about on the journey back, and when I spoke to her earlier, is that conversation. Aelia is convinced that the traitor told you something, passed along a message. That or you killed him to silence him, so he would not reveal your part in the plot."

"She wanted to give Abra a slow, painful death," Bordan answered. "She thinks I stole that chance from her."

"Possibly. She would have benefited from seeing it herself. An ending of sorts," Godewyn admitted. "What did Abra say to you? Perhaps if I can convince Aelia of your honesty and Abra's words, she will let you retire to your estate."

"He didn't say anything, my friend. He died with my sword in his groin. You stood the ranks, you fought in battles large and small. How often did you have a dying confession from a soldier stuck with a sword?" Bordan passed the wineskin back.

"When you put it like that…" Godewyn accepted the wine and offered a small smile.

"It is all soldiers' talk, Godewyn. I stabbed him, he died," Bordan said, and raked his hand through his greasy hair. "In front of all those people, those nobles, the power and wealth, the Emperor accused me of treason. She cannot back down. The loss of face, the embarrassment would undermine her rule from the beginning. An Emperor can never be wrong. It is our Empire's unwritten rule. If another had made the accusation, there would be a chance. Not now."

"You are ready to give up so easily?" Godewyn's eyebrows rose. "That is not the General I know, nor the man."

"What would you have me do? Stage a rebellion?"

"No." Godewyn's voice was low and the sadness it contained slowed its journey across the space separating them. "I saw what you did in the Church."

"For a moment," Bordan began, "I considered it. I am a soldier. I've always been a soldier and it is not in our nature to give up a fight when there is a chance to win, a chance to survive."

"Then why didn't you?" Godewyn leaned forward and picked up a piece of cheese, looking up and catching Bordan's eyes. "I saw the look on their faces. I felt their desire and the way their loyalties were torn. One word and they would have followed you. It would be Aelia here and you resting in comfort in the palace."

"Until the inevitable civil war broke out," Bordan answered. "All those needless deaths just so I could have a few more years of life."

"Your life is so easy to give up?"

"Of course not," Bordan spat, a sudden rage sweeping through his body leaving him shaking. "My whole life, Godewyn. Every action, every thought, every decision has been out of duty and service to the Empire. I've given my life and the lives of thousands of soldiers to its defence, its protection, its survival."

"And you'll be remembered as a traitor," Godewyn said, holding up a hand to forestall the anger driven response. "It is not fair, my friend, and not warranted. I know few have given as much as you to the Empire."

"And Aelia, even with her father's memories, puts that to the side," Bordan snapped, smashing his clenched fist onto the stone floor at his side.

"Let me take Abra's words to her, Bordan," Godewyn pleaded. "Let me try. Give me something I can use as a weapon against her distrust. Something I can turn her from this course of action with."

"Godewyn, he didn't say anything. My name was his last breath."

"I'll tell her that," Godewyn continued. "I'll try to convince her of the truth. The stories do not help, they say he confessed all his sins. That he cursed the Emperor to the frozen wastes. That he thanked you for saving him from a slow death on the cross."

"The girl has read too many myths and legends, too many stories of heroes of the ancients. She grew up with a scroll, not a sword in her hand. It is all she knows, Godewyn. Aelia believes in dying confessions, of noble deaths, and sacrifice. She thinks I silenced the man," Bordan answered, his anger ebbing and leaving him hollow.

"I will continue to do what I can," Godewyn said, reaching across and putting a reassuring hand on Bordan's arm.

Bordan sighed. "For what they are worth, my thanks."

"You have been my friend for many years," Godewyn's hand retreated.

"Godewyn..." Bordan started, as the thoughts he had been battling came back to the fore, "do you think it started and ended with Abra?"

"Now you are starting to sound like Aelia."

Bordan nodded. "I know."

"There have been no more attempts on her life," Godewyn mused.

"Because I am locked up?" Bordan grunted. "I've spent the journey back wondering who Abra might be working with, if anyone."

"And?" Godewyn prompted.

"I don't know, Godewyn," Bordan said. "I've considered everyone close to the Emperor."

"Me?" Godewyn's tone was strangled.

"You. Vedrix. Me. Other officers. Palace staff. Other nobles."

"And? You've a fine mind, Bordan. If not you, if not Abra, then who?"

"Aelia," Bordan replied after a silent moment.

"The Emperor herself?" Godewyn rocked back and his startled voice filled the cell.

"Power is enticing. Aelia was the second child, destined for a political marriage, some land elsewhere, out of the way. Forgotten. She is no soldier, and the army would be ill-served by her leadership," Bordan mused. "A priest, maybe, but unlikely. Her appetites and her life would never have prepared her for that life. She saw a chance, after her father's death, to take the throne for herself and acted upon it."

"Bordan," Godewyn gasped. "That is treason to speak of."

"I cannot be more condemned than I am, and this is only supposition and only if Abra was working with someone else," Bordan said with a shake of his head. "And of that, I am not convinced."

"I cannot stay and listen to this," Godewyn said, standing and looking down at the disgraced General. "Do you truly believe what you are saying?"

"There are many questions unanswered, my friend, and I am sure of nothing. All I have is time to think and let every scenario play out in the darkness."

"And what if it was you, as Aelia believes?"

"Then I would have taken the throne already with the might of the army behind me and be resting in the palace even now," Bordan pointed out, reflecting Godewyn's own words. "It would have been an easy order to give in the Church. However..." He left the word hanging between them.

"You did not," Godewyn answered at last. "I will talk to the Emperor. There may be a chance, my friend."

"I wish it were so, but it is not," Bordan replied, looking away. "I thank you for the blanket, the food, and the wine. More, I thank you for the friendship, Godewyn."

"It has been my pleasure, Bordan, and honour."

"A last piece of advice, my friend."

"Go on."

"Do not get dragged down with me," Bordan said, lifting the wine in a salute and drinking deeply from it.

LVI

The Magician

Three years ago:

They were shown into Vedrix's study. The Master Magician stood from his chair, ignoring the ink he spilt with his sleeve and hurried over to them.

"Excellent," the magician said. "Welcome, young man, to the Gymnasium of Magicians. We will teach you all you need to know, and you can find your place in the Empire here."

"I just want the dreams and headaches to stop," he said.

"And they will," Master Vedrix said. "They will."

He caught the disappointment which flitted through the old man's eyes as he looked to the man who had raised him for the last seven years.

"I want to see him." Kyron paced the outer room of Padarn's quarters. The sleeping chamber was untouched, and some servants had placed a cot in the room for Emlyn to sleep on.

"They will not let you in," Master Vedrix said.

The Master of the Gymnasium had taken the comfortable chair Padarn had always sat in to read one of the histories of the Empire or a treatise on magical theory. It was strange to see someone else there and Kyron's thoughts strayed to his late master, the late nights and lessons delivered in this room.

"He will be allowed visitors," Kyron complained.

"He is accused of being a traitor, of plotting the deaths of the imperial family. No one will be allowed in to see him," Vedrix corrected. "I am sorry, my boy, but there is little we can do. You especially. Do not think your actions in the church went unnoticed."

"What?" Kyron blurted, feeling a twist in his stomach as the memory of the motes gathering about him resurfaced.

"You're stronger," Vedrix said, raising a finger to illustrate his point, "but you've little more control. If anyone else had felt the magic drawn in the church, young Kyron, there would be a crowd at the gates, whipped up by the zealots of the Church, trying to break it down or burn us to the ground."

"I didn't," was all Kyron could manage, and the distant motes and clamouring flame made him shiver.

"And you must never," Vedrix said. "The Emperor is all that stands between us and the Church."

"The High Priest wouldn't," Kyron said, confidence in his voice. His grandfather had spoken of Godewyn as an honourable man and he had been to the house for dinner enough times when Kyron was growing up for him to believe his grandfather's assessment.

"He may have no choice," Emlyn said from her seat on her cot. She cupped a hot tea and the scent of jasmine and bergamot wafted about the room.

"That's true," Vedrix nodded. "The High Priest may be a good man, but the Church has spent many centuries speaking out against the evil of magic and its affront to the Holy Flame. If he is pushed, he will bow to the pressure of his priests and the people."

"He's my grandfather," Kyron argued. "I want to see him, to talk to him. There is no chance that he is involved in a plot against the Emperor."

"We all know that," Vedrix said. "However, he would want to keep you away from it all. Both Godewyn and I know of your relationship, but the Emperor does not."

"What's that got to do with anything?"

"He is saying you are guilty by association, by family," Emlyn said, plucking a stick from her belt and inspecting it. "They are worried that the Emperor will blame you too. After all, you were there when the first Emperor died."

"I wasn't anywhere near him," Kyron snapped. "That's just stupid."

"You struck him down with magic," Emlyn said, digging the point of her knife into the stick and flicking a tiny shaving of wood free.

"I didn't."

"But that is what they will say. You were a part of your grandfather's plot. A General who is known for clever strategy and tactics, who plans every move to secure a victory. You were just one of those moves, the first maybe or perhaps one in a long chain of plans within plans. Is that not so, Master Vedrix?"

"I'm not sure it will be quite so eloquently put, but that about sums it up," Vedrix nodded. "We cannot, you cannot risk being caught up in this. For now, we have to stay out the way and stay silent. He would want you to be safe above all."

"What if the Emperor is right, that someone else was involved?" Kyron said, clutching at straws as the thoughts passed him by with the force of a hurricane driving them.

"What do you propose, Apprentice?" Vedrix said, shuffling forward on his seat. "Conducting some type of investigation, discovering the truth and setting your grandfather free?"

"Well..." Kyron tailed off.

"The hardest truth is the realisation that sometimes there is nothing you can do," Vedrix said. "I cannot intervene with the Emperor. She barely trusts me as it is. All I can do is look harmless and trustworthy to the last. It is the best defence for the Gymnasium and all the magicians who call it home."

"The High Priest?" Kyron swiped at another straw.

"I've already spoken to him," Vedrix said. "It is the one chance, however slim. He is going to see your grandfather."

"You said no one would get in to see him."

"No one will stop the High Priest of the Flame," Vedrix said, a sad smile on his face. "It may come to nothing, but they have been friends since before you were born."

"Then what can we do?"

Vedrix lifted himself from the chair and moved to the door. "Stay here and stay out of trouble. We are doing all we can, little as it is."

After Vedrix departed there was quiet in the room. Kyron's mind whirled and dived like a flock of sparrows while Emlyn sat on her cot, knife moving in slow, methodical strokes against a new stick.

"So," Emlyn said breaking the silence, "when are you going?"

"What? Where?"

"To see your grandfather," she replied.

"You heard Master Vedrix." He glanced at her and looked towards the door. "He told me not to go. Anyway, they won't let me in."

"You are a magician?"

"What is that supposed to mean?"

"I thought it meant you might have a way not to be noticed," she answered, her carving continuing unabated. "Perhaps I was wrong."

"It is getting dark," Kyron said.

"Night will do that," Emlyn agreed.

"I might go for a walk," he said, "just for some fresh air."

"If you do, be careful," Emlyn said. "I'll go and see about some food for when you get back."

"Thank you," he said, moving over to the desk and the sheathed gladius resting upon it.

"I don't think you'll need that," she said, "but take a cloak in case it gets chilly."

Kyron nodded, leaving the gladius where it was and sweeping the cloak she offered around his shoulders. "I won't be long."

"Of course not," she said.

He turned left outside the gates of the Gymnasium, picking out the palace on the skyline and hurried in that direction. The streets were still busy with revellers, drinking and dancing in celebration of the coronation of the Emperor. As he moved through the crowds, he heard talk of his grandfather. Some were disbelieving while others saw a conspiracy where he saw none. It was a struggle, but he ignored their words and soon the walls of the palace came into sight.

There was a constant flow of people through the gates and he joined a group who passed under the guard's watchful gaze without trouble. Detaching himself, he gazed around. The open ground here had been set aside for the celebrations and there were more vigilant guards on the stairs and at each doorway. The palace dungeon was down and his urgent reading of one of Padarn's histories had given him a basic understanding of the palace's layout.

Kyron took a breath and squared his shoulders. He slipped the bound and sealed scroll from his pack and tapped it on his hand as he walked towards the guards.

"Stop," the first one said.

"My name is Apprentice Kyron," he said. "I have a message for Master Vedrix."

The second guard glanced down at the scroll. "I am not sure he is here."

"I was told by the Gymnasium that he came earlier," Kyron said. "I don't want to have to walk all over the city trying to find him."

"Don't you magicians have ways?" the first guard said, wiggling his fingers in what he must have thought was an arcane manner.

"I wish," Kyron answered with a sigh. "Can I just go to his office and leave it on his desk?"

"Well…" the first guard said with a shrug.

"I want to get back to the celebrations," Kyron added.

"And we're stuck here until the watch changes," the second guard replied.

"That's too bad," Kyron said. "I'll have a drink or two for you, if that helps."

Both guards chuckled and the second one said, "It won't, but I don't see why you should be missing out. You've got identification?"

Kyron fished his Gymnasium amulet from out under his clothes and held it up for them to see.

"Off you go then," the first guard said, stepping aside. "If Master Vedrix is there, hope he doesn't give you another job to do."

"An apprentice's work is never done," Kyron said. "At least, that's what they tell me. Usually it is doing all the things they think they're too good to do."

"Same with officers, lad," the first guard said. "Now, get along with you."

"Thank you both," Kyron said as he hurried through the door and down the empty corridor. He heard the door close behind him and only turned to check once he was at the far end.

Vedrix's office and the whole administrative section was to the right, so Kyron turned left. He kept the scroll in his hand, his one disguise and excuse for being here. However, encountering the first servant proved that he did not need it. Once past the door, it seemed, you belonged.

Stopping at another junction, he called up his mental map of the palace, placing the door to the dungeon upon it and planning his route. Now he walked with purpose, head held high, though the hood of his cloak was up to create shadows across his face and, he hoped, a bit of mystery. Magicians should always have an air of the other, Padarn had told him. Confidence and a competent demeanour was worth more than a sword at your hip, he had been fond of saying.

There were more guards and as he stepped back around the corner, he cursed himself for a fool. One stood next to the door and there would doubtless be others down the stairs and in the dungeon itself. Not many, he hoped, and they would all want to be celebrating with the rest of the populace.

Well, he reassured himself, at least he'd come prepared.

Kyron drew upon the motes and built the construct with calm urgency. Invisibility was a difficult construct, one only attempted by a master who had spent decades in study, so the tomes said. However, making someone not see or hear was much simpler, at least for a short time.

He closed his eyes and lifted the construct over the glowing form of the guard, settling it around the man's head. With a twist of his fingers he set the knots on the magic and stepped around the corner.

The guard stared straight ahead, his eyes unblinking and his chest rising and falling in a regular rhythm. It would not last long, a few heartbeats at best, so Kyron ducked around the man and slipped through the door. As it clicked shut behind him, he felt the construct come apart.

Getting out would be a worry for later, he decided.

The stairs were narrow and the air cool as he descended. His soft boots made barely a whisper on the stones and he listened out for the sounds of guards below. As the stairs spiralled deeper the air began to cool and there was a damp smell upon the air. The lanterns which lit the way were burning low and casting shadows upon the walls as he passed.

A change in the air, the way it brushed across his cheek or the smell, told him he was close to the bottom, and he drew magic to him.

Reaching out with his new sense of life, of the motes which made up everyone and everything, he felt for the presence of a guard.

There was another, sat in a chair before the last door to the dungeon. Beyond the door, as far as he could reach, there was only the hint of others.

Building the construct in his mind, he went over it again and again, making sure it would do as he required. Simply having the guard ignore him and any sounds for a few moments would not be enough. Beyond that door Kyron needed time to find and talk to his grandfather.

He took another breath, firming his course of action. The guard was just doing his job and, more than that, he was a soldier. Grandfather would never forgive him if he hurt a soldier unnecessarily.

The construct net of motes wrapped itself around the guard's neck and Kyron felt rather than saw the man lift a hand to scratch at the feather light tough. Focusing his senses, Kyron felt for the flow of life in the guard's neck, the major arteries which carried blood to his brain and closed them off.

On his chair the guard's legs stiffened and his hands clawed at his neck for a moment. Kyron gritted his teeth and held his own breath, focused upon that pulse of life in the man's neck. Constrict the flow for too long and the soldier would die, too short and he would wake up too soon.

The pulse fluttered, the heartbeat stuttered, and Kyron let the magic go. He ducked around the corner, wiping the sweat from his face which even the cool air of underground had been unable to prevent.

Slumped in his chair, the guard looked pale, but his chest rose and fell. Kyron approached with caution, stepping lightly and keeping his distance, ready to run the moment the guard shifted. When the man did not move, Kyron pressed two fingers to the soldier's neck and felt for the pulse. It was steady and his flesh was still warm. He would live but wake with a headache worse than a hangover courtesy of three days' heavy drinking.

Kyron slid the key from the guard's belt and unlocked the door. Beyond were the cell doors and only the light from the guard post's lamp illuminated the floor. Prisoners were denied even the comfort of light.

Closing the door behind him, Kyron shut his own eyes and let the motes of magic create an image for him. There were no hard lines, no greys of stone, but a rainbow of hues which flowed, mixed and swirled. Each picked out something different, something unique, but despite the confusion it made sense.

Reaching out, he found the prisoners in their cells. Most were sleeping, though one or two had shifted at the closing of the door. Kyron crept down the corridor, looking for the signature of his grandfather, certain he would recognise it above all others. If he did not, his plan would change and the risk of discovery would increase.

In the end it was not the man's signature, but the presence of an oil lamp in the cell which gave it away. Using the guard's key, Kyron unlocked his grandfather's cell and stepped in.

"What time is it?" His grandfather's voice was tired and flat.

"Grandfather," Kyron said, letting the motes slip from his grasp and in the meagre light of the oil lamp he saw the rumpled form of the old man shift on the bed of straw.

"Kyron?" The man's voice was suddenly sharp, and he sat up swiftly.

"I can get you out of here," Kyron said, stepping in and kneeling before his grandfather.

"Damn it," his grandfather cursed. "I told them to keep you away."

"Master Vedrix warned me off," Kyron admitted, "but you are my grandfather. I can get you out of here."

"To what end, Kyron?" The words were accompanied by a deep sigh.

"To get you to safety."

"And start a civil war?" His grandfather reached out and took his hand in his own. "You shouldn't have come."

"I couldn't leave you here," Kyron said, finding his throat full of sadness and the words hard to find. "You didn't do what the Emperor said."

"How do you know I did not?" his grandfather asked.

"Because I know you," Kyron answered with hesitation.

"I did not do it, but that doesn't matter anymore," his grandfather said. "You have to get away and stay safe."

"Someone else did? If I can find them and evidence, I can present it to the Emperor and she will free you," Kyron said, swallowing a sob. "You must suspect someone?"

"What and who I suspect is no matter, Kyron," his grandfather said.

"Tell me," Kyron demanded.

"No," his grandfather replied. "It will do no good. I'll keep my thoughts and suspicions to myself. They'll only serve the Empire ill."

A sudden image of the old man scribbling in that leather-bound journal he kept with him. A record of this thoughts, perhaps.

"I can help," Kyron pleaded.

"You must go. Leave the city, if you can. The coming days and years will be tough, and I would know you are safe."

"What will happen to you?" Kyron asked, a tear welling in the corner of his eye and tracking down his cheek.

"Best not to think on that," the old man said. "You've done well, boy. I never got to tell you that enough. Your father would be proud of what you've become, of who you are. Your mother too. Now, go, get out. Get out of the city and don't look back."

"I want..." he started to say and changed his mind, saying the words he knew his last relation needed to hear, "I will, Grandfather."

Kyron shuffled forward and threw his arms around the man who had raised him since the death of his parents. He felt arms wrap around him and squeeze. There were no words to say because language fell far short at moments like these. He could feel the old man's love, his pride and respect, and only hoped his grandfather felt the same from him.

After a timeless while, they relaxed their arms and Kyron stood up.

"I will see you soon enough," Kyron said, recalling the grove. "I know who we are, where we come from, and where we return to."

"Be safe, boy. I do love you," General Bordan, Grandfather, said and turned away to bury himself into his straw bed.

LVII

THE GENERAL

THREE YEARS AGO:

"You'll be fine, lad," he said, resting a callused hand on the boy's shoulder. "I think you are right, this is the place for you."

"I will visit," the boy said, looking to the magician for permission. The fat man nodded and smiled.

"We are the Gymnasium, not a prison," the magician said.

"I will make you proud," the boy said.

"I know you will," he replied. "You always have."

BORDAN AWOKE SORE and stiff. The blanket and mattress of straw had kept the worst of the chill from his bones, but age had stripped much of his natural defences. The days of laying out under the stars, only a low fire and hard earth for comfort, were long gone.

He sighed and rolled over, clambering to his feet, using his hands against the cold stone wall for balance. They came away damp and slick and he wiped them down his tunic.

In the corner, the little oil lamp still flickered. It was a small mercy and a reminder of the sun, of the world outside. At the thought of the morning sun his belly grumbled. Last night's wine was gone. Godewyn's gift was tucked beneath the straw and he swept some aside to drag out the last of the bread.

Biting down on the hard crust, he drew as much saliva to his mouth as he could. On each swallow it was harder and harder to moisten the bread sufficiently. In the end, it was impossible to eat any more, the bread turning to dust in his mouth.

Bordan paced his cell, back and forth, stretching his back and groaning in pain. It was good to move and feel the cool air of the cell brush against his face in an imitation of a breeze.

"Stupid boy," he muttered and slapped the wall with his palm, the sting giving him something to hold onto. "If he got in, he got out."

He stopped at the wall, leaning against it.

"What if he didn't?"

He resumed his walking, the pace increasing as thoughts and conjectures tumbled about his brain.

"You'd know, Bordan," he said to himself. "There would have been an outcry. Even down here you'd have heard it. Surely."

"Not if it was far up in the palace," he answered his own question on the next circuit. "What can you do about it?"

He slowed as he reached the wall once more, his breath heaving and his heart pounding in anger rather than exertion. "Nothing. That's exactly what I can do about it. Nothing."

The sound of footsteps came from the corridor outside and he turned towards the door as it opened.

"Is it time?" he asked, his voice hoarse.

"I hope not," Master Vedrix said as he stepped into the cell and turned to the guard. "Thank you, soldier. I promise not to take too long."

"What are you doing here?" Bordan stepped forward.

"I came to see you, my friend," Vedrix answered, his gaze sweeping the room. "Though I had never thought to pay you a visit here."

"Which makes two of us," Bordan said, crossing to the cell and sliding down the wall to sit on his bed of straw, gathering the blanket to him. "I'd offer you a seat, but they have yet to deliver all the furniture I requested."

"You seem in fine mood this morning," Vedrix said.

"I'm not," Bordan grunted. "I'm angry and powerless."

"To be expected," Vedrix answered, swinging his satchel around and producing a wrapped parcel of food and a water skin. "The young guard has a cousin at the Gymnasium."

"Thank you," Bordan said, "and thank him for me."

"I am sure he would have let me through with the food no matter," Vedrix said, tossing the food onto the straw next to Bordan. "They would still fight for you, you know."

"You don't want a civil war," Bordan said, pulling the stopper from the water skin and drinking. The cool and fresh water coated his tongue and a sense of hope washed through him, clearing the cobwebs of depression away. As soon as the thought occurred the little spiders returned, stringing their silken strands from one worry to another, drawing them together into a dark ball which settled in his guts once more.

"You are so sure?" Vedrix said, his voice a whisper.

"You?" Bordan's head snapped up, and his voice echoed around the cell.

"Me?" Vedrix answered, waving his hand to dispel the question. "You think I have not considered it? I spend my life protecting the Gymnasium, General. A seat of learning and knowledge. We contribute to the defence of the Empire. We bring fresh water to the city through our inventions. We have developed medicines, healing draughts and potions which have saved lives. The amulet which brings stability to the succession was created by magicians so long ago that we've lost the method." The Master Magician heaved a sigh. "And our reward? To be feared and hated. To be cast as the great evil in the Empire. The Church speaks against us from their pulpits at every sermon."

"Godewyn understands your place here, your worth," Bordan said, "and the last Emperor did too."

"And the new one?"

"I... don't know," Bordan confessed. "There are so many things about her which I do not know. Civil war, Vedrix, would you truly wish that on the Empire?"

"All I said was I had considered it, just as you did in the church. I saw it on your face. All those soldiers, armed, skilled, and ready to follow your orders. It would have been one word, Bordan. One word and you could have changed the path of the Empire," the magician said.

"For the better?" Bordan scoffed. "A civil war serves no one."

"Something with the Emperor is not right," Vedrix offered. "You see that as much as I, as much as Godewyn, as anyone who spends but a few hours in her company."

"When Aelia comes to terms with the memories in the amulet, she will calm and be reasoned in her rule," Bordan said and cursed himself for the excuses he made.

"You protect the Empire even now," Vedrix's eyebrows rose. "Look at you, my friend, imprisoned and facing a traitor's death."

"The order has been given?" Bordan looked up into his friend's eyes and sighed.

"You were not informed? The proclamation was made this afternoon," Vedrix said, with a shake of his head. "This is not the Empire you knew."

"It is still the Empire," Bordan stated. The execution order was expected, and despite Godewyn's wish to change the Emperor's mind there was only one punishment for treason. Even so, he shivered. "I have given my life to it, to keep it safe and strong. Given that, I cannot, I could not drive us into war. Too many innocents would suffer."

"And you think Aelia's rule will be stable, that the people will not suffer," Vedrix snapped, taking half a step in Bordan's direction before the sudden fire left his eyes. "My apologies. I see the end of the Gymnasium coming. I see the magicians in my care, all their knowledge and learning lost, and the Empire sliding backwards into a dark age from which it may never emerge."

"The Empire has survived poor Emperors in the past," Bordan said. "Godewyn, you, and Maxentius will keep the peace."

"And you are giving your life so that it must endure another?"

"So that it can endure," he corrected.

Vedrix sighed. "I understand the concept of a noble sacrifice, and there are many things I would let go of to preserve the Gymnasium, but this, Bordan, when there are other paths to take?"

"There are no other paths, Vedrix," Bordan answered. "The Emperor cannot back down from her order of execution, and my freedom would only come at the cost of a war. It is too high a price to pay. You say you would sacrifice much to preserve the Gymnasium? Is one life not enough when weighted against hundreds or thousands? Would you strike at the Emperor to preserve your precious Gymnasium?"

"If it would preserve it," Vedrix said after a moment, "I might. However, we know that if the Emperor dies by magic, the Gymnasium will be destroyed. Either by the army," he nodded at Bordan, "or the Church leading the people in a crusade against us. I am caught as much as you and nothing I say, I do, can change that."

"And what will you do?" Bordan squinted up at the magician, noting for the first time the optimistic, happy look in his eyes had been replaced by one of profound sadness.

"The only thing I can," Vedrix said. "I will stay silent and act the good servant. Though much good that did you, it is all I can hope will keep the Emperor's ire away from the Gymnasium."

"And," Bordan swallowed his fear in a great gulp, "what is planned for me?"

"Crucifixion on the hill before the city gates," Vedrix said, his shoulders sagging as if he lifted a great weight from it. "Tomorrow."

"A large crowd to be expected," Bordan said, trying for a light tone but it fell flat against the stone floor.

"In the pack," Vedrix pointed, "is a small pill. It will numb the pain and ease your passing. Put it in your mouth before you are taken from here. I promise it won't melt until you bite down upon it."

Bordan glanced down at the wrapped parcel unsure of the words to say.

"There is also some spiced sausage, bread, cheese and another water skin," Vedrix continued, clearing his throat as he spoke. "It isn't much, but it is all I can do."

"Thank you," Bordan choked out.

"It is not a pleasure, my friend. It is anything but that," Vedrix said. "I wish it was not needed."

"I thank you anyway," Bordan said.

"In the Church," Vedrix turned back to him, hooking his thumbs into the soft leather belt, "when Aelia denounced you, did you believe her?"

"That it was me?" Bordan answered, puzzled.

"No. That someone other than Abra had arranged the assassins," Vedrix asked.

"Did you?" Bordan fenced.

"Yes," Vedrix stated without delay. "It makes sense and I knew Abra for a long time. He was a man of wealth, of ambition. He would take every chance given, but he would consider it first. If it benefited him, if the risk met the reward, he would try."

"For the throne?"

"The risk does match the reward," Vedrix considered. "However, he was also a man who valued his possessions, his position on the council. If something went wrong, he would know there would be a heavy price."

"He paid the price."

"Perhaps he paid someone else's price, or at least their share of it," Vedrix said. "Such an endeavour was not simple, and thieves may talk about honour amongst their kind, but all know that is an illusion borne of fear."

"You know who it is?" Bordan felt a moment of hope course through his blood.

"No," Vedrix admitted, "but I know it was not me or you."

"Godewyn?" Bordan asked, meeting the magician's piercing gaze.

"He is of the Church," Vedrix said, the words slowly drawn from his mouth. "However, I think not. It does not sit well with all I know of him."

"Who then?"

"I don't know," Vedrix answered, irritation clouding his voice. "I've considered other nobles, the tribes somehow insinuating an agent into the city. One of the Kingdoms to the north. A traitor from the southern continent."

"Not the Emperor herself?" Bordan asked and saw Vedrix's eyebrows shoot up. "I've nothing to lose by suggesting it. You said yourself, I'll be dead by the end of tomorrow."

"You saw her reaction when she discovered her brother, and her mother," Vedrix said. "I do not think it likely."

"You said she was not sane at the moment," Bordan continued. "Who is to say what those driven by grief will do."

"True, however I feel you mix cause with effect. The deaths drove her to this current state, not the other way around," Vedrix said. "My time is up, my friend."

"Thank you for visiting," Bordan said, standing.

"I see I was not the first." Vedrix nodded to the blanket.

"Godewyn," Bordan admitted.

"Friends risk much for you, General. The army would do the same on your word," Vedrix said.

"I cannot," Bordan replied.

"I know."

"You will look after Kyron," Bordan said. "A last favour to me. Keep him safe. Send him away from the city if you can. The boy hasn't come to his senses yet. He has lost everything. I worry what he will do."

"He has been to see you?" Vedrix's eyes narrowed.

"I didn't say that." Bordan spoke on reflex and heard the lie the same time Vedrix did.

"Damn that boy," Vedrix snapped, stamping his feet. "I told him not to come. I forbade him to come and see you. I can feel the magic he used, the tiny flutters in the world that should not be there. What if he had been caught? What if someone saw him. You know he almost acted to protect you in the church?"

"I didn't, but if you came here, he got away safe," Bordan said, his worry only growing. "Get him away from here, Vedrix. Send him far away. Today if you can. I don't want him to see me die."

"It won't change anything," Vedrix said. "He is impulsive and stubborn. The wound will fester even if I send him far away."

"It will give him time to heal, to come to terms with it," Bordan argued. "He has had to do it before, when his parents were killed. He can do it again. Please."

"I will do what I can, my friend. For you, and because despite it all, I like the lad," Vedrix said, clapping Bordan on the shoulder. "Remember the pill. We've both been to far too many executions, we know what to expect."

"How long before?" Before what he could not say, the words would not come.

"The effects will last for many hours, but I would save it until you are on the hill," Vedrix said. "Better not to give them an excuse to put it off for another day."

"Thank you, Vedrix, my friend," Bordan said, gripping the other man's shoulder. "Keep Kyron safe for me."

"I'll do what I can," Vedrix said. "I fear for the Gymnasium when the day is out and the weeks crawl by. One spark is all it will take for them to burn us down."

"Let us hope for rain then," Bordan said.

"Always," Vedrix replied with a sad smile before he turned for the door.

LVIII

THE MAGICIAN

THREE YEARS AGO:

"I know you wanted me to be a soldier," he said.

"I wanted you to be whatever you wanted to be," the old man said, his voice gruff and his eyes darting towards the Master Magician.

"I enjoyed learning the sword and shield," he said, trying to give something back, knowing it was not enough.

"And I enjoyed teaching you, just as I taught your father," the old man said. "You both made your own decisions in life, and there is nothing more I could ask of either of you." ·

"WHY ARE WE here?" Emlyn said as dusk settled once more over the roofs of the city.

"It is my grandfather's house," Kyron pointed out, "and I want something that is inside."

"Then can't you just walk in?" she asked.

"I looked this afternoon," Kyron explained again. "There are guards on the door, and I think it is being watched."

"To catch anyone involved in your grandfather's plot?"

"He wasn't involved," he snapped back, trying his best to keep his voice low.

"You know what I mean."

"Probably, yes," Kyron said.

"Vedrix isn't going to be happy," she added.

"He wasn't the happiest this morning either," Kyron replied, wincing at the memory of the dressing down he had endured.

"He was right though," Emlyn said. "You should leave the city."

"And give up on him? No." Kyron caught the words before they erupted into a shout. "He didn't give up on me. He took me in when my parents were killed and let me join the Gymnasium even though he didn't want me to."

"He is family," she said as if that explained everything.

"The Emperor is wrong," Kyron stated, more to himself than to her. He poked his head around the corner, checking the street for the hundredth time. "My grandfather has always served the Empire. He would never work against it. He knows who set the assassins on the Emperor's family."

"How do you know that he knows? I thought you said he would not tell you."

"I used a truth spell," he lied, "and I know him."

Kyron ducked his head around the corner once more. The streets were quickly giving way to shadows and the lanterns would soon be lit. Up the street he could see the single guard stood outside his grandfather's two-storey home. It was little different to those which surrounded it in this wealthy part of the town.

There were others, close by, whose footprint was larger, which contained gardens and fountains. However, General Bordan's home was reminiscent of the man. Tall, strong, and protective. The windows facing the street had their shutters closed and locked. One door graced the front elevation and the upper windows were sealed.

"But he didn't tell you. He didn't want you to go and do something stupid," Emlyn said, pausing briefly before adding, "again."

"Something like that," he acknowledged.

"The guard isn't going to leave," she said as he looked around the corner once more, "and we look very suspicious just stood on this street corner."

Kyron looked along the street and saw a few other people trudging along its cobbles. Most were servants carrying the ingredients of the evening meal bought fresh from the market or local shops. A few were likely on errands for their employer and one or two were heading to their own homes for a deserved rest. None looked their way.

"We're not that unusual," he said.

"A magician and a woman of the tribes?" She raised an eyebrow.

"As you've pointed out before, a lot of us have a heritage within the tribes," he replied. "And I don't look much like a magician at the moment."

Which was true. He had ditched his formal attire after the coronation, and the apprenticeship tunic he had worn to get into the palace last night. Instead, he had dressed in travelling clothes, much as he had worn on the campaign, though he had left the gladius in Padarn's quarters.

"If you say so."

"Let's go," he said, across the road and heading away from the street upon which his grandfather's house stood.

"Wait. What?" Emlyn said as she moved to catch up with him. "Where are you going?"

"This way," was all he said, hurrying along the street. At the next junction he turned right along the road parallel to his target. "We can't get in that way. The guard would see us. The door is locked and, even if we could climb, the upper floor is secure."

"So how do we get in?" she asked, looking around when Kyron stopped.

"Here," he said, pointing at his feet.

There was a large stone, edged with iron, between the two of them and it was slotted into the surface of the street.

Drawing the motes to his arms and hands, strengthening them. He held out a steel hook to her and said, "Help me."

The hooks slotted into the edge of the slab and they lifted. It was heavy, even with his enhanced strength and the assistance of Emlyn, but it moved with a slow, drawn-out grating sound which set dogs in the distance to barking.

"Down," he wheezed as he lowered the stone onto the road.

"It stinks," she said, wrinkling her nose. "What's down there?"

"You don't want to know," he answered, drawing a length of cloth around his nose and mouth. He handed a similar one to her. "Down."

She glared at him and then clambered down into the hole. There was a splash and a curse as she vanished into the darkness. A small smile crossed his face as he followed.

Landing in soft liquid he wheeled his arms, catching his balance as the rank odour of shit, piss and rotting food clawed its way up his nose. Bile rose in his throat and it was an effort of will not to vomit.

"You left the stone open," she pointed out, looking up.

"We need a way out," he said, "and I couldn't think of how to close it."

"Magic?"

"I could, I suppose, but it is really heavy," he replied after a moment's thought. "We still need a way out."

"You brought a torch or lamp?"

"No," he answered. For once he felt he had the upper hand. The forests were her domain, she understood them and her place within them. Throughout the journey she had seemed so calm amongst the trees, as if she belonged. Here, in the city, it was his land, his terrain. "Everything rots down in here and there are pockets of gas which flare and explode when exposed to flame."

"Really?" She peered into the darkness. "How do they get cleaned?"

"They don't," he said, taking her by the hand and moving out of the faint illumination of the summer stars above. "We're slightly downhill of the house and water runs through the sewers towards the docks and out into the sea."

"And no one comes down here?"

"It is all the human waste from the homes around, would you come down here by choice? Well," he said, cautious, "I did read that sometimes thieves and other folks use these tunnels to avoid the militia."

"Great," she said.

"We're not going far," he said. "Just up the hill a little."

"And how will we see?"

Kyron gave her a wide grin in the last of the starlight and lifted his free hand. In it, he gathered the motes, focused and forced them together into a small ball which sat in the middle of his cupped palm.

The construct was simple and one of the first learned by an apprentice. It taught focus, strength of will, and how to manipulate the motes as they danced and wove around in the air. It only needed enough gathered in one place and a single knot to maintain it. With a twist of thought he secured the knot and light bloomed in his hand.

"Is that it?" Emlyn asked.

"What?" He looked the dull ball of light he cupped in his palm.

"It is quite small."

"Any brighter and bigger and you'll lose your night vision, plus someone outside might notice it," he explained, a little hurt. "It is enough for what we need to do."

"If you say so."

"Come on."

He turned his back on her and started up the sewer. The bricks and stone were old, built when the city expanded and constructed so well it needed little repair. Here and there, a loose stone had tumbled from the wall and in one place on their short journey a small pile of them had been overwhelmed by a much larger slick of brown muck. The top of which was above the water and had dried to a broken crust. They skirted around it and continued forward.

Every ten steps he counted, he stopped and held the small ball of illumination up to the bricks around head height.

"What are you looking for?"

"They carved the streets and house numbers into the bricks when they built it," he said. "It made joining homes with sewers easier."

"That sounds like a lot of planning just to carry the waste away."

"Thirty years of planning, so the book said," he explained. "And better the waste is carried away than rises into your home. When it was finished, it cut the rates of disease and death by half in just the first year."

"That was in the book too?"

"Yes."

"And you have more of these books?"

"Padarn had lots and the Gymnasium library is immense," he said with a touch of pride. "You want to visit it when we get back?"

"No. How far to your grandfather's house?"

"Just here," he said, crestfallen. They turned the corner and the sewer walls tightened in upon them. However, a few steps later the old brick walls gave way to a more recent construction. "He had this built before I was born. It was the escape route from the house. We used to practise evacuating every few months."

"A prudent man," she said.

"He planned, plans everything," Kyron said. "If he had organised the killings, he would have had a way out, yet he is in prison. It wasn't him."

"How do we get in?"

"There's a trapdoor ahead," he said, fingers digging into the pouch on his belt. "We both had a key."

The light from the small globe showed the wooden square in the ceiling. Reaching up, Kyron inserted the key and twisted. It moved with hardly a sound.

"He keeps it well oiled," Kyron explained. "Step back a bit."

When he was sure Emlyn had moved aside, he slid the lock bolt back and grunted as he took the weight of the door. He guided it open on smooth hinges and let it swing a little at the end of its arc.

"No rope? No ladder?" Emlyn asked coming to stand next to him and peering up.

"It was never really designed for getting in," Kyron said. "Out was just a matter of jumping down and running."

He lifted the hand which held the small globe of light and tossed it into the room above. The faint illumination showed the edge of the trap door and Kyron leapt upwards, catching the sides and pulling himself into the home.

"I'll help," Kyron said as he turned around to reach down a hand. Emlyn was already clambering through the hole, a grin just visible on her face. "Though you don't seem to need it."

"I climbed trees my whole youth," she said. "This is nothing. What are we looking for?"

"Grandfather keeps a journal, a diary," Kyron explained. "I've never been allowed to look in it, but he told me years ago he keeps his memories and thoughts in it. He may have written down the person he thinks actually organised the assassinations."

"That doesn't seem like a safe thing to do?" she quizzed. "What if someone finds it? It might be full of secrets."

"I don't know," Kyron said, pausing in his steps towards the stairs which led up from the cellar. "I didn't think of that." He shook his head. "It doesn't matter. We find it and then we can decide what to do."

"So where is it?"

"I don't know," he admitted, nearing the top of the stairs. "His study, his room, somewhere in the house. He didn't have it on him when he went to the church and hasn't been anywhere since."

"His office in the palace?"

"I already checked, on the way out the prison," he answered. "It was quiet in the palace. I think everyone was celebrating."

He pushed open the cellar door and stepped into his childhood home. The kitchen was unchanged. A long wooden counter running down one wall, some amphorae stacked in the corner and near the stove were cupboards and shelves.

A cook and cleaner had been employed in the house when he had left for the Gymnasium. Kyron realised he had no idea if they had stayed with his grandfather and were still living in the house.

"We... um... may not be alone in the house," he whispered.

Emlyn nodded, slipping her knife free and holding it ready.

"No," he hissed. "They'll be asleep and wouldn't harm me. We just have to be quiet."

"The way we smell would wake the dead," she said with a grimace and, he noticed, did not sheathe her knife. "Which way?"

"His office is on this floor," he whispered. "This way."

He led her to the door and out into the home's atrium. It was square with a tessellated floor in a simple design and the painted ceiling looked down upon them from above the second floor. In the southern Empire this room would, he knew from his classes, have an opening in the ceiling and a small, decorative pool in the centre of the room. It was too cold and too wet for such luxury here.

The front door was directly ahead and beyond that the guard. To the left were the stairs leading upwards and, he knew though could not see, a door leading into the large dining room. On the right were three doors.

One of the rooms had, from his memory, belonged to the cook, Decima, and her husband, Gressius. An ex-soldier, the man hadn't spoken much, but walked with a pronounced limp without complaint.

Next to that was the small house temple. A richly decorated room with a fire bowl which was kept burning day and night, the smoke exiting through a small chimney. Grandfather was a devout follower of the Flame and tried without much success to impress the same upon Kyron.

The last room, the one closest to the door was the old man's office. Apart from the walled garden out back, it was where he had spent much of his time when Kyron was growing.

Upstairs was given over to bedrooms and guest rooms. Some of his belongings would still be there, Kyron knew, but facing those memories would be too much for tonight's work. Another day, he promised.

"Here," he whispered, pushing open the office door and lifting his free hand to maximise the illumination. As Emlyn crept in beside him, he closed the door. "We're looking for a book, about so big with dark leather bindings. I don't recall it having any writing on it, but it looks old, battered and well used."

"His desk?" she suggested, pointing.

Kyron walked over, keeping clear of the slim tables upon which vases and statues rested, moving around the large chairs which, during the day, would be in full view of the sunlight streaming through the windows.

"It's here," he said, holding up the book, its leather straps keeping it shut.

"Well," Emlyn said, "that was easy."

There was a crash from the atrium, the sound of a door opening and metal striking the tiled floor.

Kyron stared at Emlyn who returned the shocked gaze. She moved first, turning back towards the door.

"We need to go," she said, her voice gone from a whisper to a warning, and the knife coming up before her.

"Don't hurt anyone," Kyron said, racing forward, drawing the motes from the room and building them into a spell.

"No promises," she replied as she pulled the door open and stepped into the ruddy light of an oil lamp.

"Guard!" the man shouted, as Emlyn came into view. "Guard!"

Kyron piled out of the room, book tucked under his arm and his spell of light still glowing in other hand. At the front door, there was a rattling sound as the soldier outside tried to respond to the man's shout.

"Gressius," Kyron whispered, dropping the spell he had been about to throw at the man, "it's me, Kyron."

The old soldier lowered his gladius and cast a sidelong look at Emlyn who still held her knife ready. "Kyron, you stink. What are you doing skulking around? It's your house as much as his."

"Not at the moment," Kyron corrected, stepping forward to clasp arms with his grandfather's loyal cleaner and handyman who wrinkled his face at the smell. The old soldier's eyes were bright despite his age and the scar which ran down his face. "I would say it is good to see you, but you know what is happening."

"Aye, I do," the old man said. "It isn't right, but I won't be abandoning my post."

"Are you all right in there?" the soldier outside called. "Let me in."

"I'm fine," Gressius called back. "Stop your shouting. You'll wake the whole street."

"He didn't do it," Kyron said. "What everyone is saying. What the Emperor said. He didn't do it."

"I know that," Gressius answered. "Isn't him at all."

"Let me in." The door rattled once more. "By order of the Emperor."

"I just tripped over something," Gressius called back. "Everything is fine."

"Open this door!" the guard screamed through the thick wood.

"You have to go," Gressius told Kyron, "and take your young friend with her sharp knife with you. Can't do much about the stink, but I'll think of something."

"They can't know I was here," Kyron said, shifting the book under his arm. He saw Gressius take a quick glance towards it. "It is to help him."

"You sure he wants your help, young Kyron?"

"Maybe not, but like you I am not abandoning him," he said, squaring his shoulders and standing up.

"Good for you," Gressius nodded. "Get out through the trapdoor. I'll hold up our loud friend for a moment."

"Open this door or I'll start chopping it down," the guard shouted. "Thank you, I..."

"Get going," Gressius took hold of Kyron's arm gave it a squeeze and then pushed him towards the kitchen door. The old man raised his voice and limped towards the door. "One moment. I fell over. Let me get something on and the key."

"Open this door," the soldier called once more.

"I'm coming," Gressius shouted back, "dropped the chamber pot. Give me a moment to clean it up. Wouldn't want to spoil your boots."

Kyron and Emlyn left the two soldiers arguing and slipped down the stairs into the cellar. Dropping into the darkness, Kyron passed the journal over and lifted the trapdoor back into place, locking it with the key.

"Now you'd better hope the street cover is still open," Emlyn said.

"I hope Gressius doesn't get hurt," Kyron said as they hurried down the dark sewer, his dim light leading the way.

"He's known pain before, by the way he walks and stands, but he looks like he knows its tricks," Emlyn said as she followed along.

It took an hour of negotiating the sewers and streets before they stumbled, worn out and stinking back into Padarn's rooms. The magician at the gate had covered his mouth and nose with the sleeve of his robe but asked no questions.

"Wash," Emlyn said, pointing to the bowl of water, and speaking over her shoulder as she moved to the other room. "And get changed. Throw those clothes away, that stink will never come out."

He sniffed the air and proceeded to strip off, casting glances at the closed door. Kyron raced to get clean and dragged on a new set of clothes whilst still damp.

"Well," Emlyn said as she came back in and stirred the fire back to life, "let's see what you got."

Kyron cleared a space on the desk and drew an oil lamp closer. With shaking fingers, he undid the bindings and opened the book, turning the pages and scanning the neat lines within. "I can't read it."

"Why not?" Emlyn said coming closer.

"It is some sort of code or cypher," Kyron snorted in disgust, stepping back and away. All that effort, for nothing. The last chance to find the information he needed to save the old man. The stubborn old man who had raised him, argued with him, driven him to slamming doors and raised voices, and to the Gymnasium, to magic and a future.

He staggered to a chair and slumped down. Already the tears, a mix of frustration, anger, and grief, were welling in his eyes and flooding down his cheeks. He balled a fist and slammed it down upon the arm rest. He raised it again and this time brought it down upon his own leg, the pain a punishment, acknowledgment of failure, of self-disgust. Leaning forward he put his head in both hands, covering his mouth and screamed into them.

For a time, he cried. Each hot tear was a regret for an opportunity missed, a chance lost, a moment ignored. They carried with them his sense of loss and emptiness as they dripped to the floor forming a small, lonely puddle of grief upon the cold stone.

Slowly, the sound of pages turning infiltrated upon his thoughts. He looked up to see Emlyn hunched over the book. Wiping his mouth with the back of his hand, he mumbled, "What are you doing?"

"Reading," she said without turning.

"The code?" He stood, incredulous and shocked.

"It isn't code." She turned to him with a cautious smile. "It is written in Old Galix."

"In what?"

"The old language of the tribes," she said. "Quite a few in the northern areas, like mine, still write in it. Usually in formal declarations, and your grandfather cannot spell worth a damn, but it does make sense."

"Did he say who he thinks ordered the assassinations?"

"He does," she said, her smile fading. "You're not going to like it."

"Who?" The hole in the pit of his stomach gaped wider as the thought that his grandfather had confessed his guilt to those private pages.

"Aelia," Emlyn said.

"The Emperor?" Kyron said, leaping from the chair and snatching the book from her hands. "We have to find Master Vedrix."

"He is at the palace tonight," Emlyn said. "They told us that this afternoon."

"I have to see him." Kyron turned to the door.

"They won't let you in," Emlyn called. "Not dressed like that and not stinking like you do. Also, it is late and Vedrix will be asleep. I know it is hard, but it will be best to see him in the morning."

"The morning," Kyron almost shouted. "My grandfather will be executed in the morning."

"You have time, Kyron," Emlyn said, stepping across the room and gripping him by the arms. "You have time. Let's wash, get some sleep and be ready for the morning. We'll leave as soon as the sun rises."

She was correct, he knew. It was too late, the palace would be sealed until morning and there would be more guards on the streets. It would do no good to get caught, to have the book, the evidence taken from him before he could speak to Master Vedrix.

Her being right did not make him feel any better.

LIX

THE GENERAL

THREE YEARS AGO:

The last sight of the lad in the Master's study almost broke him, but he smiled and gave the boy a wave. It was returned with hesitance and the door closed.

"He will be fine, General," the magician who escorted him to the door said. "He is not the first, nor last to come through those doors and start a new chapter of their lives."

"He is a good lad, but not always the most," he paused, "sensible."

The magician laughed. "I think that describes most boys of his age. I will look out for him. Please, do not worry."

"Thank you," he began and realised he did not know the other man's name.

"Padarn, General," the magician said. "Master Padarn."

THE SOLDIERS WHO arrived to escort him to the hill of execution did not speak. Communication between the condemned and their guards was forbidden, and he had trained his soldiers to follow orders above all else. However, the lack of chains restraining him and the manner in which each looked at him said more than simple words would convey.

Give us the order, they said. We will follow.

He shook his head and held out his hands for the chains. The soldier, uniform spotless, freshly shaved, and unsmiling, clasped them about Bordan's wrists with a sigh.

Still without a word they turned and marched from the cell. He fell into step, two soldiers ahead and two behind. Through the door and up the stairs, only the sound of their boots on the stone steps and the whisper of their breath for company.

At the top, the door stood open, and a line of soldiers guarded the passage they trooped down. He felt every gaze fall upon his shoulders with the heavy weight of expectation. Bordan, once General of the Empire, kept his gaze down, focused upon his feet and the path they followed.

The palace and parade grounds were silent, lined with more soldiers, survivors of the honour guard and those who fought in the Battle of the Bridge, whose eyes followed his every step to the gates.

Overhead the summer's day had dawned, cloud covered and grey. Rain would fall. Its scent was upon the air, and those little gusts of wind which chilled his face.

He stopped at the gates, looked up at the sky, and took a deep breath. With deliberate care and speed, Bordan let his eyes go to every man and woman who stood upon the walls and filled the parade ground.

His army. His troops. Trained and deployed to keep the Empire safe. Feared by the Empire's enemies and loved by its people. His children almost as much as his son had been. Every single one raised under his watchful gaze and each with some imprint of his personality. His proudest achievement.

Bordan raised his bound hands and tapped his chest. In a great wave every soldier returned the gesture. The condemned may not speak, but often words are the lesser aspect of language.

Keeping his shoulders straight and head high, he crossed the threshold of the palace and stepped out onto the wide avenue. Here the crowds had gathered to see the traitor conveyed to the hill. The same barriers which had been used to keep the people back on the day of coronation were in place, but no one cheered this time.

He turned with his escort and joined the larger group of soldiers who would take him to the hill.

As they marched, the whispers began. The populace had come to see a traitor executed and their view was blocked by the soldiers. Whispers became calls which grew into shouts and rage.

"Traitor," came the call.

"Murderer," another.

"Assassin," a third shouted.

"Bastard."

He felt each shout batter at his ears, but he had faced armies. In the years of service, he had stood on the front lines and lifted a sword for the Empire's sake. In battles past, he had seen friends cut down, had cut down enemies.

Blood, intestines, kidneys, the clear liquid which was housed only in the skull, the wrinkled grey of brain, the purple hue of a stilled heart, the bright red of severed muscle and the clean white of freshly exposed bone.

There was nothing he had not seen in battle or the lull after. A man crying over a lost friend. A soldier vomiting and shaking in released fear. The stink of shit and piss. Copper tang of blood on his tongue. A dying soldier whimpering for help.

Soldiers, survivors of a battle, given over to their base emotions and the need for revenge. The slaughter of enemies. The painless application of the poppy or the slither of a sharp knife across a throat.

The shouts of the crowd were nothing to those. Irritating and undeserved, but not as sharp as a sword nor as dangerous as an axe surrounded as he was by soldiers who had stood with him, or at his order, in battles of their own.

Here was his land, his domain, his safety and comfort. However short it would be, this march to his last battle would not be one of shame.

In his mouth, Vedrix's pill was as hard and cold as a pebble fresh from the beach. A passing memory of a small boy, sad, sullen, broken, lifting a smooth stone and throwing it with every ounce of anger and injustice into the crashing waves.

They marched through the city, down roads he had walked for decades, past shops he had bought food from, inns and taverns he had drunk in as soldier. The city had grown over the decades and improved. Markets had taken over squares and the people enjoyed the wealth which the Empire brought to their door. All protected by him, by his army, by his soldiers.

Now they wanted his blood, to see him die upon the cross. He should be angry with them. The thought rose in his mind like the relic of a ship exposed by the tide. He should condemn them much as they did him.

But he could not. All he could do was wish to spare them the pain of the coming years. Aelia as Emperor, even with the tempering experience of Godewyn, Vedrix, Maxentius, and the other council members, was a disaster in waiting. Soldiers who had seen battle and whose minds had snapped, or who had been overwhelmed by fear, by the horror, were given doses of poppy to keep them calm and sent back to rest. Some never recovered, but few ever held a sword in anger again.

There was no one to give Aelia the calm clarity of the dreamer's potion. Her mind would crack further under the pressure of grief and the amulet. Those who served her would ever remember this day, and know that they could be next. Some, he knew, would see this as a just punishment, but many others who knew of his lifetime of service would know this for what it was, and they would be afraid.

The eastern gate was open, and the troop passed through without pause. Glancing back, he saw a crowd of city folk had followed them through the streets. As far back as he could see there were people, an ocean of them, a flock of starlings which wheeled, twisted and turned, following the leader.

The road rose to the small hill upon which traitors were executed. Atop, Bordan could see the High Priest, the Master Magician and, in the centre, Aelia. A small crowd of workers, carpenters who had built the cross, and others who dug the hole it would sit within, milled about. The base of the hill was surrounded by a double rank of soldiers who would keep the crowds back.

The line of soldiers parted and those with him, except the original four, peeled away to add their numbers to the ranks. Underfoot, the cobbles of the road, worn smooth by feet became more rounded, slippery, and sought to send him to his knees. He steadied his legs and focused upon each step, even as he pushed the pill into his cheek to prevent an accidental bite.

Godewyn's face was impassive as Bordan crested the hill. Dressed in full regalia, a beacon of faith as much as the flame which burned in the bowl behind him.

Stood apart, Vedrix, Master of the Gymnasium of Magicians, looked at him with sad eyes. The man's beard had been combed and his robes were a colourful rejection of the simple white which Godewyn wore.

Aelia stood, shifting from one foot to the other, in her bronze armour. Ornate and burnished to a high gleam with the red cape rippling in the breeze. A gladius hung on her hip and a pugio sat in a matching sheath on the opposite side.

Through the small group and laying on the ground was the cross. Thick timbers carved and planed to a smooth finish. The upright looked to be twice his height and the cross beam was as thick as two arms. It was an effort of will to tear his gaze from it.

The new Emperor took a deep breath and Bordan saw the woman's hands clenched at her side. "A traitor's death for you, General. Upon a cross for everyone to watch."

Bordan glanced at Vedrix and Godewyn. Both met his gaze but offered no help, no words, and their faces were unchanged, unmoved.

"I am no traitor," Bordan said, pitching his words so only the three could hear. One of the workmen paused in his task, sparing Bordan a look before returning to his task.

"Denial?" Aelia tilted her head as if looking at the General from a different angle would help. "You've been set against me ever since Alhard was killed. You made him a hero to the people, General. The great warrior who put down a rebellion in the countryside. But we know my brother had little between his ears. You knew you could control him and be the Emperor in everything but name."

Bordan gaped and looked once more to his two friends.

"The man who stole the glory from even my father. It was your plans which sent him north to conquer the tribes. It is you the soldiers always look to. My father knew that. Who controls the army controls the Empire, he told me once," Aelia ranted, pacing back and forth, tapping her chest. "I know what he meant now. His wisdom guides me."

"That's not—"

"Silence," Aelia screamed. "A traitor's voice seeks only to turn the hearts of others from the truth. Alhard resisted your manipulations. He wanted to be Emperor alone. Your clever words could not sway him, so you killed him."

"Godewyn," Bordan said, holding out his manacled hands.

"No," Aelia snapped, stalking forward and battering Bordan's hands down. "My mother knew, suspected, so you had her killed. You had me fooled though, didn't you? You had me going along with your plans, your schemes. You foisted all the blame on Abra and killed him before he could be brought to justice. Even so, you gave him time to organise an army, to try and steal my father's body and the throne from me. He would have handed it all to you and your army would be there, ready to turn on me."

The Emperor's hand went to the sword at her waist and half drew it in a fit of rage before slamming it back into the sheath. "You'd like me to kill you now. A soldier's death, General. One with honour. That you will not have."

Aelia turned away and moved in staccato steps to the cross which lay upon the grass. Before Bordan could speak again, the young ruler rounded upon him.

"I saw through your delays," the Emperor said, her voice now a hoarse whisper. "Why did you want to wait for supplies? Why hold us back? Why not attack as soon as you can? Why all the worry over the soldiers whose job it is to fight and die at the Empire's command? All to delay. All to give Abra a chance. Such timidity and fear at the bridge, General. Such an unwillingness to attack."

"I am not a traitor," Bordan said the moment Aelia ran out of breath.

"Lies. Lies. Lies." Aelia's face screwed up as if she had just tasted something unpleasant, something bitter and poisonous. "We knew you would lie. Knew you would say anything to save yourself."

"Your Majesty," one of the workmen said, looking up from the cross. "It is ready."

"You see," Aelia pointed to the wooden beams. "This will be your death. The one reserved for traitors. Abra should be there beside you. Two traitors scheming for the throne and power. It was never yours to have, General. We talked," Aelia stepped around the cross and looked down upon it, "talked on the journey. It all became clear. Every action you took, you took to strip my family of power and put yourself on my throne."

Talked to who, Bordan wondered. Vedrix looked confused, worried, and despite the grey skies there was sweat upon the man's brow. Stood a little apart, Godewyn wore the expression of a priest. Serene and at peace, and when he met Bordan's eyes there was little to read in them.

This cannot be right, he wanted to shout at them. The Emperor has lost her mind to grief and anger, and you are going along with her.

Start a civil war. The words in his mind were uttered in Vedrix's voice and the chance was still there. Call out to the soldiers, order them to save him, and they would. Enough would, he knew, but some would not, and the war would begin. Hundreds would die. Cities and towns would burn. The Empire would tear itself to pieces. All that he worked for, all that service and duty, would be ground into dust beneath his feet.

There is nothing he could say. Nothing he could do.

General Bordan brought the pill between his teeth and bit down. He heard it crack through the bones in his jaw and the taste of dust filled his mouth. Swallowing, he brought more saliva to his mouth to mix with the dust and form a clag which he could force down his throat.

He turned to look out across the crowd. From the ring of soldiers at the base of the hill, over the crowd which had gathered, to the city walls and gate. Above them all the palace towers and spires of the church.

A warmth spread from his stomach along his limbs. They felt light, distant, as if they belonged to some other man. The grey light falling through the clouds brightened and the grass of summer beneath his feet became a vibrant green. He was floating yet standing still.

In his chest, every beat of his slow heart thrummed through his body, each pulse meandering its path along arteries and veins. He could hear the crash of the sea in his ears as the voices of the crowd faded away.

"Place him upon the cross." The words came to his ears from a thousand paces away, a bare whisper which was chased away by the sound of the breath in his lungs.

He felt himself lifted, but it was happening to someone else, and carried. Above his head the clouds swayed and billowed against each other. Subtle movements on the edges, blurred by distance and merging into a smear of muted greys.

Lain down, he felt the hard wood against his spine, but it was comfortable, like slipping into his own bed after a long day. Feet aching with the day's efforts, legs heavy and welcoming the soft give of the cloth stuffed mattress.

Something pinched his heels, drawing a short gasp from his lips and a chill ran up his legs and through his chest. The clouds moved above him, driven by a breeze which he thought he could see in the eddies which turned the grey cotton in upon itself.

His arms were lifted and stretched to the side. They were pulled and pushed like the finest massage in the public baths. When had he last visited the baths, the thought slipped in for a moment, before drifting away on the winds of Vedrix's pill.

There was a pop, like the bursting of a soap bubble which he both heard and felt. It was pleasant, a release of pressure he had not known he was feeling and his arms were warm.

Now the sky wheeled and danced. His stomach dropped and there was moment when he was free of weight. The city came back into view and below its roofs, the walls, the gates. Arrayed around him, a crowd and soldiers, but blurred and indistinct.

He tried to wipe the mist from his eyes, but his arms would not move. Turning slowly to the left and right, he saw his arms running red and the heads of large iron spikes jutting from his flesh.

Not his flesh, though. A stranger's. It was not his body he inhabited. He was numb to it. Unfeeling. Distant. Absent.

Thoughts drifted and meandered through his distant mind. None stayed long and few could be grasped or held up for inspection.

Dying, a thought, a word came through, but was carried away on the stream of wonder that was the sky and crowd.

A figure, a movement on the edge of the crowd came into focus for moment, but the vision ran through him like a cold stream. It chilled him. Scared him.

A moment of reality, a scream of pain, a figure he knew carrying something dear to him.

"No," he muttered, finding the use of his tongue once more.

LX

THE MAGICIAN

THREE YEARS AGO:
He stared up at the high ceiling in the dormitory. They had given him a bed, a chest in which to keep his things, and a new robe which swept the floor when he walked.

"You'll grow into it," the magician said.

"What do I do now?" he asked, lost and alone again.

"Sleep," the magician said. "Lessons begin in the morning and you'll have a chance to meet your classmates."

The other boys who had come in later, had glanced to his bed, but no one had spoken to him. A tear trickled down his face and soaked into the pillow.

THE CROWDS WERE gathering when Kyron, followed by Emlyn, left the Gymnasium in the morning. These people were not celebrating, and all the muttered talk he heard was of the execution. Some were headed to the palace to get a first look at the condemned man and others towards the hill outside the city gate to make sure they got a good spot at the front. Here and there he spied small stalls or street sellers hawking wares and souvenirs, small wooden crosses, hot food, and illustrations of the crucifixion hill lit by bright sunshine on squares of parchment.

Keeping the book tight under his arm, Kyron pushed and elbowed his way through the people. Many turned to glare, to complain or rage at him. He did not let them stop or distract him. Their eyes saw only his departing back and their words fell on deaf ears.

He ducked into a gap in the crowd and skipped out of the way of a bigger group heading his way. Lowering his leading shoulder a little, he pushed forward eliciting a shout of anger from the man he knocked out of the way.

"Are you determined to make everyone angry with you today?" Emlyn asked, catching his elbow and slowing him down.

"I have to get to the palace," he explained, wrenching his arm free.

"But not with a whole crowd of angry people following you," she said. "They won't let you in to see Vedrix if you've got to argue with two hundred people first."

Kyron grunted and tried to slow his feet. The energy running through him, speeding his heart and pulse, forcing his mind to constantly twist and turn the possibilities over until no course of action seemed right, kept driving him to a faster pace. Only Emlyn's hand on his forearm kept him slow and careful.

Rounding one corner, the towers of the palace came into view and the spires of the church rose over the homes on his right. Here though, the crowd thickened until forward movement was all but impossible.

"Excuse me," he tried, tapping a woman on the shoulder.

"If I'm not going forward, neither are you, lad," she turned and said, not unkindly.

"I need to get to the palace," he said.

"You'll be lucky," she answered.

"Try this way," Emlyn said, tugging on his arm and pointing along the street. There was a small alley of space between the building and the crowd of people trying to get to the front.

"I just need to find a guard," Kyron called as he followed her along the edge of the crowd which ebbed and flowed like the tide across the small beach of empty space. Occasionally it crashed up against the cliff of the buildings and they had to wait for the crush to ease a little.

"There," Emlyn said, pointing at a small gap which had opened in the mass of people.

Kyron dove for it, keeping his elbows out to dig into the ribs of any who tried to block his path. Amongst the people the temperature rose and the stink of unwashed bodies made him gag. It was difficult to stay upright, but he staggered forward.

"Let me through," he shouted. "Official business. Palace business. Messenger."

Any important sounding words and phrases he could conjure from the confusing mess of fear and panic in which his mind swam, he said, shouted, and screamed at the people around him. Quite a few moved aside, pushing others out of the way. One or two grumbled and an angry-faced man grabbed Kyron by the shoulder as he moved past him.

"Hey," the man shouted as he pulled Kyron around. "Stop pushing your way through. We were here first. You should have got up earlier."

Kyron drew in a sharp breath to respond, his own anger setting fire to his throat, hot words ready to burst forth like dragon's flame.

"My apologies, sir," Emlyn said, pressing a coin into the man's palm. "Official palace business."

The man looked down at the silver coin in his hand and then up to Emlyn. "That's fine. Sorry to stop you."

Kyron did not stop to enquire where she had found the coin but pushed forward. Broaching the front line of onlookers and coming up against the wooden barrier which kept the avenue clear, he went to duck underneath.

"Now then," said a voice, "where do you think you're... Kyron?"

The apprentice looked up into Cohort Borus's face and for the first time felt that there might be a chance.

"Borus," he called, reaching over the barrier to clasp the man's wrist, "I need to see Master Vedrix in the palace."

"Can't get into the palace, lad," Borus said, shaking his head. "I know what today means to you. I'm sorry."

"I have to get in," Kyron complained, feeling the frustration begin to bubble over. It was a strong effort of will to hold himself in check.

"You can't, lad," Borus said. "No one can. Whole place is locked down because of... well, you know."

"I need to see Master Vedrix," Kyron cried, bringing the palm of his free hand down upon the wooden barrier, welcoming the momentary flash of pain. "I have to see him."

"He isn't there," Borus said, covering Kyron's hand with his own. "You'd best keep calm today, Kyron. A cool head can solve a lot more problems than a hot one. You've stood in the line, you know what fear and anger will do to a soldier."

"Vedrix isn't there?" Panic welled in his throat, choking his words and numbing his tongue.

"He left earlier with the Emperor and High Priest," Borus said. "They've gone to the hill to get ready for the... I am so sorry, lad. If there was anything I could do."

Kyron did not stay to hear all of Borus's kind words but pushed back through the crowd and turned towards the gate which led to the hill.

As he crashed through the onlookers there was a sudden hush which swept like an ill wind along the avenue. The people stood stock still and it felt as though everyone held their breath at the same moment. Kyron tried to crane his neck to see over the heads of all those he had just barged out of the way.

In a momentary gap, as one in the crowd tilted their head to the side and another stepped in the other direction, he saw the reason for the sudden silence. Flanked by soldiers, his grandfather, the General of the Empire, stood in the gateway to the palace.

He wanted to shout out, to barrel forward and drag the old man to safety. With a crowd of city folk and a wide avenue between him and his grandfather, he had never felt more impotent in his life.

The gap closed and the crowd began to move towards the gate. There was nothing to do, no way to push through quicker and all he could do was tighten his grip on the journal and go along with it. A hand grabbed his free arm and he looked back over his shoulder, pulling Emlyn to his side as they were swept along.

"I saw him," Emlyn called as the silence vanished into a mass of conversation and speculation.

"So did I," Kyron answered, stepping around an old man who was using a cane to limp along with the crowd. A scar ran across the man's nose and Kyron noticed that he only had three fingers on the hand holding the cane. "Are you all right, old man?"

"Fine," the old man grumbled, looking up into Kyron's face, the wrinkles around his eyes made them seem small, hard, and dark. He nodded towards his hand and cane. "Old wound from my time in the ranks."

"Be careful getting through the crowd," Emlyn said. "Best to stick to the side."

"He wouldn't do it, you know," the old soldier muttered. "Too much honour and too stupid."

"Stupid?" Kyron almost stopped as the old man's word caught him off guard. Honour was a part of his grandfather as much as breathing was, but no one had ever accused him of stupidity.

"They'd follow him, you know," the old man lifted his cane, and the woman who was passing him on the other side was forced to duck out of the way, "the soldiers. In a heartbeat, without question. Stupid not to give the order."

"He fears a civil war," Kyron said, and when he noticed the sharp-eyed glance the old man gave him added, "probably. There would be a lot of deaths."

"That's what war is, lad," the old man said, shaking his head. "Never stood the ranks, have you? Young people today have no idea what it is to serve and do your duty."

Before Kyron could respond they were carried away and through the gate, spilling out onto the road beyond. Here the crowd widened and spread around the base of the hill where a ring of soldiers kept them at bay.

He stopped with Emlyn beside him and looked up. The grey clouds made sluggish progress across the sky and on the crest of the hill, the Emperor stood next to his grandfather. To the side, Godewyn and Master Vedrix kept a respectful distance.

"No," Kyron whispered.

"Only good end to a traitor," said a woman stood next him. She pointed up at the hill with a bone thin finger. "Hope he screams. I like it when they scream. Teaches the youngsters to behave and keep out of trouble."

Emlyn's hand gripped his wrist and he found his own hand had wrapped around the hilt of his pugio.

"No," she whispered, and he shivered, taking a deep breath. The woman darted a look at his face, her eyes widening as she backed away, into the crowd.

"Silence!" the Emperor roared, and the people obeyed, though a glance up at the hill showed the instruction had not been directed at them.

Kyron could see the Emperor, dressed in armour, speaking with his grandfather though he was too far distant to make out what was said. As he watched, his grandfather shook his head and spoke back. Neither Vedrix nor the High Priest moved or spoke. Whatever was being said was between the General and the Emperor and it was only making the newly crowned heir angry.

The conversation ended when the Emperor pointed at something on the earth and workmen, previously out of sight, gripped his grandfather's arms and lifted him. There was a drawn-out silence and then the chime of a hammer driving nails into wood.

Kyron did not need to see what was happening. The process was well known to all in the Empire, its most painful, most feared punishment. The victim's heels were nailed to either side of the upright timber and more nails were driven through the two bones of the lower arm to hold the prisoner to the crosspiece. When lifted into position, those nails kept the condemned from falling too far forward and the slow loss of blood, the pain of all their weight pulling at bones and flesh unfailingly drew screams from their throats.

"I have to get up there," Kyron said, rushing forward, book under his arm, and pulling Emlyn with him.

"It's too late," Emlyn said.

"No," he shouted and the people in front turned his way, shock on their faces. "Get out of the way."

On the hill the cross was raised, and Kyron stopped once more, all the breath in his lungs escaping in a great gust. His grandfather was pinned to the beams and blood flowed down the upright from the ruins of his feet and wrists. Strangely, there were no screams and no look of anguish upon the old man's face. Instead, there was wonder and peace.

"That ain't right," one man muttered.

"He's not screaming," said a woman.

"Mama," a small voice said, "I can't see. What's going on?"

Kyron inhaled and pushed forward once more. Letting go of Emlyn's hand, he grabbed the clothes of those in front, dragging them aside. Fear and panic lending him strength which had never been his. Those who fought, who refused to move, suffered an elbow to the ribs, a foot to the back of the knee and Kyron surged forward through the crowd.

"No." His grandfather's scream cut through the crowd's muttering and the angry voice joined those who Kyron had shoved, pushed, and felled.

He looked up to the hill once more to see his grandfather staring back down at him.

"No," his grandfather called once more. Not a scream, but a strong, parade ground voice which carried across the landscape like a trumpet's call to war. A hush followed in its wake.

"You've something to confess," the Emperor called, her voice pitched high. Around Kyron, the crowd leaned forward to catch his words.

"I confess," his grandfather said. "It was me."

"You confess," the Emperor shouted, the sibilant ending drawn out and savoured. "Does it matter, General? Will your confession save your soul?"

"I did it," his grandfather called. "I confess to being a traitor. I confess to organising the death of the Prince and Empress. It was me."

Kyron could not breathe. His grandfather's words condemned him before the city, before the soldiers who would have aided him, could have saved him. The words in the journal were worthless. The last slim chance to convince Vedrix and Godewyn was gone. No one would believe a confessed traitor's written words. They would be dismissed as nothing but excuses, the raving of a desperate man, an attempt to get away with the highest of all crimes.

All those years of service and duty were washed away in the storm of confession. Soldiers were even now turning away from their General. Godewyn's head bowed and Vedrix shuffled in place.

"No. No. No," Kyron muttered, repeating the word as if it could change things. "Why? Why? I could have saved you."

And it occurred to him in the cold spray of reality that this was exactly why he had confessed. To save the last of his family, the boy he had raised.

"No," Kyron breathed, a cavern of despair opening in his mind and his heart thudded in his hollow chest. He wanted to move, to raise his hands to his grandfather, to stride forward and take hold of the old man for one last time, but he was frozen by the sight on the hill.

"Confession." The Emperor turned to the crowd, both arms raised high to the sky. "He confesses for an easy death, for the Holy Flame to forgive him." There was a pause while the Emperor stifled a giggle. "And we should be forgiving while justice is done."

The Emperor drew the gladius at her waist and stabbed into his grandfather's stomach. The old man went rigid and every cord, every muscle in his frame strained against the pain he must have felt.

"No," Kyron screamed aloud.

Withdrawing the tip of the sword, the Emperor held it high so all could see it coated with blood which began to trickle down the blade. His grandfather sagged on the cross, not dead, not yet, for Kyron saw his head move, look up and catch his eye.

Even from the bottom of the hill, it was clear who the General, the condemned and dying man was looking at. His own call had marked him out and the crowd parted around him, creating a circle an arm's length distant.

"No," Kyron shouted again, the book under his arm falling to the summer grass, and he started forward. The despair deepened, excavated the rock of his being until it broke open his core. A sea of hot lava roiled in his centre, his soul was anger and it burned hotter than the Holy Flame.

Everything was gone. His family was dying upon a hill. Innocence, already wounded by the experience of war, was ripped to shreds by injustice. Trust was torn apart by the Emperor's hands which wielded the sword. Faith, such as it had been, was ground into dust below the High Priest's unmoving feet. Hope was extinguished by Master Vedrix's inaction.

What was the point of learning, knowledge, of trusting others, of relying on people, of magic, if it made no difference in the end, if it could change nothing? If it all came down to the disappointment and pain of this moment, then it was worth less than nothing.

A priest who watched his friend die upon a cross. A magician who had the power but did not exercise it. An old man, a soldier, a General, who could have saved himself with one simple word.

An Emperor who had killed her own family for power. Who had manipulated and schemed to become the ultimate power in the Empire. A woman to whom justice and truth meant nothing. A Princess who had stepped on the lives of so many just to be crowned. All those soldiers, Astentius, Padarn, and now his grandfather. All for power.

"It is not true power," Kyron whispered, all sense of control crumbling, despair bubbling upwards in a wave of heat and flame.

The world changed. Definition fled and his sight became only that of the motes which swirled, cavorted, danced and battled all around him. He drew them to him, stealing them from the earth, from the people, from the air, mustering his power.

The shouts of alarm, the screams, were nothing to him. He swelled, filled his body and mind with the magic, building it into a construct of instinct and anger, feeding it every last bit of power he could.

Even so, as his power rose, he felt something pressed into his hand and looked down. A single rod, a stick of twisting motes, carved to channel and funnel the power which was his.

Kyron felt its purpose and lifted his arms, taking hold of the carved stick in both hands and pointing it at the hill.

He cried out, a sound torn out of the elements which made up his world, added his pain and loss to the call, and released the construct.

The ground shook under his feet and on the hill the people staggered. Clumps of earth were torn from the ground and screams rose all around him.

"This is power," he muttered, tying off the construct.

The shaking stopped and for a moment there was silence. Nothing moved, not a cloud, not a person, and no birds flew.

A narrow pillar of flame rose from the hill, engulfing the Emperor alone in a corona of yellow and white. The woman's armour melted and flowed down her body, burning, searing the flesh. It was her turn to scream as her flesh charred and turned to ash. For a heartbeat, in that blinding column of fire, a dark skeleton formed of shadow and it was gone.

"That is justice," Kyron said, letting the knots unravel. A wave of heat and wind crashed down the hillside, bowling over people, staggering the soldiers and breaking against the city walls behind him.

There was wailing, fear-driven screams, panic-induced shouts, and a calm voice which cut through it all.

"We need to go."

LXI

The General

THREE YEARS AGO:

The streets thronged with people, but he saw none of them. The door to his home opened and he stepped in, numb, a deep pit of loneliness in his stomach.

"It'll be quiet without him here," Decima said, taking the cloak from his shoulders.

He nodded.

"He will be fine, General," Gressius said, forcing a cup of wine in his hand. "He'll come visit."

"I know," he said, "still... I'll miss having him around."

HEAT WASHED OVER his exposed skin and the acrid stench of hair melting assaulted his nose. Even the power of Vedrix's pill was unable to dull the pain. Bordan screamed.

Bright flames blinded him and the crowd at the bottom of the hill vanished behind tears. The afterimage of Kyron's outstretched hands, the clearing around him, was imprinted upon the inside of his eyelids as they snapped shut a moment late.

The heat intensified, and he felt the sword wound in his side open further as he writhed upon the cross. Even the breath he drew into his lungs was hot, turning the moisture inside his mouth into steam, burning the soft flesh of his throat.

Between one beat and the next of his pounding heart, the heat vanished. A great wave of wind buffeted him on the cross and he heard the wood rattle in its hole. There came a creak and tearing rip as the timber gave way.

He fell, the crossbeam striking the earth and his body jolted against the nails holding him to the wood. Flesh tore and blood pulsed from the open wound as another bolt of pain broke past his dulled thoughts.

For a moment, he hung, balanced, poised between falling forward on his face or backward onto the earth. The grass below, he noticed in that frozen second of time, was charred and wilted, turned brown like autumn. A cool breeze picked up, brushing against his reddened skin, sweeping past him, and he fell backwards, slamming into the ground, his head bouncing from the wooden beam he was nailed to.

It should have hurt more, his sluggish brain said. You should be unconscious.

Staring up, just the grey clouds and little flecks of ash drifted on the breeze. A lone bird took flight and crossed his vision, flying north.

"Still with us, I see," Godewyn's voice intruded into the silence and a moment later the High Priest's face came into view.

"Just," Bordan mumbled, a warm ache between his shoulder blades.

"I don't think they made the hole deep enough," Godewyn said, and the crucified man saw his friend's eyes glance towards his feet.

"Emperor?" Bordan croaked and coughed. Something warm and wet coated his tongue, but it had no taste.

"Dead," Godewyn replied, holding the amulet up in the General's vision where it appeared untouched by the flames which engulfed it.

"Not war," he tried to say.

"I'll order the soldiers to secure the city," Godewyn said, staring at the amulet. "This wasn't my plan, you know."

"Plan?" The grey clouds darkened.

"To have the Emperor dead," Godewyn answered.

Bordan watched as the High Priest lifted the chain of the amulet over his head and settled the jewel in place on his chest.

Godewyn cocked his head, took a breath, and his expression changed from calm to puzzled. "It seems the amulet does not work for me. No dead Emperor is talking to me. No memories. Perhaps your grandson's magic has damaged it?"

"Kyron."

"Quite an impressive feat," Godewyn said, kneeling and Bordan could hear the man's hands raking through the grass. The High Priest held them up and rubbed the ash between forefinger and thumb. "I will have to advance my plans somewhat due to his somewhat heated interference."

"Your... plans?" Bordan coughed again and felt a kick of pain in his lower back. He groaned.

"You can feel some pain? I hoped Vedrix's pill would have numbed you completely. You're a stubborn man, my friend. I had hoped to save you the pain, for the sake of old times, which is why I allowed Vedrix to visit," Godewyn said, glancing over his shoulder and down the hill. "Alhard would not listen to me. He worshipped you, you know. The great General of the Empire. The foremost tactician and warrior. He wanted to be like you. Tried so hard, but kept falling short."

Slow thoughts brought the truth to the surface. "You killed him."

"Of course," Godewyn smiled. "I learned strategy and tactics from the best, did I not? What you taught in the battlefield, the Church honed to a sharper edge. I used Abra, gave him money, threatened him when necessary, and offered promises of power. Priests are everywhere, General. People tell us their darkest fears, their sins and desires. From servants to nobles, they tell us everything. I used it all."

"Why?"

"The Church has worked towards this for over hundred years," Godewyn said. "The High Priest has had this sacred charge laid upon them upon anointment. A Holy Empire of the Flame, General. A Theocratic Empire. One in which everyone worships the Flame and the High Priest has ultimate power."

"For power?" He coughed, spitting out the liquid which threatened to clog his throat.

"I knew I could rely on you not to call for civil war," Godewyn sighed. "Though I had hoped to let you retire and fade away. Your replacement, Maxentius, is a Church man through and through. I have built up Aelia's trust since she was young. She was a fervent worshipper of the Flame and as High Priest she looked to me in all matters. I advised her, fed her stories of myth and legend, poetry and treatise on faith, made sure she would only listen to me, but even I cannot plan for every eventuality. When you delayed, I spoke in her ear, urged her to action. When you cautioned, I told her to be bold."

The grey clouds above turned to black, scudding across the sky, each tendril a clawed hand reaching for him.

"Kyron," he whispered.

"Your grandson has done me a favour, but condemned the magicians," Godewyn nodded. "I would save him, out of respect, but killing the Emperor is not a crime I can ignore."

The world dimmed, but Bordan heard footsteps approach.

"There you are, Livillia. Be so good as to see to the Gymnasium. Our plans must advance more quickly than I had foreseen," Godewyn's voice was faint and far away, an echo only. "General, are you still with us? I never knew you to run from a fight, but this is one you cannot win and the struggle will only cause you more pain. You should know, the magicians and their precious Gymnasium are finished. I would not save them, even if I could. It is an abomination to the Flame. The Empire will continue. Take that with you to the Holy Flame. A small comfort, I realise, but it is all I can offer you. Strange as it may seem, my friend, I will miss you."

"No," Bordan whispered, coughed, and died.

LXII

THE MAGICIAN

TWO YEARS AGO:

The Grammaticus was droning on once more about the history of the Empire on the Southern Continent. Occasional flashes of interest came when a magician or some battle happened, but other than that there was nothing to hold his attention. His eyes gazed through the windows and out onto the garden of olive trees, orange trees, and shrubs.

If he let his eyes lose focus, the motes and particles of magic would stream from those leaves and rise into the air. Their dance and play was a much more interesting spectacle.

"WHY HAVE YOU come back?" Vedrix shouted as he burst into Padarn's room, spittle flying from his mouth and cheeks red with anger. "You've sentenced us all to death. Magic killed an Emperor, Kyron. Magic. Now the Church has everything it needs to finally be rid of us. You gave it to them. For what?"

"The Emperor killed my grandfather," Kyron snapped back.

"Your grandfather knew what he was doing," Vedrix shouted. "You spoke to him. I know you did, there were traces of your magic everywhere. He told you his wishes. You should have respected them."

"He didn't do it." Kyron stood, clenched fists at his side and his own face flaming.

493

"I know that. He knew that," Vedrix sighed, and the old man's shoulders sagged, the anger draining from his face. "He saw you coming, Kyron, from the cross. He confessed to save you, to stop you doing something stupid and you did it anyway."

"It was wrong," Kyron said, choking down his anger. "It wasn't fair."

"Fair?" Vedrix's eyes widened. "Fair. Of course it wasn't fair. Your grandfather knew that and still went through with it."

"Why?" His own anger died, and the grief came welling up his throat, bringing painful tears to his eyes.

"Did you not know him at all?" Vedrix said, stepping forward and resting a comforting hand on Kyron's arm.

"I tried."

"He gave everything to the Empire," Vedrix said.

"Service and duty," Kyron mumbled.

"Exactly," Vedrix said and a sad smile split his beard. "Never a more stubborn man. I saw him too, Kyron. I tried to convince him to start a war. The soldiers would have followed him. They'd have followed him if he ordered an attack on the waves. He would not give that order."

"Why?" Kyron's voice cracked.

"Because the Empire would have fractured, and thousands would have died. It would have marked the end of everything he worked for, everything he held dear," Vedrix said, letting his arms fall. "You should have fled the city."

"I needed to see you," Kyron said. "I wanted to give you this."

He held out the journal to Vedrix who looked at it much as a mouse stares at the descending hawk.

"What is it?"

"My grandfather's journal," Kyron said, putting the book down upon the table. "He thought it was Aelia who organised the deaths of her family."

"Aelia?" Vedrix's eyebrow raised. "

"My grandfather knew," Kyron persisted. "He wrote it all down. All his thoughts and evidence."

"In Old Galix," Emlyn supplied.

"I didn't even know Bordan knew that language," Vedrix mused, turning the book with a cautious finger. "What do you want me to do with it, Kyron? The Emperor is dead, you saw to that, and now they will come for us."

"Stop them," Kyron said. "Give the book to the High Priest, convince him to help."

"He can't," Vedrix sighed. "He may want to, but he is trapped like we all are. You've set something in motion which cannot be stopped." Slamming shut the page he had opened, Vedrix stared hard into Kyron's eyes. "Godewyn will take control of the Empire. Someone has to step into the vacuum you created, but even he will not have enough support to stop the zealots amongst the Church and those in the populace. Your grandfather would have found the same."

"Then use magic and stop them. Protect the Gymnasium," Kyron demanded, his anger returning. "You cannot do nothing. You can't just wait for them to come and tear the Gymnasium down. Everyone here has power they can use."

"And kill a thousand people? Two thousand?" Vedrix said, picking up the journal. "When would it stop? When we ran out of energy? When we needed to rest or when they sent the army in to slay us all? The Gymnasium is finished, Kyron. Whether tomorrow or next tenday. The end is coming and there is little we can do."

"There has to be something you can do," Kyron said, the anger ebbing once more in the face of Vedrix's obvious grief.

"I've ordered all our valuable books, scrolls and knowledge taken to the vault. We will seal it with spells and constructs which will last a thousand years. The tunnel leading to it will be collapsed. That we can save," Vedrix moved to the door. "The magicians, I've ordered to leave, to flee for the countryside, to countries outside the Empire, as soon as they can. You should do the same. I promised your grandfather I would get you away, but there is too much to do here."

"Away." Kyron's stomach sank.

"Your guide here can take you north, if you want," Vedrix said, glancing at Emlyn. "I saw what you did. I can feel the power from you when I could not before."

Kyron saw the wry smile cross her face as she held up the remaining carved sticks she kept in her belt.

"I had to break those masking my power, or the enhancer I gave Kyron would never have worked," she confessed. "I've done what I was sent to do, though perhaps not the way I would have set about it."

"Sent?" Kyron said. "You were our guide. Your family was being held hostage."

"They know what I was sent to do, they went willingly," she said, and it was her turn to let her own grief and sadness show.

"Which was?" Kyron asked.

"To stop the invasion? Kill the Emperor?" Vedrix asked, no anger or malice in his voice.

"Whatever I could to save my people," she answered.

"You're a traitor?" Kyron blurted.

"To who, Kyron?" she answered and the look she gave him was direct. "Not to my people, nor to you. You'll recall I helped you on a course you had already decided upon."

"You used me," he replied, hurt.

"I helped," she repeated.

"My advice," Vedrix said, opening the door, "is for both of you to get out of the city tonight. They'll be searching for you, Kyron. The esteem Godewyn held for your grandfather may grant you some time, but not much."

"Master Vedrix!" The shout rushed through the open door and followed the echo of running feet along the corridor.

"What is it?" Vedrix stepped through the door and looked along the corridor.

"They're coming, Master. They're coming," the voice called. "We saw the torches and heard the chants."

"It seems your time is up, Kyron, as is ours." Vedrix turned to him. "Take what you need and go." He stepped through the door, stopped and looked back. "Get as far from here as you can. Good luck."

Before Kyron could respond the Master of the Gymnasium of Magicians was gone. Only an empty doorway faced him now, and a step into the unknown.

"Let's move, Kyron," Emlyn said, and he heard her begin to gather things together. "Don't just sit there. Vedrix told us to go and he is right. This city is no place for you anymore."

"It's my home." He shot up from the chair and turned to face her.

"Your home is about to be burned down," Emlyn answered, facing him down with her own anger. "Just like mine. Welcome to life under attack. You want to live? Then we need to get away."

"I want to," he began and realised he had no idea what he wanted. Everyone was gone. Parents, Padarn, Grandfather, and soon the Gymnasium. All the people who had given him direction were silent in death, only memories, lessons, and their imprint on his thoughts were with him. It was up to him, his decision, his life to lead. "What am I going to do?"

"Live," Emlyn answered, stuffing a warm cloak into a backpack. "Do that and you make all the choices, mistakes and successes you want. Stand there, do nothing, die, and all those choices are gone forever."

The truth of her unforgiving words struck him, cleared his thoughts like a brisk, cold wind through the leaves of autumn. He grabbed the sword belt from the table, buckling it around his hips, he checked that the gladius Borus had given him sat well in the scabbard. His own backpack was near his feet, and he raced to the shelves, picking two books from it and stuffing them at the bottom, beneath his clothes.

"Food," Emlyn said. "We'll need food."

"The stores are on the way out," Kyron replied.

Pulling his cloak around his shoulders and fastening the clasp, he stepped to the door and peered both ways along the corridor. It was empty, but the sound of movement rumbled through the stones. Somewhere, magicians were making their own preparations to leave, or to fight. No matter what Vedrix said, some would fight.

Maybe even Vedrix himself, Kyron realised. A sacrifice to appease the people, to buy time for the others to escape. The power and price of leadership.

"This way," he said and ran along the corridors of the Gymnasium. Occasionally a magician or servant would race past in the opposite direction. In the stores, they grabbed bread, cheese, smoked meat, stuffing it into the backpacks, and headed for the door.

"Not that way," said a magician hurrying past them. "They've reached the gates and are demanding we all come out. Take one of the lesser doors."

"Where are you going?" Kyron asked.

"The southern door," the magician said. "It looks out on the slums. Maybe I can vanish into the hovels there for a bit."

"We'll follow you," Emlyn said. "Come on."

The three of them raced through the Gymnasium, until they reached a door and a queue of magicians heading the same way. An armoured guard stood by the exit, a round shield propped up against the wall and a gladius upon his hip.

"Split up once you get out," he said as Kyron came up to him. "They haven't got around here yet, too focused on the main door, but it won't be long. You'll be better off if you're wearing civilian clothes. Don't draw attention to yourselves and get out of the city."

Kyron nodded as he ducked through the door, Emlyn behind him, and out into the night. The magician they had followed turned left and ran along the narrow road between the Gymnasium and the buildings which had been built alongside it. A dark shadowed alley faced them and Emlyn did not pause but grabbed his hand dragging him into it.

"Where's the nearest gate?" she hissed.

"That way," he pointed across the city. "The main gate."

"That'll be guarded," Emlyn whispered. "If this is the Church, they'll want you captured. Is there a smaller gate?"

"There's the one my grandfather went through."

"I'd rather not run around the city just to head north." Emlyn shook her head. "I've seen the land there, they'll see us from the walls, and there isn't a lot of cover."

"We could get on a ship, in the docks," he suggested as they moved carefully along the alleyway.

"To where? I'd prefer to be able to run if I need to, and you can bet they've got the docks watched to."

"There's a small gate in the north wall," Kyron said, after a moment's thought. "It isn't well used, mostly farm workers and night soil men."

"Sounds ideal," she answered. "Lead the way."

"We'll have to go around the crowd," he said, indicating the direction with a jerk of his head.

"Why not those tunnels under the city?" Emlyn said.

"I don't know the way," Kyron answered. "Only that small section by my grandfather's house."

"Best keep your cloak tight and the hood up then," she ordered as she flicked her own over her head and rested a hand on her knife.

He drew his own up, hiding his face, but cutting off his peripheral vision and put his own hand on his sword. "I don't want to hurt anyone."

"Too late for that," she whispered, hurrying forward.

They turned at the end of the alley, onto a wider road, and saw a group of townsfolk emerge from a side road ahead. He stopped, drawing Emlyn back into the dark shadow of a doorway. The people carried torches and he saw the telltale sign of the Flame upon the robes of the priests amongst the people.

"For the Flame," they were shouting. "Death to magic."

"Let's be careful," Emlyn said as they watched the group vanish in the direction of the Gymnasium.

He nodded and realised she could not see the gesture under his hood. "I agree."

They crept up the road, peering around the corner from which a group had come, and slipped across it into the road opposite. Light emanated from the apartments above, candles and oil lamps left aflame by the inhabitants, enough so they could make out their path.

"There's a large road up ahead," Kyron said. "It's the one that leads to the Gymnasium."

"Is there another way around?"

"Not to get to the gate," he answered. "We'd have to head deeper into the city."

They rounded a slight curve in the road and found the street ahead blocked by a large crowd of people carrying torches and chanting. Interspersed amongst them were the white robes of the priests.

"We're stuck," he said, already turning around.

"No," she said, grabbing his arm and forcing him to continue walking. "We just go through them."

"Through?" His strangled gasp was consumed by the chants.

"Politely, nicely, like we're supposed to be there," she said. "Chant along with them, walk for a bit, and take the road we need."

"But—"

"Your hood's up and they won't know who you are or who I am," she answered, pulling him along. "Act like you belong."

He found he had no choice as they drew closer. In the dancing torchlight he could see the faces of people driven to feverish excitement. Their mouths were open, chanting 'Death to Magic' and 'Burn them down'. Each flame-lit eye was burning with righteous anger and the few looking their way beckoned them to join.

It was a mob. These people, he would have seen them in the markets, amongst the streets he had walked without fear for all his years, in the taverns sharing a drink with friends, in the city parks, or at the Colosseum. He would have paid them no mind and they none to him. Now, whipped up by the white-clad priests who wove their way through amongst the crowd, shouting imprecations, screaming about the Flame, abominations and curses, those people had been subsumed by hatred, by the lowest and basest of their emotions. Individuals no longer. All that remained was a mob driven by fear and controlled by hate.

Kyron slipped in amongst them and a wash of emotion almost carried him along. His grip on the hilt of his gladius and Emlyn's on his arm kept him steady as they picked their slow way across the current. Swept along, he could see, above the mob, the roof of the Gymnasium come into view.

"They have lied to us all these years," a shrill voice called above the shouts. "Magic killed the Emperor and next they'll come for the Church."

Kyron's gaze snapped around in reflex and he was pinned to the spot by the returned glare of Livillia. His sword flew from its sheath into his hand and he felt Emlyn's grip torn free by the crowd.

"You," she screamed, pointing a bony finger in his direction. "There he is. The assassin of the Emperor. The magician who is coming for your Church, for your children, your wealth, your souls, for you all."

LXIII

THE MAGICIAN

TWO YEARS AGO:
"No one is denying your affinity for magic," Master Vedrix said.
"However, your teachers all comment on a lack of focus in class."

"I want to do magic, Master," he complained. "I want to learn
to build nets, constructs, and all the rest. Class is all about history,
theory, old magicians."

"And you want to do magic," Master Vedrix sighed. "Well, each
student eventually finds their own path, but you want to begin the
search before you know what to look for."

KYRON STEPPED BACK, away from her hate and the crowd gave him
space. Those who had passed by turned back his way, and those
coming up behind stopped and hissed at him. He searched the faces
of those who surrounded him seeking Emlyn, but she was gone,
vanished into the mob, carried along by its unending wave.

"You won't escape us," Livillia said, her voice a triumphal call to
the mob. "This is the grandson of the traitor crucified upon the hill.
This is Kyron, the magician who killed the Emperor upon the same
hill."

The mob bayed names like wolves at the full moon, but they did not
advance. Perhaps the memory of the pillar of flame which consumed
their Emperor kept them back.

"I don't want to hurt anyone," Kyron shouted. As he spoke, he drew the motes to him in a desperate rush of power. With slippery fingers of the mind he pinned motes to his blade and built a hasty construct. A simple knot at one end, a twist of thought and he let energy surge into it. The sword caught flame and the crowd backed up a step as one. "But I will if I have to."

He swept the sword before them and the roar of the flames brought flickers of fear to their faces.

"You bring fire against a priest of the Flame," Livillia's voice reached a higher pitch. "Sacrilege."

"Just let me go. No one needs to be harmed," he shouted, pointing the fiery sword at her. Heat washed over him and the bright flame limited his vision.

"Go," she laughed. "Where will you go, little boy? You cannot escape the justice of our Holy Empire."

Kyron saw the crowd shuffle forward, gaining courage from Livillia's unflinching disparagement. He wished for the weight of a shield on his arm, just like his grandfather had trained him to hold in the years before he left for the Gymnasium. It would do little against all these people, but it would have felt comforting.

His heart thudded in his chest and he could feel blood pulse through his body. The hand holding the sword shook and he needed to piss.

The crowd shuffled forward once more in answer to his inaction.

"Give it up, boy," Livillia crowed. "You have no way out."

Kyron cast about once more, looking for Emlyn, for anyone to assist, but all he faced was anger and hate. The fine folk of the city bitten too many times and turned rabid by the teachings of the Church. No one was going to help him. He was alone.

He took a breath, feeling the torch smoke and sweat of the city folk's tight-pressed bodies coat his throat with a burning acid. Magic came to him, drawn from the street and earth below, from the fabric of the buildings around him, and from the bodies of the mob. He saw them in his rainbow blurred vision weaken and sag as he sucked the energy from them, but they came on.

A spell, a construct, something, anything to get away.

"You move, you die," grated a voice and it took a heartbeat to realise it was not directed at him.

He looked up, drawing the sword aside to free his eyes from its glare. Kyron struggled to hold the gathered magic within his body, feeling his skin stretch thin against it.

"Emlyn," he whispered, as his eyes adjusted to the sight of the guide's face appearing over Livillia's shoulder and the knife she held pressed hard against the priest's paper-white neck.

"Tell them to back away," Emlyn hissed.

"You can kill me," Livillia replied, no fear in her tone, only pride and superiority, "but I will find everlasting life in the Holy Flame and these good people will still kill you."

"At least you won't be around to see it," Emlyn replied, her tone matter of fact as she drew the sharp edge across the priest's neck.

For the first, and only time, Kyron saw shock and pain upon the thin woman's face. An expression which faltered as the blood arced from her severed neck across the mob and cobbles.

Emlyn let the body fall as the people cried in alarm, stepping past and grabbing Kyron's arm.

"We need to run," she said, drawing him away from the sight.

For a moment it looked as though the crowd would give way to the knife-wielding woman and magician with the flaming sword. They did not. They rallied, driven by shock and anger, by revenge and outrage. Their screams shook the buildings around.

Objects flew from the mob. Stones, boots, lumps of wood, food. It all sailed over their heads and into the clearing around Kyron and Emlyn. Some was thrown too hard and landed amongst the people on the opposite side and there were groans of pain amongst the rage.

Kyron shuffled aside from a length of wood which clattered against the cobbles and felt something strike his leg. A sharp shaft of pain sped along his nerves and he stumbled. Emlyn's grip kept him upright.

He siphoned a little magic, drawing it into a shield above their heads. The knots were simple to tie, the work of a moment's thought and the next rainfall of missiles bounced harmlessly away.

Thwarted, the anger of the mob grew and weapons were drawn. Old swords, knives better suited to the kitchen, brooms and garden tools, hoes and spades, were brought forward.

A man broke ranks ahead, running forward, raising his adze-hammer over his head and shouting for Kyron's death.

Another siphon of power, enough to forge a hammer of his own which he threw with a grunt of effort from his outstretched hand. The bolt of force struck the carpenter in the face, smashing his nose flat and splattering blood across his chin, cheeks and mouth. The adze-hammer fell to the cobbles followed by its owner.

The magician turned at a call from Emlyn to see her launch one of those carved sticks at the crowd in her way. It flared with green light as it tumbled end over end, coming apart into tiny, acorn shaped ovals. They struck the three who menaced her. Each burst against their clothes and a vibrant yellow liquid spread across cloaks and tunics. Twisting tendrils of smoke rose from their clothes and they slapped at them, an instinctive reaction. Instead of extinguishing non-existent flames, the people screamed even louder as their flesh began to steam and then burn without fire.

Fire cleansed, the priests taught, but Kyron now saw the truth, heard it in those screams. It burned. It destroyed. Lumps of charred meat, scorched stone, night dark charcoal wood, the residue it left behind was a husk of all it had once been. Smoke rose upon the air, spreading the pollution, the reach of the fire, to everyone and everything, tainting all with its touch.

It was not holy to be cleansed, to be cremated, it was destruction. It was not a new beginning: it was the end. Fire did not create, it consumed.

The flames upon his sword flickered and died. He lowered the warm steel and held out his free hand, palm up. The magic flowed from him, weaving into the cobbles at his feet, wrenching them free, lifting and spinning them around Emlyn and himself. A spiral of warning and destruction. With a little change to the construct, all the debris which had been thrown at them was added to the whirling shield.

He took hold of Emlyn's arm, pulling her close as he stepped forward, pushing the tornado of rock, wood and metal, forward, keeping them at its epicentre. The crowd backed away, and he stepped again, and again, intent upon the road opposite and the tenuous safety it offered.

It was within reach when the whole city, the crowd around them, even the buildings which towered over them seemed to take a deep breath. The mob shared glances, and Emlyn's sharp fingers dug into his arm.

The ground beneath their feet bucked and rumbled. Buildings shook and a wall of wind, laden with biting dust swept over them all, obscuring everything.

His spell failed and the debris he had raised flew free, no longer held by the magic. Beneath the howl of the onrushing wind, he heard people scream as stone struck flesh, breaking bones, ending lives.

A desert heat of dry air stole the moisture from his skin, eyes, nose, and open mouth. He stumbled, falling, and dragging Emlyn to the cobbles.

Stone, plaster and wood above their heads ripped, tore and broke free of buildings. It rained down upon them, mob, magician and guide, caring not where it landed. Past the crowd and above their heads, a fireball rose into the night sky, trailing dark smoke, from the roof of the Gymnasium.

He wrapped his arms around her, letting his sword fall to the ground, and pulled Emlyn in close. His conjured shield above their heads their only protection. Every mote of magic he could draw to him, he added to the shield, and knew it would not be enough. His mind sped along the lines of his construct, strengthening bonds, twisting complicated knots which could resist the falling blocks, and knew he would fail.

"Here," she whispered, putting her faith and two carved sticks into his hands.

Her magic, the power she had hidden and which he recalled Padarn had noticed but done nothing about, joined his. The shield flared into cerulean and green, flickered yellow and red, turned egg-shell white and became all they could see as the buildings fell on them.

LXIV

THE MAGICIAN

Two years ago:
  A hand came to rest on his when he moved to open the door to the Grammaticus's room.
  "Not today," said the owner of a neat beard and stone-grey eyes.
  "Master?" he said.
  "Some learn by listening, by reading, by quiet thinking, but you learn, I am told, by doing. Today, you will do," the magician said. "And if you do well enough, I will take you as apprentice."
  A flush of excitement washed through his body, bringing heat to his face.

KYRON STAGGERED TOWARDS the gate, limping on his bad leg while Emlyn cradled her arm. Both were covered in a layer of brick and plaster dust, the ash of many fires, and scratches too numerous to count. The torches and lanterns hung on the walls cast shadows on doorways and though most citizens had barricaded themselves in their homes, there were a few about to watch them pass.

Along the street, the sounds of violence, the army trying to restore control followed them much as the smoke from the ruins of the Gymnasium. The tall buildings, those which had survived the destruction of his home, funnelled the sound and it hammered into his skull, a reminder that this was all his fault. He carried the blame of every magician's death upon his shoulders.

As they had expected, the gate was guarded. Five soldiers in lorica segmata, carrying shields, and armed with swords. Three remained by the gate, the smallest in this wall which led out of the city, and the one he had thought least likely to be busy. Most of those trying to escape the violence which was sweeping the city, the wealthy who could afford to start anew elsewhere or who had homes in safer parts of the Empire, would leave via the main gates, their carts full of possessions.

"We will have to kill them," Emlyn said, wincing as she let go her arm and reached for the last remaining wand in her belt.

"I can't," Kyron said, guiding her into a shadow. "There has been enough death, and they are my people."

"That didn't bother you when you struck down the Emperor, or the others tonight," she pointed out.

The truth was like a sharp needle in his eye, it hurt and clouded his vision with tears. His excuse sounded weak in his ears. "I didn't have a choice."

"We don't now, not if we want to live, and I do want to live, Kyron," Emlyn said. "I can kill one, maybe two of them. The others are yours, kill or disable, I don't care, but we need to get out of that gate."

"Maybe we can talk our way past?" he suggested, glad she could not see the pathetic hope he knew was written across his face.

"They are looking for us, Kyron," Emlyn whispered. "They have our description. We can't talk our way out."

"I won't kill them." He found the words contained truth, whether determined by weakness, submission, or morals instilled by his grandfather or Padarn, he could not say.

"I'm glad to hear it," a voice said from behind them.

Kyron spun on his heel, stumbling on his weakened leg, but he grabbed the hilt of the gladius at his waist. Emlyn grunted in pain as she too turned, levelling the last of her own magic at the dark figure who stood there.

"Your grandfather would not approve of killing soldiers," the figure said.

"Borus?" Kyron gasped. "How did you find us?"

"It was easy enough, I know you both well," Borus replied, stepping into a pool of light. He was dressed in armour, a parma shield in one hand, but his sword remained sheathed.

Kyron's hand trembled on the hilt of the gladius, the desire to draw it, ready to defend Emlyn and himself if needed.

"You'd kill me with the sword I gave you?" Borus asked, making no move to draw his own sword.

"I don't want to kill anyone," Kyron said.

"Walk away, Borus," Emlyn said, her wand rising to point at the soldier.

"I saw you use those at the execution, you discarded them straight afterward. If you use it against me, you'll have nothing left for the guards" Borus said, "My condolences, Kyron. He deserved a better fate."

"He did," Kyron answered. "Put it down, Emlyn, I don't think he is here for us."

"Wisdom, finally?" Borus said. Kyron saw the flash of teeth as the soldier smiled. "I can get you through the gate."

"Why?" Emlyn's question was brittle.

"For him," Borus nodded to Kyron. "For his grandfather who served the Empire faithfully his whole life."

"I am a traitor, Borus," Kyron said, lowering his voice. "I killed an Emperor."

"You won't be the first," Borus said, "and probably not the last. I've served in the army my whole life, boy, and most of that under the General's care. He never spent lives needlessly, looked after his men, and was loyal to the last. He also cared for you. He spoke to me, on the journey back. Did you know? Asked me what you'd done and how you'd served. Thanked me for looking out for you, even the little that I did. Hauling you back to face justice from whoever it is that takes power serves no purpose."

"Godewyn," Kyron said.

"Looking that way," Borus nodded. "He was a good officer, the High Priest, and the most senior council member remaining. The army and Church will follow him. It makes sense."

"The Church and army are supposed to be separate," Kyron said.

"That's what I was taught about our Empire. Godewyn will have power over everything, everyone, Church, army, and Empire. The Holy Flame only destroys, Borus. I realise that now."

Borus raised his hand. "I'm a simple soldier and a follower of the faith. Life's a lot easier that way. Don't make me change my mind."

"The Gymnasium's gone, Borus," Kyron said, "and I saw the priests with torches in hands, leading the people in, setting fire to it all."

"People need something to blame, lad," Borus explained, "and they know magic killed their Emperor, and word got out it was used against Prince Alhard too. They also need someone to look up to, and Godewyn might be that man for a time, until things settle down."

"You're letting us go," Emlyn cut across their discussion. "How?"

"All I said is, I can get you through the gate," Borus answered, "and without killing any of those men."

"I'll take it," she said.

"After that, you're on your own," Borus said. "Don't come back to the city, Kyron. There's nothing for you here anymore."

"I know," he said, the weight of loss almost forcing him to his knees.

"Good," Borus said, straightening back. "You did well, lad. Helped get us back safe and there are a few hundred men and women who owe you, even if they don't know and can never repay the debt. I'm here, doing it for them. Wait here. You'll know when to go through the gate."

Without another word, Borus swept his cloak back and strode out of the side street towards the gate.

"You men," he called as he went, drawing their attention to him, "I need four of you to get to the market square, we've got civilians thinking they'd like to get rich off the traders' stockpiles."

"We're supposed to guard the gate, sir," one of the guards said.

"I know," Borus said without a pause. "I've got five men coming to take over from you, but the market is more important. One of you stay here with me. I'll make sure the gate stays locked."

"Yes, sir," another guard said. "I've got the key."

"Then you're the one staying," Borus said. "Rest of you get moving. Try not to kill anyone but secure the market. Times are bad enough with all the merchants shutting their stalls and shops. People still need to eat, but if there's nothing to sell, no one will be able to buy."

"You think the Empire will be all right, sir?" the gate guard asked as the other men trotted away, their armour clanking and rattling as they went.

"Survived so far, don't see why it won't continue," Borus said. "It better do. I need to get paid or the wife will be wanting to sell me on the streets to earn money. I don't reckon I've got the right skills for that."

"You could always send her out, sir," the other guard said, adding a nervous chuckle.

"If I have to, but I don't think other men would pay for that dubious pleasure," Borus said.

"I don't think…" the guard began.

"Watch out," Borus interrupted, pointing with his shield over the soldier's shoulder and drawing his sword. As the man turned, Borus dropped the hilt of his gladius down upon the man's unprotected neck.

The soldier collapsed, boneless to the cobbles in clatter of shields and armour.

"Sorry about that," Borus said, and waved Kyron forward, grabbing the key from the fallen soldier's belt. "Emlyn, get the gate. Remember, don't come back."

"I promise," Kyron said. "Thank you."

"One more thing," Borus said, "draw your sword."

"Why?" Kyron stopped as Emlyn took the offered key.

"Cut me," Borus explained. "I'm not looking forward to it, but I'll need a good story."

Kyron drew the gladius and looked down into the short length of steel which Borus had given him back in the forest. "I can't. What if I cut too deep, or hit something important?"

"You need to, lad."

"I'll do it," Emlyn said, passing Kyron the key and snatching the sword from his hand.

"Now, girl," Borus said, raising his hands, "I don't want to die or get maimed."

"I'll be careful," Emlyn sighed. "Where do you want the wound?"

"Well, I was thinking—" Borus's words were cut off by a hiss of pain.

"It's barely a wound," Emlyn said as wiped the blood from the sword.

"By the Flame, girl," Borus hissed between clenched teeth. Kyron saw him clamp a hand to the wound on his thigh as blood trickled down his leg. "You could have warned me."

"Better this way," she explained.

"Get going," Borus said, limping to the wall and slumping down against it, "and good luck to you both."

With a last look at the Cohort, Kyron limped his own way through the gate.

The air outside the city carried the stench of civilisation, of ash and flame, of dust, plaster, and rot. Kyron peered into the gloom of night, seeing the faded colours of patchwork farms and a straight Empire road, heard the waves crashing against cliffs, and tried to let the guilt fall from his shoulders. It clung on, wrapping fingers around his throat, digging with clawed hands into his bones, piercing his heart with dirty fingernails.

"Where to?" Kyron asked, shaking the sadness for a moment.

"North," Emlyn answered. "There's nothing for you in the Empire, not anymore. In the forests, you can be free."

"And the army in the North?" he said. "They're going to come back through the forests."

"There are more trees than people," Emlyn pointed out. "If we need to hide, it won't be difficult."

He started to hobble along the track. "If we make it there."

"We will," she said, "one step at a time."

Kyron sighed, refusing to look back at the city where he had spent much of his life, where his family had lived, once fled from, and where his grandfather had died.

I'm fleeing too and like them I'll never return. Borus and Emlyn were right. Padarn travelled to learn, perhaps I can do the same. There is a bigger world than I know, and it is not constrained by high walls and rigid structures.

The Empire and home he had known were ash upon the wind, never to be reborn.

ACKNOWLEDGEMENTS

WRITING THESE ACKNOWLEDGEMENTS will, by the very nature of memory, be an imperfect exercise. So I will begin, as is customary, in mentioning that I will forget people—not on purpose or through any desire to not recognise their help, but purely because my memory is not the best. To all those I forget, I am sorry, and know I am still thankful.

These will also be the first acknowledgements I ever write to a book which will be found on the shelves of a bookshop. The chance may not come again to say these things, so bear with me, or skip to the end. They're going to be long whereas subsequent books will consist of "Yeah, thanks" and "refer to previous acknowledgements"—I half-promise.

Let's begin with my mother, Angela, ("The Mothership" as she is known to my brother and I) without whom I wouldn't be here (obviously), but more importantly I would not be the person I am today. Blindingly intelligent (with occasional forays in whimsy), and incredibly caring, she has always encouraged me (and my brother) to find our own path in life and I know beyond doubt that she just wants us to be happy. You can't imagine (though I truly hope you can) what that means to a growing boy, a man, and an adult—knowing she will, and continues to, pick us up when we fall, dust us down, and tell us to get back to it. Paul, you are a saint and you keep doing what you are doing, you make her happy and for that I thank you.

My father, Gordon, who is practical, full of common sense, and gives the best advice when you ask it of him. A man who can strip any machine down to its constituent parts and rebuild it better, faster, stronger. I am forever in awe of his technical knowledge, his ability to just do things that my brain refuses to comprehend. He is Scotty, whereas I am Spot (Data's cat)—and I know that's mixing the series up, but it is probably the best analogy of our relative technical skills. He proves to me again and again that if I need solid ground to stand upon, he will lay out the dimensions and pour the cement. And Wendy, I know he is a pain, but thank you for looking after him.

My brother, Jonathan, combines the best of both my parents and somehow augments with his own special ways. A musician through and through. He was born with the talent for music, into a family of musicians and rose above them all (in my humble opinion). During our younger years we fought like brothers do all across the world, never listening to our parents who told us we would be best friends when we grew up—once again they were proved right (strange, this skill of good parents, to be right more often than wrong). Jenny, you remain a wonder to me—I grew up with him, but you have made him even more than he was.

My own family leave me alone long enough to write, most of the time, and that alone is a gift. Thomas and Holly, my children, remain a constant joy (and irritation, in equal measure), and I hope I raise them at least half as well as my parents did in raising my brother and I.

In summary; my successes are theirs, the fuck ups are all mine.

I will also have to give a lot of credit to the crowd from BristolCon and those I've met through Grim Gatherings—you are all too numerous to mention, but let me pick out a few; Rob, Tom, Laura, Dyrk (for coming over the pond to see us all), Rosa, Dolly (my first Con buddy), James (from my hometown) J.P, Mike, and all the others.

I apologise now to all those authors with whom I have forged friendships and whom I may have asked awkward questions or made silly jokes to during panels—feel free to return the favour. I am looking at you, Steve, Anna, Adrian, amongst others.

Thanks also to the Purple Skies group. Mariëlle and Jude, who make me smile at least once a month, even during lockdown, and I value those talks and catch-ups. Adrian Selby, who not only helped me with my synopsis, but remains a constant source of advice, humour, and inspiration. Without you all keeping me sane, I'd be a much poorer man.

Julia, my first supporter, my beta reader, my proof-reader, my champion, and seriously folks, if you've read this far and you enjoyed this book (or any of my others) you have to know that without her help and assistance the books would be nowhere near as good as they are. Andreas too—a man of infinite patience and joy. You have my thanks, and I do owe you a good meal and some decent beer!

Marc and Jennie at Fantasy-Faction. Thank you both for taking me under your wing, for supporting me, and for letting me join your world. It really has been amazing, and continues to be so!

Mark Lawrence, for the snippets of wisdom, the beer, and that photo of us where I appear to be drinking a vase of flowers. Also for championing the SPFBO and starting that initiative off. It makes a difference.

T. O. Munro (Matthew), we got started together on this writing lark and that encouragement and sense of camaraderie through those first years set my feet securely on this path. Those first books will always be with us.

Graham Austin-King, my friend, and a man who has punched me in the face numerous times (during martial arts practice, I'll add) which knocked a good deal of sense into my head.

Thanks to Natalie, without whom a sentence would not be as perfect as it is now.

Sammy HK Smith for taking the last year of this journey together with me, sharing the fears, worries, and excitement as publication days draw closer has been a joy and a comfort. And with regard to fluttering loins, you're right, the book is better without them.

Kate Coe, my editor, for taking a chance on the book, for seeing the promise and helping turn it from a good book to a great book. It has been a learning experience, and I've done my best to take on every lesson.

Jamie Cowen, my agent, who turned down two previous books of mine, but each time with good advice, with encouragement, and words of wisdom. I promise I took it all on board as I wrote the next one, and look, it worked. Thank you!

Mark, Martin, Jon, Polly, Rhys, Simon, Tristan and Tom, my friends, RPG, and board game buddies. This year (2020) has been hell, and getting out to play has been difficult, but playing online has been a salvation; City of Mist, Adventures in Middle Earth, Invisible Sun, Star Trek. We live in different worlds for a short time, but the fun stays forever. Thank you all.

Also, to some of my oldest friends, the members of Arte; Andrew (Ty), David (Ed), Mark (Garth), and Alan (Cal)—we fought for Albion, amongst other realms and worlds, in wars too numerous to mention. The Roman skeletons on Salisbury Plain, the monsters of Darkness Falls, all fell before us, but we should never forget the Black Dog which ended up being one of our number's greatest foe.

Lastly, to friends I see but very rarely but always have a place in my heart and take up a large portion of my memories; Claire W, Claire H, Tony, Paul, Justin, and Gi. I love you all and miss you.

And those who've read this book and supported my writing—my eternal thanks!

That's it. I'm done.

Thank you for reading this far and I hope to see you in the next book!

GLOSSARY

THE EMPIRE

The Emperor
The Empress
Alhard: First born, son and heir to the Imperial Throne.
Aelia: Second born, daughter and second in line the Imperial Throne.

Historian's note: Imperial law and tradition dictate that only a direct blood relative may sit on the Imperial Throne. However, a careful reading of Imperial History would indicate this has not always been the case.

Ruling Council: Comprised of the Emperor, General of the Empire's Army, High Priest of the Flame, Master of the Gymnasium of Magicians, Dukes/Duchesses, and those of rank invited by the Emperor.

General of the Empire's Army: Bordan
High Priest of the Flame: Godewyn
Master of the Gymnasium of Magicians: Vedrix

Historian's note: The presence of the Military, the Priesthood, and the Magicians on the Ruling Council is both historical and practical.

The Emperor can be assured that all realms of advice and points of view are explored in Council, while balancing the three major branches of Empire power against each other.

ARMY RANKS AND ORGANISATION

Emperor
General
      In charge of the three armies
Legion (3)
      In charge of an army
      An army is 15,000 Foot
Commander (3 per army)
      A Command is 5,000 Foot
      Each Commander leads 5 Prefects
Prefects (15 per army)
      A Prefect is 1,000 Foot
      Each Prefect leads 2 Spears
Spear (30 per army)
      A Spear is 500 Foot
      Each Spear leads 10 Cohorts
Cohort (300 per army)
      A Cohort is 50 Foot
      Leads 5 Shields.
Shield (1,500 per army)
      A Shield is 10 Foot
Foot: A single soldier.

Immunis: Possess a specialised skill; Carpenter, Quartermaster, Musician, Hunters, Engineers, and do not have daily duties.

Historian's note: While the number of 15,000 Foot is regarded to be a Legion, the true number of each Legion is higher. Those of the Immunis are not counted amongst the Foot, nor are the civilian labourers and others who service the requirements of the army. Similarly, a Shield is considered to be 10 Foot, but in reality, can vary between 7 and 14 Foot. Amongst the Immunis are those who have completed their requisite years of service but elected or been chosen to remain part of the military—quite often the General or a Legion will employ Immunis for specialised tasks or duties.

WEAPONS AND ARMOUR

Gladius: a short stabbing sword. The main weapon of the soldiers.
Spatha: a longer sword.
Pugio: a dagger.
Pila: throwing spears, javelins.
Lorica segmentata: the usual armour of the soldiers. Metal strips formed into circular bands and fastened to leather straps.
Lorica hamata: made from alternating rows of rings and rows of riveted rings.

Historian's note: The weapons and tactics of the Empire Army have developed over the years and through contact with other peoples. Most recently, the Lorica hamata was adapted from armour worn by those of the tribes who used to call the old, long since felled forest near Sudrim, home.

RANKS IN THE CHURCH OF THE HOLY FLAME

High Priest
Bishop
Deacon
Curate
Priest

Justice/Inquisitor: Outside of the formal ranks and report directly to the Bishops and High Priest.

Historian's note: The Church of the Holy Flame is the dominant religion of the Empire. Arising over eight hundred years ago, it is regarded as the cause of the Old Empire's schism. Promising a life eternal with the Flame, the simple message of this new religion quickly swept aside the old household gods whose complicated and imprecise worship was viewed as heretical and paganistic.

RANKS IN THE GYMNASIUM OF MAGIC

Master of the Gymnasium
Master
Journeyman
Apprentice

Magister: Outside of the normal hierarchy and report directly to the Master of the Gymnasium.

Historian's note: In the scrolls of the Old Empire, it is clear that the Magicians held much more power and were in the ascendency when compared to the centuries since the Schism. The Gymnasium itself is maintained by the Emperor and the Empire, its members protected by law. A recent survey of magician numbers indicates a decline in the amount of apprentices joining the Gymnasium; however, the reason for this is unclear.

FIND US ONLINE!

www.rebellionpublishing.com

/rebellionpub   /rebellionpublishing /rebellionpublishing

SIGN UP TO OUR NEWSLETTER!

rebellionpublishing.com/newsletter

YOUR REVIEWS MATTER!

Enjoy this book? Got something to say?

Leave a review on Amazon, GoodReads or with your favourite bookseller and let the world know!

THE SIX KINGDOMS

N

THE LANDS

1. AELEDFYR
2. CLAN LANDS
3. FORESTS OF THE TRIBES
4. STEEPWALL
5. ESADALE
6. THE EMPIRE